MRS.

GEORGE
CANTERBURY'S
WILL

Volume 2

Elibron Classics
www.elibron.com

Elibron Classics series.

© 2005 Adamant Media Corporation.

ISBN 1-4021-7881-6 (paperback)
ISBN 1-4021-2692-1 (hardcover)

This Elibron Classics Replica Edition is an unabridged facsimile
of the edition published in 1870 by Bernhard Tauchnitz,
Leipzig.

COLLECTION

OF

BRITISH AUTHORS

TAUCHNITZ EDITION.

VOL. 1085.

GEORGE CANTERBURY'S WILL BY MRS. H. WOOD.

IN TWO VOLUMES.

VOL. II.

A NOVEL.

BY

MRS. HENRY WOOD,

AUTHOR OF "EAST LYNNE," "TREVLYN HOLD," ETC.

COPYRIGHT EDITION.

IN TWO VOLUMES.

VOL. II.

LEIPZIG

BERNHARD TAUCHNITZ

1870.

CONTENTS

OF VOLUME II.

———

GEORGE CANTERBURY'S WILL.

CHAPTER I.

A painful Interview.

The twelvemonth went by, and Thomas Kage was ready to resign his executorship: some law details had thus protracted the settlement. The deed of release was forwarded for Mrs. Canterbury and the other parties to sign, and Mr. Kage also left London for the Rock: there was no legal necessity for his presence there, but he chose to spare the time for the journey. The railway was now extended to within two miles of the Rock; and an omnibus, as Mr. Kage was informed, plied between the terminus and Chilling. He was hastening to look for the conveyance when he ran across Mr. Carlton. That gentleman had long been disabused of his resentment against Mr. Kage on the subject of the executorship; for the lawyer, Norris, told him how craftily the appointment had been made.

"Don't get into that jolting omnibus," cried the warm-hearted squire; "let me drive you in my pony-gig; there's room for you and your portmanteau too. I came to look after a parcel of books, and it has not arrived."

They were soon bowling along the road, Mr. Carlton full of gossip, as he loved to be. In relating some news, he mentioned the name of Captain Dawkes.

"Captain Dawkes!" exclaimed Mr. Kage. "What! is he here?"

And Mr. Kage found, to his very great surprise, that Captain Dawkes was not only there at present, but had been there ever since, or nearly ever since, his first appearance in the place twelve months before. Just for a few moments he could scarcely believe it: that Captain Dawkes should remain at Chilling had never crossed the mind of Thomas Kage. A certain five pounds borrowed, had been intended to take him to some remote fishing-town on the Welsh coast; at least, the Captain had said so.

"Do you know him?" questioned Mr. Carlton.

"A little. What is he doing here?"

"Fishing and sporting, *he* says. He does fish; but as to being a sportsman, why he is the greatest muff in the field you ever saw. The fact is, he is fonder of indoor sports than outdoor ones," continued Mr. Carlton significantly. "I fancy he is likely to become a relation of yours."

"A relation of mine! In what way?"

"Rumour goes that he will marry Mrs. Canterbury."

"Ridiculous!" involuntarily burst from Thomas Kage.

"I suppose she does not think so. He is a good-looking man, very; and is heir to a large fortune, they say."

"Who says it?" quietly asked Mr. Kage.

"Who? I don't know. Everybody; and he says it himself."

"How has he become intimate with Mrs. Canterbury?"

"Through living in the neighbourhood. He has been here a long while: ever since Mr. Canterbury's death, it seems to me."

"How and where does he live?" questioned Mr. Kage, who appeared to be absorbed, and not pleasantly, in what he heard.

"First of all, he was at the inn, and then he removed to a little furnished box there was to let, and had his sister down. He took it from month to month at starting, but now he seems to have it altogether."

"And is intimate, you say, at Mrs. Canterbury's?"

"Uncommonly intimate," was the answer of Mr. Carlton, who relished a dish of gossip more than anything. "Is at the Rock every day of his life. Folks say that Mrs. Kage went up there, and took her daughter to task about it; but Mrs. Canterbury is her own mistress, and will do as she likes."

"But surely Mrs. Kage is living at the Rock?"

"Not she."

"It was decided that she should, as Caro—as her daughter is so young."

"There was some such arrangement made, I remember. Mrs. Kage fished for it, and got it. But it did not last long,—nobody thought it would,—and she went back to her own home at the cottage. Mrs. Kage assumed too much domestic control, and the young mistress of the Rock would not put up with it. Mrs. Canterbury visits a great deal, and is extremely popular in the county."

"In spite of the unjust will."

"She and Mrs. Kage got a great deal of blame at the time, but people seem to have forgotten it now."

"Ay," mused Thomas Kage, "time is the great obliterator of human actions, whether they be evil or good."

He fell into a reverie as he spoke, and Mr. Carlton found he had the talking to himself; which was what he liked. The hint just given troubled Mr. Kage, in spite of its utter improbability. Barnaby Dawkes, with his debts and his ill-living, and sweet Caroline Canterbury with her marvellous wealth! The thing was utterly absurd, painfully incongruous; but, nevertheless, Thomas Kage would have given a great deal to be made sure that nothing was in it, or ever would be.

How was it, he wondered, that he had not heard until now of this lengthy sojourn of the ex-captain's at Chilling? His own correspondence with the place had been confined to a few business letters exchanged with the lawyer, Norris; for Mrs. Canterbury seemed to have taken umbrage at something or other on the day of the funeral, and had never written him one. Still, he thought he might have heard bits of gossip through Sarah Annesley, now Mrs. Richard Dunn. But Mrs. Dunn's chief friends, the Canterbury family, were all in Germany. Mrs. Rufort's health necessitated a change, her condition gave great anxiety to her husband and sisters; and Mr. Rufort got leave from the bishop of the diocese to substitute a clergyman in his place for twelve months; so that from them Sarah Dunn could hear no home news. Another circumstance, not explained to Mr. Kage until long after, had also tended to keep the fact of Captain Dawkes's residence there a secret from London ears. At first, he had been called

Mr. Barnaby. That he had, in his desire for privacy, given this name, was more than probable: *he* said the people at the inn had taken it up from seeing it on a letter, and assumed it to be his surname. The public called him "Mr. Barnaby" still; and the Captain made a joke of the same to the very few acquaintances he made down there, Mrs. Canterbury, her mother, and Mr. Carlton nearly comprising the whole. At any rate, whatever might have been the inducing causes, Mr. Kage had never known or suspected that Captain Dawkes was at Chilling. Now that he knew it, his thoughts were busy. Mr. Carlton talked on, and he answered Yes and No at random, as one who hears not.

When they reached the Rock, Mr. Carlton halted, and shouted for the keeper to open the lodge-gates. The wife came running out.

"I will walk up to the house," said Mr. Kage. "I should prefer it, for my legs are cramped. Thank you for bringing me."

He took out his portmanteau, and carried it inside the lodge, observing that he would despatch a servant for it. The woman took it in her hand to test its weight.

"It's not heavy, sir. My boy can run up with it at once."

"Very well," replied Mr. Kage.

Close upon the house he heard the sound of voices at some little distance, and saw a gentleman playing with a child: now running with him, now tossing him, now carrying him on his shoulder. It was growing dusk, but Thomas Kage had no difficulty in recognising Barnaby Dawkes; and the child was, beyond doubt, the young heir to the Rock.

Mrs. Canterbury was alone in the drawing-room; she had just come down attired for dinner. The article she had called a widow's cap was discarded; and with the expiration of the twelve-month, a few days ago, also her heavy mourning. She wore a black-lace evening dress, with jet necklace and bracelets, and some jet beads in her sunny and luxuriant hair. Her emotion at sight of her visitor was vivid, and he could not fail to observe it.

"O Thomas! this is indeed unexpected."

"I wrote you word last week I should be coming."

"But you did not say when. And I never thought you meant so soon."

"Am I too soon, Caroline?"

"O no, no; my surprise is all gladness. Have you come from London to-day?"

"I will answer as many questions as you like, when I have taken off some of this travelling dust; but I had better do it first, for it must be close upon your dinner-hour. You will like me to stay for that?"

"Stay for that! I hope you have come for longer by a great deal. Remember how often you have promised to come to the Rock."

"I had intended to stay one night at it; but—"

He did not finish the sentence. Caroline was looking at him with her wide-open blue eyes; dusk though it was, he could see their depths of beauty.

"What do you mean by 'but,' Thomas?"

"Well—yes; I will remain until to-morrow. How is Mrs. Kage? I thought she was living with you, Caroline."

"She comes in most days to dinner. I have long wanted to see you, Thomas; to thank you for acting for us as executor after all, in spite of your scruples."

A strange gravity came over his face with the introduction of the subject. His voice took a colder tone.

"If my declining to act would have changed the provisions of the will, I should have declined. But, in striving to perceive on which side my duty lay, that fact, above all others, forced itself upon my notice. The refusal would have brought no good to any one; only some trouble on you; and so I put aside my personal feelings, which were all against it, and went on with the task."

He quitted the room as he spoke, to be shown to the chamber assigned him; and, on descending again, found himself in the presence of both Mrs. Kage and Captain Dawkes.

Dinner was announced immediately. Captain Dawkes—we give him his title from habit—was advancing to Mrs. Canterbury; Mr. Kage stepped before him quietly, but with unmistakable decision. The gallant Captain fell behind to Mrs. Kage, her fan, her essence-bottles, and her mincing affectation.

Mrs. Canterbury, from the head of the table, asked Thomas Kage to take the opposite place. Captain Dawkes was on his best behaviour, subdued and gentlemanly. Mr. Kage caught, at odd moments, a glance of the eyes directed surreptitiously towards his quarter, and he knew that his appearance at Chilling was just about as welcome to their owner as snow in harvest.

"I hear you have been making a long stay in this neighbourhood, Captain Dawkes."

"Pretty well. I rather like it."

After dinner the boy was brought in, little Thomas Canterbury. He was too gentle to be what is called a spoilt child, but his mother seemed wrapt in him. Mr. Dawkes appeared equally fond: he took the boy on his knee, fed him with sweet things, kissed him, petted him, and kept him there until the ladies retired and carried him away with them. As Thomas Kage returned to his seat from closing the door, the Captain took a five-pound note from his pocket-book and laid it on the table.

"Kage, I owe a thousand apologies for not having repaid you before. I am so glad to see you—and relieve myself of the debt."

"You might have sent it," observed Mr. Kage.

"I know I might; but negligence is one of my failings. Thanks for the loan. You never got it repaid by that ancient relative of mine, I suppose?" he added, as an after-thought.

"I never mentioned the matter to her."

"Keziah writes me word that she is only waiting my presence in London to kiss and be friends. I thought she would come-to. For the past twelve-month, you see, I have got along without asking help from her, and that has put her in good-humour."

"But how have you been able to get along?"

"I had a windfall from a brother officer. A fellow who owed me a lot of money, and came down like a brick with it. I had given it up for a bad job; but he suddenly came into a fortune, and paid up his debts."

This was true. But Captain Dawkes did not think it necessary to add that the "windfall" arose from a former bet at gambling; or that its payment had enabled him to make for a time a show at Chilling, and pass off for a tolerably rich man; or that Keziah's means had been sacrificed bit by bit to keep the show up.

"Do you see any signs of decay?"

"Decay in what?" asked Mr. Kage.

"In the deaf party. It's an awful shame of her to live so long, keeping a fellow out of his own!"

"Are you sure that Mrs. Garston's death would benefit you?"

"Yes. To the extent of the greater portion of her fortune."

"I think you are mistaken, Dawkes."

"No, I am not," said the Captain, smacking his lips as he put down his glass. "Capital wine this of old Canterbury's! You don't seem to appreciate it, Kage."

"A short while ago, Mrs. Garston began talking to me about her will," resumed Mr. Kage, passing over in silence the remark on the wine. "I did not ask her for it: I didn't care to hear about it, for it was nothing to me. But she then said as solemnly as it is well possible for a woman to speak, that you would *not* inherit her money. If I tell you this, Dawkes, it is in kindness—that you may not deceive yourself with false hopes."

"Perhaps you imagine that *you* will inherit it," rejoined the Captain with a scarcely-suppressed sneer.

"I am sure that I shall not," was the quiet answer. "Mrs. Garston will bequeath her money without reference to me. Rely upon one thing, however, Dawkes: that you will not have it any more than I shall. Were

I not persuaded of the positive truth of this, I would not have mentioned it to you."

"Were I not persuaded of the positive truth that I *shall* have it, I should not be living at my ease as I am," was the retort. "She may have changed her mind since telling you this, or perhaps only said it in momentary pique; but I do know for a certainty, through Keziah, that Mrs. Garston will do right, and make me her heir."

The assertion was utterly devoid of truth, though the Captain's bold face was a marvel of candour as he delivered it. The fact was, it suited him to pass off at Chilling for a man whose large expectations could not be imperilled. Mr. Kage silently supposed there might be some inadvertent misconception on Keziah's part, or that her hopes deceived her.

"You do not ask after your little friend, Belle Annesley, Dawkes."

"Hope she's well," was the careless comment. "Had nearly forgotten her. Nice little girl enough: wonder when she's going to get married."

It was not Thomas Kage's province to tell Captain Dawkes he ought to be the bridegroom. In point of fact, he did not know how much or how little had passed between the two. Belle might have given her heart without due inducement; a not entirely uncommon case.

"Yes, she is a very nice girl," he said warmly. "Something seems to ail her, Dawkes. All her childish ways are put aside; and she is as staid as she was once light-mannered. Sad, in fact."

"Sad, is she? It's through living with that wearying old mother. How's town looking?" he added, deliberately passing off the subject. And Mr. Kage was content to let it pass. They rose from table together, and went into the drawing-room.

It was not altogether a merry evening. Thomas Kage was silent and thoughtful; the ex-captain like one under some constraint; Mrs. Kage shot keen glances, and not always pleasant ones, at the assemblage generally, from over the top of her smelling-salts. Calling Thomas to her, she made room for him on the sofa near the fire. A large one was kept up every night that Mrs. Kage was there.

"You have not told me how I am looking," she said, tapping him playfully with her fan.

Had Thomas Kage told, and truly, he would have said, very ill. Of all battered, worn-out old creatures, the late Lord Gunse's daughter was the worst. Her head nodded involuntarily. Mrs. Garston, over twenty years her senior, looked younger. In this past year she seemed to have aged ten.

"I hope you feel well, Mrs. Kage," was all he could bring himself to say to the appeal.

"Perfectly charming. Don't I look so? When Fry settled this white feather in to-day,"—pointing to the top of her withered old head,—"she said it became me in a wonderful manner, making quite a girl of me. Some of us never grow old, you know.— Thomas, I don't like that man."

The transition rather startled him. Her simpering face of affectation had changed to a sharp one, her self-sufficient voice to a dissatisfied whisper behind her fan; her eyes cast forth gleams of rage at Captain Dawkes, who stood for the moment at the far end of the room with his back to them.

"He makes himself too much at home here. I tell Caroline so, but she does not see it. Sometimes I think he must have designs on Caroline and her money. And that, you know, dear Thomas, would be undesirable."

"Entirely so."

"I wish he'd go away, and leave the place. He doesn't like me, and I don't like him. He is heir to Mrs. Garston's great wealth, poor deaf old object!— but still I don't like the unpolite man. Do you know much of him?"

Certainly Thomas Kage did not know much good of him, had he chosen to say so.

"I took a dislike to his rolling black eyes; it was the first day, when he as good as told me I'd got paint on. I do assure you, Thomas, my complexion is sweetly natural."

Thomas Kage bit his lip to hide a smile, and the tête-à-tête was broken by the gallant Captain himself, who came up too near to be talked of.

Both the guests left early. Late hours were getting to be barred luxuries to Mrs. Kage; and the Captain gave her his arm to the little close carriage that brought and took her, taking his own departure at the same time. It was scarcely ten o'clock when Mrs. Canterbury and her cousin were left alone. She caused the chess-table to be brought forward, and set out the men.

"You will play, Thomas, will you not?"

He drew his chair up, and they commenced the game. In five minutes Mrs. Canterbury had checkmated him. Then he began to put the pieces up.

"But will you not play again?" she asked.

"Not to-night. My thoughts are elsewhere."

He finished his employment, pushed the table back, and dropped into a musing attitude, his elbow on the arm of his chair. Mrs. Canterbury glanced at him as she played with the trinkets that were hanging from her chain. Her own spirits throughout the night had been gleefully high.

"Is anything the matter, Thomas? You have been as solemn as a judge all the evening."

"Is it true that you are likely to marry Dawkes?" was his abrupt rejoinder.

"My goodness! what put that in your head?"

"Is it true, Caroline?" he more sadly repeated.

"No, it is not true," she emphatically said. "How came you to think of such a thing?"

"A hint of it was whispered to me since I came down here."

"O, then, I know—it was by mamma," she slightingly said, her lip curling.

"No, Caroline. It was by a stranger."

"I am surprised at your taking it up, seriously, Thomas; there's not a shade of truth in it. But why cannot people keep their mischief-making tongues within due bounds?"

"It was not prudent, Caroline, to allow a man, of whom you know nothing, to become so intimate here. In the first place, you are too young for it."

"No, not too young in position. I am mistress of the Rock, and a widow; I have a child of three years old. You were always ultra-crotchety, Thomas."

"Let me tell you a little of what I know of Dawkes," was his calm rejoinder. "He has been a wild gay man; up to his ears in debt and embarrassment; has lived

2*

in little else for years past. Mrs. Garston has come
to his relief on occasion, but it has not seemed to
serve him much. When he came to this neighbourhood, it was to be safe from his creditors."

"Few men have been exempt from embarrassment
at some time or other of their lives," observed Mrs.
Canterbury. "Captain Dawkes's having been in debt
ought not to tell against him, now he is free from it."

"How do you know he is free from it?"

"Of course he is. He lives here openly, and seems
to have plenty of money."

"He may have paid his debts in part; he may have
some ready-money to go on with; I do not know that
it is not so, and you do not know that it is. But I do
know that plenty of money he cannot have. It is only
a very short while ago that his sister Keziah—I mention this in strict confidence, Caroline—applied to Mrs.
Garston for help for him."

"And if she did—it would be like asking for his
own. He will inherit Mrs. Garston's large fortune."

In the most earnest words he could use, Thomas
Kage assured Mrs. Canterbury that Captain Dawkes
would *not* inherit it; that his own expectation on the
point would inevitably prove a fallacy. Knowing the
old lady so thoroughly, he was convinced, beyond
danger of mistake, that Captain Dawkes would never
be her heir after the words she had spoken, and he
deemed himself justified in saying as much to Mrs.
Canterbury.

"I'm sure he may be cut off with a shilling for
aught I care," was Mrs. Canterbury's answer. "Captain
Dawkes and his prospects are nothing to me, Thomas."

"I thought it strange if he could be. But reflect

for one moment, Caroline—to such a man as this, with his, at best, uncertain future, what a temptation a fortune like yours must hold out! The—"

"What a shame it is people can't mind their own business!" interrupted Mrs. Canterbury. "They interfere with me in the most unwarrantable manner; they say I visit too much, and they say I left off my ugly widow's caps too soon—I wore them nearly twelve months, and they were spoiling my hair. And now they have been talking to you about Captain Dawkes."

"I was about to observe that the tastes and pursuits of Captain Dawkes—I have seen something of them—are not calculated to bring happiness to a wife, Caroline."

She smiled; a bright laughing smile. Mr. Kage was vexed; he thought it a derisive one.

"Caroline, I speak for your sake only—for your happiness."

"Then you really do care for my happiness?"

"I have never cared for any one's so much in life. You knew it once, Caroline."

Mrs. Canterbury had risen to stand on the hearthrug before the large pier-glass, and the red glow of the fire deepened to crimson the blushes on her cheeks. Or had they deepened of themselves? anyway, they were rich and beautiful. Thomas Kage thought so as he stood near to her; far too innocent and beautiful to be thrown away on Barnaby Dawkes.

"I *thought* it once," she hesitatingly said, "until—"

"Until when?"

"Until I married. But it was all over then."

"Not so; I am anxious for your happiness still, and I wish you would let me try and guide you to it."

"How would you begin?" she merrily said.

"First of all, you should break off the intimacy with Dawkes—How was it brought about?" he interrupted himself to ask.

"It began by his taking a fancy for my boy. He made acquaintance with him and his nurse in their walks, and the child grew so attached to him, nothing was ever like it. How could I help being civil to one who is so fond of my child?"

"Let there be truth between us, Caroline," he interrupted in a pained tone.

"I am telling you truth; I will tell you all. I care nothing for Captain Dawkes, and I only like him because he loves the boy. But he has grown to like me in a different way," she added; "and last week he asked me to become his wife."

"What was your answer?"

"My answer! It was such that I do not think Captain Dawkes will ever venture to speak to me in that manner again. He begged my pardon humbly for his mistake. It was then that he told me—but I had heard him say it before—that he would to a certainty inherit Mrs. Garston's fortune."

"This having been your answer, how is it that he is still intimate here?"

"He begged me to bury what had passed in oblivion, to pardon him for it, to let it die out of my remembrance as a thing that had never had place, and to allow him to continue his friendship with the Rock. It would grieve him painfully, almost kill him, to part with the boy, he said. I told him it was so entirely a matter of indifference to me, that he might continue to come here on occasion if he chose."

"Then you do not love him, Caroline?"

"No; it is not to him that my love is given."

"That tone, Caroline, would almost imply that it is given elsewhere. Is it so?"

She had spoken incautiously; and the flush of crimson rising in her face was so vivid that she turned it from him. Thomas Kage took her hand and held it between his.

"Would you have me go through life alone?" she sadly asked. "Why should I not marry again? Some mothers call girls at my age too young for wives. I am not three-and-twenty."

"My dear, I hope you will marry again; my only anxiety is that you should marry for happiness. What is the matter?"

Mrs. Canterbury had burst into tears.

"It is such a lonely life," she whispered; "it has been so lonely all along. I married,—you know about it, that I did not care for him,—and I found I had grasped the shadow and lost the substance. I tried to carry it off to others and be gay; but there was the aching void ever in my heart. Since I have been free, it has been the same: no real happiness; nothing but a yearning after what I have not. Sometimes hope springs up and pictures a bright future; but it flies away again. I have never," she continued, raising her eyes for a moment, "breathed aught of these my feelings to man or woman: I could not to any one but you."

"Caroline, you are indulging a love-dream! Who is its object?"

She was trembling excessively: he could feel that, as he held her hand, which she had not attempted to remove. Alone with him in that quiet evening hour, her heart full of romance and sentiment, Caroline Canterbury may be forgiven if she betrayed herself. Though she had heartlessly rejected Thomas Kage to marry a rich man, she had loved him passionately then, and she loved him passionately still.

"Who is it, Caroline?"

"Do not ask me."

"Who is it, Caroline?"

"*Need* you ask me?"

No, he need not; for in that same moment the scales fell from his own eyes. Her agitated tone, her downcast look, told him what he had certainly not had his thoughts pointed to. He dropped her hand, and went and leaned his own elbow on the mantelpiece, with a flush as rosy as hers.

Thomas Kage was no coxcomb—never a truer-hearted man than he in the world. His first feeling was surprise; his second self-blame for having himself provoked the avowal. But that Caroline Canterbury should love him still, after her deliberate rejection of him to marry another, after all these lapse of years, and the time she was a wife, never once entered into his mind. Rather would he have expected her to avow a love for the greatest stranger—for this man Dawkes, even—than for him.

"Caroline," he whispered, breaking a long silence, "was *this* your dream?"

Vexed at having betrayed so much, her sobs increased hysterically. He waited until she grew calm. "It cannot be," he continued in agitation. "Whether it might have been, whether the old feelings might have been renewed between us, I have never allowed myself to ask. There is an insuperable barrier."

"In my having left you to marry Mr. Canterbury?"

"Mr. Canterbury is gone and has left you free. The barrier lies in his unjust will."

"I do not understand you," she faintly said.

Thought after thought came chasing each other through his mind: some of them Utopian, perhaps; but, as she used herself to tell him, that was in his nature.

"Our former attachment was known to some people —or, at least, suspected," he remarked in a low tone. "Were I to make you my wife now, who but would say that will was a work of complicity planned between us?—the money bequeathed to you, and I the executor! Caroline, were you as dear to me as formerly, as perhaps you might become again, I would die of heartbreak rather than marry your money, and so sacrifice my good name."

Her face and lips had turned of a stony white; her heart felt turning to stone within her. Mr. Kage resumed:

"In my mind there has always been a kind of fear connected with the will. When it flashes into my memory suddenly, as events will so flash, I seem to shrink with dread. It is a strange feeling; one that I have never been able to account for. Caroline, rather than be connected with that will, in the way of benefit to myself, I would fly the kingdom."

She had turned her face to look at him: it expressed a kind of puzzled wonder.

"Yes, I see how inexplicable this must sound to you. But the aversion to the will, the dread of it, lies sure and fast within me. Mr. Canterbury bequeathed me, as you may be aware, one hundred pounds for my trouble as executor. What little expense it entailed upon me, I honestly repaid myself; and the rest of the sum I have sent to one of our most necessitous hospitals. I only mention this to prove to you how impossible it is that I could, under any circumstances, consent to reap benefit from that unjust will."

"Answer me one thing," she rejoined in agitation. "When you urged me so strongly to induce Mr. Canterbury to make a more equitable will, was this—this—in your thoughts?—that perhaps, sometime, as—as he was an old man, and I almost sure to be left free when still young—that this question of to-night might arise between us?"

"No," he earnestly answered, "I spoke alone in the interests of justice. I wished you to be just in the eyes of men; to endeavour to be so in the sight of God. From the day of your marriage with Mr. Canterbury, I have never thought of you but as lost to me; and I schooled my heart to bear."

Recollection, remorse, grief, were telling upon her. She shook as she stood, and turned to lay hold of something by which to steady herself. He could but walk across the rug to support her. But it was done without the smallest tenderness.

"I suffered then as you are suffering now," he whispered.

"Let me make it up to you," she returned, heeding little what she said in her despair—"let us make it up to each other. You do care for me still—I have riches, I have my love. O Thomas, let me make it up to you!"

"Don't you see it is those riches that make it impossible? Caroline, do not tempt me; it can never be."

"I will give up my riches; and think it no sacrifice."

"You cannot give them up. The greater portion are held in trust for your son."

Yes, she saw it; quitting his side to lean against the mantelpiece, she saw it. The riches must cling to her like some foul thing that could never be shaken off. The gold, so coveted and deceitfully planned for, was already turning to bitterness in her mouth, like the apples of Sodom.

"Then you reject me," she faintly said.

"As a wife; I have no other alternative. But, Caroline, we can be dear to each other still—as brother and sister."

"Brother and sister! brother and sister!" she wailed. "That is not a tie to satisfy the void of an aching heart."

"Caroline, my darling sister, you must school your heart," he urged in his faithfulness. "*I* had to do it. I have to do it still. Why! do you think this, now passing between us, is not bringing me the most exquisite pain?" he broke off, giving way for a single moment to his emotion. "But for the barrier that Fate has raised up around you, I should take you to my breast with rapture, now as we stand here, thanking God that sunshine had come into my life at last. It has been cold and bleak enough without you, all these years."

The jet necklace on her white neck heaved and fell. But for the utmost control, but for the reticence of action that never forsakes a modest, right-minded woman, she had fallen on his breast then.

"As brother and sister," repeated Mr. Kage, retaining his distance; but he was quite sure of himself. "Any warmer feeling, any more sacred tie, between us is impossible. Be composed, Caroline; be yourself."

"Yes, I will be myself," she answered, pride coming to her aid. "Farewell, Thomas."

She was walking rapidly to the door to seek her chamber. Thomas Kage opened it for her, and held out his hand as though nothing had happened.

"Good-night, Caroline. To-morrow we will meet as usual, and forget all this. I shall have to leave you very soon after breakfast."

In attempting to return his good-night, a smothered sob of anguish escaped her. His own heart echoed it as he closed the door and went back to the fire for some few minutes. The rejection he had had to give was as painful as any ever spoken by man.

And poor Mrs. Canterbury? As she tossed on her sleepless pillow, recognising at last the upright worth, the value of the man she had once rejected, retribution seemed to have laid hold of her with its piercing fangs. Throughout the whole of the live-long night she bewailed the possession of the vast riches that were not justly hers. Fatal, worthless, molten riches; as they seemed to be in her eyes now. They had brought the reproach of the world in their train; they had heaped this present misery and mortification on her head; they had thrown up an impassable gulf against him who had alone made her day-dream.

Pretty well, all this. But Mrs. Canterbury—looking

upon them in that bitter moment as a sort of evil gift, a fatality—caught herself wondering what else of ill they might bring in the future.

CHAPTER II.

Captain Dawkes in Town.

FACE to face with each other—she bolt upright in her richest brocaded silk, on the stiffest of her drawing-room sofas, he tilted forward from a small chair—sat Mrs. Garston and Captain Dawkes. Their faces nearly met. It was a momentous interview; and the Captain always had the idea that she could not hear one word in ten unless he were within an inch of her.

The year had grown older by a week only since Thomas Kage's visit to Chilling. Captain Dawkes, weighing plans and projects, ways and means, had at length brought himself to town, braving the danger that might accrue if his creditors caught sight of him. But he had learnt caution of old.

His large dark eyes wore a gloomy light as they gazed into the cold gray ones of Mrs. Garston. She had been telling him, in terms not to be misunderstood, that the inheritor of her money would not be himself.

"You never ought to have looked for it, Barby Dawkes; never. But I don't blame *you* for doing so, so much as I do those who flattered you up that it would be yours. Keziah, to wit. I told her, when she was last here bothering me, that if you'd come and see me you should hear what I would and would not do."

"And I have come, ma'am."

"You've took your time about it," was the old lady's retort. "But that was your business, not mine. And now I will fulfil my part of the bargain: First of all, though—is it true what Keziah tells me: that she has sunk some of her small capital for you?"

"That is true."

"And more shame for you to let it be true, Barnaby Dawkes! What?—no other means? Most men would have gone and broke stones in the road before they'd have robbed a sister."

"I live in hopes to repay her," said Barnaby.

"Do you!" spoke Mrs. Garston with irony. "What do you suppose Keziah said to me the other day?"

"I can't imagine. She says queer things on occasion."

"That if you were a married man you would be as steady as old Time."

"And so I should be," rejoined Barnaby eagerly. "I should be as steady and saving as you are, Aunt Garston."

She did not speak at once. Her bright gray eyes were gazing into his, as though she sought to know whether trust might be placed in his words.

"If I were fortunate enough to get married—that is, if my circumstances allowed me to do so—it would be the turning-point in my life," he impressively said. "My future safeguard."

"Barnaby Dawkes, I think it might be."

To hear even this concession from one who never spoke of him, or to him, but in terms of the most utter disparagement, rather surprised the Captain, and very much gratified him.

"It is true, Aunt Garston, on my honour. Let me

get the chance of becoming a married man, and you would see how good a member of society I should make. You might safely leave your fortune to me then, without fear that it would ever be wasted."

"What do you say?" she asked, bending her best ear. And Captain Dawkes repeated his words.

"Listen, Barnaby. I told you just now, as plain as I could speak, that the bulk of my fortune would not go to you. Take you heed of that once for all: *it never will.* When my will is opened, after my death, you will find two hundred pounds a-year secured to you; and, besides that, a sum of five hundred pounds down, which you may use to pay your debts with."

If ever a blank look settled on man's face, it did on that of Captain Dawkes.

"You cannot *mean* it, Mrs. Garston," he said after a pause.

"It is all you will inherit from me, Barnaby," was the cold resolute rejoinder. "I shall never make it another shilling—except on one condition."

"What's that?" he gloomily asked.

"That you marry. Now don't you mistake me, and think I want to urge you into marriage," added Mrs. Garston, rapping with her stick violently; "I'd be sorry to do it by the person dearest and nearest to me in the world. People should look out for themselves in such serious matters, and then nobody else is responsible for consequences."

"The devil take Keziah!" was the Captain's mental comment. "She must have been letting loose that tongue of hers."

"You fell in love with a girl in London, Barnaby; *made* love to her, that is. Considering that you are worthless in conduct, and hampered by debt, it was three-parts a swindle to have done it."

"But I—don't know what you mean, ma'am," replied the surprised Captain. "How came you to hear such a thing of me? It has no foundation whatever."

"How I came to hear it is nothing to you. Perhaps I saw it for myself. I can see one thing, Barby Dawkes—that the foolish child is pining her heart away for you."

"But—who is it, Aunt Garston?"

He knew quite well, and there was an untrue ring in his voice as he asked it. Down came Mrs. Garston's stick, ominously near his foot.

"It is Belle Annesley. How dare you pretend ignorance to me, sir! Do you suppose it will serve you?"

His face grew a little hot. He would not acknowledge to this; he might not venture, in the teeth of her insistency, to deny it. "It was quite a mistake," he lamely muttered; "quite a mistake."

"If it's the want of money that keeps you from marrying her, I'll remedy the bar," said Mrs. Garston. "She will inherit three hundred a-year from her mother; I'll settle on you both jointly, and your children after you, seven hundred more; which will be an annual income of one thousand pounds. If you can't think that enough, you deserve to die in the workhouse. Over and above, I will pay your debts, Barby, on the wedding-day."

Some twelve months before, Barby Dawkes would have leaped at this offer as a boon. Now, in the teeth of greater and grander visions, it only perplexed him. He stroked his purple moustache.

"But—suppose, Aunt Garston, that I were to decline the marriage; that I were— in short—to find it would not suit either myself or the young lady—what then?"

"What then? Nothing. *I* don't urge it; I've said so. If a word from me would marry the pair of you, I'd not speak it. The decision lies with you and her. But if you are both set on it, and you intend to be what you ought to be to her, you shall not be hindered for want of means."

"You are very kind," muttered Barnaby. "What I wished to ask was—about money-matters in regard to myself, if I don't marry her."

"Were you deaf?" roared out Mrs. Garston. "Didn't I tell you that, not married, you'd get two hundred a-year at my death? Where's the use of my repeating things?"

"And—until your death?" he ventured to urge. "I am in embarrassment now."

"Until my death I'll allow you one hundred a-year, Barnaby Dawkes. Not another penny, though it were to save you from hanging."

There ensued a silence. To attempt to contradict Mrs. Garston never brought forth good fruit; as Barnaby knew. He saw another thing—that what she had said now would be irrevocable for life. It was the first time she had explicitly stated her intentions, and he knew they would be abiding ones.

"Would you make me the same offer, Aunt Garston, if I married some one else?"

"If you did what?"

"Married another lady; not Belle Annesley?"

The question put Mrs. Garston into such a rage that he was fain to withdraw it, saying she had comprehended him wrongly.

"I hope I did. But I don't think it. If you could go and marry another, after what you've led that child to expect, you might look for Heaven's vengeance to come down upon you. She'd be well quit of a man who could act so, but it would break her heart. You may be a villain, Barnaby Dawkes; but I'd advise you to keep it to yourself in my hearing. And that's all I've got to say."

Barnaby Dawkes pushed his chair back, and fell into thought. A minute or two, and he lifted his head again.

"Marriage is a serious matter, Mrs. Garston; few of us, I imagine, like to enter upon it rashly. I must take a week or two for consideration."

"That's the most sensible thing you've said this evening, Barby Dawkes."

"And go back to Wales while I reflect; I dare not stay in London. You will help me, Aunt Garston? I cannot live upon air."

Mrs. Garston grunted. Air was certainly not very substantial to live upon.

"I'll give you fifty pounds."

"Thank you. If you would but make it a hundred!"

"Now don't you try my patience too much. What I've said I mean, Barby. Will you take some dinner?"

"Thank you. With immense pleasure."

"Then just ring that bell to let them know I'm ready for it. I'd have left out the "immense," if I had been you."

When the announcement of the dinner's being served was brought, the Captain gallantly held out his arm. Mrs. Garston put it aside with her stick and stalked on, leaving him to follow behind.

"I go in by myself when Thomas Kage is not here."

"Crush him for a snake in the grass!" mentally uttered the rejected Captain. "*He*'ll get the bulk of the money, the smooth reptile."

To partake of Mrs. Garston's good dinner was one thing; to remain the whole evening with her was another; and Captain Dawkes rose to leave with the table-cloth, making an excuse that he had a pressing engagement.

"I thought you were afraid of meeting some sheriff's officers in the streets," spoke the old lady in her open manner.

"There's not so much danger, ma'am, after dark."

But nevertheless, when the Captain reached the gate, he looked cautiously up the road and down the road, pulling his coat-collar high about his ears.

Little did Belle Annesley, enshrined within the safety of her mother's home so short a distance away, dream of the joy that the hour had in store for her. Mrs. Annesley, whose health was failing much, spent the greater portion of her time in her own chamber. On this day she had been downstairs for a few hours, but went up again, and to rest, at dusk; so that Belle was alone.

Time had been when Mrs. Annesley would have scrupled to leave her so much without a companion, but Belle's random days were over: never a lady in the land more staid, tranquil, home-sick, than she

3 *

now.   Mrs. Lowther and Mrs. Richard Dunn were
always more than glad to see her; but she did not go
to either very often; sometimes they ran in to sit with
her.

Seated at work by the light of the lamp, her fingers
slow and listless, her countenance hopelessly sad, was
she.   But she was not less pretty than of old.   The
face was young and fair; the blue ribbons—she cared
for no other colour—were still adorning the fine light
hair with its golden tinge.   Her dress this evening was
a white sprigged muslin, and altogether she looked in-
finitely charming.

"That's Sarah Dunn," she softly said to herself,
as a ring was heard. "I thought she would be coming
in."

"Captain Dawkes, miss," announced the servant.

One moment's gaze, as though she had not heard,
and then Belle dropped her work, and rose.   Her
pulses were tingling, her heart bounding, her face turning white as death.   She felt sick with the rush of joy,
her hands and frame were alike trembling; for a
moment sight left her, and she grasped the table for
support.

Standing before her, when they were shut in alone,
Captain Dawkes, experienced man that he was, read
the signs, read the love.   It brought him pleasure; for
if his heart had a preference, it was for this girl.   He
took her hands in his, he bent his face with a soft
whisper.

"You are glad to see me, Belle?"

Glad! An instant's struggle to maintain her calmness, as a well-trained young lady should, and then
poor Belle gave way.   She burst into tears, and Captain

Dawkes gathered the pretty face to his shoulder. He scrupled not to kiss it, and kiss it again; although he had as much intention of marrying her as he had of marrying you.

"It has been so long—so long!" murmured Belle, ashamed of her emotion, and sitting down to the work. "I thought you were never coming again."

"As did I," responded the Captain, taking a chair in front of her. "Things have been going cross and contrary, my little one."

"Are they straight now?"

"Anything but that. If that wicked old party would but do her duty by me, I should have been all right long ago. I've just come away from her; been undergoing the penalty of dining with the mummy."

"And have you come to London to remain, Barnaby?"

"Only until to-morrow."

Her face fell sadly. He drew his chair a trifle nearer.

"You know, my pretty one, where I would be if I could—where my heart is. But if the Fates are unpropitious, what's to be done?"

"It must be very dull for you, away from everybody."

"A frightful exile."

"I am dull too," she added in a plaintive tone. "Mamma is always ill; Sarah has her own home now, and her baby; and I am mostly alone."

"What's the matter with Mrs. Annesley?"

"The doctors call it a break-up of the constitution. She is sadly weak and spiritless. How do you manage to amuse yourself, Barnaby?"

"Fishing," answered the Captain shortly. "That and the bemoaning of my hard fate fill up the time."

"Have you many friends down there?"

"Friends! There? You never saw such a miserable, lonely, out-of-the-world place as it is, Belle."

The colour in the fair cheeks was going and coming; the fingers, plying the needle, began to tremble again. Belle's voice was faint as she spoke:

"Do you know what I heard? I want to tell you."

"Tell away, child. What did you hear?"

"That you were going to be married."

"Married! I!" And the Captain acted well his perfect astonishment.

"I thought it could not be true. Forgive me for repeating it, Barnaby."

"Why, you silly child, *you* might have known it was not."

The words and the reassurance caused her whole heart to thrill with rapture. O, but it was good to undergo the past doubt and suffering for *this* relief! The dark days gone by were as nothing now. One shy glance at him from the loving pretty blue eyes, and Belle sat on in silence. A question actually crossed Captain Dawkes's mind for the moment—should he accept the offer made by Mrs. Garston, and take this girl to his heart as his wife? He cared for her more than he could ever care for any other. The next minute he nearly laughed at himself: a thousand a-year and domestic bliss would not suit Barnaby Dawkes.

"What work is that you are so busy over, my fairy?"

"One of mamma's new handkerchiefs; I am hemming them for her," was the simple answer.

"Wish I'd got somebody to hem mine!"

Belle smiled and glanced at him. In her heart she was feeling ten years younger. Captain Dawkes suddenly bent down, and kissed the hand that held the cambric.

"Halloa! who's this, I wonder?"

A visitor's step in the hall called forth the exclamation. Captain Dawkes was in the act of pushing his chair back to a respectable distance, when Mrs. Richard Dunn entered, in a pink-silk hood. Belle's face wore some conscious confusion; and Mrs. Dunn thought she must have interrupted a scene of love-making.

And Captain Dawkes, who did not particularly like Mrs. Richard Dunn, took up his hat and went forth, braving the danger from the sheriff's officers.

CHAPTER III.

Playing for high Stakes.

In her own favourite room at the Rock, with its soft carpet of many colours, and its beauteous furniture, its rare and costly surroundings, sat Mrs. Canterbury. The French window was opened to the ground, and the gay autumn flowers were wafting in their sweetest perfume. On the lawn beyond, the young heir to the Rock was sporting with his attentive friend, Captain Dawkes. The blue sky was overhead, the warm sunshine shed delight around. Pleasant things, all; but to Caroline Canterbury they seemed as dismal as a dark night. For her the world had lost its charm.

She sat in a low chair drawn back from the window, dressed for gaiety. It was afternoon yet, but she had

a drive of ten miles to keep a dinner engagement, and
the carriage to convey her was already coming round.
It was only yesterday that Thomas Kage had quitted
her after his brief visit, and yet it seemed to her that
she had since lived a lifetime.

None, save herself, might know what fond dreams
she had been indulging since the death of Mr. Canterbury; dreams of which Thomas Kage was the hero.
There was no sin in doing it, as she would softly
repeat over and over to herself: she was as free as air,
and there could be no sin. None, save herself, could
ever know or conceive what awful pain, mortification,
and repentance his rejection inflicted on her. Bright
was she to look at in her gala-robes; the black-net
dress with its white-satin ribbons, than which nothing
could be more attractive to the eye, and the diamonds
gleaming in the hair where the widow's cap so recently
had been; but the heart within was encased in sack-
cloth and bitter ashes. What were all the jewels and
gauds of the world to her, since she might not enjoy
them?

She could not enjoy them alone. Whatever might
have been Caroline Kage's greed of gain, one great
need was implanted in her by nature—that of companionship. It might be, that until this moment she
never knew the full extent of her love for Thomas Kage:
we rarely do find the true value of a thing until we lose
it. He was lost to her for ever. The money for which
she had sold herself was hers; but it had deprived her
of Thomas Kage. In that moment it seemed that the
beautiful things in the room, the Rock itself, the fine
lands she looked out upon, had all grown hateful to

her. One balm amidst it alone remained, and that was her little boy; her love for him approached idolatry.

When she and Mr. Kage had met at breakfast, the morning after that painful and decisive interview took place, no allusion to it was made by either of them. Caroline chose to have the child at the breakfast-table, perhaps as a break to what might otherwise have been an embarrassing meal. But Mr. Kage, for his part, seemed to retain no remembrance of it; he was calm, kind, self-contained in manner as usual; ready of speech, talking of indifferent things, and still very solicitous for her comfort and welfare. They spoke of business matters before his departure; his closed executorship, and the future of the child, to whom he was trustee. And this morning Caroline had received a letter from him, which must have been written, she thought, on his journey to town. It concluded as follows:

"Your life at the Rock must indeed be very lonely. When you alluded to it this morning, I felt the fact just as forcibly as you. I had thought your mother lived with you. You do not please to have her, you say; but is there no one else that you could have? I do not like to suggest one of the Miss Canterburys, say Millicent; but she would be very suitable, and you used to be the best of friends and companions. Think of it, Caroline. If not one of them, take some other lady: and a desirable inmate would not be difficult to find.

"Meanwhile, I beg you to remember what I said to you in regard to Barnaby Dawkes. Dismiss him at once from intimacy, and gradually drop his acquaintance altogether. I should not bid you do this, Caroline, without good and sufficient reason.

"One thing more. If you are ever in need of advice or counsel, or aid of any sort, send for me. Whatever my engagements may be, I will not fail to come to you without delay.

"Give my love to my little namesake, Thomas. Train him well—O, Caroline, train him well in the best sense of the word: you will find all comfort in doing it. And believe me ever to be your faithful friend and affectionate cousin,

                                "THOMAS C. C. KAGE."

This note lay in Mrs. Canterbury's bosom, now as she sat. She was in a very humble frame of mind, and counted the friendship of such a man as something.

But it was a great deal easier to say, Dismiss Barnaby Dawkes at once from intimacy, than it might be to do it. Besides, Caroline could not quite see the urgent necessity for this step. He was little Tom's friend and playmate—there they were now, playing on the lawn—and what harm could it be? So that portion of the letter, and it was the only one calling for prompt action, she disregarded.

"Mamma, there's the carriage at the door," said the little fellow, running in, with his imperfect speech.

Mrs. Canterbury took him on her knee, kissing him passionately. Beyond this child, she had nothing in life to satisfy the longing of an aching heart; and hers was so young still! The many years to come looked long and dreary enough when she cast a thought to them.

"Be a good boy, my darling. Mamma must go."

Her maid appeared with a cloak, and Mrs. Canterbury rose. Captain Dawkes, coming in through the open window, took the mantle and asked leave to place it on her shoulders. Then he offered his arm to conduct her to the carriage, and assisted her in. It was all done in a quiet, almost deprecating kind of way; neither Mrs. Canterbury nor anybody else could have taken alarm at it. The last sight that met her view, as she drove away, was her boy kissing his hand to her from Captain Dawkes's shoulder.

Within a week of this time, Captain Dawkes left Chilling for London, to hold his interview with Mrs. Garston—as was before related. On the third day he was back again. Mrs. Canterbury was genuinely pleased to see him; the little boy had felt sadly dull, and in truth so had she. She had no love for Captain Dawkes, but she liked him; and such was the monotony of her life, that he, their daily visitor, had been sensibly missed. He told Mrs. Canterbury that he had made it all right with that old aunt of his, and that she had placed his succession to her fortune beyond doubt.

The autumn days went on, and with them Mrs. Canterbury's sense of isolation. When the first sting of Thomas Kage's rejection had in a degree worn away, she grew to resent it, and her mind filled itself with bitter feelings towards him. She began to contrast his heartless rejection of her with Captain Dawkes's unobtrusive homage. O, but Barnaby Dawkes was playing his cards well! And the stakes were high.

Mrs. Kage, looking on with sharpened eyes, took alarm. The Captain's visits to the Rock grew, in her mind, more suspicious. One evening, going there to dinner at dusk, she saw Caroline on his arm, pacing the dim walks; and the two seemed to be talking confidentially. Mrs. Kage made her way to a private room, and sent a mandate for her daughter. Caroline received the reproaches coolly.

"There's not the slightest cause for this, mamma. Even if I were going to marry Captain Dawkes, as you seem to insist upon it that I must be, what should you have to urge against it?"

Mrs. Kage was in too great a passion to say what. She broke her choicest smelling-bottle.

"Captain Dawkes is a gentleman, mamma. Looking after my money? O dear, no; he has no need to look after it, he will have plenty of his own. All Mrs. Garston's will be his, you know."

"That's just what I don't know," shrieked Mrs. Kage. "And if I did, I don't like the man, Caroline. I'm sure there's something or other against him. What has he been staying at Chilling for, all this while, I'd like to know? He's playing a part, that's what he is; and his pretended love for little Tom is all put on— it's as false as he. O my poor nerves! why do you excite me, Caroline?"

Caroline only laughed in answer, and said that dinner was waiting. Mrs. Kage liked her dinner very much, and did not keep it waiting long.

But, to Mrs. Canterbury's intense surprise, she heard the next day that her mother and her mother's maid, Fry, had gone to London. Captain Dawkes held his breath when *he* heard it, and asked what they had gone for. O, just a whim, she supposed, was Caroline's careless answer; and after that she thought no more about it.

Mrs. Kage, more energetic than was her usual custom, had taken a sudden resolution to clear up the mystery that, in her opinion, surrounded Captain Dawkes. She and that gentleman owned to a kind of subtle instinct against each other; and it would not be too much to say that she had hated him since the day he was bold enough to insinuate that her delicate complexion did not owe its lovely tints to nature. For the rude man to aspire to Caroline and her wealth, was worse than gall and wormwood to Mrs. Kage; and she determined to go and learn a little about him from Mrs. Garston. To whose house she proceeded amidst a dense November fog on the day subsequent to her arrival in London.

But, what with Mrs. Kage's mincing affectation, always in extreme flow in society, what with Mrs. Garston's deafness, always worse when under any surprise, the interview was a little complicated. Compliments over—which Mrs. Kage entered upon and Mrs. Garston received ungraciously, inwardly wondering, and very nearly asking, why so battered-looking an old creature, her head nodding incessantly, should have come out from her home—the visitor entered upon her business; explaining, rather frankly for her, the motive of her visit—that she feared Mrs. Garston's relative, Captain Dawkes, was casting covetous eyes on her daughter, with a view to marriage and to the grasping of her daughter's wealth. She prayed Mrs. Garston to feel for her, and candidly tell her *what* there was against Captain Dawkes—it was something bad, she felt sure —that she might "open Caroline's eyes to his machinations."

But now, between the mincing tone, and the frequent application to one or other of those auxiliaries

to weak nerves, the scent-bottles, all that Mrs. Garston
comprehended of this harangue was, that Barnaby
Dawkes was going to be married.

"O," said she, "made up his mind at last, has he?
He has taken his time over it. It's a good two months
since he sat where you do, talking it over with me."

Mrs. Kage felt inclined to faint. "Did you approve
of it, then?"

"Did I *what?*" asked Mrs. Garston.

"Uphold him in his crafty scheme? I'd never have
believed it!"

Had Mrs. Garston caught the word crafty, her answer might have been explosive. It was only hard.

"Barnaby Dawkes told me he wanted to marry.
Keziah as good as told me; promising he would then
be as steady as old Time. I neither said to him 'do'
nor 'don't;' but I told him, if he did marry the girl,
he might look to me for an income."

"Dear me! Do you think it right to play with a
lady's name in that free way?" demanded Mrs. Kage,
gently touching her nose with essence of lavender.

"Right!" retorted Mrs. Garston; "the girl's dying
for him."

Mrs. Kage's head nodded ominously.

"Well, I'm sure! How dare you say such a thing
of my daughter?"

"Say it of *whom?*"

"My daughter; Mrs. Canterbury. Deaf old mo-
del!" added the honourable lady for her own especial
benefit.

"Who did say it of your daughter?" retorted Mrs.
Garston, bringing down her stick with such force that

the visitor leaped upwards. "It was of Belle Annesley!"

Mrs. Kage thought they must be at cross-purposes,
and blamed the deafness.

"I don't think you understand, ma'am."

"I don't think *you* do!" was Mrs. Garston's irascible
answer. "It's Belle Annesley that Barby Dawkes is
going to marry, if he marries at all. He has been
courting her for these two or three years past."

Bit by bit, it all came out; at least the version of
it that lay in the old lady's mind. They wanted, she
was told, to get married; and she had smoothed the
way by promising to settle on them seven hundred a-
year, which, with Belle's three hundred when her mother died—and that might not be long first—would
make their income a thousand. The relief to Mrs.
Kage was something better than perfume. She opened
her fan, and gently wafted a little cool air to her
heated face. As she was doing this, a question arose
to her, and she put it openly: "Why, if Captain Dawkes
were going to marry Belle Annesley, should he remain
so long at Chilling?"

Mrs. Garston was at no fault for an answer; the
reason, to her mind, was clear enough.

"I said I'd pay his debts on the wedding-day; but
I expect my gentleman has such a pack of them, that
he is trying to make an arrangement with his creditors
to take less than their due, because he is ashamed of
letting me know the extent of the whole."

"O, Captain Dawkes has debts, then!" said Mrs.
Kage.

"Bushels of 'em; he never was without debts, and
he never will be, that's more. The money I settle will

be settled upon *her* and her children.   I'd not trust it
to his mercy."

"He tells society at Chilling that he is to be your
sole heir."

"Does he! 'Society' needn't believe him."

"Will he be?"

"My heir!" and down came the stick with a flutter.
"No, he never will! I'd not make Barby Dawkes my
heir to save him from perishing.   If he marries Belle,
he gets what I told you; otherwise, he'll never have
more from me than will keep him on bacon and eggs
in lodgings. Barby knows all this just as well as I do.
I went into it with him when he was last here."

"I think he must be—if you'll excuse my saying it
—rather given to tell boasting falsehoods," spoke Mrs.
Kage.

Out it all came.   Thus set off on the score of
Barby's boastings and doings, Mrs. Garston told all the
ill she knew of him: his fast living, and his many accumulations of debt; his meannesses, and deludings of
his creditors; his startings afresh on his legs, through
her, and his speedy topplings-down again.   Mrs. Kage
placidly folded her hands as she listened, and hoped
Miss Belle Annesley would get "a bargain." Any lady
was welcome to him, provided it was not her own
daughter; and in her intense selfishness she would not
have lifted a finger to save Belle Annesley from him.

"It's the best thing he can do; they'll get along
on a thousand a-year; very—ah—generous of you, I'm
sure! I suppose he is—ah—attached to her."

"If he's not, he ought to be," snapped Mrs. Garston.   "He made enough love to her, they say; and

she has been pining out her heart for him, silly child!"

"Vastly silly," assented Mrs. Kage, surreptitiously flinging some pungent drops on the carpet.

"Barby seemed to be doubtful about the marriage when we were having matters out together, and said he must take time to consider—afraid of his mass of debts, I suppose; I'll answer for it, some of them are not of too reputable a nature. He soon made up his mind, though; for he went straight from me that night to Belle Annesley, and Dickey Dunn's wife found him there love-making. Every mortal day since, have I been expecting him here to claim my promise, and get money-matters put in train for the marriage; and I know by the delay he is in some deep mess that it's not so easy to get out of."

"No doubt," murmured Mrs. Kage. "And he has found the Rock good quarters to dine at while he's doing it. Won't Caroline listen when I open the budget!"

"He will contrive it, though; he is crafty and keen," pursued Mrs. Garston, not having caught a syllable of the intervening words. "I shouldn't wonder but they'll be married now before Christmas. I told Belle so when she was here two or three days ago; it made her blush like a robin. She confessed to have had a letter from him that very morning."

Perhaps no diplomatist ever went away from an interview more completely satisfied than Mrs. Kage from hers. Her fears in regard to the gallant Captain and Caroline were laid to rest. She purposed returning to Chilling on the morrow and carrying her budget with her, making herself comfortable meanwhile at her hotel.

But now, whether it was that the journey up had been too much for her strength, or that the London fog had struck to her, Mrs. Kage, on the evening of this same day, found herself feeling ill. The following morning she seemed very ill; and Fry, her maid, called in a doctor. That functionary decided that she had taken a severe cold, and said she must not attempt to quit her bedroom, or to travel for at least a week. Lying at rest, and being petted with nice invalid dishes —game and jelly, and suchlike good things, and plenty of mulled wine—was rather agreeable than not to Mrs. Kage. The week passed pleasantly enough, in spite of its solitude. She sent to ask Sarah Annesley, that was, to come and see her; but learnt that Richard Dunn and his wife were staying at Brighton.

At the week's end Mrs. Kage went home. Fry wanted her to break the journey by sleeping on the road, but Mrs. Kage did not like strange inns, and pushed on. She got home at nine at night, too much done up for anything but bed.

Breakfast was taken to her in the morning. Poor wan old thing she looked in her nightcap, sitting up to eat it! Without her face embellishments, she did not like to be stared at, even by Fry; and she sharply told the maid to come back for the tray when she should have finished. Between the intervals of her going and returning, Fry chanced to hear a piece of news; and when she went in again it was with a face as white as her mistress's, though not so haggard.

Report ran that Mrs. Canterbury had gone out of

the Rock on her way to church, to be married to Captain Dawkes.

"Eh?" exclaimed Mrs. Kage, too much startled to realise the words, and looking up in a helpless manner.

"I think it's true, ma'am," said Fry. "The sexton's boy is telling them downstairs."

How Mrs. Kage was rushed into her clothes, and her bonnet put on, and her face made passable, and got down to the church in the space of a few minutes, Fry says she shall never know to her dying day. The news was true, and Mrs. Kage was not in time.

Very, very true. Captain Dawkes, taking alarm no doubt at the mother's sudden journey to London, had made good play with Mrs. Canterbury, and persuaded her to a quick and quiet marriage. That the sore feeling induced by the rejection of Thomas Kage urged her on in fatal blindness was, no doubt, the secret of her acceding. But that was known only to herself, and is of little moment to us. The unhappy step was taken, and already past redemption.

The ceremony had just concluded, and the bride and bridegroom, with Keziah for bridesmaid, and a friend of Captain Dawkes's as groomsman, were quitting the altar for the vestry. Caroline wore a quiet gray-silk dress and white bonnet; Keziah similar attire. Mrs. Kage, a variety of emotions giving her wings, flew into the vestry after them; Fry sitting down in a pew to wait.

That a scene of confusion ensued will readily be imagined. Noise, reproaches, tumult. Captain Dawkes and Keziah, their end attained, were cool and calm as unbroken ice; but for the clergyman, Mr. Rufort's sub-

4*

stitute, they had politely, but forcibly, conducted Mrs.
Kage from the church again.   The Rev. Mr. Jennings,
a middle-aged, fresh-coloured, capable man, stood by
Mrs. Kage and protected her.

"I *will* speak," panted that lady; "I am her mother;"
and Mr. Jennings told them decisively that the speaker
ought to be heard.   But perhaps he was not prepared
for quite all she had to say.

Every accusation that Mrs. Garston had made on
Barnaby Dawkes, every disparaging epithet she had
applied to him, Mrs. Kage repeated; affirming that it
was as true as gospel.   She was really agitated, and
for once in her life affectation was thrown aside, as
she demanded whether the ceremony could not be un-
said.   Caroline, between fright and emotion, burst into
tears.

"You have cause to cry, child, Heaven knows.   He
has been hiding down here all this while from his
creditors; he is engaged to that sweet girl, who is
breaking her heart for him; they were to have been
married before Christmas.   O Caroline, it is not you
he wants, but your money, to help him out of his
debts!   He has millions of them.   Deny it if you
dare!" she added with a shriek, stamping at Barby.

And, with that shriek, Mrs. Kage broke down.
She sank on a chair, white and cold; the exertion had
been rather too much for the worn-out frame.   Nobody
saw anything was amiss; it was only supposed she had
no more to say.

Caroline, utterly bewildered, doubting, sick, not
knowing what to believe or disbelieve, looked at her
new husband.   It had not been Barnaby Dawkes if he
had failed in his powers of rhetoric now.   With a smile

of calm contempt at the mass of words, and of sweetness for Caroline, he put her hand within his arm, and spoke a few low earnest syllables of reassurance. He turned to the clergyman, and quietly declared the whole thing a mistake; a tissue of misrepresentations from beginning to end—as the future would prove. And such was his cool self-asserting manner, that the clergyman yielded belief to it as well as the young wife.

"These stories have been concocted by Mrs. Garston," spoke Keziah boldly. "She was bitterly against my brother's marrying, and hoped to stop it. The poor ancient lady is in her dotage."

With a sob of relief, Caroline looked at her husband as he led her down the aisle of the church. She implicitly believed in him, and a smile rose to her face to chase away the tears. Fry stood up as they passed her, and curtsied. The groomsman led out Keziah; the clergyman followed slowly at a distance, his surplice on still.

It was not in Fry's nature to stay behind. The bride and bridegroom were going away from the church-door direct on their wedding-tour; the carriage had post-horses to it, an imperial was on it, a man and maid-servant behind. Captain Dawkes handed in his bride, and they set off at a canter. Keziah, who would be going back to London in the course of the day, started on foot for her brother's cottage to change her attire, the groomsman by her side.

"But where's my mistress?" exclaimed Fry, turning round when she had sufficiently feasted her eyes, and could see only the back of the carriage fading away in the distance.

"She is in the vestry," said Mr. Jennings. "I held out my arm to her, but she would not notice it. It is a sad pity, Fry, she should be put about like this by the marriage."

"It has come upon her so sudden, you see, sir, for one thing," was Fry's answer.

"So it seems. When Captain Dawkes came to me last night about the arrangements—and that was the first intimation I had of it—I'm sure I thought he said Mrs. Kage was privy to it. My mistake, I suppose."

Fry hastened on to the vestry. Mr. Jennings, returning more leisurely, and unbuttoning his surplice as he walked, was surprised to see her dart out again, livid with fright.

"What's the matter?" he asked.

"O sir, please come and see! My mistress is fallen sideways, with the most dreadful face you ever saw."

The Reverend Mr. Jennings made but one step to the vestry. Mrs. Kage had been seized with paralysis.

CHAPTER IV.

Breaking the News to Belle.

THE handsome carriage of Mrs. Garston, with its fat old coachman on the box in front, and its footman behind, holding his gold-headed stick slantwise, was steadily making its way along the Strand. But that Mrs. Garston was a little eccentric, ordering her carriage out at all hours as the mood took her, her servants might have wondered what took her abroad so early this morning. St. Mary's Church was striking eleven as they bowled past it.

Thomas Kage felt surprised, if the servants did not.

He was hard at work in his chambers on the dull November morning, when Mrs. Garston's footman penetrated to the room, saying his mistress was coming up. Hastening down, Mr. Kage met her on the first flight of stairs, ascending by help of her stick. She took his arm without a word of greeting, and pointed upwards. He stirred his fire into a blaze, and brought forward the most comfortable chair for her to sit in.

"Have you heard the news?" she shortly asked. And they were the first words she had spoken. Mr. Kage replied that he had heard none in particular.

Upon that Mrs. Garston dived into her pocket, and brought forth two letters, which she placed on the table. She was relieving herself of some weighty emotion by emphatic thumps with her stick. Thomas Kage wondered what in the world had happened.

"She'll repent it to the last hour of her life. Mark you that, Thomas—though I may not live to see it. I thought her a fool for making that other marriage, but she was not half the fool then that she is now."

And still Thomas Kage was in the dark.

The two letters before Mrs. Garston were written, one by Barnaby Dawkes, airily announcing his marriage with Mrs. Canterbury; the other by Keziah. Keziah very briefly mentioned the ceremony at which she had assisted; and followed it up by telling of the seizure of Mrs. Kage. She, Keziah, intended to remain with the sick woman that one night; and a despatch had been sent after Mrs. Dawkes, who might be expected to return on the morrow. Altogether, what with one untoward event and another, Caroline's second marriage did not seem to have been inaugurated happily.

"Married! To *him*—and in this indecent haste!"

Thomas Kage could not help exclaiming. "What can have induced it?"

"Induced it!" wrathfully echoed Mrs. Garston. "Why, his persuasive tongue, his cajolery—that's what has induced it. Barby Dawkes, with his rolling eyes and his tongue of oil, would wile a door off its hinges. I understand now the reason for his burying himself alive in the place, and concealing it from everybody. I understand why Keziah made a mystery of it to me, and pretended that the place was in Wales, and she couldn't pronounce the name. He has been at Chilling all the while, practising his arts on George Canterbury's widow."

Thomas Kage, standing against the window and looking dreamily out, remembered how he had heard the news of her first marriage in this self-same spot. *This* did not shake him as that had done; proving how well time had exercised its healing properties. Brought face to face with her the night that they stood together lately at the Rock, some of the old passion cropped up in his heart, and it had almost seemed to him that he loved her as of yore: in that hour of sentiment, when practical reality was lost sight of in romance, it could scarcely have been otherwise. All his present grief was felt for Caroline, and it was intensely keen. He saw, with a certainty so great as to partake of the nature of prevision, that this marriage was nearly the worst mistake she could possibly have made.

Mrs. Garston rose from her chair and came towards him, tapping his arm with her forefinger, her eyes and face almost solemnly earnest.

"Look you, Thomas,—this marriage will not bring Barby good. It has been brought about by deceit.

He has been deceiving her all along as to himself, his character, his means; he has been miserably deceiving that unhappy child Belle Annesley. Grand stroke of fortune though it may be in his opinion, it will never bring him good."

"I am sure it will not bring her good," cried Thomas Kage impetuously.

"I know now what his game was. He has been playing fast and loose with Belle, intending to take her if the richer scheme failed. I know now why he wanted his time to consider of it; and who he meant when he asked me if I would make the same terms if he married another. Ah, ha, Mr. Barby; you would afterwards have persuaded me it was my deafness that heard the question amiss! You and Keziah have been acting together to deceive me and gain your ends: it may not serve you much in the longrun."

Thomas Kage gave no answer.

"She has got a waggon-load of wealth, but he'll get through as much as he can of it," proceeded the shrewd old lady. "I've never had much love for Barby, or Keziah either; I dislike them now. What have they cared for playing with the feelings of Belle, so that their turn was served? He liked her too, he did. And it is not Mrs. Canterbury he has abandoned the girl for, but Mrs. Canterbury's money. Old Canterbury was a fool ever to leave her such a prey."

Very true. From first to last the will seemed to have brought nothing but ill. Last? The last was not come yet.

"I'm sorry for the poor old woman, Thomas. It seems she has got some feeling, for all her affected folly. You should have seen her the day she came to me—with her painted cheeks and her girl's white bonnet and flowers; and her palsied head nodding nineteen to the dozen over all. She brought in a fan and a cargo of smelling-bottles—it's as true as that I'm telling it. I'm afraid, too, I misled her—saying that it was Belle Annesley Barby was going to marry; but then, you see, I thought it was. O, but they are crafty, he and Keziah! But for hoodwinking me, and causing me to say what I did, Mrs. Kage might have gone back at once to Chilling, and stopped the marriage."

"Yes, it might have been so," Thomas acknowledged. But he remembered what he himself had told Caroline of Barnaby Dawkes, and therefore he felt that she was almost as much to blame as he. What infatuation could have blinded her?

"And now I'll go," said Mrs. Garston. "And, Thomas, you'd better call in at Belle Annesley's and break the news to her. It will be a blow: mind you that. Better not let it come upon her suddenly. I'm sorry for the child. So long as she was no better than a stage dancing-girl, flirting with every man she came near, I'd have nothing to say to her except abuse; but she was wise in time, and put all that aside. You break it to her; you know how to do such things; and so did your mother before you."

"I shall not be able to leave my chambers until late in the day."

"Very well; it will keep. Dickey Dunn and his wife are away, and there's nobody else would be likely to tell her. For the matter of that, I don't suppose it's known to a soul in London except you and me. There'll be a flaming paragraph in the *Times* to-morrow, as there was last time she had a wedding, but it couldn't be got in to-day.   O, Barby Dawkes is a crafty one!"

Seizing Thomas Kage's arm, Mrs. Garston moved a step towards the door.   Suddenly she dropped it again.

"You are trustee to the child's money, I think, Thomas?"

"Yes."

"Take you good care of it then, or Barby will be too many for you.   He'd wring the heart out of a live man, if it were made of gold."

Thomas Kage smiled; but there was nevertheless a very determined tone in his voice as he gave his answer.

"So long as I am in trust, he shall never wring a sixpence out of me belonging to the boy, Mrs. Garston.   Rely upon that."

Mrs. Garston nodded with some satisfaction; and stood to take a look from the window.   The river flowed on drearily, the grass looked poor, even Mr. Broome's chrysanthemums, dying away, had a sombre aspect as of the dead.

"It's a dull look out, Thomas.   I think I'd rather see plain bricks-and-mortar."

"All things look dull on these dark November days.   You should see it in the spring sunshine."

"I can't think, for my part, how old Broome gets his flowers to such perfection.   They must have been a show a month ago."

"Indeed they were; a very fine one."

"I'll go, Thomas, now.   I suppose I'm only hindering you.   Show me where you sleep first."

He opened the door of his bedroom, and Mrs. Garston and her stick marched round it, making her comments.

"Not bad for a makeshift: sheets and counterpane a tolerable colour; places tidy. Who makes your bed, Thomas?"

"A woman comes to do all I want. She is the boy's mother."

"Does she shake up the feathers well? Some of 'em are too lazy to give it more than a turn and a push."

"It's a mattress," he answered, laughing.

"Ah, that was one of Lady Kage's crotchets, I remember—mattresses. Well, I'm glad to see there's some approach to comfort for you, Thomas: but you'd be better off in your own home."

"Indeed I am glad that Mr. Rashburn has remained my tenant so long. The lease will be out next year, Mrs. Garston—"

"Do you suppose I don't know that?" was the interruption. "Mine will be out as well as yours."

"And I am not sure but I shall give it up," he added. "A single man does not need a house of that sort."

"Give it up, will you? Just as you please, Thomas Kage. Your mother thought you'd be a good son and neighbour to me; but her wishes and mine don't go for much, I see."

"Indeed they do, dear Mrs. Garston."

"Indeed they *don't*. Would you ever have gone out of your house, else, and let it to strangers?"

She walked rapidly through the rooms as she spoke, ungraciously accepting his arm at the stairs.

Mr. Kage helped her into her carriage—to the admiration of a small collection of urchins, who had assembled to stare at the equipage and the attire of the imposing footman.

"Good-bye, Thomas Kage. You'll come in to dinner, and tell me how the child takes it." And he nodded assent as the carriage rolled off.

Mr. Kage did not by any means like his task; for he knew that he should inflict pain. But he accepted it as a duty. Some one would have to be the inflictor —better himself than a stranger.

He did not get up westward until long after dusk had set in, which came on early that gloomy day. Belle Annesley, quite unconscious of the shock that was in store for her, was at that time in her mother's chamber. Mrs. Annesley, in an invalid wrapper, her feet stretched out to the warm fire, had dozed off in her easy-chair. Belle, seated on a low stool on the other side, was indulging herself with a peep at Barnaby Dawkes's last letter, not yet a fortnight old, holding the pages noiselessly to the fire-light, when a servant came in and said Mr. Kage was below. The noise, slight though it was, aroused the sleeper; and Belle, as if by magic, had nothing at all in her hands.

"What did Ann say, my dear?"

"Mr. Kage has called, mamma. Shall I go down?"

"Of course. He has come to see me, Belle; but I am very tired to-night. Perhaps, if he does not mind, he would let me be till another evening."

"I'll tell him," said Belle gleefully, the soft passages of the hidden letter—meaning nothing to an impartial ear—making melody in her mind. "But,

mamma dear, I think he might do you good. I am
sure you want rousing, and Thomas Kage is very
gentle."

"Not this evening, dear; not this evening. Is it
tea-time, Belle?"

"It will be soon. I'll dismiss Mr. Kage in a whirlwind of hurry, and come and make it."

"Ah, child, what spirits you have! And you were
for a long while so down-hearted. I never knew why,
or what the reason was; but you've got all your natural
gaiety back of late."

"The reason?—why, mamma, I was lamenting for
my sins!" spoke Belle, with a light laugh. "Don't
you know what a naughty girl I used to be? Don't
you remember the uneasiness I gave you? Sarah often
said I frightened her: but we called her an old maid
in those days."

Mrs. Annesley was looking at her daughter. The
gay tone, the glad countenance, the dainty dress—a
pale-blue gleaming silk—all told of a mind at rest
within.

"What are you dressed for, child?"

"This is Mrs. Lowther's night."

"To be sure. You are going there."

"But not for ages yet, mamma. I shall have tea
with you first, and go in at my leisure: seven o'clock
or so. The children won't leave till nine or ten.
Perhaps Thomas Kage has come to go with me. I
never thought of that."

Glancing at her pretty self in the glass, touching
her golden hair and the blue ribbons that mingled
with it—for Miss Belle was a vain little coquette still

at heart—she ran lightly down. Thomas Kage was standing by the dining-room fire.

"Have you come to accompany me to Mrs. Lowther's?" she asked, as he shook hands.

"To Mrs. Lowther's? No."

"She has a child's party to-night. I shall make mamma's tea and take some with her before I go in. Perhaps you came to see mamma, then? But she is tired; she has been very low and weak all the afternoon."

"No, not your mamma. My visit is to you, Bella."

He had never smiled once: tone and face were alike remarkably grave. She could but notice it; and one of those instincts of ill, that perhaps we have all experienced, stole over her.

"Have you brought me any bad tidings, Thomas?" she asked, calling him by the familiar name, as she had done before at earnest moments. "Mrs. Garston is not ill?"

"Mrs. Garston is quite well. She has had some news from the country to-day, and I—I have come to tell you what it is."

"Good news, or bad?"

"It relates to a wedding; but I call it bad. Won't you sit down, Belle?"

"I'd rather stand. I've been sitting all day in mamma's room. Well?"

"A friend of yours has been getting married, Belle," he continued, thinking how very badly he was performing his task, now that the critical moment had come. "Can you guess who it is?"

"A friend of mine! O, I can't guess. It's nobody

that I care much to hear about, I suppose. I have no very close friends, Thomas; except married ones."

She was perplexingly unsuspicious. Thomas Kage did not speak for a minute, and the young lady took occasion to call his attention to her attire.

"Is not this a lovely dress?" pulling the skirt out with her two hands to show its beauty. "If mamma were as particular as she used to be, she'd grumble like anything at my wearing it to a child's party. But she's not. She says I am changed; I'm sure *she* is."

"Belle, I must get my news out," he said with sudden resolution. "I am beating about the bush, my dear, because I dislike to have to give you pain. Of all the people in the world, whose marriage would you be the most unpleasantly surprised to hear of?"

"Of all the people in the world?" repeated Belle, dropping her dress and lifting her innocent face. "Do you mean the women?"

"No; the men."

"O, I—I don't know."

The colour was beginning to flush her face, her voice to hesitate. But still Belle had not the least suspicion of the astounding news. To connect any one in ideal marriage now with Barnaby Dawkes was simply impossible, unless it had been herself. Looking at Thomas Kage from a hopeless sea of mist, the notion suddenly flashed over her that some harm had happened to the gallant gentleman.

"Have you—come to tell me anything bad about —about Captain Dawkes?" she timidly whispered, hanging her head.

"You may call it bad. I would not pain you with it if I could help, Belle."

"He was not in that—O Mr. Kage, there was an awful railway accident in the *Times* this morning! He was not in that?"

"No, no. Captain Dawkes has been behaving like a villain: it is neither more nor less. Can't you take my hint, child?"

Belle's face was growing whiter than chalk.

"You must tell me, please," came from her trembling lips.

"Dawkes is married."

O, the sound of anguish that broke from that poor girl's heart! Mr. Kage thought she was going to faint, and threw his arm round her.

"My dear child, be calm. You see now how utterly unworthy he has always been of you."

"Will you please put me in a chair?" she gently said.

He was just in time. She did not quite faint, only lay like a dead weight for some minutes, and then her heart began to beat frightfully. Thomas Kage would not call assistance for her sake. Presently she sat up, trying to be brave, and leaned her cheek upon her hand. He drew his chair close.

"Now tell me all about it, please. I must know. Whom has he married?"

"Mrs. Canterbury of the Rock."

"Mrs. Canterbury of the Rock!" almost shrieked the girl in her surprise. "O—then—it may be for her money. It—may not—have been—for love."

"Be you very sure that money would outweigh love in his estimation any day," spoke Mr. Kage with scornful emphasis.

"But she is young, and very lovely," came the

bitter rejoinder, the one grain of comfort losing itself in torment. "Nearly as young as I am."

Mr. Kage took the listless, trembling hands in his, speaking gently. "You must regard me as a brother, Belle,—I have asked you this before,—and pour out your soul's trouble to me. It will make it easier for you to bear. I went through the same ordeal once myself, child, and can give you back sympathy for sympathy, sigh for sigh. I was the fittest person to break this to you—and badly enough I've done it—but I knew I should be more welcome than a stranger. All that you are suffering *I* suffered: suffered for years."

Belle bent her head and let her cold forehead rest a moment on Mr. Kage's hands as they held hers. It was a token that she understood and thanked him.

"Was it for *her?* I can feel more at ease if you tell me. We will keep each other's secret for ever."

"Yes, it was."

"I think I'll go to mamma, please," she said, attempting to rise; and her bosom was heaving, and her voice seemed to have lost its life. But Mr. Kage detained her.

"An instant, while I speak to you of Barnaby Dawkes. I can now give you my opinion freely. While there was a possibility that—that a nearer tie might sometime exist between you, my tongue was tied."

"You have never thought well of him."

"Annabel, there exists not a man in the world whose conduct I think much worse of than I do of his. I do not believe that he has the smallest sense of honour. He is a false, pitiful, self-indulgent coward.

Had you married him, I feel persuaded he would have made your life a misery."

"And she? Will hers be that?"

"I fear so; but in a less degree, perhaps, than yours would have been. With her vast wealth they can live as fashionable people—he going his way, she hers."

A moment's pause. Was Belle about to faint again? Her wan face suggested it. Thomas Kage rose, holding her hands still and bending over her.

"My dear, believe me, and try to realise what I say to your own heart. A marriage with Barnaby Dawkes would have been nothing but a great misfortune. Take comfort. Your pain just now is difficult to bear, but I think you will be able, regarding him as entirely lost to you, to throw it off day by day. *I* had to do it."

She wrung his hands with a lingering grasp, and turned to quit the room. As he was opening the door for her, she stopped.

"I cannot go to Mrs. Lowther's. Do you mind telling her? Say—say—O Thomas, I don't know what you can say! I had so faithfully promised to go."

"I will say that Mrs. Annesley is very tired to-night, and you do not care to come out. Leave it to me. God bless and comfort you, child!"

She went straight to her own chamber—not at present was she fit for mortal eyes—and there she strove to battle out the first fury of the pitiless storm. Desolation! desolation! Amidst all the tumult of her unhappy heart, Annabel Annesley was conscious that it would be nothing less for ever.

When she emerged from the room, her silken robe

5*

had been replaced by one plain and soft, the blue ribbons were no longer in her hair. There was no emotion visible, no sign left of the anguish she had passed through; her face and herself were alike strangely quiet.

"My love, how long you have been!" exclaimed Mrs. Annesley, glancing' at the yet unused tea-tray that waited on the table.

"I am very sorry, mamma. You shall have your tea in one minute. I have been taking my dress off."

The tone of the voice seemed changed; it was so meekly subdued as to sound like one of despair. Mrs. Annesley glanced at Belle, busy with the tea-cups, and noted the change of attire.

"Why, what's that for?"

"I don't care to go to Mrs. Lowther's, after all. I will stay with you instead, mamma."

Her mother alone henceforth. Belle had nothing else left in life to cherish now.

CHAPTER V.

At Mrs. Richard Dunn's.

ANOTHER year had come in, and was coursing onwards. The sweet May flowers were above ground, the May sunshine was making gay even London streets; those fine white houses in Paradise-square seemed ablaze with its light.

In one of the best of the said houses, the one owned by Richard Dunn, there sat, in what is called an American chair, a young girl in deep mourning, who was coughing sadly. Her face, surrounded by its golden hair, was painfully thin, her form shadowy.

She was tired of sitting by the fire, and had dragged the chair to the window to sit in the sunshine. You would scarcely have known her for the Belle Annesley of six months before.

Mrs. Annesley had died in March. The home was broken up; and Belle, with her portion of three hundred a-year, had been staying since with her cousin, Mrs. Richard Dunn. Where her home would eventually be fixed was not decided; all concerned were content to leave it to the future. It was proposed that in the autumn Belle should go on a visit to her brother in the West Indies, and so avoid the cold of the next English winter, for her chest seemed delicate.

Her chest seemed delicate: it was said from one to another. The girl was wasting away to death before their eyes, and yet it was all they saw! "She coughed too much, and her chest was weak, and she grew thin grieving for her mother!" O, but they were all blind together.

The first to see any cause for apprehension was Mrs. Garston; what was there that the keen old eyes did not see? Belle—poor, sick, weary, hopeless, grieving child—had been strangely averse to going out for a long while. Before her mother died, the plea of remaining with her was an excuse; since her death, *that* had been the plea. But Mrs. Garston drove one morning to Richard Dunn's, gave them a sound trimming all round for yielding to Miss Belle's inertness, and carried the young lady off with her for the rest of the day; at least, until dusk approached. She sent her back in the carriage then, telling her to keep the windows shut; and when Thomas Kage came as usual in the evening, abruptly met him with the announce-

ment that Belle Annesley was dying. Mr. Kage, seeing
Belle often, for he generally went in to Richard Dunn's
two or three evenings in the week, rather disputed this;
and it aroused Mrs. Garston's ire. Contradiction always did. He had certainly thought Belle looking ill
when he got home from circuit, but he attributed it to
her mother's death, and perhaps somewhat to the
mourning robes.

"How long is it since you saw her by daylight?"
demanded Mrs. Garston.

Thomas Kage could not remember. Not, he
thought, since last winter.

"If you are not entirely overdone with work to-
morrow, you just quit it for an hour, Thomas Kage.
To hear you talk of the amount of business on your
shoulders, one would think you must be making your
fortune as quick as it 'ud take an air-balloon to get
from here to Jericho."

"I have to do a great deal of work for a very little
pay," he answered laughingly. "It is only the great
guns amid us who make fortunes."

"You 'don't see much change in her!' she has
'a bright colour of an evening!' You are a fool,
Thomas Kage!"

"But—"

"Now don't you begin a dispute. Anybody, *not* a
fool, would know that invalids like Belle always do
pick up in an evening. If you can spare a couple of
hours of that precious time of yours, you go and see
her to-morrow by daylight, and then come and tell me
whether I'm right or wrong. Will you do this?"

"Yes, I will."

And accordingly on this very day, when Belle had

just drawn her chair into the sunshine in Mrs. Dunn's handsome drawing-room, Thomas Kage walked in. He talked of indifferent matters with as cool an air as if he were conscious of no secret motive for calling; chiefly to Mrs. Dunn and Mrs. Dunn's baby, a little damsel who sat on her mamma's knee, fiercely biting away at a coral and flinging her small fat arms about.

But he took the opportunity to glance between whiles at the rocking-chair opposite him, and at her who sat in it. Wan, white, shadowy; her blue eyes weary, her golden hair somewhat neglected; the thin hands lying inert on the black crape of the lap; so sat she. A pang of regret darted through Thomas Kage.

"How long has your cough been so troublesome, Belle?" he asked, as the baby grew restless, and Mrs. Dunn rose to carry it about. Not that it was a violent cough; but hacking and frequent.

"O, I don't know. I had it last spring. It went away when the hot weather came in."

"I shall feel your pulse, young lady, being a bit of a doctor."

He crossed over, and took her hand in his; a hot, damp, fragile hand, its palm very pink. Thomas Kage laid it down again, and put his gentle fingers on her forehead.

"I have had a doctor," said Belle. "Mr. and Mrs. Dunn called in Dr. Tyndal, in spite of my saying there was nothing the matter with me. There is nothing, Thomas, except the cough; and that will go away with the advent of warm weather."

"What did the doctor say to you?"

"Say! That nothing did ail me, that he could find out. He says it every time he comes."

"He really does," interposed Mrs. Dunn, jogging the baby in her arms as she spoke. "I tell him that Belle gets thinner; but he seems to think there is no cause for it. He says he has several young patients suffering from coughs; through the coldness of the spring, he thinks. Why, here's May, and we have had no warm weather yet. If the sun shines, it is only with a cold brightness."

"I should say he is a muff," remarked Thomas Kage. "The doctor I mean; not the sun."

Mrs. Dunn laughed, Belle laughed; and the laughing appeared to offend the baby, who set up a defiant cry. Upon which Mrs. Dunn left the room to consign her to ignominy and the nursery.

"Belle," said Thomas Kage in a low tender tone, seating himself near her and bending forward, "you are letting past troubles lay hold of you."

The wan face became lovely with a crimson flush.

"No," she said evasively; "no."

"Nay, Belle, speak the truth, as to your own heart. *It is so.*"

There was just a little feeble battle with the instinctive effort to maintain the denial, and Belle gave it up for ever. For a moment she looked into the kind dark eyes, bent in true concern upon her, and then hid her face in her hands.

"And if it be so? Will you tell me how I am to help it?"

"But, my dear child—look up, Belle; this is serious. If you do not make head against it, it will make head against you."

"Do you see that I am looking very ill?" she asked.

"Yes, I do. It did not strike me until to-day."

"Do you think that I am dying?"

"O Belle, you should not say foolish things!"

"But I feel like it."

She was looking at him now earnestly, and he at her; her sad eyes wore a strangely peculiar light.

"There's nothing to live for. I have felt that since —you know; and now that mamma is gone, there is less and less. But it is not that, Thomas. Though life had everything to make me wish to stay in it, to strive to stay, I feel that it would be of no use. It is drifting away from me."

"It is wrong of you to think this."

"But if it be so, and if I cannot help feeling and knowing that it is, where's the wrong then?" she persisted.

"Are you conscious of any malady?"

"No, not of body. I lose strength, and I get thinner and thinner; that's all."

"Then why should you feel that you are dying?"

"I don't mean dying yet. Only that I shall never get up again and be as I once was—as other people are. Thomas, will you believe that I have come to long for death? Heaven only knows what I have gone through—what my pain has been."

"You told me a minute ago that you had no pain."

"Neither have I of body—except the cough."

He took her left hand very tenderly within his, and stroked it, as a mother might soothe a sick child. The right hand was raised, shading her face.

"The pain and anguish are killing me, Thomas. I cannot help it. Indeed, I did try to take your advice to throw things off, and to forget gradually; but I could

not do it. I'm afraid I was not strong, and it has
worn me out."

"You must make a true, earnest, *prayerful* effort,
once for all, and rally."

"I have not prayed to rally. I have prayed for
death—but only if God pleases. There is no sin in
that. I believe He sees that I could not live on with
my broken heart."

"Hearts don't break so easily, my dear girl. I
once thought mine had snapped right asunder, but I
fancy it is whole yet."

She shook her head sadly.

"It has been breaking ever since that time—breaking and breaking; night and day, night and day. I
did not think any one could go through what I have,
and live. I could not go through it again."

"I am afraid, Belle, this state of mind is sinful,"
he rejoined, really not knowing what to say that would
make any impression on her.

"I hope not. The horrible pain is upon me always, Thomas; always. It is wearing out my heart;
it is killing me; it prevents any desire to live. If the
pain were lifted off me—and O, how willingly I would
lift it if I could!—then I should be happy again, and
wish to live on; but I cannot lift it; it is not in my
power: instead of leaving me, it seems only to grow
more real. Don't you see? I and my will are, as it
were, helpless."

"Yes, I see," he murmured, his tone partaking of
the pain she spoke of.

"It is making me wish for death, Thomas. There
can be no other relief. O, I know how good you are,

and how good Lady Kage was; but don't blame me, please don't blame me!"

"Blame you!" he interjected feelingly.

"And sometimes I think that God is not blaming me; that He is sending all this in love. I was such a wicked girl, you know: doing what I could to plague my mother, to ridicule and annoy everybody. It was well that punishment should come to me—that I should see my sin. With heaven in view, Thomas, it seems like sin now."

"*Is* heaven in view?"

"I think it must be," she softly said. "I think God means me to see it, and to long for it. I have taken lately to dream of being in the sweetest place; where the sense of perfect rest is upon me, and pain and tears are over; the light is beautiful, softer and brighter than anything on earth, and the flowers are sweeter. It is heaven, nothing less. When I wake up, and my real pain rushes back on me, I stretch out my arms feebly to God, and ask Him to please to take me to it. I think He will."

Thomas Kage sat for an instant in silence. This was difficult to deal with.

"Listen to me, Belle. If you mean that you really and truly think you are in danger of death, it must be seen to. We must call a consultation."

"A consultation! *It would be worse than useless.* What I am suffering from is nothing within the scope of a physician. I am just drifting out of life without any malady—except that of a broken heart."

"But—"

"Thomas, believe me," she earnestly pursued, "nothing can be done for me; there is no disease to

work upon. If you called in all the doctors in London,
they could say no more than that. Dr. Tyndal sees
me every other day: he will preach to you by the hour
about want of "tone," and spring's deceitful winds,
and young ladies' fancies; and finally tell you there's
nothing else the matter with me. Go and ask him.
Many a girl has suffered, and wasted away to death as
I am wasting, and the doctors have never known what
she died of. It is not their skill that is in fault."

"Granted; but—"

"And mind, Thomas, you must not speak of this:
you know that there's no one else in the wide world
that I would breathe it to. I could not have told you
but for what you disclosed to me that night. We—"

A servant came in, bringing the cards of visitors.
Not seeing his mistress, he presented them to Miss
Annesley.

"Yes, I suppose they must come up," she answered, wishing the house was her own, so that she
could be denied.

As the man left the room again, she cast her eyes
carelessly on the cards, and started up with a faint
cry. Thomas Kage bent to look.

Captain Dawkes—Mrs. Dawkes.

Since the inauspicious marriage (if you knew all,
my reader, you would indorse the word) of Mr. and
Mrs. Dawkes the previous November, they had chiefly
resided at the Rock. Mrs. Kage recovered in a degree
from her attack of paralysis, but only to be more
battered in look than ever, more dilapidated in constitution; and to pay her a visit daily Mrs. Dawkes found
an intolerably wearisome task. How Captain Dawkes
contrived to reassure his wife on the score of his ac-

credited ill-doings, he best knew: woman is credulous, and man is wary. He did contrive to do it; and after the accusations in the vestry, Mrs. Dawkes heard no more. Those who would have spoken the truth to warn her from the man, found their lips sealed as soon as he had become her husband. If Mrs. Dawkes had cause for any suspicion, it was confined to her own breast. She had committed the great imprudence of marrying without having her available money settled on herself, and if Captain Dawkes made free with it, why the law would have said it was his own to do with as he pleased. They went in for a vast deal of show and expense; and the Captain was a gentleman at large again, to display his face in the London world at will, and get as much credit as he chose. He had re-purchased into the army, and was altogether grand. Their London house, the lease of it bought recently, was one of the most fashionable mansions in Belgravia; and Captain and Mrs. Dawkes had now come up to take possession of it, with the intention of being a very fashionable couple. Caroline had always loved show and glitter; and it may be that she loved it all the better since her heart had grown a little seared with a certain blight Fate had cast upon it. But for the cold spring, and the rather delicate health of little Tom Canterbury, Mrs. Dawkes had been up before May. The Captain had been a good deal away from the Rock himself, pleading his soldier's duties. However, here they were now in London, and had come to make a call on Mrs. Richard Dunn.

The crimson flush of emotion burning in Belle Annesley's cheeks was already fading to an ashy whiteness. She had started up to quit the room, but the

sound of voices and steps close outside the door cut
off her escape. Thomas Kage laid his restraining hand
upon her in calm composure, and it almost seemed to
give her strength.

"Be still, Annabel. You have nothing to do but
keep quiet. I will shield you."

And as if to receive the visitors, Mr. Kage placed
himself before her. Mrs. Dunn unconsciously helped
matters by coming in at the moment. There was
greeting and much talking; and it was only when they
separated to place themselves in chairs that the invalid girl in her deep mourning was perceived.

"Ah, Miss Annesley!—how are you?" said the
Captain, putting out his hand as coolly as though he
had never played fast and loose with her.

Caroline took a step forward in curiosity when she
heard the name. She had never seen Belle Annesley,
but she could not forget that it had been said she was
Barnaby Dawkes's love. Barnaby, when asked about
it by his wife in private, had burst out laughing at the
very idea; had made game over it, game also of Belle.
But Mrs. Dawkes was curious, nevertheless; and she
came across the room to see.

Belle had risen. A fragile girl with a mass of
golden hair, and a transparent face whose delicate
cheeks were shining with a hectic glow. But if Caroline had been calling up incipient ideas of jealousy,
they went out at once as she stood; for there was
something about the girl that seemed to say she was
not very long for this world, and Caroline's heart filled
itself with a wondrous pity.

"Sarah, is this your cousin?" she asked, calling
Mrs. Dunn by the old familiar Christian name.

"Yes. Miss Annesley, Mrs. Dawkes."

The two had stood looking at each other, apparently waiting for the introduction, or Mrs. Dunn had surely never been so formal as to make it. She felt a little confused herself, remembering what Barnaby Dawkes's conduct had been.

Belle sat down again, her bosom heaving and fluttering; the leaf-like hectic fading out of the cheeks. Thomas Kage moved near her; the Captain crossed over and took a chair by Mrs. Dunn.

"I cannot think how it is we never met during the six months that I passed in London, when my boy was a baby," began Caroline, who seemed as if she could not take her eyes off the sick girl. "I feel quite sure I never saw you. We called twice on Sarah—who was then staying with your mamma—but I do not remember you at all."

Belle cast her thoughts back, to the time spoken of by Mrs. Dawkes, in a kind of transient shame. Too well she remembered that spring: it was in the very height of her thoughtless and flirting days, when she had no care for aught save her admirers. The advent of Barnaby Dawkes and his love had not dawned then.

"I must have happened to be out when you came," she replied. "I know I once went with mamma and Sarah to call on you in Belgrave-square, but you and Mr. Canterbury were not at home. I was very young then, and mamma did not take me out much. But I saw you once, Mrs. Dawkes."

"Ah, you mean in the old, old days when we were little mites of children, and you came down to Chilling

Rectory on a visit. That was just after mamma settled at the place. Of course we saw each other then."

"No. I meant when you were in town. You had been calling upon Mrs. Garston, and Mr. Canterbury was putting you into the carriage. I stood inside the gate and watched you away; but you did not notice me," added Belle, losing herself in the reminiscence.

"You don't seem well," said Caroline, a little abruptly. And the remark seemed to scare Belle's senses away.

Thomas Kage came to the rescue, speaking quietly.

"I was just telling Miss Annesley that her cough was making her look ill and thin; but she says she had it last year, and only got strong when the warm weather came in. It has been a late spring."

"It has not been much of a spring at all, down with us," observed Caroline, playing with her watch-chain, and never looking at him as she spoke. Face to face with Thomas Kage, it could not be but that remembrance should lie upon *her*. "Little Tom has had a cough too; they think his chest is weak."

"Have you brought him to town?" asked Mr. Kage.

"What a question, Thomas!" she answered, with a laugh that seemed not to be very real. "As if I should go anywhere without my boy! You'll come and see him, will you not?"

"Certainly."

"Mamma says I had a delicate chest myself when I was a child; she was always afraid for me. Papa died of consumption. But I grew up to be strong and well, and I don't see why Tom should not."

"The boy has always seemed to me to be a particularly healthy child," observed Mr. Kage. "Though small and slightly formed, he is quite sound."

"Of course he is," acquiesced Caroline. "Captain Dawkes says sometimes that Tom is *not* strong, but I am sure it is all fancy."

"Shall you make a long stay in town?"

"Until August, I suppose. I want to spend September on the Rhine. By the way, can you tell me whether Mrs. Dunn is in London?—Lydia Canterbury, you know."

"She is."

"The Miss Canterburys are abroad still. Austin Rufort and his wife came back to the Rectory just as we left Chilling. I did not see them; we crossed each other on the road."

"The Miss Canterburys are in London, staying with their sister, Mrs. Dunn," spoke Thomas Kage. "I seem to know more about your family than you do, Mrs. Dawkes," he added, with a slight laugh.

Mrs. Dawkes bit her pretty lip. She did not like his calling her "Mrs. Dawkes," or the coolly civil indifference that characterised his tone and manner, as if she could never be an object of the smallest interest to him henceforth for ever. Neither did she care to hear that the Miss Canterburys were in London. A sense of the wrong inflicted on her late husband's daughters lay dormant in a remote corner of her heart; the sight of them invariably woke it up, and Caroline would rather have been spared the meeting.

"O, staying with Lydia Dunn, are they? Do they look well?"

"I have not seen them, Mrs. Dawkes."

"Mrs. Dawkes" again! Mrs. Dawkes drew her chair round, and joined in the conversation with her husband and Mrs. Richard Dunn.

But Captain and Mrs. Dawkes soon rose. Perhaps neither felt quite at ease in the present company. In the movement,—the slight bustle of the farewells,— Captain Dawkes got an unobserved moment behind with Belle. Clasping her fragile hand within his, so warm with strong life, he bent his face until it nearly touched hers, speaking in a sweet and tender whisper:

"Do not blame me until you know how I was tried. The misery has been worse to me than to you. Heaven bless you, Belle!"

And when Thomas Kage came back across the room to say his own adieu after they had disappeared, he wondered what had come to Belle Annesley. Her blue eyes were shining as with the light of love; the dead weariness had momentarily left her face; and her cheeks were bright with a soft rose colour.

CHAPTER VI.

At the Festive Board.

THE crowded and prolonged season gave no signs yet of drawing to a close. If the spring had been cold and dull, the summer was lovely. London was very full; Hyde-park shone with beauty; frivolity reigned everywhere.

Amidst the gayest of the gay were Captain and Mrs. Dawkes. In their fine mansion in Belgiavia, they reigned a king and queen of fashion, entertaining frequently the world, regardless of cost. From the state

and expense kept up, by the way the money was
squandered right and left, it might have been thought
their purse was without end. There's an old saying,
"Lightly come, lightly go;" and both of them were
new to riches. The most absurd stories of Mrs. Canterbury's wealth had flown about, and society deemed
her revenues to be at least regal. Possibly in her in-
experience she fancied them so herself.

The Captain was in clover. Unlimited wealth, and
a high position amidst his fellow-men, had been the
dream of his ambition from boyhood. A dream of
fancy, however, rather than of hope; for Barnaby
Dawkes had never thought to be more wealthy than
Mrs. Garston's money would have made him. And,
even that he had not looked upon as a certainty. Although Keziah and others had told him he was sure
to succeed to the old lady's inheritance, in his own
heart there had always lain a doubt of it. She herself
had never led him to expect it—never by a single
hint; on the contrary, words had many a time fallen
from her lips from which he knew he might draw a
totally opposite deduction. And therefore Mr. Barnaby
could never in reality plead expectations as an excuse
for the spendthrift ways he took up. But what was
Mrs. Garston's moderate wealth compared to this that
he had come into by his marriage with Mrs. Canterbury? Barnaby Dawkes estimated that, now, much
as he did a few ashes from his cigar. He could at
length afford to snap his fingers at the old lady; and
did so metaphorically.

To marry Barnaby Dawkes was an imprudent step
of Mrs. Canterbury's; to marry him in the haste she
did, and without any kind of settlement, was im-

prudence terrible. For see you not that by so doing
all moneys, not secured to her separate use by her
first husband, passed into his power? Reviewing this
desirable fact in his mind while he shaved, the morning after his marriage, complacently regarding himself
in the glass, the Captain called it a "godsend." Possibly: but he had not the sense to foresee that to a
man of his lavish tastes and self-indulgent habits it
might prove a dangerous one. He paid his debts,—
more, were they, than the world or Keziah knew of;
he repurchased into a crack corps; he flung money
about as inclination dictated, without the slightest
stint; and he and his wife, quitting the Rock, set up
their gorgeous tent in Belgravia for the season, to live
on the scale of princes.

They were a fashionable couple in other respects
as well; politely indifferent to each other, rather than
cordial. That Caroline had found out her mistake in
marrying him, was only too probable; and the very
listlessness in which her days were passed caused her
to enter the more eagerly into gaiety. If she repented,
she did not show it; woman-like, she buried it within
her breast; and talked, and dressed, and laughed, and
was the gayest of the gay. She liked the life; possessing, in point of fact, an innate genius for it. A late
breakfast in the morning, she and Barnaby lounging
over it together, glancing at their plans for the day
and picking out the most agreeable ways of killing
time; very fine and fashionable both, in look and
manner and speech, and intensely heartless; he away
afterwards, she devouring some charming novel; a few
select morning callers; a grand luncheon, taken nearly
always in company; next the real visiting and being

visited; then going out to buy dress and flowers and sweetmeats—anything attractive that shops can display; the Park later; dinner (always a sumptuous one), out or at home; the Opera and evening assemblies; and to bed in the morning sunlight. This was the life; it was, in fact, nothing but a whirl of excitement, and both Captain and Mrs. Dawkes thought it paradise. He, of course, had other pursuits—billiards and wine-drinking and gambling.

But it is not entirely of Captain and Mrs. Dawkes that this chapter must treat. Looking on at all this extravagance and gaiety were the inmates of a house in a less fashionable quarter, but not so very far removed either; and that was Mrs. Dunn's, of Paradise-square. Mrs. Dunn had her two sisters staying with her—Olive and Millicent Canterbury. It was natural that they should see all this lavish waste of money, *their* money, with grievous heart-burning. Yes, their money; they could not but look upon it as theirs still of right, for they had been born to it. Who were these strangers, these interlopers, Caroline Dawkes and Barnaby her husband, that they should be revelling in the sisters' birthright? Olive and Millicent did not suffer their lips to put the question even to each other. Mrs. Dunn, less reticent, asked it a dozen times a-day. But, like many another bitter wrong, it had to be endured, for there was no remedy; and two of them at least strove to make the best of it.

The two houses kept up a show of friendship. Stay; not friendship, acquaintanceship. Miss Canterbury willed it so. It was better, she urged; and, after all, what good would be gained by showing resentment? Millicent, following her eldest sister's lead

always, acquiesced without a word. Mrs. Dunn grum-
blingly yielded; not to comply with Olive's advice, but
because in her curiosity she would see a little farther
into Captain and Mrs. Dawkes, and Captain and Mrs.
Dawkes's ménage. So a call had been exchanged
twice or thrice, and now there was going to be a
dinner. Caroline felt a kind of uneasiness in their
presence always, her husband none. Indeed, he personally could not be changed with offence to them.

The fine June day was drawing, like the month itself, to a close, as Keziah Dawkes picked her way
across the watered streets of Belgravia to her brother's
residence. However gratified Barnaby Dawkes might
be with the substantial good resulting from his marriage, Keziah was less so. In the abstract she had not
wished her brother to marry at all; she felt, to this
hour, the keen pang that shot across her heart the
evening that he had first spoken of Belle Annesley as
his possible future wife; for Keziah loved him jealously.
But when Barnaby cast his covetous eyes on the wealthy
Mrs. Canterbury, and sent for Keziah to help him scheme
to get her, she had entered into it with her whole
spirit. What precise good Keziah pictured to result
from it for herself, she never said; but she certainly
looked for a great deal. And she was feeling disappointed: for as yet the good had not come. To be
welcomed as an inmate of this Belgravian mansion,
she had confidently anticipated; but she had not got
there yet. In point of fact, Mrs. Dawkes did not like
Keziah, and she told her husband that she would not
have her there. Keziah thought he might have taken
the reins into his own hands; and she intended to
suggest it to him. Reaching the door, she gave a

knock and then a ring; and a smart footman, in the smart Canterbury livery, appeared.

"Is Captain Dawkes at home?"

"No, mem."

"Mrs. Dawkes?"

"Mrs. Dawkes has not come in yet, mem. There's nobody within but Mrs. Kage."

Keziah felt a little surprised.

"Mrs. Kage! Is she here?"

"She come up three or four days ago, mem," said the man. "I think she is in her room, a being dressed for dinner."

"I will wait," said Keziah.

Making herself at home in the house, as she chose always to do, she turned into the dining-room. The table was already laid, and for several people.

"There's a dinner-party to-day, I see," observed Keziah quickly, the. beautiful glass and silver glittering in her eyes like so many diamonds.

"Not much of a party, mem; a family assemblage, I believe," answered the servant, who minced his words affectedly like some of his betters. "The Misses Canterburys is to dine with us, and one or two more."

Keziah passed into a small room that her brother called his "study." Pipes and pistols, and suchlike curiosities, lay about; but of materials for other kinds of study there appeared to be none. She sat down by the window, which had a lively prospect of the back yard.

"When my brother comes in, say that I am waiting here to see him," she said.

And the man left her.

Captain Dawkes and his wife arrived together. He

had been driving her in the Park. As Mrs. Dawkes passed upstairs, the servant delivered the message to his master.

"Well, Keziah," said the Captain, beginning to unbutton his gloves slowly as he entered.

Keziah shook hands with him. Since the marriage her manners had become, perhaps unconsciously, more formal. Time was when her only greeting to him had been a loving kiss.

"I have been waiting in for you every evening for a week past, Barnaby," she began, some resentment in her tone. "You promised to come and talk one or two things over with me."

"Awfully sorry for it," said the Captain, with a great show of repentance. "Haven't been able to come, 'pon honour."

Keziah took her bonnet-string in one hand and stroked it with the other,—a habit she had when in deep thought,—while her eyes were fixed reproachfully on Barnaby.

"The matters must be talked of between us, Barnaby, for my sake, if not for yours. I have never thought but of you through life; but I—I must consider a little for myself now."

"To-morrow, or next day, I'll come for certain, Keziah. We get up awfully late here, and the morning's gone before one can look round."

"I suppose that is a consequence of your going to bed late?" said Keziah, alluding to the getting up. "I am out of my bed at eight every morning in the year."

"Jolly freezing that, in winter!" remarked the

gallant Captain. "Look here, you'll stay dinner. Go up and take your bonnet off."

"You have a party to-day, and I am not dressed for it."

"A party? no. The Canterburys and Dunns and Tom Kage. Don't think there'll be anybody else. No need of particular dress for them."

"I did think you would have asked me to come here and stay a few days with you, Barnaby," she broke forth, the sore feeling finding vent at last. "It would be a relief after my poor lodgings."

"Fact is, Caroline objects to have people staying with her," spoke the Captain with indifference.

"*You* might invite *me*."

"I'll see later. No time to think about things. Hands full of engagements always. You'll stay to dinner though?"

"Barnaby, do you ever look back to the old days," she asked in a low tone, her gray hard face bent forward with an expression of intense pain, "when you and I struggled on together, with very few comforts and no dainties, and you went in fear of your liberty? Do you ever recall that time?"

"Why, on earth, should I?" demanded the Captain. "I'm only too glad to send it amidst the bygones. What's the matter with you, Keziah?"

The matter with her! Keziah Dawkes was only learning the hard lesson that many another woman has had to learn. His turn served, the wealth and position he had coveted his at last, Barnaby Dawkes's entire selfishness displayed itself in its true colours. He cared no more for the sister who had sacrificed so much for him than he did for the rest of the world.

Self it had been always with Barnaby; self it would be to the end.

"I did think you might have liked to have me for a short while in your house, Barby, now that you have one worth coming to," she said a little plaintively.

"Ah—tell you, got no time to think about it just now, Keziah," was the supremely independent answer. "Such a lot to do in town always. You shall come and stay with us at the Rock."

A gracious promise apparently, but not a sincere one. Barnaby's private belief was, that his wife would no more have Keziah at the Rock than she would in Belgravia. For himself it was a matter of nearly perfect indifference; of the two, he would rather prefer Keziah's room to her company.

"O Barnaby! what a splendid diamond!"

Captain Dawkes did most things with the drawling slowness of a man of fashion, and he had by this time got off one of his gloves. A diamond on the third finger of his right hand flashed in the light.

"Rather nice," acquiesced the Captain listlessly, as if diamonds were as common with him now as debts once were. "It's a little too large: got to wear it on this finger; shall have it taken in."

"It must have been a priceless diamond," remarked Keziah.

"No; cheap, for what it is. Gave three hundred and fifty for it. Saw it by accident at Garrard's the other day, and nailed it on the spot. Ordered a set of studs to match; doubt if they'll get 'em as fine as—My dear, what's the matter?"

For Mrs. Dawkes had come into the room in a

kind of commotion. She did not at first see Keziah, and began to speak very rapidly.

"Did you ever *know* anything like mamma? She says she is going to dine at table, and is being got up for it in a low dress.—O, how do you do, Keziah?"

"I was telling Keziah to take her bonnet off and stay to dinner," remarked the Captain. "Not dressed for it, she answers: as if that mattered!"

"O, don't think of your dress," said Caroline graciously.—"But about mamma, Barnaby; what's to be done."

"Let her dine at table if she wants to," was Barnaby's comment.

"But she'll look—she'll look—such an object," returned Mrs. Dawkes, hesitating to apply the word to her mother, but finding no ready substitute.

"And if she does?" said the easy Captain. "There'll be no strangers."

Mrs. Dawkes and Keziah went upstairs together. The latter unbuttoned her mantle, and glanced at her tight-fitting brown-silk dress. Good of its kind, but not quite the thing for a dinner-party. Keziah Dawkes, however, had outlived the age of vanity. She never possessed much; all hers had been concentered in her handsome brother.

She went and sat in the drawing-room alone, and there waited for the appearance of the company, indoor and out-door. What a beautiful room it was! Keziah was engaged in a mental calculation as to how many hundreds of pounds the furniture and fittings-up had cost, when her attention was attracted by the entrance of Mrs. Kage.

Keziah's eyes took a startled stare of surprise, and

she drew back involuntarily. Was it indeed Mrs. Kage?
or some poor puppet fantastically attired to frighten
the world?   Sure such a painted face was never seen
in connection with paralysis!   For the remains of that
seizure were still upon her: the legs were uncertain,
the arms shook, the mouth twitched incessantly.   Fry,
the maid, dragged rather than led her across the room
to a seat.   Keziah, in her humanity, went up and
helped.

"O dear!—much obliged—who is it?" asked the
poor cracked jerking voice, and the dim eyes looked
up; eyes too near their final closing to be tricked out
as they were with belladonna.

"It is I—Keziah Dawkes.   I am glad to see you
can be about again, Mrs. Kage."

"O, I'm quite well, thank you; quite blooming.—
Fry, where are you putting me?"

Fry and Keziah were putting her into the easiest
and safest chair they could find, one with large elbows;
from an unsafe one she might have tumbled out.   O,
what a mockery it was!—her bedizened face; the
flowers and feathers nodding on the head never still;
the bare neck with its thin black-lace covering; the
jangling beads on the skeleton wrists!   When Mrs.
Kage should be attired for her coffin, lying in it at
rest, she would be more seemly to the eye than she
was now.

"Fry had scarcely fixed her, or finished picking up
the fans and scent-bottles that would keep falling from
her hands and lap, when Mrs. Dawkes entered—a
lovely vision she, in pearls and blue satin.   Something
like dismay rose to her beautiful face.

"Fry! how could you think of bringing mamma

here?" came the vexed question. "She should have been taken at once to her place at table."

"She'd not go, ma'am," answered Fry. "She would not hear of it."

"But how is she to be got down when the people are here?—Mamma"—bending low her face to the palsied one—"you had better go to the dinner-table at once, it will be more comfortable for you."

"What do you mean?" asked Mrs. Kage shrilly. "I am going down with the rest; I am not a child. O, the ingratitude of daughters! After I have schemed for you, Caroline, to put you in your beautiful position, and got you loads of wealth, and—"

"There, there, mamma; that will do.—Fry, pour some eau-de-Cologne on mamma's hands."

Mrs. Kage was ever ready for scent in any shape, and the "pouring it on her hands" took her attention from undesirable reminiscences. Caroline, biting her pretty lips, walked to the window and looked out.

She was just in time to see the stoppage of Mrs. Dunn's carriage underneath. One, the first to step from it, caused her heart to thrill even then; it was Thomas Kage. He turned round to give his hand to the rest. Millicent Canterbury jumped lightly down; Olive came next; Lydia Dunn last. Captain Dawkes, entering the room close behind them, found himself pulled gently by the coat-tails.

"May I come in, papa?"

"No, certainly not," growled the Captain angrily. "We don't want you, sir. Be off back!"

The child—it was little Tom Canterbury—shrank away timidly. He had his mother's blue eyes and her fair hair. Mr. Kage, who had lingered a moment to

give Mrs. Dunn's footman his directions, came just in
the boy's way, and stretched out his arms playfully on
either side to make a barrier. They were alone on the
landing. Something like a sob burst from Tom.

"Why, my little fellow, what is it?"

"Papa won't let me go in; he is always cross
now. Mamma is there, and I've got to go away to the
nursery."

"I'll take you," said Mr. Kage. "We'll go together."

Picking up the child in his arms, he carried him
up the stairs very tenderly. Some instinct whispered
to him that Captain Dawkes's show of love before marriage for this unfortunate child had faded into air. In
point of fact it was so; Captain Dawkes was not deliberately harsh or cruel to the boy—his wife would
not have permitted that; but he was coldly indifferent,
sometimes very cross. Judith, the nurse, sat in the
nursery, mending a pinafore.

"Back again, Master Tom! I knew it was of no
good your asking."

She turned round, saw Mr. Kage, and rose. The
little boy ran to a box of bricks, and began showing
Mr. Kage what a good house he could build. They
were the best of friends, rare though their meetings
were; and Mr. Kage never failed to bring some delightful book to please the child's eye or ear. He
drew one from his pocket now, and took the boy on
his knee. Tom—he was always gentle—pressed his
little hands together with delight at the first picture.

"What's that, Mr. Kage? An angel?"

"I never see such a child," interposed Judith in a
superstitious semi-whisper. "He's always wanting to

talk of angels and heaven, sir; one would think they
had called him to go up there."

"Well, this is an angel," said Thomas Kage, smiling pleasantly. "See, Tom—he is standing at the top
of the ladder; and Jacob is asleep at the foot, with his
head on the hard stone."

"Does the ladder reach right up into heaven?"
asked little Tom.

"Right up. And the angels, though we cannot
see them, Tom, will help us all to climb it in our
turn."

"I dream of the angels sometimes," said Tom; "I
like to."

"Just hark at him!" interjected Judith to herself.

"Nobody tells me about them but you," said Tom.
"I wish you'd come here oftener."

"I have to stay at home and work," said Mr.
Kage. "Ask mamma to tell you."

"Mamma says she has no time."

"You audacious little Turk, taking mamma's name
in vain!" interposed a fond voice at this juncture; and
the child slid off Thomas Kage's knee to fly to it.
Caroline clasped him in her arms, kissing him passionately. *Her* love for him could not fade or weaken.
With a laughing apology for not speaking to him at
once, she held out her hand to Mr. Kage.

"I thought I might find you here. But what kind
of manners do you call it, sir, to pay your respects to
Mr. Tom before you pay them to me?"

"He waylaid me on the stairs, and I carried him
up here."

"Papa would not let me go into the drawing-room.
I wanted you, mamma."

"Not let you! Nonsense, Tom! The dinner's not quite ready; you shall go down with me."

"I don't care now," dissented Tom. "I've got a book with some angels in it. Mr. Kage gave it me."

"You are very kind to him," exclaimed Caroline, a mist of gratitude rising in her eyes. "I think you wish to be a true friend to him."

"It is what I mean to be, Heaven permitting me."

Tom sat down on the carpet, picture-book on lap, and Mrs. Dawkes and her cousin descended the stairs together, her vain glance lingering in any mirror they happened to pass. Thomas Kage had rejected her for his wife; but she liked to look her best in his eyes, for all that. Whether she were more vain of herself or her precious boy, it would have puzzled Mrs. Dawkes to tell.

"He is a queer little darling," she suddenly said. "Fancy his staying up there from choice, to 'look at the angels'!"

"He could not look at better things, Caroline."

"O, of course not. I think it must have been you who first gave him the fancy. Judith says he would always be talking of angels and heaven."

"I think, in these rare cases, it is Heaven itself that gives it," gravely spoke Mr. Kage. "Caroline, are you doing your duty by him?"

The question sounded rather an abrupt one. Mrs. Dawkes turned her face to the speaker.

"My duty!"

"I mean in the higher sense of the word. A child should be trained to think of these solemn things. Are you training him?"

"Thomas, how old-fashioned you are! What do I know of angels, more than anybody else knows?"

His good dark eyes rested for a moment upon hers. That she certainly knew next to nothing, had never been taught to know, he was only too well aware.

"The child has just said to me, talking of angels, 'Mamma has no time to tell me about them.' Caroline, you must make the time. It is the solemn duty of every mother to endeavour to train her child for heaven."

"I wish you'd not preach as though you were in a pulpit, Thomas. I do train him. He says his prayers, and all that. One would think you feared I meant him to be a heathen!"

"His father is dead; you alone are left. If Mr. Canterbury can look down on this world, Caroline, think what his grief and agony might be at seeing his little son left untaught. The training of children is the most solemn duty that can be assigned to us in this world. Very few fulfil it as they ought."

"How earnest you are in this!" she involuntarily exclaimed.

"Because my mother trained *me*," he whispered. "Caroline, for your boy's sake, I beseech you look to it."

Mr. and Mrs. Richard Dunn had arrived when they got back to the drawing-room; also two gentlemen invited by Captain Dawkes. The butler was coming up to announce dinner.

"Mind, Thomas, you go in with me," said Mrs. Dawkes hurriedly, as she went forward to shake hands with Sarah Dunn.

"And your young inmate, Belle Annesley?" she asked. "I wrote word that we hoped to see her."

"She is past going out to dinner now, Caroline," was Mrs. Dunn's answer. "She gets weaker and weaker."

"Poor girl! When does she start for the West Indies?"

"I fear, never. I fear she will not live for it."

"Is she so ill as that?" exclaimed Caroline, all sympathy. "What can have induced it?"

Mrs. Dunn said nothing. Her eyes chanced to meet those of Thomas Kage; both could have answered what, had they chosen.

After all, Thomas Kage did not take first place, as proposed. There appeared to be so much difficulty in getting down Mrs. Kage and her fans, that he went to Fry's assistance. Her poor legs were dropping beneath her at every stair, but she was landed in safety. He took a seat by her; no one would have smoothed difficulties for her as he did: Caroline was tolerably content that it should be so, and bade another gentleman to her side in his place. But a sharp cloud passed momentarily over her brow when she saw that Thomas Kage had Millicent Canterbury on his other hand, and that they appeared to be on terms of assured friendship.

What a display it was!—the fantastic, shaking puppet at the festive board, amidst the lights and the flowers and the gala dresses! A death's-head, more than anything else, by contrast looked she. The shaking fork rattled against the shaking teeth, the food fell, the wine was spilled; and she, poor thing, strove to make a pretence of being juvenile with the rest, and tapped Thomas Kage's arm with her fan, and thought she was flirting with him. He did his best to cover her deficiencies, and got very little dinner for his pains; but she was a pitiable object, tottering on the edge of the grave.

Was it for *this* that she had schemed and plotted, and lost the favour of good men? Had her grasping and her basely-acquired wealth brought her no other or better reward? The means and the end were in fitness with each other; and Mrs. Kage in horrible fitness with them.

CHAPTER VII.

Mrs. Garston's Purchase.

THE streets were comparatively empty, comparatively cool; for the London great world had not yet come out to throng them, and the burning summer's sun had scarcely attained to its midday heat. Traversing the shining pavement, with the deliberate step of one who talks as he goes, was Thomas Kage; and by his side a young lady, whose gentle face and cool muslin dress were equally pleasant to look upon. Never saw man a nicer face than hers; for it was Millicent Canterbury's. Miss Canterbury and Lydia Dunn were on in advance.

Take it for all in all, the days of Mr. Kage were greatly occupied just now; on this, the day after Mrs. Dawkes's dinner, he would be very busy. Labour always accumulated when he prepared to depart on circuit; and for once in his life he had lately been striving to unite business with pleasure, for he went out a good deal with the Miss Canterburys.

7*

Accident in the first instance led to his doing so. Dining one evening at Mrs. Dunn's soon after the Miss Canterburys came on their visit to her, Olive happened to remark—in answer to a question of whether they had seen some show-place—that they did not go about so much as they would, in consequence of having no gentleman to accompany them; Mr. Richard Dunn, who was always kind and polite, being very much in Wales at his mines just now, and only running up occasionally. Upon that, Mr. Kage offered himself as Richard Dunn's substitute, and was with them as often as leisure allowed.

The expedition this morning was nothing formidable; only the calling upon Mrs. Garston. That active lady, rebellious to fashion's habits, preferred to see visitors literally in the morning; after ten o'clock she was ready for any who might call. At Mrs. Dawkes's dinner-table the previous evening, Mr. Kage, hearing that the Miss Canterburys purposed going there, had made a half promise to come round and fetch them. He was living in his own home again, as a temporary arrangement. The friends who had tenanted it were gone, and Mr. Kage slept at home for safety. He had now written to the landlord, saying he should resign it at the approaching expiration of the lease.

Absorbed in conversation, their steps lingered, and Olive and Mrs. Dunn were first at Mrs. Garston's gate. It did not surprise Thomas Kage to see the old lady with them, for she liked to pace her garden in fine weather. Leaning on her stick, her gray bonnet tilted a little forward on her head, she watched their approach with her keen eyes.

"So, Thomas Kage, you are taking holiday to-day!"

"Not whole holiday," was his answer, as he held out his hand to her. "I am going to my chambers by and by."

But the venerable lady did not respond to the movement. She despised the formality of hand-shaking, except when people met but rarely. Thomas Kage was used to her, and he thought the rejection meant no slight. Walking to a shady path, where two benches faced each other, Mrs. Garston seated herself, and they grouped themselves around her. It was within view of that tree where poor Belle Annesley had leaned her aching forehead, the day she met Keziah Dawkes and her cruel words.

"What makes you so late?" was Mrs. Garston's first question to Miss Canterbury.

"Do you call it late?" replied Olive. "I thought it early."

"Why, it is not twelve o'clock yet," put in Mrs. Dunn. "I said to Olive, coming along, that you would take us for Vandals."

Mrs. Garston's stick struck the smooth hard gravel. The latter speaker was no more in favour with her than she ever had been.

"I've never taken *you* for much else, Lydia Dunn. You'd go in for fashion and frivolity yourself, if you were not so restless. I wonder you come here."

"But I like to see you now and then," laughingly answered Mrs. Dunn, taking the reproach in good humour.

"Then behave yourself when you come, and don't talk false nonsense about the day's being early when it's half gone. It is disrespectful to me, Lydia Dunn. I am old enough to be your grandmother, and with some years to spare."

"I wish we could bring our country habits with us to London, and find them welcome here," remarked Miss Canterbury with a smile. "We are earlier there than even you, Mrs. Garston. Chilling is but a primitive place."

"Earlier are you?" returned the venerable dame. "I am down to breakfast every morning at nine o'clock, Olive Canterbury, and often in my garden at ten. And so you were out at dinner last night?"

"Yes; we dined with Mrs. Dawkes."

"With her that was Caroline Kage, and next Caroline Canterbury, and then went and made a fool of herself by marrying Barby Dawkes," commented the old lady. "Well, they are not ill-suited to each other; heartless frivolities, both of 'em. *You* had an escape there, Thomas Kage."

The colour flushed sharply into his face at the allusion; as was to all eyes perfectly visible, standing there with his back against the tree-trunk. Mrs. Garston lifted her stick, but not in wrath.

"You needn't redden up so Thomas. Many a man as good as you has had his fancy taken by a pretty girl—and his heart too. But you were too good for her; and I b'lieve Heaven saw it, and spared you. Barby has got her; and she is too good for him. She'll find it out, too. Well, I didn't envy you your dinner last night."

"We did not envy ourselves," remarked Lydia Dunn. "It is never very pleasant to us to meet Caroline. The remembrance of certain wrongs recurs with more force at the sight of her."

"I don't mean for that," retorted Mrs. Garston, with a few violent knocks. "Nobody supposes it would be pleasant; but if you choose to go in for it, you bring the consequences on yourselves, whether they are pleasure or whether they are pain. I spoke of Mrs. Kage. *I* should not like to sit down to dinner, and have a skeleton at the same table with painted cheeks and rattling bones! 'Twould have upset my stomach."

Millicent burst out laughing, somewhat irreverently. Olive lifted her finger in reproof, and turned to Mrs. Garston.

"You have heard about the dinner, then?"

"I have heard all about it. Early as you may consider it, Mistress Lydia Dunn, Keziah Dawkes was here more than an hour ago. She happened to call at Barby's yesterday, and they asked her to stay dinner."

"I don't like Keziah Dawkes at all," spoke Mrs. Dunn, with her usual blunt candour.

"You like her as well as I do, I'll lay," said Keziah's great-aunt. "She knows it too, and does not come here often—a'most never, but when she wants anything. There's some trouble up about the money she advanced for Barby before his marriage; the people are claiming some of the charges twice over, and Barby has managed to lose the papers. Daresay he never kept 'em. Keziah came here to ask if I remembered a certain date."

"Keziah Dawkes always gives me the idea of being a thoroughly good sister," interposed Thomas Kage.

"She's that. She has been to Barby one in a thousand. Keziah Dawkes would sacrifice all the world to him, herself included; but she is hard-natured in the main—ill-conditioned also. You should have heard her sneers this morning at Mrs. Kage. Why did they let a poor object, like her, dine at table?"

"I think Mr. Kage has the most cause to ask that," said Lydia Dunn. "He had all the trouble of her."

"Had he! Serve him right. He gives enough trouble to other folks."

Of course the aspersion caused Thomas Kage to look up. His old friend was glaring at him with no sweet expression.

"What have I done now, dear Mrs. Garston?"

"Now, suppose you put that question to yourself, Thomas Kage. Just think over your actions of the last day or two, and perhaps you mightn't need to ask it of other people."

"I really do not know what you mean," he resumed, after a pause.

"Have you wrote a notice to your landlord to quit your house, or have you not?" she asked, lifting her stick in his face.

"I have done that. "I told you that I should do it, Mrs. Garston."

"But I didn't suppose you were in earnest," she angrily said. "I never thought you'd have the heart to give up the house that your mother died in; or the face to abandon me. I thought better of you, Thomas Kage. What's the matter with the house? Answer me that."

"Not anything. If I were at all likely to settle in life, I should like none better. For me, a single man, it is a great expense, and I feel that I should scarcely be justified in renewing the lease."

"And the leaving me counts for nothing, though I've been as good to you as a mother!"

"But I shall not leave you, dear Mrs. Garston. I can be with you just as much as though I lived next door."

Mrs. Garston's head was nodding ominously—not after Mrs. Kage's helpless fashion, but in anger. Thomas Kage had expected some such explosion; but he wondered how she had got to hear of the notice so speedily, since it was sent only on the previous day.

"What are you thinking to do with your sticks and stones, pray?"

He did not answer for the moment, for the subject was rather a sore one. "Sticks and stones" that have been for years in our old homesteads can be parted from only with lively pain.

"Some of the furniture—it is not of much intrinsic value—I shall sell; and the articles that were prized by my mother must be warehoused," was his tardy answer. Anything but a satisfactory one to Mrs. Garston, who was bending forward to listen.

"Warehoused! You would warehouse the good old articles that were dear to your mother! I wonder what you'd call that, Thomas Kage? Sacrilege?"

"They shall be well taken care of, somehow," he murmured.

"And you'll sell the rest! Sell! D'ye suppose there's anything among 'em that might suit me?" she resumed in a pleasanter tone. "Let us step in and have a look. I'm going to rebuild my coachman's house, and shall want furniture for it."

She went marching off with her stick, taking Thomas Kage's arm when he held it out to her. The rest followed. Mr. Kage smiled at the sudden invasion of his premises, and hoped they would be found in order.

He need not have feared; for old Dorothy, in renewed health, was back again, and ruled over matters with a critical eye. Mrs. Garston, without the smallest ceremony, went from room to room till the whole house had been visited, making her comments aloud. All very disparaging comments, and tending to the point that it wanted "doing up."

"It is as I say—the place must be redone," she observed, coming to an anchor in the dining-room. "Just you get a pencil and paper, Thomas Kage, and jot down what the landlord will have to do before it's taken by a fresh tenant."

"But—it will not be any business of mine," dissented Mr. Kage.

"Now you do as I bid you," she arbitrarily rejoined. "I know that landlord too well; and so do you, Lydia Dunn, I expect, for he is yours. He'll give a single coat of paint and a dab o' varnish, and call a room done."

"I thought tenants had to put a house habitable at the expiration of a lease," interposed Miss Canterbury.

"That's as the lease may be worded," said Mrs. Garston. "Ours is the other way.—Now then, Thomas Kage, where's that pencil and paper?"

Putting the paper before him without so much as

a smile, he sat down to write what she desired: he had grown to obey her almost implicity. It must be waste of time, he knew; and tedious, he feared, to the Miss Canterburys.

The house, she decided, was to be papered and painted throughout, and thoroughly renovated, all in the best style and manner; drains were to be looked to; a scullery, much wanted, should be built out at the back; the premises altogether made complete.

"Is that all?" asked Thomas Kage, looking up with a laugh as she came to an end.

"It's all I think of for the present," she answered. "How ever you and poor Lady Kage could have lived with this horrid red paper on the wall" (striking it with her stick), "I can't think. And your mother had good taste in general, Thomas."

"We did not like the paper because it lighted up so badly; but it is handsome of its kind."

"Handsome of its kind! You may say that of a dancing-bear. If I had a red-papered room in my house, I should whitewash it over. Give me the list."

As he handed it to her, she caught the look of smiling incredulity on his countenance. It a little annoyed her.

"I see: you deem this quite useless. Waste of time, as you said just now."

"I am sure the landlord will never do so much, nor the half of it," he answered. "And in any case, dear Mrs. Garston, it cannot concern me."

"I'll answer for this much, Thomas Kage—that the landlord will do every item you've written down here. Whether it shall concern you, or not—that is, whether you shall choose to stop on in the house, or whether you go out of it—it shall be put into proper repair."

"You must have made it a condition with him, then, in renewing your own lease."

"Never you mind whether I have or haven't; don't you be so fond of contradicting me.—We will go back again now."

When they reached her garden, Mrs. Garston led the way indoors to her own dining-room. Its beautiful paper of white and gold was cheerful to see in the midday sun. She called their attention to it.

"This is the right sort of paper. I like large-looking rooms, and I like light ones; and you don't get either when the walls are red. This self-same pattern, if it can be got, shall be put into that parlour of yours, Thomas Kage."

"If you can get the landlord to do it," he answered, humouring her.

"The landlord happens to be myself."

The avowal took them by surprise. Mrs. Garston made it from her large chair, in which she had put herself; her gray bonnet was thrown back; her keen gray eyes sought theirs; her stick, held in both hands, gently tapped the carpet before her. Never did a more self-asserting old lady sit for a portrait. But if some doubt appeared in Thomas Kage's face, he might be pardoned. She saw it; perhaps had been watching for it.

"You'd like to tell me to my face that I am asserting what is not true, Thomas Kage. What would your mother have said to such manners? *she* always trusted me. I have bought the house next door, and I have bought this. Now then!"

"I'm sure I am very glad to hear it," he murmured.

"I wished to buy them years ago: your mother knew that. But that landlord, scenting the wish, put such a price upon them that I'd not give it him. You have left me no resource now, Thomas Kage."

"I!"

"You. Don't you be insolent—staring at me as if I talked Dutch! Could I submit to the chance of having any kind of people next to me?—and you said in my ear months ago, you know, that you should give up the house when the lease ran out. A travelling circus might have come and took it, for all I could answer—the grounds are big. So I sent for the landlord, and said to him, 'Put on your own price;' which he did, and a nice price it was: but I paid it, and the property is mine."

"Dear me! that was going to work in a very costly manner," commented Mrs. Dunn, who never could refrain from interfering in other people's business.

Mrs. Garston rewarded her by a sharp reproof.

"It was my own affair, Lydia Dunn. If it had cost me ten times as much, I should have done it. Once my mind is set upon a thing, who is to say me nay?"

"But the waste of money?" persisted Lydia.

"Money! I've got enough of *that*—more than I know what to do with sometimes. And now—a last word with you, Thomas Kage. Ah, you little thought when you penned that fine notice yesterday that it was coming to me. I wish you to remain on in the next house. I've bought it that you may; and whether you pay me rent, or whether you pay me none, is a matter of indifference to me. If I were to say I'd not receive any, your pride would rise up all cock-a-hoop; so I don't say it. But I beg you to understand this one thing—if my wishes go for naught and you quit the house, it will remain empty, for I shall never suffer any other tenant to enter it while I live."

As if to give effect to the assertion, Mrs. Garston brought her stick down with a thump so emphatic that Millicent Canterbury, standing by the chair's elbow, started backwards. They rose to depart; the visit, including the time they spent in the other house, had been unconscionably long, as Lydia Dunn expressed it. Thomas Kage, feeling rather bewildered, prepared to attend them. In going down the garden he found himself pulled back by Mrs. Garston. The others were well on in advance.

"You made a mistake once in your life, Thomas," she said. "Are you thinking to remedy it?"

"What mistake, dear Mrs. Garston?"

"In falling in love with that Kage girl. You see how she served you. Many a one before you has thrown away the kernel for the shell."

He smiled a little. What kernel?—what shell?

"She." And the stick was pointed at Millicent, who had turned round at the end of the path to wait. "If I can read countenances—and I used to do it— that girl is one of the best living. She'd make you happier than the other ever would; ay, though you had married that 'un in the heyday of love."

He flushed a very little, laughing lightly.

"Millicent Canterbury must be as a forbidden star to me, my dear old friend."

"And why must she?"

"She has ten thousand pounds. I have nothing; or next to nothing."

Never had Mrs. Garston been nearer going into a real passion than then. Her gray eyes flashed sparks on the speaker.

"Ten thousand pounds! and you nothing! Are you saying this to enrage me, Thomas Kage? It's false sophistry, every word of it. Though the girl, or any other girl, had ten times ten thousand, and you had but the coat and breeches you stood up in, you'd be more than her equal. A husband such as you'll make, a good man as your mother trained you to be, is worth, to the woman who gets him, a king's ransom. Ten thousand pounds!—ten thousand rubbish!"

Mortally offended, Mrs. Garston turned in and slammed the door in his face. He went forward with rather a conscious countenance.

"What is Mrs. Garston angry with you for?" asked Millicent.

"I said something that did not please her," he answered, glancing at the sweet eyes cast on him with unsuspicious inquiry.

For some little time now he had esteemed Millicent Canterbury above everybody else in the world; not with that early passionate love that can touch man's heart but once, but with a far more lasting friendship. To what end? since, in spite of Mrs. Garston's anger, he did not look upon social problems exactly as she did.

"We must step out, Millicent. Your sisters have got on the length of the street."

CHAPTER VIII.

Not quite heartless.

THE window was thrown open to the summer sun, and a fire burnt in the grate. To every one but the poor sick invalid the heat seemed stifling. Richard Dunn, a fine portly man, mentally pronounced it to be so, as he paced the room with gentle steps. *She* was cold; and a suspicion was dawning on those around that it might be with the advance shadow of death.

She was passing away very gently: the painful adjuncts that too often attend even young girls to the grave spared Belle Annesley. The maid dressed her still, and combed out the soft curls of her pretty hair, and now and again tied a bit of ribbon in it. The cough had left her: there seemed absolutely nothing the matter with her but weakness. Wise Dr. Tyndal, paying his visit this morning, had declared to Mr. Dunn that if they could only fight against that, she might recover. But Mr. Dunn knew quite well that they could not against it. The child herself knew it.

She really looked but a child; more so than ever, in spite of the huge shawl that wrapped her up, and her black-and-white muslin dress. She lay back in the easy-chair, her feet on a footstool; the trembling fingers of her delicate hands plucking at the white handkerchief that lay in her lap. Richard Dunn, happening to notice the restless movement, and not liking the look of it, stood still for a full minute regarding her.

"What is amiss with the handkerchief, Belle?"

"Nothing," she listlessly answered, pushing it aside. The next minute she had begun again—at the shawl this time. Mr. Dunn sat down by her, and took her hand in his.

"Do you feel worse, my dear?"

"No. Why?"

"You are very silent," he answered by way of excuse.

"I was thinking. Thinking of the past. Of those old days, when I was so wild and heartless and wilful. They seem to be ages ago now."

"Past time often does, my dear."

"Always, I should think, to one like me—leaving the world for ever. I want you to say that you forgive me," she added in a whisper.

"Forgive you! What for?"

"O, you know. I did cause you pain in those days, and I caused it wilfully. A vain, mocking, ridiculing thing—that's what I was; nothing else. I—I don't care to recall it all in words; but I want you to say you forgive me."

Richard Dunn stooped over her and kissed her forehead. "My dear child, if there is anything you need forgiveness for, take it heartily: but I think you are fanciful to-day. I wish—I wish you had been spared to us. Sarah and I would have striven to make life pleasant to you."

"Thank you for all your kindness; thank you for ever."

The trembling fingers, entwined in his, presently released themselves and began to work again. Mr. Dunn did not altogether like the signs. He quitted the room to find his wife. During the interval, little Tom Canterbury came in with his nurse.

When the boy had been taken down to dessert the previous evening at the dinner in Belgravia—for we have not got beyond the day spoken of in the last chapter—Mrs. Richard Dunn asked him to go to them on the following morning; and Judith was told to bring him. In the old days at Chilling, when Miss Annesley was the rector's daughter, she had taken part in trying to teach Judith to read. The instruction, as previously hinted, had not come to much, but Judith was grateful all the same. During this present sojourn in London, she had occasionally, when out with her little charge, found her way to Mrs. Richard Dunn's. Tom had grown to like to go there and to see Belle Annesley, between whom and himself a great friendship had arisen; in point of fact, it was Belle who, when her cousin was starting for the dinner-visit, had asked her to bid Tom come.

And so Judith and he had arrived, nothing loth. Tom wore his morning attire: a plaid dress reaching to the knees, his straight legs incased in little white socks; in the afternoon Mrs. Dawkes would have him decked out in velvets and gewgaws; but Judith had her own way till then. A quiet, thoughtful, mild child was he, whose disposition and temper were admirable.

Belle Annesley kissed him; she took off his straw hat with her own fragile fingers, and stroked the falling curls of his light hair. Tom looked at her wistfully: it might be that he detected a change in her countenance, for a child sometimes sees signs hidden from older eyes.

"Lift him up, Judith."

There was ample room for the two on the large chair, and the boy was placed side by side with Belle. After considerable tugging, he succeeded in getting a book out of some mysterious underpocket.

"I brought it for you to see," he said, as Judith left them to go and enjoy a gossip with Mrs. Dunn's nurse. "It has got an angel in it, and Jacob's ladder. Mr. Kage gave it me last night. Look: that's the angel, and that's the ladder, and its end is right up in heaven."

Belle Annesley's eyes were riveted on the picture with as much earnest interest as though she had been a child herself. Tom, waiting for sympathetic admiration, heard none.

"Isn't it pretty, Belle? I should like to be an angel."

Dropping the book, she clasped both his hands in hers. Her face and voice were alike strangely earnest.

"We may both be so shortly, Tom. *I* shall. You may not be long after me."

The words were remarkable—taken in connection with what the hidden future was destined to bring forth. But the dying sometimes speak with a curious prevision.

Tom Canterbury, to judge by his eyes, did not know whether to be most awed or interested. Belle had fallen back in her chair, and was plucking at the shawl again. He thought his book neglected.

"Judith didn't want me to bring it, Belle. Mrs. Dunn said last night I was to come."

"Yes, I wished for you," answered Belle. "I

8 *

thought you were not coming, though: it is nearly afternoon."

"Judith didn't get ready. She went in to help Fry with grandmamma."

Belle rose from her seat, and tottered to a desk that was on a side-table, holding by the furniture as she went. Her strength for walking had almost passed away. Standing up before the desk, the shawl fell off her shoulders, and she looked like a shadow. The child got down with a jump and picked it up. She tottered back again, holding something in her hand.

It was a beautiful little box of mother-of-pearl, made in the form of a shell, and inlaid with silver. Inside was a raised fretwork of silver enclosing a miniature painting in bright colours—a baby borne by two angels, who were gazing upwards. Sitting down, Belle put it into the boy's hand: the toy was so small, that his hand easily clasped it.

"My brother brought it for me, when he came over from the West Indies at mamma's death. Tom, I give it to you. You must keep it always for my sake."

Tom, opening the lid, stood entranced with admiration, oblivious of everything but the picture that so charmed him. He had an eye for bright colours, which were wont to impart to him a strange delight.

"It's angels too," he said breathlessly. "They are carrying the baby up to heaven."

"When you look at it sometimes after I am gone, Thomas, remember that they have carried me up there," she whispered.

"Do you like to go?" asked the boy, somewhat dubious on the point, now that it seemed to be coming to action.

"Yes."

"But wouldn't you like to stay here, and have playthings? Such things as this?"

"No, not now. It is so weary here."

She was feebly endeavouring to fold the shawl around her, and said no more. The little exertion had fatigued her; she lay back panting for a few moments, and then, as if it brought relief, her fingers were at work at the shawl again. Mrs. Dunn, who now entered, took in all the signs with a rapid, searching glance.

"Belle, my darling," she said, pushing the hair from the pale damp brow, "you seem a little restless."

"Do I?" returned Belle with apathy. "I am very tired, Sarah."

Tired indeed! Tired sadly in body, and very tired with the world and its cares. Poor Belle Annesley was dying, with all her trouble upon her—that unfortunate love for the man who had played her false. It racked her still; not as it had done, but more than was good for her comfort. One great wish lay ever upon her— that she could see him once again. It almost seemed to her that she could not die without it. Foolish, foolish girl! if her death, she thought, should but bring a pang of repentance to him, a bitter loving regret, why, then to herself it would be welcome. Sentiment clung to her to the last; and she wanted Barnaby Dawkes to see the wreck she had become for his sake. But she had not been able to call up the courage to ask for him.

It was to be, however. When Judith departed with little Canterbury, Mrs. Dunn went downstairs with them.

She was standing for an instant at one of the front windows, and saw Thomas Kage pass. He had just left the Miss Canterburys at their door after that visit to Mrs. Garston. She made a sign to Mr. Kage, and he came in.

"Go you up to her, Mr. Kage," she said, after telling him that both she and her husband fancied some change for the worse was approaching in Belle Annesley. "See what you think, and then come down and tell me; I'll wait here. Mr. Dunn has had to go out, but he will not be long."

When Mr. Kage entered the room, Belle had her eyes closed. He noticed the movement of the fingers spoken of by Mrs. Dunn. They were slowly at work. She gave a great start as he approached, and stared wildly.

"O, is it you?" she said in a minute, an accent of disappointment in her tone. "I—I—I think I had dozed and was dreaming."

"Of whom were you dreaming, Belle?" he asked very gently, as he sat down near her and took one of her wasted hands in his.

The pale cheeks took a tinge of bright colour at the question; the blue eyes, getting a little glassy now, fell downwards. But she gave the true answer. She generally did give it to Mr. Kage.

"I was dreaming of Captain Dawkes. I fancied he stood at that door talking to me; and when you came up, I—in the confusion of awaking—I really thought it was he."

"Would you like to see him, my dear?" asked Mr. Kage after a pause.

Another faint flush of hectic.

"Perhaps he would not care to come. But—if he would, I should like to say good-bye to him."

"And how do you feel to-day?" resumed Mr. Kage, changing the subject without comment. "Brave and strong?"

"O, I feel about the same," she answered listlessly. "I'm very tired."

"It is a pity I disturbed your snatch of sleep. And for nothing either, for I cannot stay. I have a hundred-and-one things to do to-day and to-morrow."

"But I shall see you again?" she said, as he stood up.

"Of course. I will come in this evening."

Happening to look back at her as he turned to close the door, Thomas Kage could but mark the eager, questioning, yearning look in the eyes that seemed to follow him. But still he said nothing about Captain Dawkes. That worthy gentleman might not choose to pay the visit, although bidden.

"Well, what do you think?" asked Sarah Dunn anxiously.

"I do not see much difference in her," was Mr. Kage's answer. "Nevertheless I think the end will not be very long delayed."

"Did you notice what I said about her fingers?"

"Yes. But I have seen the same thing in patients who have subsequently got well."

"You are sure of that?"

"Quite. She would like to see Dawkes."

"*Would* she!" exclaimed Mrs. Dunn in astonishment. "Were the case mine, I would rather send him miles away than see him. I do not understand it."

A peculiar expression crossed the face of Thomas

Kage. Matter-of-fact, rather than imaginative, Sarah Dunn was just one of those who could not be likely to understand.

"Dawkes may not be willing to come," observed Mr. Kage. "*He* probably would rather go miles any other way."

But Barnaby Dawkes was not altogether heartless, and if he had cared for any one in the world, it was certainly Belle. As Thomas Kage was bending his steps across one of the squares, he accidentally met him in his mail-phaeton, two grooms seated behind. Mr. Kage made a sign that he would speak with him; and afterwards the Captain changed his course, and pulled up at Mrs. Richard Dunn's door.

Her head lay upon his arm, and the tears were trickling down her flushed cheeks. Barnaby Dawkes was a selfish man by nature and by habit, indifferent to all that did not concern himself, utterly careless of any world save this present one; but, looking on the wreck of that once sweet girl, on the unmistakeable signs that said the life would so shortly close, he went into a fit of remorse and tenderness, both genuine.

"You will not quite forget me?" she sobbed, clinging to him. "I mean no treason against your wife, Barnaby; I would not for the world; only—only —that you will think of me at an odd moment now and then."

Incredible as it may be deemed, little as the gallant Captain might ever believe it of himself afterwards, a tear dropped from his eyes on her upturned face. Belle saw it, and felt repaid for her lost life and the agony that had shortened it.

"Don't grieve for me too much, Barnaby; I should not like that. I hope you will be happy always, you and your wife. If she ever hears about me—about me and the past—give my dear love to her, and say I said it."

"I wish I had never met you, child! I was an awful brute to leave you and marry another—and that's the fact. My love was all yours, Belle; but I was in a fearful state of embarrassment, and wanted the money. Why did you care so much for me? Why did you let it prey upon you? I was not worth it."

Never a truer word spoke he than that. Belle's restless fingers, at peace for the moment, were entwined within his.

"I daresay it was all for the best," she murmured. "I might have died just the same."

Voices were heard on the stairs, and the Captain prepared to take his departure.

"Say you forgive me," he whispered.

"I forgive it all—the death, and the pain, and the weariness. I hope we shall meet in heaven, all of us, and live together in happiness for ever and for ever. God bless and keep you, Barnaby, until that time shall come!"

It may be that Barnaby Dawkes, irreligious man though he was, echoed the wish for the passing moment. Whether he did or not, was known to him alone. He kissed her cheeks, her brow, her lips, as he had been wont to kiss them in earlier days, and laid her wan face back on the pillow, and resigned her hands the last.

"Good-bye, Belle. Good-bye, my best and dearest!"

The voices were those of Mr. Dunn and Dr. Tyndal.

Captain Dawkes exchanged courtesies with them as he passed, and went out to his carriage.

When Thomas Kage got there in the evening, according to promise, the hands of the dying girl, in her bed then, were working feebly at the counterpane; the advance shadow of death, no longer to be mistaken, lay on the face. But the shadow seemed to have brought peace with it.

CHAPTER IX.

A few whispered Words.

On the pseudo-mosaic floor of a place of worship—that was neither Protestant church, nor Roman-catholic chapel, nor curiously-decorated mediæval drawing-room, but partaking something of all three—knelt Keziah Dawkes. A hard cold woman looked she, as she rose and sat down to listen to the sermon, with never a smile on her gray leaden face. The services did not seem to bring much cheer to her. When the short sermon of ten minutes was ranted through—and which Keziah and every other one of the scattered worshippers present might have been defied to make top or tail, or any sort of sense of—she quitted her seat and glided into the street; into the pleasanter light of a spring twilight evening. The place she had just quitted was almost dark at midday; else how would the lighted candles on the communion-table have borne effect? For some time now, Keziah Dawkes had been a lonely, disappointed woman, finding her heart and her love thrown back upon her. She had never had but one object of affection throughout her life—and that was her brother Barnaby. Worthless Barnaby!

But it often happens that the more worthless a man is, the closer somebody or other clings to him. Barnaby Dawkes had done nearly as much as he could do to throw his sister's affection off; at least, so it seemed to her perhaps exacting heart. Wounded to the core, ready to die with disappointment and weariness, Keziah in sheer ennui took to attending one of the ultra-ritualistic daily services that were springing up around her as rapidly as mushrooms.

Time has gone on, reader. Nearly four years have elapsed since the marriage of Barnaby Dawkes and Mrs. Canterbury. They have latterly been staying almost entirely in London: more fashion to be met with in Belgravia than at the Rock, and both Major Dawkes and his wife are votaries of it. He is Major Dawkes now—having got up a step; and the world looks upon him as one of the most wealthy and flourishing officers in her Majesty's service. A few people—money-lenders, lawyers, and the like—perchance could tell a different tale—that there existed not a more embarrassed man in secret than he.

Keziah suspected something of this embarrassment; but not to its fullest extent. When we love any one very deeply, we seem to see, as by intuition, any ill that may surround him. Keziah was very little with Major and Mrs. Dawkes; less even than she used to be, although their mansion was not far removed from her home. Sometimes she would not call upon them once in two months. She had paid them one visit at the Rock in the earlier days of their marriage, but the invitation to her had never been repeated.

That a man with Major Dawkes's propensity to spend—that any one living on the scale he did, fling-

ing away hundreds, ay and thousands, of pounds—
should have gone on from three to four mortal years,
and not have burst up, might have been deemed one
of the marvels pertaining to Major Dawkes. Mrs.
Dawkes's was almost what might have been called a
regal income, though in truth not so much as the
world set it down at; but Barnaby had fingered it in a
lavish style. If I had ten thousand a-year, and spent
twenty thousand, it would not need a conjurer to fore-
tell what must come of it. Keziah, sharp and calcu-
lating, knew pretty well what the state of affairs must
be; and she was looking for the explosion of the
bombshell. To her, it seemed almost like retribution;
a judgment upon them for their neglect of her.

But in that well-appointed Belgravian mansion nothing was suspected of its master's embarrassment. He
kept it to himself. He had no other resource in de-
cency but to do so, since the troubles were wholly his
own. For, it was not the state and style in which they
lived that could have hampered them, but Major Dawkes's
private pursuits. Neither mistress nor servants knew
aught of the matter: the latter were aware that some
people, shabby men and others, intruded often on the
Major, who avoided them when he could; and when
he could not, held private colloquies with them in his
study, and showed them out of doors himself. The
household bills, too, were being pressed for.

Keziah Dawkes left the chapel—or what she might
please to call it—behind her, and walked steadily on
to her lodgings: the same lodgings where you once
saw her, reader. She had lost them during that long
absence, when she was down at Chilling, helping Barnaby to scheme for Mrs. Canterbury; but she had re-

gained them again. The evening was chill; the clouds chased each other across the sky; the wind blew round the corners with a wintry sound. Passing a gay shop-window, its wares lighted up with the blazing gas, Keziah's eyes were caught by something, and she stopped to look in.

"It's a sweet bonnet," she exclaimed after a long gaze; "and only ten-and-sixpence! I could not make it for much less myself; and somehow my home-made bonnets have always a dowdy look. It's not so high but I could afford it; and spring's getting on. Suppose I come by daylight and look at it? But then"—pausing—"there's aunt Garston! I *don't* think she can last much longer; and it would be waste of money to buy it, if I had to go in mourning soon afterwards."

With a lingering look, Keziah turned away, and continued her course towards home, revolving the bonnet argument in her mind, for and against the purchase. The wind took her cloak, the chilly air seemed to penetrate her; but Keziah was used to wind and weather. Arrived at her door, she opened it, and went upstairs; taking off her cloak on the landing, and shaking it. The tea-things were on the table, glowing pleasantly in the fire-light; and some dark form, to which her eye was not accustomed, filled the easy-chair with its washed-out, thin chintz-cover.

"Barnaby! Is it you?"

"What an awfully long time you've been coming in!" was the Major's responsive greeting. "Thought you must have gone out to make a night of it."

"I have only been to evening prayers."

"Been to what?"

"The evening service at a new chapel. A place we have got opened here."

"It's not Sunday," said the Major, staring.

"I know that. What am I to do, alone here always? never a soul to speak to! The evening services break the monotony; it's an object to get out for: but I don't go every evening. I'd not have gone now had I thought you were coming."

She put her bonnet on the bed in the inner room, came back, and began to make the tea. The shining copper kettle stood singing on the brass plate; a new loaf and some butter were on the table.

"You will take a cup of tea, Barnaby?"

"Not I. Wishy-washy stuff!"

"Some bread-and-butter, then?"

"That's worse."

"Is there anything else that I can get you?"

"No; thanks. I'm going home to dinner."

Keziah took the candles from the mantelpiece, and lighted both in honour of her company; when alone, she generally contented herself with one. That Barnaby had come for some aid or other, she was sure of; but she did not see what he, the great man, could want from her now. The candles lighted up his face; the same handsome face, with the shining black eyes and hair as of yore; but somewhat of perplexity sat on his features. He was leaning forward towards the fire, and pulling at his moustache moodily, as if in a brown study. Keziah poured out her tea, and sat sipping it.

"Do you think you could do anything for me with the old party?" he suddenly began.

"In what way?" coldly asked Keziah; knowing that the "old party" meant Mrs. Garston.

"I don't believe she'll last a month longer, Keziah."

"She will not last long; I am sure of that. When those vigorous old women begin to fail—as she is now failing—their time is drawing to a close."

There ensued a pause. Keziah, brimful of her wrongs and Barnaby's ingratitude, would not prompt him by so much as a word. She cut herself a piece of bread-and-butter.

"I want you to see her for me, Keziah."

"To see her for you!"

The chilling tone grated on the Major's ear. He turned his head.

"What's the matter with you, Keziah?"

"The matter with me?" repeated Keziah, as if bent on reëchoing his words. "Nothing more than usual."

"You have not been pleasant with me for some time, Keziah."

"What have you been with me?"

"I!"—the Major turned to the fire again in a frightful access of gloom—"I've not meant to be anything else. But—I am awfully worried, Keziah."

"You bring you worry on yourself, I expect."

He did not attempt to gainsay it; he had never been otherwise than tolerably candid with his sister.

"I am in a mess, Keziah. If I cannot get helped out of it, Heaven knows what the end will be."

"You have been in many a mess before."

"Never such as this. I want to talk it over with you: as I used to talk over the troubles of the old days, Kezzy."

"Yes! You come to me when you need anything—never else. Barnaby, I do not believe Heaven ever created your fellow for selfishness!"

"I am not selfish!" snapped the Major.

"Not selfish! Listen, Barnaby: I may be the better, perhaps, for letting loose a little of the grievances long burning within me. When we were brother and sister together, who helped you as I did—and loved you—and cherished you? Who stood between you and aunt Garston, and told her lies without end to cover your faults, and divert her shrewd suspicions from you? Who parted with all available means, that you should be pulled out of ditches and straits? Who helped you to your rich wife; and shielded you in all ways when you wanted shielding? Answer me that."

"You did," avowed the Major, fancying an open policy might be the best in the awkward situation.

"Yes; I. You married your wife, and came into what would once have seemed to you incalculable wealth—what was so, in fact; and how did you recompense me? By throwing me over, as if I were some menial that you had no longer work for."

"Don't talk nonsense, Keziah!"

"*Is* it nonsense? You know better. It is true you repaid me the bare money I had advanced; but not a fraction over, for thanks or interest. Without the repayment I could not have lived, for it was my income that I forestalled and risked for you; had it not been my income—had it been saved money—I don't believe you would have ever troubled yourself to repay it at all. Since your marriage you have not treated me as a sister—I was nobody in your fresh ties."

"'Twas not that," burst forth the Major. "Ties! The ties have never been to me half what you were."

"It has been self with you always, Barnaby—self, self, self," she resumed, the hard tone subsiding into a plaintive one, for the avowal had somewhat appeased her. "It of course was nothing for your wife to neglect me—it was to be expected, perhaps: but I did not look for it from you; and the pain has been hard to bear."

"I don't see why I should not tell you the truth," he said, "though I've never told it before. The neglect has been Caroline's. She—she took a dislike to you, Keziah, goodness knows why; and I never have been able to prevail upon her to have you with us, except for that short visit when you came to the Rock. *My* will has been good to have you—to have you always; but she would not."

It was all very well to excuse himself in this way. He had been quite as willing to neglect her as his wife was. Keziah was coming round. The old love for him had only been smouldering; it would never leave her but with life.

"It may be as you say, Barnaby; but your wife is not you. *You* might have come to see me—you might have been generous to me; it was in your power to make my life bright, and you have not attempted to throw even a ray on it. A hundred times have I sat here, by my solitary fire, on a winter's evening, repeating over to myself that old song of Shakespeare's: "Blow, blow, thou wintry wind; thou art not so unkind as man's ingratitude.'"

Apparently the remembrance overcame her. Keziah Dawkes burst into tears, and put her handkerchief to

her face. Barnaby could not remember ever to have
seen her cry in all his life. A sudden impulse of affection—if such could exist in the man's nature—or of
self-interest well acted, caused him to put out his hand,
and clasp fondly the one lying unoccupied on her lap.
Almost at once she dried the tears, as though ashamed
to have given way to them.

"Let bygones be bygones, Keziah; there's nobody
in the world I care for half as much as I do for you;
there's no one else I would tell my troubles to. Will
you hear, and help me?"

"I am willing to hear you, Barnaby. But as to
help, I should not think any of *that* lies in my power."

"Substantial help of course does not. You need
not fear I wish to ask for the advance of your poor
little income again. It would be of no use to me; but
as a bucket of water to the flowing Thames. What I
do want is, that you would see Mrs. Garston, and get
her—get her to make her will in my favour. Not a
stone must be left unturned, Keziah."

"You want it badly?"

Badly! Worse than Keziah, happily for her, had as
yet any notion of. The Major drew a sketch of his
embarrassments and difficulties; and Keziah grew a
little frightened.

"Barnaby! How can you have been so mad?"

"Money melts," said the Major gloomily. "It is
only when a man pulls himself up that he sees how
much has gone."

"But how can you have got into this state?"

"The pigs know," he wrathfully answered; "*I*
don't."

"I suppose—it is—the play," she said in a hesitating whisper. "O Barnaby! and you so faithfully resolved to leave it off when you married Mrs. Canterbury!"

"A man could leave off many things, but for the cursed temptation that surrounds him on all sides in this miserable town. What's the good of his resolves then?"

"I suppose it has been going from bad to worse— bad to worse?"

"It is pretty bad now, I know that."

"What can be done?"

"I must get some money. If I don't get that—" here the Major stopped.

"Well?" said Keziah.

"I *must* get it; that's all," repeated he.

"I suppose it is a great deal that you want?"

"Tolerable."

"And have you any idea how it is to be had?"

"I've run it over in my mind; I have been doing nothing else for some time past; and I see only two ways possible. That Kage should advance me some of Tom Canterbury's hoards; or that old Mother Garston should put me down for a pot of money in her will."

"Is either likely?" asked Keziah, in a tone that said volumes.

"Deuced unlikely. I have tried Kage: went down to his chambers, and put the matter to him in as favourable a light as circumstances allowed. He did not entertain it; it would not have been him if he had, hang him! He stopped me off-hand, in his coldly civil manner, and as good as showed me the door."

Keziah shook her head.

9*

"You would find it difficult, I am sure, to get anything of that kind out of Mr. Kage; he sticks up for principle. He would be afraid of not getting it paid back; and that either he must refund, or little Canterbury be a loser."

"He was afraid of something—and be shot to him! I hate the man. Any way, that outlet seems closed; and there's only Mrs. Garston to fall back upon."

Keziah, in her secret heart, knew there was no more chance of Barnaby's getting money from her, by will or otherwise (beyond what she might have already left him), than there was of his getting it from Mr. Kage. Less, in fact: of the two, she considered there would be more hope with the barrister.

"Barnaby, you may put aunt Garston out of the question, for she will never lend you any, or leave you much."

"You must try what you can do," said the Major irritably.

"She would not hear me. If I persisted in pressing the question, she would call her servants to show me out of the house. Since that—that unhappy affair, she has never once allowed me to mention your name."

Barnaby Dawkes lifted his eyes in surprise.

"What affair?"

"Of Belle Annesley."

A minute's silence. Keziah turned round, and drank what tea was left in her cup.

"Keziah," he said hoarsely, his black eyes taking quite a fierce gleam as he looked at her—a gleam born of trouble—"I tell you that I must have money, though I move heaven and earth to get it."

"My will is good to give it you, Barby," she an-

swered, all the old affection coming back with a rush;
"but when I know—I know—that the notion of getting
it from Mrs. Garston is more visionary than that wind
now sweeping past the window, it would be foolish of
me to deceive you with hope. Could you not borrow
money upon your income? Upon your wife's income,
I mean."

"I have done a little in that way," acknowledged
the Major. "Can't get another stiver on it from any
money-lender breathing; have tried the greater portion
of 'em. Don't you see? if she died to-morrow, it
would not come to me, but to the boy; and they are
cautious."

"I don't quite understand."

"Should Caroline die in the boy's lifetime, the
income she enjoys lapses to him; should he die in
hers, while he is a minor, his money lapses to her.
When old Canterbury made his will, he seemed to
forget that anybody existed in the world but those
two."

"And should the boy die after he is of age, to
whom does it lapse then?"

"To whomsoever he shall will it. It's an awful lot
of money, his is; and Kage will take sharp care of the
accumulations. By Jove! when I remember sometimes
that that miserable little unit of six years old is keeping me out of wealth, I'm—I'm—savage."

"Don't, Barnaby."

"Don't what?"

"Talk in that way. You should keep such thoughts
down," added Keziah sensibly. "The thing is so, and
you cannot alter it. You ought to have begun at first

to put by out of your wife's large income, and insured her life."

"How I hate Kage!" growled the Major. "Any other trustee would have accommodated me under the circumstances."

"I don't think there has ever been much love lost between you and him."

"Curse him! It is he who hopes to come in for that old creature's money. He has her ear always. I'd not bet a crown that it is not he who is keeping up the ball against me."

Keziah shook her head.

"Wrong, Barnaby. I do not fancy he will come in for her money; and, though he is no favourite of mine, I believe he is too honourable to touch the ball against you, let alone keep it up."

Major Dawkes rose.

"Will you see her to-morrow? Do as I bid you, Keziah: move heaven and earth to get her to remember me well. I'd say almost *forge* a will!" he added impulsively—though, it must be confessed, without any real meaning—"for money I must have."

"Don't be angry with me, Barnaby, if I suggest to you another course. I do so, only in the conviction that the two you mention are hopeless."

"Well?"

"Be made a bankrupt at once."

Major Dawkes glared a little. *He* a bankrupt!

"You don't know what you say, Keziah."

"I see the social disadvantages just as well as you; but at least you would be clear. Of course I don't mean a regular bankruptcy as tradespeople have to go through—I mean privately; what they call whitewashed."

"I can't be."

"Can't be?"

"Will you help me, or won't you?" he repeated in desperation. "There's more necessity for help than you know yet."

"What necessity? Tell me all, Barnaby, if you have not told it. It may be better. Perhaps we are at cross-purposes."

It is possible that the Major thought it might be better. He hesitated for half a moment, looking at her up-turned face; then he whispered two or three words in her ear, and went out, whistling softly, leaving Keziah as white as ashes.

CHAPTER X.

Called out of the Reception-room.

LAMPS at the door and carriages dashing up to it, and the shouting of clashing coachmen, and the sweet scent of exotics through the hall and up the staircase, proclaimed that Major and Mrs. Dawkes were holding a reception. Strictly speaking, it was hers. When the Major got home, after his interview with Keziah, he had barely time to get his dinner-coat on. Half-a-dozen people dined with them, and the reception came later. The Major had quite forgotten there was to be a party, if indeed he had ever been made aware of it.

He was beginning to hate these crowds at his own home. Careless-natured though he was, there were certain dangers besetting his path that half frightened him; and the mob jarred upon his nerves.

Mrs. Dawkes did not consult him when she should hold her receptions; and was not likely to. As yet

the dangers were at a tolerable distance; and the
Major, always sanguine, hoped to avert them.

Not one person do we know amidst the crowd.
Satins, feathers, fans, bouquets, jostle the black coats
of men; a goodly company; but to us they are
strangers. Mrs. Dawkes, in white silk and lace, her
golden hair worn carelessly—and perhaps that is the
chief reason of its looking so wondrously beautiful—
stands to receive them. But now some one comes in
whom we do know—Thomas Kage the barrister. And
his presence in that house is so very rare—at least at
its gay doings—that Major Dawkes lifts his supercilious
eyebrows, and wonders audibly what the dickens has
brought him.

This. Somebody had said in his ear lately, that
Mrs. Dawkes was killing herself—killing herself with
the dissipated life she led: that she was looking just
as though she had one foot in the grave, and might
be in it now before her mother, if she did not take
care.

For that poor old shaking scarecrow was alive yet.
A sad burden to herself, a wearing trouble to all
around her, she existed on, never moving out of the
one room she occupied in her house at Chilling. Fry,
her maid, had quitted her place, strength and patience
alike reduced, and had taken service with Mrs. Dawkes.
But it is not with Mrs. Kage that we have anything
to do.

So Thomas Kage came to see. He generally had
a standing card for Mrs. Dawkes's assemblies. In spite
of his non-attendance, she always sent them; and he
thought he would for once make use of it. He also
wanted to say a word to the Major. Drawing aside to

let the crowd pass in advance, he stood against the wall while he scanned her.

Even so. She was looking thin, worn, ill. Dark circles were round her eyes; her lips were feverish; her cough—she coughed three or four times—had a hollow hacking sound. A strange pang shot through the heart of Thomas Kage.

"*You* here!" exclaimed Caroline, her face lighting up with pleasure as she met Mr. Kage's hand. "I should think it would rain gold to-morrow."

"Because my appearance here is so rare?"

"You know it is. If my poor receptions were poison, Thomas, you could not eschew them more than you do."

"I wish I could induce *you* to eschew them, Caroline."

"I! That *is* good!"

"You are looking very thin."

"Yes, I am thin. I have not been well lately."

"What has been the matter?"

"O, a cold, I think. I have spit a little blood once or twice."

"Caroline!"

She laughed at his look of consternation.

"It was ever so many weeks ago. Nothing but the cough brought it on. One night, coming out of St. James's Hall, the carriage could not get up. Major Dawkes was in a hurry to go somewhere, so we walked to it. I had nothing on my neck but a thin lace cape, and the cold caught my chest. I am quite well again. It is the sitting up late and the rackety life we lead that makes me look thin."

"Caroline, I am glad to hear you acknowledge that

fact. To lead this life always would injure one twice as strong as you are. There's reason in roasting eggs, you know."

"Apropos of what?"

"But there's no reason in leading it without cessation," continued Mr. Kage, following out his argument. "Why don't you go down to the Rock?"

Caroline shrugged her pretty shoulders. The diamonds resting on her neck (Olive Canterbury's diamonds by right) glittered in their marvellous brightness.

"Do you want me to die of ennui, Thomas? I should if I went there."

"You did not die of it when you lived there in the days gone by."

"But I had not then tried a London life. It *is* dull for me there, Thomas. You cannot say otherwise; and the Major never stays there with me. The last time I went there, if he came down for a couple of days, he was all restlessness until he got off again. He has his pursuits here, his brother officers and that, and cannot bear to tear himself away from them. In July, or August at the latest, I shall go with little Tom to one of the quiet German baths for two months. It will set us both up."

"Tom is not very strong," he remarked.

"He was as strong and healthy a little fellow born as could be, but he has ailed somewhat lately. They say his chest is weak."

"I know what I should say—if you will allow me, Caroline."

"Say on," she laughingly rejoined.

"That it is the confinement in London that disagrees with him. For the first three or four years of the child's life he was kept chiefly in the healthy country air, and then you transplanted him to this close town. Suppose you treated a plant so. It would soon droop, if not die."

Mrs. Dawkes grew grave. The argument struck her.

"There is really nothing amiss with the child, Thomas; except that he has lately looked delicate."

"But he should look hardy, and not delicate. I say, Caroline, that he requires country air. And so do you."

"He has a wonderful affinity with me, that child," exclaimed Caroline fondly. "If I droop, he seems to droop. You come to see him oftener than you do me, sir."

"Is it my fault if you lie in bed of a morning?" asked Mr. Kage in a laughing tone. "In going to the Temple I sometimes walk round here: it is the most convenient time for me and for Tom. 'Mamma's not up,' he always says."

The soft strains of a band in another apartment rose on their ear. Caroline passed her arm within her cousin's.

"You will go through a quadrille with me, Thomas?" she whispered.

And Mr. Kage heard it with intense surprise.

"A quadrille! I! Why, do you know how long it is since I danced one?"

"How long is it?"

"So long that I cannot recollect. Yes, I do. The last time I danced a quadrille was that long bygone year when I was staying with my mother at Little Bay. I danced it with you, Caroline."

Their eyes met, quite unintentionally on either side; and for a brief moment the sweet fantasy of that departed time was recalled to either heart.

"I have never danced one since," said Mr. Kage.

"But you will this evening?"

"I do not think you ought to dance at all. You give yourself too much fatigue without that."

"I will be good, and have but this one, if you will dance it with me. There; that's a promise."

"Really, Caroline, I do not remember the figures."

She gently drew him on, and he stood up with her. Two or three very young men, embryo barristers, put up their glasses when they saw him, and laughed with each other. There was nothing to laugh at, either in him or his dancing; but they had never seen the sight before.

Later, when Mr. Kage was looking about for Major Dawkes, in the rooms and out of them, and unable to find him, Judith appeared in view, coming down the stairs.

"I never see such a child," she exclaimed to Mr. Kage, between whom and herself there was much confidence on the score of her little charge. "Just look, sir"—indicating a bit of folded paper in her hand. "Because his mamma did not have him in to say good-night, he has been writing this to her, and made me bring it.—O, it's you, ma'am."

Mrs. Dawkes opened the paper, holding it so that Thomas Kage could see.

"My dearest mamma, I say good-night to you. You must come and kiss me when the people are gone. I shall lie awake looking at the angels. I have said my prayers."

"What does he mean by 'looking at the angels'?" questioned Mr. Kage of Caroline.

"O, he means that little toy that poor Belle Annesley gave him. He never goes to bed without it, does he, Judith?"

"Never, ma'am; there he is now, set up on end in his little bed, and the thing open before him."

"You ought to make him go to sleep, Judith."

"I should like to know how, ma'am," replied the girl respectfully; "he's a'most as fond of music as he is of his angels. There'll be no sleep for him till the tunes have shut up for the night."

"I will come to him before I go to bed," said Caroline, escaping to her guests.

But Mr. Kage thought he should like to see the boy then, and turned towards the stairs. It was a frightfully high house, this Belgravian mansion; the roof pretty nigh in the clouds. This floor was devoted to reception-rooms; on the next were the best bedchambers; on the one above that, slept Tom; and there were the cloud apartments yet, no end to them. The day and the night nursery opened one into the other; they were rather small, for on that landing were crowded several rooms.

Tom was sitting up in bed, the purple-silk curtain at its head drawn between his face and the door. Mrs. Dawkes was careful of her treasure, as though he were some rich toy, and surrounded him with comforts. He thought it was his nurse coming back.

"Did you get to see her, Judith?"

"Yes, and gave the document."

The answer was in Mr. Kage's voice, and the boy put aside the silk curtain with a joyful shout. Not a

loud shout; he was never boisterous, as boys mostly
are. His fair curls were brushed back; his white night-
gown lay smooth on his shoulders; before him, on the
counterpane, was the pretty toy given him by Belle.

"What do you mean by this line of conduct, young
sir? Sitting up like this, when you should be fast
asleep!"

Tom laughed. "I am hearing the music!" he
said.

"Do you make a point of listening to it always at
these hours, when it may be going on?"

"Yes, always," said Tom stoutly; "I wish they'd
play 'Here we suffer grief and pain'!"

"What may that be?" asked Mr. Kage.

"It's a song Fry taught me. Shall I sing a verse
of it to you?"

There was a lull in the downstairs music at the
time; and the boy began, in his weak, gentle, but very
sweet voice: a voice that would be worth hearing some
day if he lived—

> "Here we suffer grief and pain,
> Here we meet to part again,
>   In heaven we part no more.
> O, that will be joyful, joyful, joyful!
> O, that will be joyful!
>   When we meet to part no more."

The boy, who had clasped his hands as he sang,
unclasped them, and looked up.

"You are a curious child," thought Mr. Kage.

"The other verse is about little children; but I
don't know it quite yet. It begins, 'Little children
will be there.' In heaven, you know."

Thomas Kage made no answer. He was gazing
down, lost in thought, on the boy's delicate face. An

idea came over him, almost like a prevision, that the lad would not live beyond the age of childhood. For a moment regret had full place.

"God knows best," he said, in his inward heart; and he laid his hand on the child's head, and kept it there.

"Where's Judith, Mr. Kage?"

The question recalled him to present things; and Judith's step was even then heard. Mr. Kage went down, intending to find Major Dawkes as he departed, and say the word he wished to say. But the Major seemed not easy to be found.

A short while before this, one of the servants had made his way quietly to his master, saying in a whisper that he was wanted below. The man, Richard by name, was attached more than any of the rest to his master's personal service, and knew pretty well about his embarrassments.

"Wanted at this hour!" exclaimed the Major haughtily. "Who is it?"

"It's Mr. Jessup, sir."

"Mr. Jessup! Did you admit him?"

"He admitted himself, sir. The front doors are open to-night."

"You are a fool, Richard," said the Major wrathfully.

Mr. Jessup was the Major's principal lawyer. His coming at that late hour boded no good; and, good or ill, the Major resented being disturbed. There were times for business, and times for pleasure. Richard had put Mr. Jessup into the Major's study—the room with the pipes and pistols. Many an unpleasant interview had it been witness to lately: Major Dawkes was beginning to shun it.

Only one of the gas-lights was burning; and Mr. Jessup, a portly man with a flaxen wig, stood under it. Major Dawkes had just told his servant Richard he was a fool; Mr. Jessup, waiting for his audience, was thinking that, of all fools the world ever saw, his client Barnaby Dawkes was about the greatest.

Standing together, the conference was carried on in a low tone—almost a whisper; dangerous secrets cannot be discussed at a high pitch. A certain matter —or rather a suspicion of a certain matter—had got to Mr. Jessup's ears that evening, and he came down to the Major.

"Is it so, Major? You had better tell me."

The Major would a great deal rather not tell. He shuffled and equivocated, and finally subsided into silence. Mr. Jessup did not make a pretence of listening to him: he knew what he knew.

"No earthly thing can patch up this and avert exposure, save one, Major; and that is, money. You must get it. No light sum, either."

It was the lawyer's parting mandate. Major Dawkes, left alone, took a rapid survey of his situation, feeling something like a man desperate. Money he must have; it was as true as heaven.

A sharp glance upwards, as the door opened; and an angry frown. He had thought it was the lawyer coming back again; but it was Mr. Kage. Richard had said where his master might be found.

"I will not disturb you for a minute, Major Dawkes. I have but a word or two to say. Are you giving it out that I am going to advance you some of Thomas Canterbury's money?"

"No!"

"Two or three applications have been made to me —from your creditors, I presume—asking whether it be true that I am about to accommodate Major Dawkes with funds from the estate to which I stand trustee. I could only think you had been spreading the report."

"I may have said that I wished you would do it," said the Major. "People jump to conclusions."

"I wish you would undeceive them, then. It gives them trouble, and me too."

"What was your answer, pray?"

"That they were under a misapprehension altogether; that I had neither the power nor the will to advance any money belonging to Thomas Canterbury."

Major Dawkes bit his lip.

"It would so oblige me, Kage—if you could be induced to do it. The money would be as safe as the Bank of England; I would give you security, and repay the whole within a year."

"You had my answer before, Major. I told you then that I must decline discussion on the subject; pardon me if I adhere to it. Could I allow even that, I should be scarcely a true trustee. Good-night."

"Good-night," was the Major's answer. "And I wish you were dead, I do!" he growled, as a parting blessing.

————

CHAPTER XI.

An old Warning recalled.

SHRUNKEN and wasted now. The fire had gone out for ever from the once fierce gray eyes; the strong hands were as feeble as a child's: but the will was vigorous yet, and the body strove to be. Mrs. Garston, with her all but ninety years, was better than are some at seventy.

She sat by the fire in her handsome chamber, in a warm dressing-gown of quilted gray silk, her nightcap on her head. Towards evening she *would* get up, in spite of Dr. Tyndal—in spite of everybody. Her hands lay on her lap, her head was bowed forward—the old stiff uprightness could not be maintained now.

"It's time I was gone, Thomas. The silver cord's loosed, and the golden bowl's broken. A few more weary days and nights, and you'll put me in the grave."

In his sense of truth, in the strong opinion he held against attempting to deceive the dying with false hopes, Thomas Kage did not attempt to refute her words. He sat near her, having called in, as was his custom, on coming home from the Temple.

"I should like to lie by your mother. We lived side by side in life; why not repose together in death? Mind about that, Thomas—but it is in the directions I've written. She was young enough to be my daughter, and she was called away years before me. Only a little while to wait now."

The fire played on the fresh colours of the hearth-rug. Mrs. Garston liked bright things yet. Its flame flickered on the face that would never more be winsome.

"It seems a dark road at starting, Thomas—this setting out for the journey of the Valley of the Shadow of Death. Once the gate's passed through, it will be light eternal. A many have gone through it before me; a many have got to come after."

Something in the words struck oddly on Thomas Kage's heart. He bent forward, speaking in a whisper.

"You do not fear the passage?"

"Me! Fear it? I hope not, child. God help my ingratitude if I did!—He'd have given me my patriarch's years in vain. I am setting out for the golden city, Thomas; and I don't care how soon I'm there."

She held up one of her hands. He drew his chair nearer, and sat clasping it.

"You've been like a son to me, Thomas. You were better than a son to your mother; and, mind, God's blessing will go with you always. I'm sure of that. You are another that need not fear the summons to the Valley; no, not though it came to you to-night."

Mr. Kage grew slightly uneasy. She had never talked in this way before. He thought there must be some hidden and perhaps unconscious cause for it—that the summons she spoke of might be already overshadowing the spirit.

A pause ensued—rather a long one; her eyes were turned to the fire in thought. When she began to speak again, it was of other things.

"I'd like you to move into this house, Thomas, remember. You can let your own."

"This house! It would be too large for me."

"Not it. When a man marries, and gets a family about him, he wants plenty of room. Don't you forget that I wish you to come to it. You'd hardly bring Millicent Canterbury home to the next door if you could bring her here. She'd go with you to a hovel, that's my opinion; but she may like elbow-room for all that, when there's no reason why she shouldn't have it."

Not a word said Thomas Kage in refutation. That Millicent Canterbury would be his wife some time— certainly his wife if he married at all—he had grown to think very probable. While his prospects were un-assured he would not marry, in spite of Mrs. Garston's sharp orders to do so; but he was getting on well now.

"You'll walk up together once in a way on a summer's evening, you and your wife, Thomas, to take a look at my grave. So will Charlotte. Mind you keep it in good order; but I know you will, because you so keep your mother's.—What's the news?"

The transition was sudden. Thomas Kage, smiling slightly, said he knew of none in particular.

"Heard anything about Barby Dawkes?"

"No. Is there any to hear?"

"That's what I asked *you*," said Mrs. Garston, with a touch of her old retort. "I fancied there might be; that's all. Barby's in a mess again, Thomas; a deep one, too."

Mr. Kage thought this more than probable; indeed he as good as knew it. It was but the day after the one spoken of in the last chapter, when he had been at the reception in the Major's house.

"Keziah called this afternoon. They told her I was in bed, not well enough to see any one, and asleep too. She said she must see me, and waited. So when my tea came in, she came with it, for I had but then awoke. What do you think she wanted, Thomas?"

Money, he supposed, but did not say so. He slightly shook his head.

"She had got a face, Thomas; but Keziah always had when it was to serve Barby. You'd not believe it unless I told you with my own tongue—she wanted me to alter my will in Barby's favour! Something's up with him, Thomas: as true as we are here, something's up. What he has been getting into now, she wouldn't say; I asked her: but it's something bad. She prayed for money for him by gift or by will, as if she was praying for her life; and her voice and hands shook like leaves in the wind."

"I conclude he must be in debt again," observed Thomas Kage.

"Debt of course; and pretty deep. It's not a little thing would move Keziah. I did feel a bit sorry for her."

"Major Dawkes should fight his own battles; not trouble his sister."

"Major Dawkes knows he'd not dare to put his foot inside my door with any such petition," sharply returned the old lady. "I've kept him at my stick's length, I can tell you, since that matter of little Belle Annesley. She's better off in heaven, poor child, than she'd have been with *him*."

She sat silent a minute, thinking perhaps of the past, and the girl's blighted life. Mr. Kage did not interrupt. He would have preferred to hear no more of Major Dawkes and Keziah's petitions. Mrs. Garston began to nod her head.

"Yes, she had a face—to come asking for money for Barby. He has got the fingering of an income half-a-dozen times as heavy as mine; and hasn't made it do, it seems! "What did I say to you, Keziah?" I asked her—"that if Barby had one hundred thousand a-year, he'd want two." And so he would, Thomas. "He is in *great* need, aunt Garston," cried Keziah— and upon my word, her lips seemed to be turning blue as she said it—"he may have to fly the country if he does not get it!" "And the sooner he flies it, the better for them that remain, Keziah," I answered; "if Barby had been sent out of it years ago at the Queen's cost, he'd only have got what he deserved." And so he would, Thomas. "Would you save him from such a fate as that now, aunt Garston?" says she to me. "No, I would not," I told her. And so she got my answer, and went away—it's not above an hour ago. But, Thomas, you take my word for it —that bad man is in for it, shoulder deep. To help him would be a great mistake, next door to a sin; he goes through the world scattering ill both sides his path; and if he gets stopped, so much the better."

What she said was true enough. Money would never help Barnaby Dawkes—never do him any real good. The more he got, the more he would need to get.

Wishing Mrs. Garston good-night, Thomas Kage proceeded to his home, hungry enough; for he had not yet dined, and it was later than usual. He had for some time thought that the staying in his house (as Mrs. Garston in a sense compelled him to do) was all for the best; he was making an ample living now, and his name stood high in his calling before the world.

Opening the house-door with a latch-key, he was about to enter the dining-room, when a maid-servant ran up.

"A lady is there waiting for you, sir. She says she wants to see you on particular business."

"Who is it?" he asked.

"I don't know, sir. She has been here above an hour. We showed her in there, as there was no fire in the drawing-room: and so the cloth's not laid."

When a man, starving for his dinner, is told the cloth's not laid, it is by no means agreeable news. Thomas Kage made the best of it, as he was wont to do of most other ills in life. But he did wonder what lady could be wanting him. Seated before the fire, her back to the door, he saw some one in a gray-plaid shawl. She got up as he entered, and turned her head. Keziah Dawkes!

Gray though her shawl might be, it did not equal the gray hardness of her face: but that had grown habitual. Mr. Kage closed the door, and sat down near her, the recent remark of Mrs. Garston's passing through his mind—that Keziah's voice and hands trembled and her lips turned blue when pleading for Barby. Her voice was not trembling now, as she apologised for taking his house by storm to wait for him. He said a few courteous words, and then left her to tell her business.

"I have come to request a great favour of you," she began. "I know how vast is the liberty I am taking in meddling with what you may deem cannot concern me; but interests are at stake which—which—"

Keziah broke down. Not from emotion: she was not one likely to be superfluously agitated, even for Barby; but because she doubted *what* she could say to justify her plea, and yet not say too much. It had to be done; those calm, honest, steady eyes were patiently fixed on her. She went on a little more quickly.

"You are the sole trustee to Mrs. Dawkes's little son, I believe, Mr. Kage."

"The trustee to his property? Yes."

"It is accumulating largely, they say."

"Of course. With so large a fortune it could not be otherwise."

"I want you to lend a very, very infinitesimal portion of those savings to the child's stepfather," continued Keziah.

"To Major Dawkes?"

"Yes.'

"I am truly sorry you should have come here to prefer any such request to me, Miss Dawkes. It is not in my power to grant it."

"In your power it is, Mr. Kage; in your will it may not be."

"Indeed you are in error. It is not in my power to touch a fraction of Thomas Canterbury's money, to lend to Major Dawkes or to any other person. If I did so, I should be false to my trust."

"Not false really; only in your own estimation."

"False really; I think you must see that, Miss Dawkes. But, put it as you suggest, I like to stand well with my conscience," he added, smiling, wishing to pass the matter off as lightly as he could.

"I have come to beg, pray, entreat of you to do this," rejoined Keziah with deep earnestness, as if the smile offended her. "I have come to *wrestle* with you for it, Mr. Kage, if need be."

She half rose from her chair as she spoke. Mr. Kage got up and put his elbow on the mantelpiece. He foresaw the interview might possibly turn out more painful than pleasant.

"To wrestle with you, as Jacob wrestled with the angel on the plains of Peniel," she continued, her voice falling, her cold gray eyes searching his. "To say to you as *he* said, I will not let you go unless you bless me."

"Were it a thing I could do, Miss Dawkes, I should not need this persuasion. Being what it is, no entreaty or persuasion can move me."

The voice was all too quietly firm. Keziah's heart began to fail within her.

"I never thought you a hard man."

"I do not think I am one. This is not a question of hardness, but of right and wrong."

"To grant the request would cost you nothing."

"The cost to me we will put out of sight, please, Miss Dawkes, as a superfluous consideration. The request is—pardon me—one that you have no right to make, or I to suffer. See you not," he added, bending his head a little in the force of argument, "that if I were capable of lending (say) one hundred pounds of this money lying in my charge, I might, in point of principle, as well lend the whole? If I could bring myself to touch any of it, what is there to prevent my taking it all?"

Of course Keziah saw it; she was a strong-minded woman of sense and discernment. But Barby's position made her feel desperate, obscuring right and wrong.

"The position I stand in, as sole trustee to so large a property, is a very onerous one," he pursued. "When I found I was appointed to it by Mr. Canterbury's will, the responsibility that would lie on me struck me at once, and I hesitated, for that and other reasons, whether to accept it. Eventually I did so; but I was quite sure of myself, Miss Dawkes. Had I not been, the world would never have found me acting."

Keziah sat forward in the chair, her head resting on her hand. Mr. Kage, still standing, faced her. He seemed firmer than that celebrated mansion pertaining to the boy's property—the Rock.

"It is so trifling a sum that I ask you the loan of! Only three or four thousand pounds."

"The amount, more or less—as you must perceive—has nothing to do with it."

"Do you think that Major Dawkes would not pay you back?"

"I think Major Dawkes neither would nor could," fearlessly replied Mr. Kage. "But—pardon me for repeating it—the question does not lie there."

"Can you suppose that you are fulfilling your duty to the child, when you thus refuse this poor little meed of aid to one who stands to him as a father?" flashed Keziah, temper getting for a moment into the ascendant.

"My duty to the child, my duty to his dead father, lies in refusing it," said Mr. Kage quietly. "But that Mr. Canterbury felt perfectly secure in my faithfulness, he surely would not have placed in my sole hands this great amount of power."

Argument seemed useless, and Keziah sighed heavily. Her face began to take a hopeless look, and Thomas Kage felt for her. But he would have given up his life rather than his probity.

"When Major Dawkes applied to me upon this subject—which fact, I presume, is known to you, by your coming yourself—I stopped him at the onset, Miss Dawkes. I told him that the matter was one that did not admit of argument; neither would I permit any."

Keziah did not take the hint. Tenacious by nature in all that concerned Barnaby, she was persistently so now.

"Put yourself in my brother's place, Mr. Kage," she pleadingly said, her tone taking a degree of softness. "If you had some desperately pressing need of temporary help, how would you feel if it were denied you—as you are denying me?"

"I must really beg of you not to pursue this farther," was his rejoinder. "It gives you pain, and is utterly useless."

"Did you understand my hint?" she asked, dropping her voice. "He is in desperate need of it; *desperate!* Nothing else would justify my persistency after your refusal. It is not common debt."

"I am sorry to hear it," said Mr. Kage. "I suspected something of the kind."

"*Will* you not lend it him?"

"No. I regret you should make me repeat my refusal so often. There is no alternative."

Keziah began to understand that there would be none. She lifted her face to his.

"Could you lend him any of your own money, then? *I* would be responsible as well as he for its return."

Mr. Kage smiled.

"You would find me much less hard in regard to my own, if I had any to lend. A struggling barrister does not put by money."

"For 'struggling' say 'rising.' You are that now."

"But I have not been so long enough to grow rich," he rejoined; involuntarily thinking that, if he were rich, Major Dawkes would be the last person to whom he would lend money.

"Do you know any one who would? any client, for example? Barnaby would pay high interest."

"I do not, indeed. A solicitor would be the proper person to apply to—or a money-lender."

Keziah's private belief was, that Barnaby had exhausted those accommodating gentlemen. She sat on, never attempting to move, and at last began to say a good word for Barnaby.

"There is every excuse to be made for my brother; you must acknowledge that, Mr. Kage."

"Excuse for what?"

"For running into debt. He has been placed in the midst of temptation. Married to a woman who has so large an income, what else could be expected of a man?"

Thomas Kage stared a little.

"I should have considered it just the position that a man might find safety in, Miss Dawkes. Every luxury of life is provided for, without cost to himself."

"You forget his personal expenses—gloves and that."

"Not at all. He reckons, I believe, to draw two thousand a-year from his wife's income for them. And there's his pay besides."

"Who told you that?" asked Keziah, quite sharply.

"Mrs. Dawkes. I had occasion to consult her on a matter connected with the estate, and she incidentally mentioned that Major Dawkes drew two thousand a-year for his private pocket."

Keziah bit her lip.

"Well, what's two thousand a-year to a man of my brother's habits? He has to do as others do."

"I question if Major Dawkes confines himself to the two thousand," rejoined Mr. Kage significantly. "Mrs. Canterbury married him without being secured, and her money lies at the bank in his name. As we are upon the point, Miss Dawkes, it is as well to be correct."

"You wish to make out that he draws just what he pleases of it!" she said resentfully.

"I wish to make out nothing. I have not the smallest doubt but that he does do it."

Keziah stood at bay. She had risen to leave; was she to go in her despair, resigning every hope? Once more a piteous appeal for help went out to Mr. Kage. And yet she knew it would be useless as she spoke it. At length she turned to go, Mr. Kage attending her.

"The mystery to me is, how he can get rid of so much money," he remarked on impulse, as he laid his hand on the lock of the door.

"He gambles," whispered Keziah, forgetting Barnaby's interests for once in her bitter abandonment.

"Gambles. Ay, there it is."

But Thomas Kage had no doubt known as much before. He closed the street-door on his guest, and Keziah went into the bleak night, wondering what now could be done for her brother.

Thomas Kage returned to his room, and while standing over the fire until they should bring his dinner, recalled a certain warning in regard to the boy's money that Mrs. Garston had given him years before. He had thought it superfluous then.

"Take you care of it, or Barby will be too many for you. He'd wring the heart out of a live man if it were made of gold."

CHAPTER XII.

Very unsatisfactory.

SOMETHING like a week went by, and then Mrs. Garston's house was closed. The hale old lady had gone to her rest.

Down came Mr. Jessup, her solicitor; the same man of law who acted (but not always) for Barnaby Dawkes. Major Dawkes was sometimes involved in odds and ends of affairs that he would not have taken to him, a respectable practitioner. Before her death, Mrs. Garston had said to those about her, "When anything happens to me, send for Jessup, and let him look in my desk for instructions."

Keziah Dawkes was with her when she died. Whether in any hope that a second appeal might be of use to Barnaby, whether in solicitude for the old lady's precarious state, Keziah presented herself at the house one morning, and found her aunt dying—all but gone. Keziah was very angry that she had not been summoned; but Mrs. Garston's maid—who had grown old in her service—said her mistress had forbidden her to send to either her or the Major. Mr. Kage had taken his leave of her the previous night; when he called in that morning, she was already insensible. Keziah listened, and could but resign herself to fate.

In less than an hour all was over. Keziah, taking off her bonnet, remained. She felt to be more mistress in the house than she had ever been before; she went peering about surreptitiously in various places, thinking she would give the whole world to know how things were left. A faint foolish hope had been growing up in her heart—that perhaps, after all, her aunt had relented in favour of Barby.

Mr. Jessup searched for the paper of instructions. They were found to have reference chiefly to her funeral. Keziah looked over his shoulder. Mrs. Garston directed that she should be buried by the side of Lady Kage, and that Thomas Kage should follow her as chief mourner.

He the chief mourner!—a pang of dread shot through Keziah's heart. Could this be an intimation that she had made that man her heir? Barby had said it would be so.

And yet, one slight circumstance gave Keziah some little courage: she gathered from the servants that Mr. Jessup had been summoned to a conference on the Friday in the past week. Counting back the days,

Keziah found this must have been the one following that pleading visit of hers for Barby. A burning hope sprang up again within her; yes, Mrs. Garston might have relented.

"Can you tell me whether my aunt has altered her will lately?" inquired Keziah of Mr. Jessup, who was putting a seal on an Indian cabinet, where Mrs. Garston's principal papers were kept.

The lawyer turned and looked at the speaker, as if questioning her right to ask.

"You think the inquiry an indiscreet one, I see, Mr. Jessup. In truth, it is almost needless, considering that the will must be so soon made public. But as Mrs. Garston sent for you last week, I thought, perhaps, she might have wanted some alteration made in her will. The summons was a peremptory one, I believe."

"That's just what she did want, Miss Dawkes."

"Did it concern my brother?" quickly cried Keziah, holding her breath.

"I cannot say but what it did," was the lawyer's answer. "That is all I can tell you now, Miss Dawkes," he added, interrupted her as she was about to speak. "For particulars on that and other points you must be content to wait for the will itself."

Well, Keziah could do that; there were some grains of hope to live upon. Very anxiously did she search the lawyer's countenance, if by good luck she might gather from it courage or disappointment; but it gave out neither. A wax face in a barber's shop could not be more expressionless than his.

Tying on her bonnet with eager fingers, pulling her gray-plaid shawl around her, she made her way to

the street-door, and met Thomas Kage in the garden.
A few words passed between them concerning the old
friend gone, and then Keziah put a home question.

"Do you know how things are left, Mr. Kage?"

"No."

"Jessup is in there sealing up the places," continued Keziah, looking hard at Thomas Kage, almost
as though she doubted his denial. "I find that my
aunt altered her will last week, and that the alteration
concerned Barnaby."

"Indeed!" was all he answered.

"Of course, after our recent interview, you cannot
but know that this is of the very utmost moment to
me, Mr. Kage, for my brother's sake," she resumed.
"To him it is almost a matter of life or death. If you
do know how Aunt Garston's will is left, it cannot hurt
you to tell me."

"But I do not," he replied. "I assure you, Miss
Dawkes, that I know nothing whatever about the will
—absolutely nothing. She never told me how her
affairs were settled; never has given me so much as a
hint of it."

Keziah saw that he was speaking truth, and continued her way, leaving him to enter. Barnaby Dawkes's
communication to her that night at her house—the few
whispered words as he was leaving—had nearly scared
her senses away. Unless help came to him—Keziah
shivered as she strove to put away the thought of what
might follow after. Her great anxiety to ascertain
whether he was left well off was this, that Barnaby
might be able to quiet unpleasant creditors at once
with the news.

"Barby, she's gone!" exclaimed Keziah, bursting

in upon him as he sat in his study looking over some
letters, a cigar in his mouth.

"Who's gone?" returned the Major, thinking of
any one at the moment rather than Mrs. Garston.

"The poor old deaf creature. She died about an
hour ago."

Major Dawkes got up and stood with his back to
the fire, into which he threw the cigar. Keziah thought
he looked startled.

"Dead, is she? Rather sudden!"

"No, they say not. It's a shame I was not sent
for."

"You see now there was not so much time to lose,"
remarked the Major. "You might as well have done
as I asked you, Keziah."

"I did do it, Barby dear. I went to her the day
afterwards. She'd not give me the slightest hope; was
just as rudely abusive of you as ever. So then I went
to Mr. Kage."

The Major lifted his eyes. "What for?"

"To get him to lend you a small mite of the trust
money; or rather to try to get him. It was of no use;
he was as hard as adamant."

"I could have told you it would be no use going
to him," was the rough answer; "and I'm sorry you
went."

"Well, I did it for the best," she said, thinking
how thankless he was—ready to swear at her rather
than be grateful.

Major Dawkes gave the fire a stamp with his heel.
A habit of his.

"Old Jessup is at the place sealing up the things,"
continued Keziah. "He had to come and open the

instructions for the funeral. Thomas Kage is to be the chief mourner. If——"

"And the chief heir too, I expect," explosively interrupted the Major. "A sly, sneaking, greedy hound!"

"He's not that, Barby. If she has left him her heir, depend upon it, it is without any connivance of his. But I think there's a chance for you."

"It's to be hoped there is."

She told him what she had learnt, about the lawyer's being summoned to make some alteration in the will, and his acknowledgment that it concerned Major Dawkes. The Major shouted at the news. He looked upon it as a certainty in that sanguine moment, and his spirits went up to fever heat.

The funeral was over. The fine spring day was drawing to a close as the carriages came back again. Thomas Kage, according to appointment, was the chief mourner; just as he had been many years before at another grave lying close beside.

The mourners assembled in the drawing-room. Keziah Dawkes, the only lady present, looking very grim in her black robes; Mr. Kage; Richard Dunn; Major Dawkes; Charlotte Lowther's husband; Mr. Lynn-Garston, a wealthy country squire, whose brother, Harry Lynn-Garston, was to have married Olive Canterbury; and the lawyer. The will, exciting so much hope and fear in Keziah's breast, was at last about to be made public.

Mr. Jessup unfolded it before them. Within it was a sealed paper, which, according to the deceased's directions, was to be read before the will. It was

written in Mrs. Garston's own stiff hand. Mr. Jessup
explained that Mrs. Garston had handed him this paper
sealed up, giving him no intimation of what the contents might be—only directions to put it with her will,
and read it first. The lawyer looked at it with evident
interest. His audience listened eagerly. It turned out
to be a kind of will, or transcript of her will, inter-
spersed with various remarks, and curiously worded.

"Whereas" (it began, after a few introductory
sentences) "Thomas Kage refuses obstinately to be my
heir, as I wished and intended to make him, I dispose
of my property amidst others, and I do it unwillingly.

"To Richard Dunn five thousand pounds. He is
an honest man, and has been my good friend.

"To Charlotte Lowther, the step-daughter of my
late dear friend Lady Kage, five thousand pounds.

"To Dr. Tyndal five hundred pounds.

"To Mr. Jessup, my lawyer, five hundred pounds.

"Legacies to all my servants—as my will specifies.
They have been faithful.

"To Olive Canterbury my case of diamonds, in
remembrance of Harry Lynn-Garston. There are few
young women I respect as I do Olive Canterbury.

"To Millicent Canterbury my set of pearls, and
the emerald ring that I am in the habit of wearing on
my little finger.

"To Lydia Dunn a plain Bible and Prayer-book,
which my executors will purchase—hoping she will
read and profit by them.

"To Keziah Dawkes an annuity of one hundred
pounds for her life. Also a present sum in ready-
money of two hundred and fifty pounds; to be paid to

her within twenty-one days of my death, free of legacy
duty. Also my set of corals and the two rings lying
in the same case. Also four of my best gowns (she is
to choose them) and the black-velvet mantle, and the
lace that is contained in the top drawer of the ebony
miniature set of drawers in the blue bedroom. Keziah
Dawkes would have got three hundred a-year instead
of one, but for the way in which she has joined Barby
to deceive me through a course of years.

"To Thomas Charles Carr Kage I leave these two
houses—this and the one he lives in. He has been as
a son to me these many years, and I thought to make
him heir to the greater portion of my money. He refuses absolutely—having had enough of unjust wills, he
says, in old Canterbury's—but I know that he would
have used the money well. If he refuses these houses,
I direct that they shall be razed to the ground. It is
my earnest desire that he should not refuse; and I
cannot think he will so far disregard my last wishes as
to do so.

"To various charities, as specified in my will, I
leave five thousand pounds.

"Barnaby Dawkes. I declare in this my last
testament, that it never was in my thoughts to make
Barby Dawkes my heir. Had he shown himself worthy
of it, I would have left him amply well off; but my heir
he never would have been. As he is unworthy, he will
not find himself much the better for me. I bequeath
to him an annuity of two hundred and eight pounds;
and I further bequeath to him a present sum of five
hundred pounds, free of duty, to be paid to him within
twenty-one days of my death.

"The rest of my property I leave to Arthur Lynn-

Garston, and make him my residuary legatee. And I appoint Richard Dunn and himself my executors.

"MARGARET GARSTON."

Arthur Lynn-Garston looked up in mute astonishment. He had not expected to be remembered at all: certainly not to this large amount. But this was not the true will. Very rapidly the lawyer was proceeding to read that, as if desirous not to give time for comment.

It proved, so far as the bequests went, a counterpart of the paper. And Barnaby Dawkes's legacy of two hundred and eight pounds a-year was to be paid to him by weekly instalments.

"That's all," said the lawyer, folding it up.

Keziah's pale lips were trembling. She approached him with an angry tone.

"You told me Mrs. Garston made some alteration in my brother's favour only a week before she died. Where is it?"

"I did not say whether it was in his favour or against him, Miss Dawkes: only that it concerned him," replied Mr. Jessup in a low tone. "The alteration Mrs. Garston desired me to make was this—that Major Dawkes's annuity of two hundred pounds should be increased to two hundred and eight; and be paid to him weekly. She remarked that Mrs. Dawkes would not live for ever, and he might come to want bread-and-cheese."

What could Keziah answer? Nothing. But her face took an ashy turn in the shaded room's twilight.

CHAPTER XIII.

Mrs. Dawkes at Home.

THE clocks were chiming the quarter before midnight, as a gentleman splashed through the mud and wet of the London streets, on his way to a private West-end gambling-house. It was the barrister, Thomas Kage. He was not given to frequent such places on his own account, but he was in urgent search of one who was—a man he had once called friend, and who had brought himself into danger. Not a cab was to be had, and his umbrella was useless; glad enough was he to turn into the dark passage that led to the house's entrance, and shake the wet from his clothes. Dark, cold, and gloomy as it was here, inside would no doubt be all light and warmth, and he was about to give the signal which would admit him, when the door was cautiously opened and two gentlemen came forth.

One of them—he was in her Majesty's regimentals —wore a scowling aspect. It was Major Dawkes; earlier in the evening he had been to an official dinner, which accounted for his dress. More and more addicted had he become to that bad vice, gambling; the worst vice, save one, that man can take to himself; and this night he had lost fearfully. To lose money now was, in the Major's case, simply madness; but the fatal spell was upon him, and he could not shake it off. Not caring to be seen, Mr. Kage drew into a dark corner. At the same moment from the opposite corner stepped some one who must have been waiting there.

"Major," said this latter gentleman, "I must speak to you."

"What the—mischief—brings you here?" demanded Major Dawkes with a hard word.

"I have waited for you two mortal hours. I was just in time to see you enter; and got threatened by the doorkeepers for insisting upon going in after you. I had not the password. Can I speak a word with you, Major?"

"No, you can't," was the defiant answer of the Major. But that he had taken rather more wine than was good for him, he might have been civil for prudence' sake. "I'll hear nothing. Go and talk to Jessup."

"Major Dawkes, this will not do. You know perfectly well that Jessup won't have anything to do with the affair; 'twould soil his hands he says."

"You know where I live," stamped the Major. "Come there, if you want to see me. Pretty behaviour this is, to waylay an officer and a gentleman."

"Excuse me, Major, but if you play at hide-and-seek—"

"Hide-and-seek!" interrupted Major Dawkes. "What do you mean, sir?"

"It looks like it," returned the other with a significant cough. "You can never be seen at your house, and you will not answer our letters. It has not been for pleasure that I have waited here, like a lackey, this miserable night; we might have sent a clerk, but I came myself, out of regard to your feelings. If I cannot speak with you, I will give you into custody; and you know the consequences of that."

Though not quite himself, the Major did know the consequences. Drawing aside into the dark corner that the lawyer—as he evidently was—had come out of, a few whispered words passed between them.

"To-morrow, then, at twelve, at our office," concluded the lawyer. "And you will do well to keep the appointment, Major, this time," he significantly added. "If you do not, we will not wait another hour."

The speaker turned out of the passage into the pool at its entrance, and then waded through other pools down the street. Major Dawkes and his friend stood watching him. The Major's cab waited, but his man, probably not expecting him so soon, was in the public-house round the corner. Somebody else's man flew to fetch him.

"Horrid wretches these creditors are!" cried the Major's friend in warm sympathy. "But it is the most incomprehensible thing in the world, Dawkes, that you should suffer yourself to be bothered in this way. Of course it is no secret that you are up to your eyes in embarrassment; there's not a fellow in the regiment owes half what you do for play, let alone other debts. Why don't you pay up, and get clear?"

"Where's the money to do it?" retorted the Major. "I don't possess a mine of gold."

"But your wife does. She has thousands and thousands and thousands a-year. Where does it all go to?"

"Nonsense! My wife's income is not half so much," peevishly said Major Dawkes, possibly oblivious that no particular sum had been specified. "It might be, if her child died."

"Ah, yes, I forgot; the best part of the ingots are

settled on little Canterbury.   Can't you touch a few of his thousands?"

"No; or I should not have waited until now to do it.   His thousands are tied up to accumulate.   His will be a lordly fortune by the time he is of age."

"But with so much money in the family—your own son's, as may be said—surely there are ways of getting at it.   You might have the use of some to clear you, and pay it back at your leisure."

"So I would, if it were not for the boy's trustee," returned the Major.   'He's as tight a hand as you could find.   The point was put to him some weeks ago; I broached it myself, not taking Mrs. Dawkes into my counsels; and Kage cut me short with a haughty denial.   He's a regular curmudgeon."

Little thought the Major that the "curmudgeon" was in the dark passage behind him and his confidential friend.   To play the eavesdropper was particularly objectionable to Thomas Kage, but he would very decidedly have objected to show himself just now.

"But if things are like this, Dawkes, how on earth can you expect to get clear?" demanded his friend.

The Major did not answer.   He bared his brow for a moment to the damp air: a whole world of care seemed to be seated there.

"Pull up while there's time, Dawkes," was the prudent advice next offered.   "How can you go on, plunging farther into the mud, at the rate you do? To-night you must have lost—"

"It is in my nature to spend, and spend I must, let who will suffer," fearlessly interrupted the Major.

"Well," said the other candidly, "it does seem

hard that a sickly child should be keeping you out of this immense wealth."

So hard did it seem, that Major Dawkes gave a curse to it in his heart; and another curse, spoken, to his servant, who now dashed up. He entered his cab, and giving his friend a lift, was driven away, while Mr. Kage was admitted to the hidden mysteries of the house. But with his business there we have nothing to do.

Several weeks had gone on since Mrs. Garston's death, when we last saw Major Dawkes. How *he* had gone on was a different affair altogether, and not so easy to discern. At that time he had thought it an impossibility that many days could pass over his head without the mine, he always trod on, exploding; and yet they *had:* the flame had only been smouldering until now. But things were growing more ominous hour by hour; and perhaps the Major continued to enter into undesirable expenses as much to drown care as from infatuation.

Mrs. Dawkes had been ill—seriously so. A return of the chest attack she had early in the spring came on; the result of late hours and her own imprudence, as the doctors told her. She was not strong naturally, and she was doing what she could, in the shape of turning night into day in her pursuit of gaiety, to bring her lack of strength conspicuously forth. For three weeks she had been confined to her bed, but was getting better now.

When Major Dawkes's cab deposited him at his house in Belgravia—returning now to the present night, making itself so agreeable with rain—he ascended at once to his bedroom; one he had been occupying temporarily since his wife's illness. It was on the floor above hers, and immediately opposite the day-nursery of little Tom Canterbury. Putting off his regimentals and other things as quickly as he could, the Major got into bed. But not to sleep: anxiety prevented that. He had taken nothing since leaving the gambling-house, and his brain was getting somewhat clearer. It is at these moments that any trouble that a man may have shows itself with redoubled force. Time had been when Major Dawkes sent away trouble with what he had an hour before bestowed upon his servant—a curse. He was of a selfish, reckless nature, and would not let things worry him. Ah, but *then* his worst trouble had been debt; now it was something else, and he had dwelt on it until it had made him painfully nervous. His position was looking fearfully black, and the Major did not see how to improve it.

In saying he was by nature a spendthrift, Barnaby Dawkes spoke only partial truth; it would have been more correct had he said by habit. To launch out into sinful expenses was only customary with him; but these expenses had at length brought their consequences behind them. Very unhappy was it for Barby Dawkes that the consequences did not consist of debt alone.

At the turn of the past Christmas, Major Dawkes, to get himself out of some frightful pit of embarrassment, obtained money upon a bill, which—which—had something peculiar about it, to speak cautiously; and which, later, perhaps nobody would be found to own. So easy a way did it seem to Major Dawkes of relieving himself of a load of temporary care, that he tried the process again, and once or so again. *This* was the secret breathed to Keziah that night when the

Major visited her. This was the secret that Jessup, the lawyer, got access to. The Major used superhuman efforts, and patched up matters for a time, and so averted an explosion. But the secret had now been discovered by two or three most undesirable people who were interested, and public exposure was looming ominously near.

A firm had innocently discounted one of these bills—solicitors in sharp practice. One of the partners it was who had lain in wait for the Major in the dark passage. Perhaps they might be induced to hush the affair up for "a consideration," in addition to all the money and expenses, otherwise they were threatening criminal proceedings; ay, and as the miserable Major knew, they would inevitably keep their word. For the bill, you see, had got somebody's name to it, and that somebody had never written it, or heard of it. That was only one of the bills; there were one or two more quite as doubtful. Other parties to whom the Major was under terrible obligations, legal, if not criminal, had become tired out, and were about to take very unpleasant steps. What with one thing and another, it seemed to the man that a fortune almost as great as Tom Canterbury's was needed to extricate him.

It was a perilous position; more than enough to disturb the Major's rest. He knew quite well that if all came out that might come out—and there were matters besides the peculiar bills—things must be over with him. His wife would quit him; the army would drum him out of it; society would scout him.

"A nice state of affairs!" groaned the Major. "Something must be done. What a fool I have been!"

Something! But what? The help he wanted was no slight sum; and he saw but one hope—and that not a real hope; only a possible one. A persistent mind, indeed, must be Major Dawkes's to cherish it still—though in fact he did not cherish it, but only glanced to it in sanguine moments; for it was the old scheme of getting some of the child's money from Mr. Kage. Only a few thousands out of the boy's large fortune, he would say to himself—only a few thousands! The thought of this fortune, so close at hand, yet so inaccessible to him—for, if the child died, you remember, the whole of it reverted to Mrs. Dawkes—had begun to be to the Major as a very nightmare: it haunted his dreams, it haunted his daily thoughts; it was ever present to him, sleeping or waking. Like unto the gold-fever that fell on some of us years ago, and sent us out to Australia little better than eager madmen, so had a gold-fever attacked Major Dawkes. As the value of a thing coveted is enhanced to a fabulous height by longing, and diminished by possession, so did this fortune of little Tom Canterbury's wear, to his stepfather, an aspect of most delusive brightness. In its attainment appeared to lie the panacea for all ills; the recompense for past and present troubles; a charming, golden paradise.

Major Dawkes had a particular dislike to children; but in feigning a love for little Tom Canterbury before the marriage—to ingratiate himself with the child's mother—he had really acquired a liking for him. This in a degree wore off later; and he was often severe with the child—a mild gentle little fellow whom any one might love—but on the whole he liked the boy. However, since this hankering after his fortune had arisen, Major Dawkes had almost grown to hate him, looking on him as a deadly enemy who stood between him and light.

In spite of his fast habits, few men living cared so much to stand well with the world as Barnaby Dawkes; certainly none so dreaded to stand ill with it. There was one ugly word moving ever before his mental sight in fierce letters of flame—F-o-r-g-e-r-y. Rather than have such a word brought home to him, he would have died—and Major Dawkes was very fond of life. It was not the act itself he repented, but the chance of exposure. Safe from that, he would have done the same thing to the end of time. Dropping asleep towards morning, he dreamt that he was in the midst of some surging sea, whose waves were perpetually going to overwhelm him. He wanted to turn his head and look behind, but the waves would not let him. He knew that some awful phantom was there in his pursuit, to overtake him unless he turned to confront it; and yet he could not. A fresh and curious epoch must have arrived in Major Dawkes's life when it came to dreams.

Remembering his engagement for the morning, Major Dawkes rose in time to keep it. *That* might no longer be ignored—as he knew too well. Swallowing his breakfast with what appetite he had, he took his departure. Of the two, Barnaby Dawkes would rather have gone to an hour's recreation in the pillory than to the appointment in the house of this legal firm, with the brand of guilt and shame on his forehead.

And yet, in one sense, the interview must be utterly superfluous. All the argument in the world would but have amounted to this—that the full indemnifying money must be produced, or the Major would be made a nine days' spectacle. He knew it himself, as he dashed there in his carriage, driving his high-mettled horses. Humble pedestrians, glancing admiringly up from the pavement, thought what a great man the Jehu must be, and how silky was his fine black moustache; but they could not read his heart, or see the cankering care eating it away. The carriage drew up in Lincoln's-inn, and the Major went in to purgatory. The consultation was a pretty long one; the lawyers were uncompromising, and the client was almost helpless; but he argued and denied and equivocated; and then they rang a bell, and desired a clerk to hold himself in readiness to perform a certain mission at Scotland-yard. The Major was brought metaphorically to his knees, and he came forth at length with a knitted brow.

"Where the devil am I to get it?" was the puzzling question put to himself, and spoken unconsciously aloud as he ascended to his carriage. Again and again he saw but one solitary opening—the appealing to Mr. Kage. Look where he would, around the whole wide world, he saw no other.

He drove straight home, regardless of a pelting shower that was coming down upon him, and found a bevy of visitors in the drawing-room. Mrs. Dawkes, lovely still, but pale from her recent illness, sat in their midst, her attire—mauve colour—charming as usual; a lame apology for mourning, worn for Mrs. Garston. Talking with one, laughing with another, exacting admiration from all: an adept was she in the wiles and the petty nothings of frivolous existence. The Major saw no chance of private conversation with her then, and shut the door with a suppressed growl, not caring whether he had been perceived by the guests or not.

When these idlers were gone and the sun was shining again, Mrs. Dawkes called for her boy. He had been sitting on the stairs, patient, loving child, hoping for the summons. Indulged though he was by his mother, never was there a more obedient, modest, good little son than he, never presuming upon her affection. He wore the Scotch dress, and his fair curls floated on his neck: nearly seven years old now, he scarcely looked his age. Mrs. Dawkes once said to Mr. Kage that the child had a strange affinity for her; if she drooped, he drooped. Certain it was that, during this recent illness of hers, the boy had seemed pale, languid, anything but well. Exceedingly delicate he looked to-day, as she took him on her knees.

"Did you eat a good dinner, Tom?"

"O yes, mamma."

"What did you have?"

"Some fowl and some custard-pudding and some jam. I've been reading my fairy-tales since. Judith's mending my puzzle."

"Is she getting ready to take you out, Tom? It's time."

"I told her I'd not go," said Tom. "I'd rather stay with you, mamma. When will you come out with me again?"

"When this showery weather is over," replied Mrs. Dawkes, who had not been allowed to go out of doors since her illness. "But Tom—"

What she had been about to say was arrested by the appearance of Major Dawkes. Putting his head in to reconnoitre, and seeing the room now clear of visitors, he came forward.

"Caroline," said he, "send Tom away. I want to speak with you."

"Is it something you cannot say before him?" she asked; for there was no longer much cordial feeling in her heart for her husband, though they maintained a show of civility.

"Are you so infatuated with that child that you cannot bear him out of your sight?" angrily demanded the Major, who was in a most wretched mood, and particularly bitter against the child.

Mrs. Dawkes was surprised: his ebullitions of temper had usually been restrained in her presence. She did not condescend to retort.

"Go to that table, Thomas, and amuse yourself with the large picture-book," she said, pointing to the far end of the room, where he would be out of hearing. "What is it?" she apathetically said, addressing her husband.

"My dear, you must pardon me; I am in much trouble and perplexity," resumed the Major, remembering that to provoke his wife was not exactly the best way to attain his ends. "It is frightful trouble, Caroline; and nothing less."

"O, indeed. Have you broken your horses' knees? I saw you drive away rather furiously this morning."

"I have been answering for the debts of a brother-officer, Caroline, and have got into difficulties through it," he avowed, having mentally rehearsed the tale he meant to tell.

"Rather imprudent in you to do so, was it not?" interrupted Mrs. Dawkes.

"I suppose it was, as things have turned out; for he died, and it has fallen on me."

"The liability?"

The Major nodded.

"I have been trying to pay it off, as I could, and have run into debt myself in consequence. Caroline, my dear," he added in a sepulchral tone, "your husband is a ruined man."

To Mrs. Dawkes, who had a splendid country mansion and some thousands a-year in her own right, of which nobody's imprudence could deprive her, husband or no husband, the above announcement did not convey the dismay it would to many wives. Not to mince the matter, the Major, looking at her from the corner of his eye, saw that it had made no impression whatever.

"How will you get out of the mess?" quoth she.

"I can get out of it in two ways. One is by paying up; the other, by shooting myself."

"Ah," said she equably, "people who *talk* of shooting themselves rarely do it. Don't be an idiot, Barnaby."

"Caroline," he rejoined in a tone that was certainly agitated, "if I make light of it to you, it is to save you vexation: but I speak literally and truly, that I must pay, or—or—disappear somewhere—either into the earth or over the seas."

"What can be done?" she inquired, after a pause of consideration. "We have no ready-money to spare: our expenses seem to swallow up everything. Often I can't make it out."

"*Our* ready-money would not suffice. The poor fellow was inextricably involved; and," he added, dropping his voice to a faint whisper, "ten or twelve thousand pounds would not more than pay it."

12*

Mrs. Dawkes gave a scream of semi-dismay. As to the "ten or twelve thousand," the Major did not think it prudent to mention a higher sum then, but that much would prove but a sop in the pan.

"But for that deceitful old aunt of mine dying, and leaving me nothing in her will (I hope there's a Protestant Purgatory, and that she's in it!), I should never have had occasion to tell you this. Indeed, but for the expectation of inheriting her fortune, I should not have answered for the poor fellow."

"What is to be done?" repeated Mrs. Dawkes, returning to the practical consideration of the dilemma, and leaving the bygone "expectation" in abeyance; for it was a question upon which she and he entertained opposite opinions.

"One thing can be done, Caroline; you can help me out—if you will."

"I!" she repeated.

"You can get Tom's trustee, Kage, to let me have the money. I will repay it as soon as I possibly can. There will be no difficulty in that, and no risk."

"He will not do it."

"He will, if you bid him. For me he would not."

"He never will," she repeated. "I know Thomas Kage too well. He is the most perfectly straightforward, honourable man breathing: ridiculously so. I am right, Barnaby, cross as you look over it. Tom's money is not his to lend, and I am sure he would not advance a pound of it."

Major Dawkes nearly lost his temper. It was a way of meeting the request that he did not at all admire.

"Will you ask Kage?"

"No. Ask him yourself."

"An ill-conditioned worthless man! He never ought to have been made the boy's trustee," spoke the Major in a suppressed foam.

Mrs. Dawkes smiled equably. "If you were but half as worthy as he!"

"Will you lend it me?" demanded the Major.

"I have not the power. And if I had, I would not suffer Tom's money to be played with."

"You have this much power: any request preferred to Kage by you, and made a point of, would be complied with."

"Nonsense! I'll do nothing of the kind. My child is my child, and his interests are identified with mine. You should not get into these liabilities. No man would, with common foresight, unless he knows that he will have the means to meet them."

Angry and wroth, Major Dawkes broke out in a temper. The little boy, most sensitively timid, shivered at the raised voices, left his picture-book and stole forward, halting in the middle of the room.

"You see now how necessary it is that Tom's trustee should be a man of firmness, that he may guard against such emergencies as the present," spoke Mrs. Dawkes rather tauntingly—at least it so sounded to the Major's pricking ears. "I am very sorry, Barnaby, that you should have got yourself into this dilemma; but it is not my boy's money that can extricate you from it."

Biting his lips to control his fury, Major Dawkes turned round and stepped against the child, not knowing he stood there. It wanted but that encounter to set him off. Out came the passion.

"You little villain," he cried with an imprecation, "do you dare to stand between me and—and—your mother? There's for you!"

It was a cruel blow he struck the child, and it felled him to the ground. Quite beside himself in the blind hatred of the moment, the irrepressible passion, Major Dawkes gave him a kick as he lay—one of contempt more than of violence—and went from the room, a furious man. Mrs. Dawkes raised the boy in her arms, and tottered to a seat; weak from her late illness, it was indignation that gave her strength to bear him. For several minutes neither of them spoke. The child sobbed on her neck, she sobbed on his.

"Mamma, what had I done?"

"You had done nothing, my darling. He wants to spend your money," she added in her indignant resentment.

"O mamma, let him have it; let us go away from here! Papa is never kind to me now."

"Yes, we *will* go away," she emphatically rejoined. "We will go to the Rock, my boy: your own home, and mine. If papa likes to follow us, and behave himself, he may; and if not, he can stay where he is."

"Let papa have my money," repeated Tom Canterbury. "I don't care for money."

"You do not understand, dear. The money is Mr. Kage's at present; he would not give it to Major Dawkes if he asked him ever so."

In came Judith at this juncture, ready to attend Master Canterbury on his walk. She saw the tears and the red eyes.

"Why, what has taken him now?" cried she in surprise.

"He has been vexed," replied Mrs. Dawkes hastily; "a little thing seems to vex him now. I don't think he can be quite well, Judith."

"It's the warm weather, ma'am," said Judith. "He'll get up all right after a bit. What he wants is fresh country air."

"And he shall have it too. The streets are damp after the rain, Judith," continued Mrs. Dawkes, "too damp for him to walk. You had better order the carriage."

So the carriage came round, and the young heir of the Rock was driven away in it to take the air, his nurse sitting opposite to him. When the sound of the wheels had faded away on the ear, Major Dawkes entered the drawing-room. He was ready to strike himself down, as he had struck the boy, for giving way to so impolitic a gust of passion. His wife listened to his apologies in haughty silence.

"Caroline, believe me, I was betrayed out of my senses; but it arose from over-anxiety for your peace and comfort."

"It it for my peace and comfort that you ill-treat my child!" sarcastically rejoined Mrs. Dawkes.

"He is an angel, and I love him as such," proclaimed the Major emphatically. "I was in a whirlwind of passion, Caroline, and did not know in the least what I did. I was agonised at the prospect before you: yes, my dear, before *you;* for if I can't pay that poor dead man's creditors, they'll come in. Into this very house, and seize upon it, and all that is in it."

"Seize our house and all that is in it!" exclaimed Mrs. Dawkes in an access of consternation.

"Every earthly thing the walls contain."

"Will they seize me and Tom?"

Major Dawkes gave vent to a dismal groan: but for his state of mind it would have been a laugh. Mrs. Dawkes, shielded always from this kind of the world's frowns, utterly inexperienced, had put the question in real earnest.

"They'd not touch you and Tom, my dear; but they would take every stick and stone in the place. They are frightful harpies. You would be left here with bare rooms, and I should be in prison, unable to protect you. It is not that; think of the shock such a scandal would cause in society!"

The last sentence told on her ear. Society? Ay, there's the terrible bugbear of civilised life. What will society think? what will society say? But for society our "sticks and stones" would often be lost with less intense pain than they are. Major Dawkes enlarged upon the frightful prospect, painting the scenes of the canvas in strong colours, until his wife shrank from it as much as he did. Writing a note, she despatched it by a servant to Mr. Kage's chambers.

When little Tom Canterbury got home from his drive, his stepfather lifted him from the carriage himself, and carried him in to his mother. He did feel sorry for having struck the blow.

CHAPTER XIV.

A Flood of golden Sunlight.

SITTING alone together in the evening twilight, Mrs. Dawkes explained the embarrassment to Thomas Kage, who had answered her summons speedily. Years ago—he remembered it well, and so did she—he had bid her send for him, if in need of counsel, at any hour of the day or night. That is, she explained the embarrassment as far as she was cognisant of it; and then preferred the request—that Mr. Kage would advance some twelve thousand pounds of Tom's money to her husband.

"Major Dawkes has been prompting you to ask this," was the barrister's answer.

"He pressed me to ask it to-day; I refused to do so at first, and it caused an unpleasant scene between us," she said, her cheek reddening with the remembrance. "But when he explained the frightful position we are in—that rude rough men, harpies he called them, will break in here and seize upon our things, and leave the house empty, of course it startled me into feeling that something must be done to prevent it. The Major says they'll bring vans to take the furniture away, and pitch beds and suchlike out of the window into the street. Only think the uproar the neighbourhood would be in, seeing that."

"Caroline," rejoined Mr. Kage in a low tone, "when I finally decided to act as the child's trustee—and you know I at first wished to decline it—one reason for my doing so was, that I might identify my-

self with, and protect, his interests. I informed you
that I should never, under any inducement, be prevailed upon to advance you, or any future husband
you might take, or any other person whatsoever,
any portion of the money. You must remember
this?"

"Certainly, I remember it; it is not so long
ago."

"Then, remembering this, how can you prefer such
a request as the present? I have foreseen that a man,
with your husband's extravagant habits, would probably
become embarrassed, and—"

"*Did* you?" interrupted Caroline, in great surprise;
"I'm sure he has had enough to spend. But this
trouble is not caused by the Major's own debts;
they are liabilities he has entered into for a brother-
officer."

Mr. Kage looked at her. "Did Major Dawkes tell
you this?"

She knew her cousin well, every tone of his countenance and voice.

"Thomas, you don't believe this!"

"I prefer not to discuss the matter with you,
Caroline."

"Whichever way it may be, however contracted,
the debts are not the less real," she continued; "and
nothing but the scandal likely to arise in our home
would have induced me to apply to you for a loan
to him of Tom's money. Will you let him have
it?"

"No. And I am sorry that Major Dawkes should
have suggested this to you. He had already had a
decisive negative from me."

"Has he asked you before?"

"Yes.   Several weeks ago."

"O, indeed," she uttered in a tone of pique; pique against her husband.   "He might have had the grace to consult me first, considering whose money it is."

Mr. Kage had thought so at the time.   He made no remark.

"You will advance it now, Thomas, for my sake."

"I would do a great deal for your sake, Caroline; but not this.   I will not be a false trustee, or part with my own integrity."

Some thought, some recollection, came over Mrs. Dawkes, and she betrayed for a moment vivid emotion. Thomas Kage took up a book that lay on the table and turned over its leaves.   He would not so much as glance at her.

"What am I to do, if people do come in here and take the furniture?"

"Go to the Rock, Caroline; that is my advice to you.   Go at once, and leave the Major to fight out the battle with his creditors!"

"They cannot come into the Rock?" she exclaimed in sudden apprehension.

"Certainly not.   The Major's liabilities could no more touch that, or anything it contains, than mine could.   It is yours for use until your boy shall be of age: after that, his absolutely."

"But would not the seizing these things be like a lasting disgrace?"

"It is a disgrace occurring every day in families higher in position than yours, and it is thought little of.   But in this case, Caroline, no disgrace will be reflected on *you*. You are shielded from it by your own position. It is a peculiar one. You have your large fortune; you are in possession of the Rock. The Major's embarrassments cannot touch you; they are his own exclusively, and people regard them as such."

"Regard!" she interrupted, quickly taking up the word. "Are they already known?"

"Somewhat of them, I fancy. But I ought to have said 'will regard,' for I was thinking of the contingency we have been speaking of. If these things must go, let them go, Caroline: it may serve as a warning to the Major to be prudent in future."

"Thomas, you know that all the things are mine. They were bought with my money."

"They were purchased in his name, and the law can take them."

"That's a great shame. The law must know they really belong to me."

"There was no marriage settlement, you see, Caroline."

"Well, well, I know how stupid *that* was; no good going over it again."

"None in the world. I am sorry your husband should have troubled you with this."

"He said if he could not have the money he would shoot himself," said Mrs. Dawkes.

Mr. Kage's eyes twinkled with a merry expression.

"I remember, some years ago, when the Major was in want of money, he said he must have it, or drown himself. I don't think he had it; and he is alive yet. Tell him, Caroline, he will do well to forget that Tom

has money. And do you go at once to the Rock,
where the Major's grievances cannot disturb your
peace."

"It has just come to what I anticipated; for I did
not really expect you would advance him any," she
observed with equanimity; "and I know you are right.
But won't he be in a passion when I tell him!"

"I will tell him myself, if you like," said Mr. Kage.
"Indeed I would prefer to do so."

Mrs. Dawkes acquiesced, glad to have the matter
taken out of her hands. And the next day the bewildered Major received a short decisive note, which
convinced him that all hope from that quarter was
really over.

Many a time since has Thomas Kage asked himself the question, whether, if Major Dawkes had gone
to him and revealed the whole truth of his peril, and
pleaded to him for salvation, as a man just condemned
sometimes pleads to the judge for his life—whether he
might have been tempted to prove false to his trust,
and save him. And he has always been thankful that
the difficulty was not brought to him.

The next scene fated to be enacted in the drama
was the illness of little Tom Canterbury. Not quite
immediately did Mrs. Dawkes act on Mr. Kage's advice—to go to the Rock. She could not tear herself
all at once from her fashionable friends; and she had
a ready excuse in the fact that she was yet rather
weak for travel. Just a few days she intended should
elapse first. Before they were over, Tom was taken
ill with a malady he had been attacked with before—
inflammation of the chest. He was in great danger.
Mrs. Dawkes hung over him, scarcely quitting his bed-

side; now giving way to hope, now to all the anguish of despair.

But see you not what a flood of golden sunlight this same dangerous illness opened on the Major? It could not be said, perhaps, that he positively prayed for the child to die; but the possible contingency lay on his heart continually in a kind of wild wish, never leaving it. To temporise much longer with those men whom he so terribly feared would not be in his power.

Mrs. Dawkes sat at the child's bedside, the purple-silk curtain drawn between him and the meridian sun. There appeared to be little doubt that he was dying. A wan white face it was, laid on the pillow, the blue eyes half closed, the fair hair falling around. One hand, stretched out on the counterpane, held the mother-of-pearl shell given him by Belle Annesley. It was open; and the vivid colouring of the angels' robes in the picture, bearing the child to heaven, shone brightly in a stray sunbeam that fell across the bed. It was strange the hold that this simple toy had taken— or rather the picture it contained—on the imagination of the boy: he was, in good truth, too susceptible.

He had been lying for some time without moving, his mother watching him, tears in her eyes, a dull pain in her aching heart, when the eyes fully opened, and some slight animation appeared in the still face.

"Let him have my money, mamma."

The words, suddenly breaking on the previous stillness, startled Mrs. Dawkes. She did not catch the thread of what he meant.

"Let who have your money, my darling?"

"Papa. O, let him have it! He'll not be angry with you then."

She understood now. His mind was running on that unhappy scene of a short while before, when Major Dawkes had struck him down, and terrified him with furious words. It had laid hold of his imagination for ill.

"We shall not want money in heaven, mamma."

"No, that we shall not."

"And heaven's better than the Rock."

"Much better," she said from the depths for her weary heart.

"I wish I was there," sighed the child. "See how good the angels are!"—with a movement of the shell towards her. "They take us up without any pain."

"Tom, my darling, don't talk of dying. It will break my heart."

But the boy did not seem to heed the words. He lay with his eyes wide open, as if looking for something in the distance, presently repeating again the burden of his song.

"I wish I was there! It is full of flowers and sunshine; and no one is cruel; Jesus will not let them be. Mamma, I wish I was there."

And Mrs. Dawkes bent her anguished brow on the pillow by his side. The wish sounded in her ears like an ominous prevision.

In the afternoon Major Dawkes came up. Tom was worse then; lying almost without motion, and breathing with difficulty.

"There is no further hope; I am sure of it," moaned Mrs. Dawkes in her heartfelt anguish.

The Major felt entirely of the same opinion. He

was looking at the small white face, when one of the servants appeared and cautiously beckoned him out. He was wanted downstairs.

"You did not say I was in?" uttered the Major, after closing the door on the sick-room.

"The gentleman would not listen to me, sir. He walked straight in, when I answered the door, and sat down in the dining-room. He says he shall sit there till he sees you. It is Mr. Rosse."

Major Dawkes nearly fainted. Mr. Rosse was a lawyer, and one of those dangerous enemies he so dreaded. Go to him, he was obliged: and yet—he scarcely dared. He shrank from the interview like the veriest coward.

"You are worse than a fool, Richard," foamed the Major. "If you cannot contrive to keep people out of my house that I don't want to see, you may quit my service."

"It's not possible to keep the door barred, sir, with visitors and doctors and other people coming to it perpetual," was all the answer Richard ventured to make.

The conference was a stormy one, though carried on in cautious tones, and within closed doors. Things had come to an extremity.

"Only a few days more; only a day or two!" implored Major Dawkes, wiping his forehead, which had turned cold and damp. "It is impossible that he can survive, and then I shall have thousands and thousands at command, and will amply recompense you. You have waited so long, you can surely accord me this little additional grace: I will pay the bill twice over for it, and twice to that."

"Upon one plea or another we have been put off from day to day and from week to week. This may be as false an excuse as the others have been."

"But it is not a false excuse; the child is lying upon his bed, dying. If Mrs. Dawkes were not with him, you might go up and see for yourself that it is so. Hark! that is the physician's step."

The physician it was; he had been upstairs, and was coming down again. Major Dawkes threw wide the door of the dining-room.

"Doctor, what hope is there? I fear but little."

"There's just as much as you might put in your hand and blow away," replied the doctor, who was a man of quaint sayings, and knew that Major Dawkes bore no blood relationship to the child. "The only hope that remains lies in the elasticity of children; they seem ready to be shrouded one hour, and are running about the room the next. We can do nothing more for our little patient; and if he does rally, it will be owing to this elasticity, this tenacity of life in the young. I do not think he will."

The doctor passed out at the hall-door, and the Major turned to his visitor.

"You hear what he says; now will you give me the delay?"

"Well—under the circumstances—one day longer," replied the lawyer, whose firm would prefer their money, even to the exposure of the Major. Let them once get clear of Major Dawkes, and he might swindle all the bill-brokers in London afterwards for what they cared. He stepped across the hall towards the door, and the Major attended him.

"But if the child should not die—if he should

recover—what then?" Mr. Rosse suddenly stopped
to ask.

The Major's heart and face alike turned sickly at
the supposition; it was one he dared not dwell upon—
literally *dared* not.

"There is no "if" about it; he is quite sure to die.
When I was up with him just now, he looked at the
last gasp; the nurse thought he was dead then, up to
the knees. I'll drop you a note as soon as it's over."

Night drew on. The child lay in the same state—
his eyes closed, and quite unconscious—battling with
death. The medical men came and went, but they
could render no assistance; and it seemed pretty certain that no morning would dawn for little Tom Canterbury. Mrs. Dawkes would sit up with him, in spite of
her husband's remonstrances, who told her that the in-
cessant fatigue and watching would make her ill again.
He went to rest himself, and slept soundly; for his
troubles seemed at an end. The sick-room, as may
be remembered, was near his own; and Major Dawkes
was suddenly aroused by a movement in it. He heard
the nurse come out, call to Richard, and tell him to
run for the doctor. The man had been kept up all
night, to be ready if wanted. The Major looked at
his watch—five o'clock.

"It's over at last," thought he. "What a mercy!
I did not think he'd hold out so long. Ah, they may
send, but doctors cannot bring the dead to life. And
now I am a free man again!"

He would not go into the death-chamber; he did
not care to witness death-scenes; and it would be time
enough to condole with Mrs. Dawkes by and by. So
he lay, indulging a charming vision of the golden

paradise which had at length opened to him, which was partly imagination, partly a semi-dream.

The return of Richard disturbed him. He heard the latch-key placed in the door, and the man come up the stairs. Major Dawkes rose, put on his slippers, opened his door an inch or two, and arrested his servant.

"You have been round to the doctor's, Richard?"

"Yes, sir. He'll be here in a minute or two."

"There was no necessity to disturb him, only that it may be more satisfactory to your mistress. The child is dead, I suppose?"

"Dead, sir! no. He has took a turn for the better."

"What?" gasped Major Dawkes.

"He seems to have took a turn, sir, and has rallied; and that's why my mistress sent for the doctor."

"I—I—don't understand," cried the bewildered Major.

He really did not. So intense had been the conviction of the child's death, that his mind was unable at once to admit any different impression.

"When the doctor was here the last thing, sir, he thought there might be a change in the night, for the better or the worse. If it was for the better, he was to be sent to, he said," explained Richard.

"And—it is for the better?"

"O dear yes, sir, happily. Judith says she's sure he will get over it now."

Major Dawkes withdrew into his room, and softly closed the door. He felt as though the death-blow,

13*

which was to have overtaken the child, had missed its
aim, and fallen upon him.

CHAPTER XV.

"Died in a Fit."

A WEEK elapsed; and little Tom Canterbury, owing,
no doubt, to the "elasticity," appeared to be getting
well rapidly.   Mrs. Dawkes, heart and spirits alike
raised, caring not even for folly and fashion in comparison with her darling child, gave orders that pre-
parations should be made for removal to the Rock.   If
the Major was unable to leave London, he could remain behind, she obligingly told him; but Tom wanted
country air, and Tom should have it.

To depart for the Rock, or to depart for Kamt-
schatka, would have seemed all one to the Major, provided either place would shield him and his reputation.
Scarcely once during this last week had he dared to
show himself out of doors.   His time had been chiefly
spent in writing bulletins of little Canterbury's state to
sundry people interested, every one of which represented the child as "slowly going."   So long as this
farce could be kept up, and his enemies be deceived
into believing it, he felt tolerably safe.   Tolerably only:
it was Major Dawkes's misfortune never to feel quite
assured upon the point at any moment, night or day.
But, in fact, he was so.   With the prospect of Tom
Canterbury's thousands and tens of thousands slipping
speedily into his fingers, to be squandered as Major
Dawkes knew how to squander, people considered that
it lay in their interests not to proceed to extremity with
him.   And such an extremity!

How harshly Fate was dealing with him in thus restoring Tom to life, Major Dawkes felt to the back-bone. He looked upon it as a grievous wrong; an injury done him: in the perversion of mind caused by need, he had come to regard the fortune as his by right. Did it stand to any reason that this sickly infant ought to keep him out of what would put him straight with the world, and relieve him from this horrible night-mare? Children who died were happier than children who lived: little Tom wanted to go to heaven; he was saying so continually; and heaven could not be kind when it thus renewed the lease of his poor frail life on earth. So reasoned Major Dawkes. There were moments now when he wished *he* had died in his childhood, before worry and debt had come; and in pursuing this line of argument he was honest enough.

But—*what was he to do?* Tom Canterbury's recovery could not be kept secret for ever. The period when it must be known, was looming all too near; advancing close, even then, to his threshold. And it was bringing with it an abyss of agony and shame, than which to Major Dawkes nothing could be more terrible. It seemed that he must forfeit life, rather than meet it.

At this, the week's end, the medical men pronounced it safe for Tom to travel; Mrs. Dawkes at once fixed the following morning for their departure; and gave the Major that obliging permission, to go or stay behind, mentioned before. Soon after hearing it, Major Dawkes was crossing the hall, when a knock and ring startled him; startled him, as it seemed, to abject terror. His first impulse was to dart into the nearest room and bolt himself in; his next to dart out again and seize Richard's arm, who was coming along to open the door.

"Richard," he whispered—and the man stood amazed at the wild alarm, mingled with entreaty, in his master's aspect and accent—"don't open the door, for your life. Go into the area and see who it is. If it's any one for me, say I went out of town at seven this morning, and sha'n't be back till—till late to-night. Swear to it, man, if they dispute your word."

Richard descended the kitchen-stairs, and his master strode up the upper ones, four at a time, stealthily, silently, like a man who is flying from danger. Up to the second-floor went he, as if the higher he went the more secure he should feel from it. Instead of entering his own room, he turned into the one opposite, the day-nursery. It opened into the little boy's bedchamber, but the door was closed between them.

Judith stood at the round table by the fire—which Mrs. Dawkes thought well to have lighted daily, though summer weather had come in. She was measuring a dessert-spoonful of mixture from a small green medicine-bottle. Little Tom Canterbury was by her side, watching her.

"What's this?" asked Major Dawkes, taking up the bottle, when she had recorked it, and put it on the mantelpiece.

"I don't know, sir; I can't read writing," replied Judith, thinking the Major meant the direction, which he was looking at. If he had meant anything, it was probably the mixture; but he had spoken in total abstraction, for his mind was a chaos just then.

"The Mixture. Master Canterbury," were the words written there.

"Does he require medicine still?" exclaimed Major Dawkes. "I thought he was well."

"It's only some stuff the doctor sends to comfort his inside, sir, which has been out of order," replied Judith. "He takes a spoonful three times a-day: morning, afternoon, and before he goes to bed at night."

Major Dawkes took out the cork, smelt the mixture and tasted it, simply by way of doing something, while Tom drank up his spoonful. But, as Richard was heard coming up the stairs, the Major hastily returned the bottle to the mantelpiece, and went out to meet him.

"Was I wanted?"

"Yes, sir. The gentleman was that one who never gives his name; and I saw two men standing off, as if they belonged to him," added Richard, in a confidential tone. "They are a-waiting opposite now."

"You said I was out of town?"

"I told him I'd take a oath to it, sir, if he liked— as you desired me. And he said it would be none the nearer truth if I did."

Major Dawkes wiped his damp brow and turned into his bedroom; his perplexities were growing fast and thick. This present matter was one of simple debt; and simple debt would have been as nothing compared to the other thing he dreaded. Exposure could not be more than a day's course off now.

"Agony, disgrace, punishment!" spoke he to his own soul, as he glanced to the future. "The abhorrence and contempt of my wife; the haughty condemnation of my brother-officers; the cool scorn of the world; the hulks for me! I am in dread danger of it all; and only because the weak thread of a wretched child's life is not broken! Why could he not have died? It was but the hesitation of the balance; a turn the other way, and—we should both have been the better. There has been a devil abroad since that night, ever at my elbow, whispering temptation."

Even so. And the devil had never stood closer to Major Dawkes than in this self-same moment. To give him his due, he struggled against the fiend as well as he knew how.

The Major did not go out that day; he did not dare; what was to become of him on the next—and the next—and the next, he shuddered to contemplate. He dined at home with his wife at six o'clock, in her dressing-room. She felt very unwell, and had been lying there on the sofa all the afternoon.

"It is the fatigue of nursing Tom," said the Major. "I knew it would bring its reaction."

"It is nothing of the sort," retorted Mrs. Dawkes. "I have taken a violent cold, or else caught Tom's complaint, for 'my chest feels sore. Country air will set both me and Tom to rights. We start in the morning. Do you intend to go with us?"

"I—I don't think I can," replied the miserable Major.

He quitted the room after dinner; and went prowling about the house like a restless spirit, not venturing to go out before dusk. Mrs. Dawkes lay down on the sofa again and rang for her boy. Judith brought him, and her mistress began talking about the arrangements for the morning.

"The carriage will be at the door before half-past nine, you know, Judith."

"Yes, ma'am; I shall be quite ready. What about Master Tom's physic?" added Judith. "Had he better take it in the morning, ma'am?—there'll be just one dose left."

"No, I think not. To-night he must."

"O yes, I shall give it him as soon as he is undressed," said Judith, "and that won't be long first: it's ever so much after seven. I think he had better come now, ma'am, that he may have a good long night's rest.—Master Tom, won't you say good-night to your mamma?"

Of course it was right that the boy, still so weak and delicate, should have a good night's rest to fortify him for the morrow's journey. Mrs. Dawkes strained the child to her; and the child's little arms strained her. It was a long and close embrace, and he cried when he was taken from her: which was somewhat remarkable, as it was not a usual thing for him to do.

"God bless you, my darling! We shall both get well at the Rock."

Mrs. Dawkes, left alone, drank a cup of tea brought by her maid, Fry, and then went into her bedroom to prepare for rest. She was irritable and impatient; so much so, that the maid asked whether she felt worse.

"O, I don't know!" was the querulous answer. "Since I drank that cup of hot tea, my tooth has begun to ache again. It is enough to distract me."

"I would have it out, ma'am, if I were you," cried Fry. "It's always a-distracting of you."

"Have it out! have a tooth out at my age!"
echoed Mrs. Dawkes, "I'd rather suffer martyrdom.
Be quick over my hair, and don't say such things to
provoke me."

So Fry went on with her duties, and her mistress went on groaning, and holding one side of her
face.

"Perhaps, ma'am, if you were to put a little brandy
to it, it might ease you," Fry ventured to say again.
"Some cotton steeped in brandy, and put into the
tooth, has cured many a toothache. Laudanum's best,
but I suppose there's none in the house."

"It would do me no good," fretfully answered Mrs.
Dawkes.

Fry left her mistress to rest. But there was no
sleep for Mrs. Dawkes; the pain of her tooth prevented
it. She tossed and turned from side to side, five
minutes seeming to her like an hour.

Now it happened that there was some laudanum in
the house; at any rate, some preparation of opium,
though the maid had been unconscious of it. It had
been brought in for some purpose several weeks before,
and had stood since then in the Major's dressing-
room. Mrs. Dawkes, in a moment of desperation,
rose from her bed, resolved to try it. Her own dressing-room opened on one side the bedchamber, the
Major's on the other; and she snatched the night-light
which was burning—for Fry had closed the shutters to
shut out all the remains of daylight—and went into
the latter.

It was a very small place, little better than a closet,
and had no egress save through the bedchamber. Her
own dressing-room was large, and had two entrances.

Over the Major's washhand-stand was a narrow slab of white marble, and on that had stood the bottle required by Mrs. Dawkes. His tooth-powder box and shaving-tackle usually stood there; but since he had occupied the room upstairs, they had been removed, with various other things pertaining to him, the unused laudanum-bottle alone being left.

Mrs. Dawkes went to the slab, and stretched forth her hand to take the bottle. Most exceedingly astonished was she to find that no bottle was there. The slab was perfectly empty.

"Why, what can have become of it?" she exclaimed aloud. "The bottle is always there; I saw it there this very day. And the servants do not come in here since the room has been unused."

She looked about with the light, but could see nothing of it—the shelves and places were bare. Exceedingly cross, she returned to her bedroom, steeped a bit of cotton-wool in some spirits of camphor, put that to her tooth, and lay down again. The pain subsided at once, and she was dozing off to sleep, when some one came cautiously into the room from the passage-entrance. Mrs. Dawkes pulled aside the curtain, and saw her husband. He started back.

"Is it you?" she exclaimed.

"What brings you in bed now?" cried the Major, looking still like a man startled.

"I could not sit up. I wish you'd not come disturbing me. Is it late or early?"

"It is not yet nine."

He went into his dressing-room as he answered, but came out again immediately, and stayed to speak.

"Caroline, I am going down to Kage about the

matter we talked of the other day—to see if he won't
help me. He ought, and he must."

"It will be of no use."

"At any rate, I shall try. I really want help very
badly. Have you any message for him?"

"None," she answered drowsily. "I don't care to
talk; it may set my tooth on to ache again."

"Well, good-night; but I am sorry to have disturbed you. I shall see you in the morning."

The Major descended the stairs. Calling up
Richard, he gave him sundry commissions and in-
junctions; and then went out, peering into the dusk to
see that the coast was clear. Bolting round the corner
and into a hansom, he ordered the driver to take him
to Mr. Kage's house. There he learnt that the barrister was not expected until late, and would probably
be found at his chambers. The hansom dashed down
to the Temple.

Mr. Kage was at work late. Rather surprised was
he to see his visitor; much more surprised to hear
what he had come for.

Why, what amount of impudence must the man
possess, thus to persist in this annoyance! He had
come to press for that loan again; and sat down and
did it. Mr. Kage may be forgiven if he answered
sharply.

"Thomas Canterbury's money!" echoed the Major,
in reply to some words. "You speak as though I
asked for all his coffers, and the Rock into the bargain.
I only wish to borrow a very trifling portion of it—
three or four thousand pounds."

"The sum, more or less, is not of any consequence; but Mrs. Dawkes mentioned twelve thousand," spoke Thomas Kage stiffly.

"Mrs. Dawkes must have mistaken what I said I should like, for what I said I wanted. From three to four thousand pounds will be sufficient."

"Were it but three thousand pence, it would be all the same. I am surprised at you, Major Dawkes. Permit me to say that no gentleman would persist in these applications, in the teeth of my refusal and its reasons."

"I shall pay you back, long before little Canterbury is of age. Kage, my good fellow," added the Major, wiping the perspiration from his brow—and, indeed, he had done little else since entering, for he seemed full of agitation—"consider the strait I am in. If I can't get money, and don't get money, there'll be nothing for it but—but—the Insolvent Court. Mrs. Dawkes would never hold up her head again."

A half-contemptuous smile crossed the barrister's lips. He peremptorily declined further appeal on the subject.

"Were the money my own, you should have had it before now," said he finally; "but my trusteeship I will hold inviolate."

"Then to-morrow morning I must see about filing my petition," gloomily responded the Major.

"Quite the best thing you can do," said Mr. Kage.

"Your cousin, Mrs. Dawkes, will have you to thank for it."

No reply to this. The Major moved to the door as slow as a bear. Mr. Kage took the lamp to light him downstairs.

"I suppose Tom is all right again—getting stronger daily?" he observed, stretching the light out beyond the railings.

"O, he is quite well; he wants nothing now but change of air. His mother takes him to the Rock to-morrow. Good-night to you."

The Major jumped into the hansom that had waited for him, and was driven off. Having been immured in-doors for days, he thought he needed some indemnifying recreation, and intended to "make a night of it."

The morning dawned brightly. At seven o'clock Fry was in her mistress's room, according to orders. Mrs. Dawkes did not like getting up at seven any more than do other people who are accustomed to lie late abed; but her child's welfare just now was paramount, and she was determined the journey should not be deferred through delay on her part, or on that of the household. She was gracious this morning, telling Fry that her toothache was gone and that she felt stronger altogether.

"Now, Fry, is everything ready?" she asked, while she dressed.

"*Quite* ready, ma'am," emphatically responded Fry; "leastways all that lies in my department to get ready. I am only too glad to be off to Chilling myself, ma'am. It. seems an age since I saw my relations there. I'd like to see my poor old mistress, too."

Did Caroline Dawkes take that last sentence as a reproach to herself? It was not meant as such. She rejoined, rather peevishly,

"In the sad state poor mamma lies, it is so very

distressing to see her, you know, Fry. I'm sure I did
not get over the pain for days, when I left her last. It
is not good for her to see me, either. It excites her;
the doctor says so."

"Very true, ma'am," acquiesced Fry.

"Is the Major going with us or not, do you know?"
resumed Mrs. Dawkes.

"I fancy not, ma'am. I don't think Richard has
got any orders about packing."

"That tells nothing. A gentleman's things can be
put together in five minutes. The Major must be
called, Fry."

"The Major did not sleep at home, ma'am."

"Not sleep at home!"

"And he is not come in yet," added Fry, who was
no particular friend to the Major, and had not the
least objection to put in a word against him if opportunity offered.

"How do you know he did not sleep at home?"

"Because, ma'am, his room is just in the state it
was last night when the housemaid left it ready for
him, with the door stark staring open."

Mrs. Dawkes, albeit caring very little for the Major,
was no better pleased than are other wives when told
their husbands have not slept at home, and continued
to dress in silence. Presently she sent Fry to see
whether the nurse was getting up. Certain though she
felt of the fact, it was as well to be on the safe side,
and ascertain it. Judith had passed many nights of
late in watching, and sleep might be reasserting its
claims. While Fry was absent, she threw a warm
wrapper over her petticoats, and went into the Major's
dressing-room to ring the bell there, knowing that it

would bring up Richard. An unexpected object met her eyes.

Great as had been Mrs. Dawkes's surprise the previous night to find the laudanum-bottle absent from the slab, far, far greater was her present surprise to see it in the exact place it had always occupied, as if it had never been touched. Mrs. Dawkes mechanically took it in her hand: it was the veritable bottle, labelled as usual, "Tincture of Opium. Major Dawkes."

Had she only dreamt that she came to look for it? —the question really occurred to her. None of the servants had been through her room in the night. But on her own dressing-table lay the cotton and the phial of camphorated spirit, to prove that it was no dream.

"Judith has been up ever so long, ma'am, and she's soon going to dress Master Tom," said Fry, coming back. "There's Richard standing outside, saying the Major's bell rang. I tell him his ears must have heard double."

Mrs. Dawkes went to the door. What she wanted with Richard was, to ask whether his master had said where he was going. Richard replied in the negative: he had supposed his master was coming home to sleep as usual. Mrs. Dawkes went back to her dressing-table, and sat down for Fry to begin her hair.

Directly afterwards the Major came in, laughing gaily. He seemed determined to put a light face on the absence. His wife kept her head fixed under Fry's hands, looking neither to the right nor the left, not condescending to notice him in any way whatsoever.

"Did you think I had taken flight, Caroline? After leaving Kage, I went up to Briscoe's rooms. We got to cards; and, upon my word, the time passed so unconsciously, and it grew so late, that he gave me a bed. I feared I might disturb you, coming in between two and three o'clock."

Caroline did not see the point of the speech. All an excuse, thought she. Three o'clock was no absolutely unusual hour for the Major to come in; and as for disturbing her, it was not her room he had to come to.

"Very accommodating of Captain Briscoe to keep beds ready made-up for his friends," she coldly remarked.

"And that was a sofa," laughed the Major. "You will have a splendid day for your journey. The wind is in its softest quarter for Tom."

"You don't go with us, then?"

"I wish I could. I daresay I shall follow you within the week."

"O, do you!" cried Mrs. Dawkes, her temper a little ruffled. "Just as you please."

Major Dawkes stood for a moment, watching the process of hairdressing. Caroline fancied he must want something, but would not ask.

"What of Mr. Kage? Did you see him?"

"I saw him. Had to go down to his chambers. He is a regular *rat*, Caroline; he will do nothing."

"I told you he would not," she gravely rejoined; "and he is quite right not to do it. As to a rat—if all people were as little like one, the world might be more comfortable."

"Is that a slash at me?" asked Major Dawkes, smiling gaily, and seeming fully determined not to be put out. "I and Kage never could hit it off well together, you know, Caroline; therefore it was hardly likely he would go out of his way to do me a service. Perhaps I may get what I want through Briscoe. He—"

"Whatever is the matter?"

The interruption came from Fry, who at that moment was facing the door. The nurse, Judith, had stolen quietly inside the room, and was standing there with clasped hands, and face wild and white. Major and Mrs. Dawkes turned round.

"What do you want, Judith?" inquired her mistress.

"I got up at six, ma'am," began Judith, "and when I had dressed myself, I put up the things I had left last night, thinking I'd let the child sleep as long as I could. I said to myself, what a long night's rest he was having; what a beautiful sleep! And I—I— went to take him up now; and I—sir—ma'am—I can't awaken him."

She had spoken just as she looked, in a wild, bewildered sort off manner; and she appeeared to shake all over.

"It is the remains of his illness," remarked Mrs. Dawkes; but she gazed hard at Judith, thinking her manner, and her coming at all, very strange. "Children are sure to sleep well after an illness. Take him gently up; he will awake as you dress him."

"But I can't take him up, ma'am," returned the trembling Judith. "He—he—won't awake."

Fry stared at her with open mouth, in private persuasion that she had lost her senses.

"Will you please to come, and see, sir?" added Judith, addressing her master.

"Nonsense, Judith girl; why should I come?"

demanded the Major. "Surely you don't want my help
to arouse a sleeping child! Take him up yourself, as
your mistress says. Splash a handful of cold water in
his face; that will wake him soon enough."

"O sir, come!" pleaded Judith. "Please come.—
Not you, ma'am."

The Major quitted the room in answer to the appeal.
No sooner had he got out than Judith, shutting the
door, seized upon his arm, and spoke in a whisper:

"Sir, I think he's dead."

"What?" retorted the Major, as if angry at her
folly.

"It is so, sir, if ever I saw death yet. I did not
dare to speak before my mistress. He is stiff and
cold."

Major Dawkes pushed her aside with his elbow,
and ascended the stairs, Judith at his heels. There
was a noise behind, and they turned to look: Mrs.
Dawkes and Fry were following them up.

"She had better not come in, sir," whispered
Judith. "It may be too much for her."

The Major went back to stop his wife. Judith
stood at the room door. It was of no use. Caroline
broke away from the detaining hand, and went resolu-
tely onwards.

Thomas Canterbury was lying in his little bed,
shaded by the purple-silk hangings, cold, white—and
dead. The shell, with the angels carrying the child
to heaven, was clasped in his hand. The angels had
been down now to carry him.

"He must have died in a fit," cried Fry.

And Mrs. Dawkes fell across the bed with a low
cry of piteous anguish.

14*

CHAPTER XVI.

Enshrouded in Mystery.

LATE in the afternoon of as brilliant a day as London can produce, when the spring is merging into summer, Thomas Kage, in his professional costume, might have been seen ascending to his chambers in the Temple with the fleet steps of one who runs a race against time.

Mr. Kage was then doing little less. He had a vast amount of business on his shoulders just now, legal and private. Only the past night Major Dawkes (as we have already seen) found him late at his chambers, hard at work. This evening he would have to quit London on some private matters connected with his friend Lord Hartledon, and he would be away for some three or four days.

Dashing off his wig and gown, he was about to settle down to his table, and go over certain papers, there waiting for an opinion, when his clerk, Mr. Taylor—for he could afford one now—accosted him.

"One of Major Dawkes's servants has been here, sir, to ask if you would go up there as quickly as you could. Mrs. Dawkes—"

"But I can't," interrupted Mr. Kage. "With what I have yet to do to-day, it is not possible. Did you say so?"

"No, sir. I said I would give you the message. I told him you were busy. The little boy is dead!"

"What little boy?"

"Mrs. Dawkes's, sir—little Canterbury."

Thomas Kage's hand ceased rattling the parchments. He looked up as one who believes not.

"What do you mean?"

"He is dead, sir, sure enough, and all that pot of money lapses. He died in the night."

"But what did he die of? What was the matter with him?"

"The man couldn't say. It was that Richard who has brought notes her once or twice."

"The boy was well again," reiterated Mr. Kage, feeling utterly bewildered. "Dawkes said so when he was here last night; besides, I know it."

"What the man said was, that the nurse found him dead in his bed this morning," pursued Mr. Taylor. "Mrs. Dawkes was in a very terrible state, and her maid sent him to ask you to go up."

A rapid argument in his own mind, whether he might venture to put off his journey until the morrow, and sit up that night to complete his work, was decided in the affirmative. At almost any cost he would go to his cousin in her sore need. He could, by taking the first train in the morning, perform his journey in time.

"I shall want you to stay late to-night, Mr. Taylor."

"Very well, sir."

He went up to Belgravia as fast as a cab could take him, and was shown at once into the presence of Mr. Dawkes. Her state was pitiable to witness. Just as she had been when the alarm came, and she had run to the child's room, so she was still—a loose robe on, and her hair hanging down. She had remained since in the very extremity of anguish—now in a semi-fainting state; now rushing to the death-room and calling on her child to live—to live! In short, she was frantic. Could she but have wept—could she but have fallen into a real faint, and so have induced weakness—it had been better for her. Fry said all this to Mr. Kage in a few rapid sentences, as she stood with her hand on the door-handle.

"I can scarcely believe it to be true, Fry, that the child is dead," he whispered.

"And that's like us, sir. We cannot believe it now."

"But what was it?"

"O, it must have been a sudden fit, sir. There's nothing else, that I know of, could kill a child in his sleep."

With a kind of choking cry, something like what may be heard from one in an attack of epilepsy, Mrs. Dawkes sprang forward when she saw Mr. Kage, and flung herself into his arms. The sight of him brought the reaction that had been wanted; and she began to sob frightfully, piteously imploring Thomas Kage to bring *him*—her lamb, her angel-boy, her all—back to life. With difficulty could he unwind her arms; with difficulty attempt a word of consolation. He did not know what to do with her. Fry, hearing the sobs of emotion, came in. Mr. Kage sent her for water and other restoratives. Where was the Major? he mentally wondered in deep anger. Surely his proper place was by his wife's side at such an hour as this!

Major Dawkes had gone out to see, as was understood by Fry, about some necessary arrangements.

"I don't care now how soon I die myself, Thomas," exclaimed the poor mother, at the end of a prolonged and exhaustive fit of violent sobbing.

"Hush, Caroline! May God temper the trial to you!" he added, more as a prayer than in answer.

The next to come in, with a whiter face than usual, as if stricken to fear, and words of condolence that seemed genuine enough on her lips, was Keziah Dawkes. Keziah had heard the news by pure accident. Happening to meet one of the servants in the streets, she stopped him to inquire after the health of the house, and learnt what had taken place. Caroline was lying on the sofa then, in another of the semi-fainting fits, utterly exhausted. Fry, kneeling by her side, strove to put teaspoonfuls of weak brandy-and-water within her lips. Mr. Kage took the opportunity to slip away in search of Judith.

He found her in the day-nursery; her hands lying idle on her knees, the tears slowly coursing down her face. She stood up when he entered, and strove to dry her eyes.

"What has the child died of, Judith?"

"Sir, I know no more than the dead—no more than he does, pretty pale lambkin. Fry insists upon it that it must have been a fit; but I don't believe it. He never had a fit in his life; and it stands to reason, that if he'd had one last night I must have heard him. The least noise awakes me. Since his illness he couldn't move in his little bed but I started up. All last night I never heard him stir, never once, and I was awake twice myself. This morning, when I got up, he was still sleeping, as I supposed, and I went on putting things ready for the journey."

"You did not discover it immediately, then?"

"No, sir. I thought I'd let him lie as long as I could, for he had seemed dead asleep last night. I'd

hardly laid him down in his bed, before he was off.
I might have let him lie longer too, but for Fry's coming up with a message from my mistress, that we was
both to be ready without delay. I finished what I was
about, and then went to his bedside. "Master Tom,"
says I, "it's time to get up; and your mamma's astir
already, and the morning's beautiful." But he never
answered. "Wake up, my darling," says I then, and
put the bedclothes down. Sir, you might a'most as
well have killed me: there he lay dead!"

"What did the doctor say?"

"The first thing he said after seeing that the child
was really dead, was to ask what I'd been giving to
him; he asked it sharply too. As if I should give him
anything that could hurt!"

She proceeded to recount the few facts connected
with the last day of the child's life, Mr. Kage listening.
He had eaten his meals well; the last thing he took
having been a basin of bread-and-milk for his tea.
Judith had seen him take them all—having, in fact,
taken her own meals with him; and not for a minute
the previous day had the boy been out of her sight.

"There's the last thing I gave him," she sobbed,
pointing to the medicine-bottle on the mantelpiece.
"He sat on my lap after he was undressed, and took
it as good as gold. I little thought I should never
give him anything again."

"What is it?" asked Mr. Kage.

Judith explained. It was a bottle of mixture sent
by the doctor, a dessert-spoonful of which the child
had been taking three times a-day. Mr. Kage took
the bottle in his hand, examined it, and read the label,
"The Mixture. Master Canterbury."

"He had took it every drop but that one dose that's left; and a great deal of good it had done him," said Judith, in her deep sorrow, as Mr. Kage returned the bottle to the mantelpiece. "O me! there's moments, sir, when I think it can't be nothing but a dream."

In truth, it seemed quite like one to Thomas Kage. "Will you see him, sir?"

He nodded assent; and Judith, unlocking the door of the next room, stood aside for him to pass. Many a time and oft had Mr. Kage gone in, to be greeted with the loving words of the gentle child.

At rest now; an angel in the heaven where he had so often wished to be.

"You have been up to see him!" cried Mrs. Dawkes, almost passionately, when Mr. Kage returned to her. "Why did you not tell me? I'd have gone with you. I wanted to go."

It seemed that some of the old excitement was coming on again; he laid his restraining hand on hers to enjoin calmness. Keziah Dawkes, sitting at the curtained window with her bonnet-strings untied, looked gray as before. Mrs. Dawkes had not invited her to take the bonnet off. This death would bring no end of good to her beloved brother Barby, but she did not seem to be making a festival of it. Caroline moaned faintly again and again, and let her fingers entwine themselves within those strong ones, in which there seemed to be at least protection.

"What did he die of, Thomas—what did he die of?"

"In truth, I see nothing that he can have died of,

except God's visitation," was his honest answer. "No
harm seems to have come to him in any shape or form,
to account for the death."

"And we were to have gone to the Rock to-day,
he and I! By this time we should have been there."

"Try and realise one thing, Caroline—that he
is now in perfect happiness; and let it comfort
you."

"Comfort! for me!" she rejoined, opening her
eyes on him for a moment. "Never again in this
life!"

And poor Caroline Dawkes turned her face down
upon the sofa-cushion, to moan out the anguish that
seemed as if it must kill her there and then.

The dusk of evening had come on before Mr. Kage
went down to take his departure. He encountered
Major Dawkes in the hall, who was then entering.
They turned together into the Major's study.

"This is a very strange and sad event," observed
Thomas Kage.

"It is the strangest thing that ever happened in
this world," returned the Major; "and the saddest too
—for my wife's sake."

"You can throw no light upon it, I suppose; or
conjecture what can have been the cause of death?"

"I! I am the least likely to of anybody," spoke the
Major with volubility. "I never saw the child but once
yesterday, so far as I can remember; and I have been
taxing my memory over it. That was in the morning.
He went out with Judith, I hear, in the carriage in the
afternoon; but I know nothing about it personally. I
was shut up in my study the best part of the day, writing letters and going over ac—"

A movement of Mr. Kage's caused the Major to stop. Looking quickly behind him, he saw the gray face of his sister. And it certainly wore a scared expression—an expression that she seemed unable to keep under. A hasty greeting—which the Major never looked in her face to give—and he went on with what he had been saying.

"I am telling Kage that I never saw the boy but once yesterday, Keziah; never saw him at all, in fact, after the morning. It is most unfortunate. Not that my seeing him could have shown me what was to happen, or prevented it. As ill-luck had it, too, I did not sleep at home last night.

A slight movement of surprise in Mr. Kage's eyes. No other answer.

"Of course I'd give a good deal not to have been out last night. I've not done it for ages. Things are sure to happen crossly. After leaving your chambers, Kage, I went up to Briscoe's. We sat late at cards, and he gave me a bed. My wife had seemed very poorly when I left her, and I did not care to go home when it got so late, lest she should hear me and be disturbed. I came round betimes this morning, knowing of the day's journey; and before I had been five minutes in the house, the alarm took place. When Judith came in, saying something was the matter with the child, and then called me out to whisper he was dead, I thought she must be saying it for a farce."

Keziah Dawkes drew a long deep breath, as if of relief. "O, Barnaby dear! and have you *no* idea of the cause of death?"

"What I think is this. That the child's late illness, or something connected with it, must have been the cause; and that the doctors were mistaken in supposing he had recovered."

"Yes, yes; it must have been so," sighed Keziah.

"Possibly so," admitted Mr. Kage, speaking slowly. "There seems to be no other way of accounting for it. I fear it will have a sad effect on Mrs. Dawkes."

"For a time," said the Major, showing a long face. "But she'll get over it after a bit; she'll get over it. Other mothers do."

A coroner's inquest would have to be held on the child; very much to the resentment of Major and Mrs. Dawkes. More to that of the former, however, than of the latter. But for his enlarging in his wife's presence on the degradation of Tom's being "inquested," as though he were a common pauper's child, she would never have thought of it, one way or the other. Major Dawkes's resentment, however, could not stop the law's demands; and an inquest was fixed for the Thursday afternoon, the child having been found dead on the Wednesday. Early on Thursday morning the doctors made the post-mortem examination; and they came to the astounding conclusion that the child had died from some narcotic poison—say opium. An overdose of opium.

The first frantic violence of Mrs. Dawkes's grief had spent itself, and on this morning, Thursday, she was tolerably calm—calm, save for a restless nervousness that prevented her from being still. Her medical attendants recommended her to remain in bed; but Mrs. Dawkes paid no heed to them, and by ten o'clock she was up, and in her dressing-room; which was, in fact, a kind of boudoir.

Here she sat, the breakfast-tray before her, making believe to sip her tea, and to bite small morsels of the thin toast. Major Dawkes had breakfasted below as usual, and was just now closeted in the dining-room with the two doctors who had been making the examination. On coming from the room above, they had requested to see him, and were shown in to him in the dining-room. Major Dawkes was not holding the doctors in much favour just now, for they were at the root of this, to him, offensive proceeding, the calling of the inquest. In the absence of all certainty as to the cause of death, they had declined to give the requisite certificate.

Never for a moment, save during the intervals when she slept the sleep of exhaustion, was her child's image absent from Mrs. Dawkes's mental sight, or its memory from her heart. It seemed to her that Heaven had been bitterly unkind; and the more she told herself it was wrong to think so, the more she thought it.

"Only two days ago, and he was with me in this very room," she moaned; "prattling to me while I ate my breakfast. I divided a bit of my toast between us, him and me. Judith, standing by, said hot buttered toast was not good for him. O my boy, my boy!"

Fry came in with an expression of face that attracted even the attention of her desolate mistress. It was a mixture of intense surprise, of puzzled curiosity, and of mortification.

"What is the matter?" asked Mrs. Dawkes.

The matter was this. The doctors, having to ask two or three questions bearing on the conclusion they had come to regarding the death of the child, had chosen to put them to Fry, knowing she was in a degree a confidential servant, and had caused her to be called in. There Fry learnt—but she was the only one of the household to whom it was suffered to transpire—that the death was the result of opium. The declaration displeased Fry beyond everything: she had formed her opinion that the child had died in a fit, and would not part with it easily.

"It's a nice thing they are saying now, ma'am," replied Fry in answer to her mistress, closing the door softly and speaking in a covert tone. "It wouldn't be doctors if they didn't have some crotchet to invent. What he died of, sweet child, was a fit, and nothing else."

Mrs. Dawkes paused in some surprise. "Why, what do they say it was, then?"

"They say he was poisoned, ma'am. Leastways that he took something that was as good as poison; senseless idiots!"

"They—say—he—was—poisoned!" echoed Mrs. Dawkes, leaning forward in her chair with dilating eyes. "Take care what you assert, Fry."

"I think it's them should be told to take care of that, ma'am," was Fry's rather resentful answer. "They declare he must have died from taking an over-dose of opium; which amounts to pretty nigh the same thing as saying he was poisoned. I'd like to ask them who was likely to give him opium. There was not such a thing as a drop in the house; but doctors must have their say. It was a fit."

A faint noise, curious in its sound, caused Fry to turn sharply. She had been putting the breakfast-things together while she talked. Was her mistress going to have a fit? She looked like it.

"Opium! He died from opium! Do they say *that?*"

"They do, ma'am. They are telling the Major of it now in the dining-room; but I don't believe it's true."

With a face white as ashes,—with hands lifted up before her as if to ward off some dreadful blow,—with a strange terror pervading her whole aspect, stood Mrs. Dawkes.

"But—but—"

Not another syllable. Utterance failed; and she fell back on the seat in a dead faint.

"And enough to make her, poor dear, when such atrocious things can be said of her own child!" ejaculated the sympathising Fry, flying to the rescue.

When the coroner's inquest met in the afternoon, the medical men declared their opinion—that the child had died from the effect of some narcotic, probably opium. Judith, as nurse, was very sharply questioned —turned inside out, as may be said—as to what food the child had taken the evening of the day preceding his death. She was to the full as indignant as Fry— more so, indeed, at their supposing anything of the kind could have found its way to him by any chance whatever; but Judith, unlike Fry, was not loud. Swallowing down her tears and striving for calmness, she was very quiet and respectful, only insisting upon it that the doctors must be wrong. Neither bit nor drop had approached the child's lips but what she herself had given him—saving a small bit of his mamma's buttered toast in the morning, which both she and her mistress had watched him eat.

"He never was out of my sight during the whole day for one minute, gentlemen," she earnestly reiterated to the jury; "and I can take my oath that he had nothing but his ordinary and proper food. The doctors say that what he took to harm him must have been taken at night; but after his tea at five o'clock, which was bread-and-milk, he had nothing whatever—except the dessert-spoonful of physic when he was undressed; and the doctors know that that couldn't have hurt him, for it was their own physic, sent in by themselves, and he had been taking it for two or three days."

Judith's simplicity and earnest manner made its own favourable impression on the coroner's court. Major Dawkes, who was present, testified that she was a truthful, faithful servant, valued by her mistress, and fond almost to idolatry of the child. The medicine-bottle, remaining in its place on the mantelpiece with the one dose left in it, had been examined at once by the medical men, and found to be exactly as they had sent it in—right and proper and harmless medicine. In fact, so far as reliable testimony went, nothing could be more clearly proved than that the child had taken nothing improper; and, moreover, that there had positively occurred no opportunity whatever for anything else to be administered to him.

No one could have had access to him. When the child was in bed—and the nurse testified that he fell asleep almost as she laid his head on the pillow—she, Judith, had remained in the room. Closing the door between the two nurseries, she had set to work to turn out her drawers and pack up her own things, all of which were in the bedroom. The child never stirred, she said; he was sleeping sound and fast. Of course, it was now known that he was in the sleep of stupor, passing quietly on to death. At ten o'clock—she heard the hour strike from the churches—she ran downstairs for her supper—some bread-and-butter. Bringing it up on a plate, she went on arranging her things, and went to bed between eleven and twelve.

A juryman interrupted to inquire how long she remained downstairs, and whether any one meanwhile could have had access to the child.

"I was not down two minutes, sir," was Judith's answer; "and no one could have had access to the child. Only my mistress was upstairs—she was in bed in her own room; and the Major was not at home. It happened that I saw every one of the servants downstairs, except Richard; and I've heard since that he had gone out on business for his master."

Major Dawkes nodded a corroboration of this. Before going out himself that evening, he had given his servant Richard a commission to execute out of doors.

"No one can regret more than myself that I should have been absent on this particular evening and night," added the Major with some natural emotion. "It was getting on for nine o'clock when I left home. I had business with Mr. Kage the barrister, and went down to his chambers in the Temple. I slept at Captain Briscoe's, and got home between seven and eight in the morning."

"So that, personally, you know nothing of the sad event, Major Dawkes?" spoke the coroner with civility.

"Nothing whatever, I am sorry to say. I consider my absence most unfortunate. Not that, had I been at home, I could have done any good, or prevented the death. The chances are—nay, I may say the certainty—that I should not have known of it one moment earlier than I did; but I nevertheless regret that it should have fallen out so."

"Did the child appear to you to be as well and lively as usual that day, Major Dawkes?"

"Quite so; what little I saw of him. I did not see him at all after the morning. Once or twice, in passing to my bedroom, I heard him chattering to his nurse, the two shut up in the nursery; but I did not see him myself during the latter part of the day."

"Can you at all account for this fact—that he must have taken opium?"

"So little can I account for it, that when the medical men informed me it was the case, I could not, and did not, believe them. Even now I am loth to admit it; for it seems to me absolutely impossible that the child could have been brought into contact with any opium, or taken it. His nurse, as you have heard, says she never quitted him at all; and I believe it to have been so. She is a perfectly reliable woman."

The coroner and jury were evidently at a nonplus. Judith was recalled, and told to re-state minutely the events of the evening from and after the boy's tea-time. Particularly was she pressed upon the point, whether she was positive she did not lose sight of him *at all* before he was in bed; one of the jury remarking that children were apt to taste at anything they came near if not watched; *his* were.

"We had tea together, in the nursery, gentlemen —him and me," said Judith in obedience. "Both of us had bread-and-milk: it's what I'm fond of, having been brought up in the country, where milk's a plenty. Little Tom read to me after tea—it was what he liked doing—first a fairy tale, and next a Bible story. Soon after seven, his mamma's bell rang for him to go down to her. I took him; and my mistress began talking to me about the morrow's journey. We stayed there ten minutes maybe, or a quarter of an hour. I went back with him then, and soon undressed him—"

"Was he as lively as usual?" came the interruption.

"Yes, that he was, sir—talking about the Rock—and didn't want to go to bed. But when I told him how tired he'd be on the morrow, and what a long way it was, he said no more. He was the most tractable child a body could have to do with—as good as gold. He said his prayers at my knee; and I gave him his spoonful of physic; and then he got drowsy, and I put him into bed. Nobody came near him, gentlemen; and there was not the smallest chance that anybody could come. After he was in bed, I shut myself into his room, and began putting the things together, as I've already said."

"Did any of the servants come up during this time?" asked a juryman.

"I don't know, sir. They might have come into the day-nursery without my hearing them. I don't think they did; for I noticed nothing touched in the room when I got back to it."

"Were the servants in the habit of coming up?" resumed the same juryman.

"Sometimes they'd come and talk a bit. None of them came that evening, sir, that I know of."

"If all the servants came to the nursery after the boy was out of it, it could make no difference to the question at issue," interposed the coroner impatiently. "So far as the testimony goes,—and it seems to me

15*

that we may rely upon it,—neither person nor thing could have approached the boy to harm him."

"I am certain that it didn't," answered Judith, hot tears gathering in her eyes.

There appeared to be no farther evidence to sift— nothing more to be learnt. The case presented a shroud of impenetrable mystery; and after some discussion, the coroner and jury were fain to give it up as a bad job, and return their verdict:

"Died from opium; but how administered, there is no evidence to show."

And little Tom Canterbury's body was buried in Brompton cemetery, his soul having departed with the angels. And Major Dawkes was a free man again, and a wealthy one.

CHAPTER XVII.

The Postern-door.

THE wild wind was whistling and booming round the station at Chilling as the train came rushing along in the dusk of a fine evening, when autumn was merging itself into winter. Time, working its changes and changes, had extended still farther the branch of the Aberton railway; and Chilling itself had a station now. It was not much more than a bleak little shed and a telegraph-box; but Chilling was proud of it, and at least three trains a-day stopped there.

It brought freight this time. Out of one first-class compartment stepped Thomas Kage, out of another Mrs. Dunn—Lydia Canterbury in the days gone by; neither of whom had known that the other was in the train. It sometimes happens so. Both of them had come down unexpectedly—that is, unknown to their friends in Chilling. A solitary fly was waiting outside. Mrs. Dunn made for it in haste, lest anybody else should appropriate it first, and was calling out to the porter to bring her luggage, when Thomas Kage went up to her.

"Goodness me!" cried she in her off-hand manner, "what brings you here?"

"I have come down on a little business," he answered. "I did not know you were in the train."

"I'm sure *I* did not know you were. I wish I had known it. Would you like a seat in the fly? I am going to surprise them at Thornhedge Villa; they don't know of my coming."

"No, thank you. I shall see you soon."

The fly, laden with its luggage, was rattled off. Mrs. Dunn ordered it to stop at Chilling Rectory; it lay in the line of route to Thornhedge Villa; and indeed, in her usual free-and-easy independence, she had not quite made up her mind which dwelling to honour with a visit first. Thomas Kage thought she must have come to surprise some of them with a tolerably long sojourn, as he looked after the pile of boxes on the fly's roof.

Turning away, he found himself greeted by a respectable, portly man, wearing the black clothes and white necktie of an upper servant. Mr. Kage knew the face, but could not remember where he had seen it.

"Neel, sir; butler at the Rock."

"To be sure," said Mr. Kage. "I remember Mrs. Dawkes told me you remained at the Rock."

"Yes, sir. They wanted a responsible person to

take charge at the Rock during their long absences
from it, what with the valuable paintings and furniture,
so I have stayed; and the Major took on a London
butler up there, who robbed them frightfully, we
hear."

"Is Mrs. Dawkes staying at the Rock now?"

"She is, sir. She has never been away from it
since she came down when the poor little heir died in
the summer. I think she is very ill, sir."

"I will see her to-morrow," said Mr. Kage.

He walked away with Neel's last words ringing in
his ears, carrying his small travelling-bag in his hand
—for he had the same propensity to wait on himself
as of yore, when practicable. He had not seen Mrs.
Dawkes since the day of the child's funeral, for she
had quitted London immediately. Twice he had written
to her at the Rock, friendly notes of inquiry as to
her health and welfare; but Mrs. Dawkes had not answered either. When he met the Major in town, as
would happen sometimes by chance, he was told Mrs.
Dawkes was pretty well, and enjoying the country.

During the long vacation a matter of pressing business connected with Lord Hartledon had taken Mr.
Kage first to Switzerland and then to Scotland. He
returned to London in October, was up to his eyes in
business for a fortnight, and had now travelled down
to Chilling for a specific purpose—to ask Millicent
Canterbury to be his wife.

Turning into the modest inn, the Canterbury Arms,
he washed some of the dust off him, changed his coat,
bespoke a bed, and then went forth again; for he
wished to put the question at rest without delay. Taking the nearest way to Thornhedge Villa—the Miss

Canterburys' residence since their father's ill-omened second marriage—he was entering the garden-gate, when a young lady, running up with fleet footsteps from the opposite direction, nearly ran against him.

"Millicent!"

She gave a little scream of surprise, and started in the dusk from the extended hand. But it was truly and veritably Thomas Kage—his voice, his hand, himself—and Miss Millicent timidly begged his pardon, and blushed like a schoolgirl.

"It has so surprised me. There's scarcely any one in the world I should have less thought of seeing than you. I have been to the schools," Millicent added rapidly, as if wishing to cover some agitation that she was very conscious her manner betrayed. "My sister Jane is not strong, and I take the trouble of the schools from her."

"I think there is another surprise in store for you. What would you say if I told you your sister is here?"

"Mrs. Rufort?" asked Millicent, looking towards the windows of the house.

"Mrs. Dunn."

"Impossible!"

"Quite possible, and quite true," said Thomas Kage.

"But she is in Germany. We are beginning to think she intends to take up her abode there for good."

"*I* think she must be intending to take it up here for good. I judge by the trunks that have come with her."

Millicent laughed. He explained about the meeting as they walked along. In point of fact, Mrs. Dunn, obeying one of her many sudden whims, had taken it into her head to quit Germany, and come down to see her relatives. The writing to inform them she had looked upon as quite superfluous.

Millicent's pulses were beating. Hers had in truth been a lasting love, enduring through many years and no encouragement. No encouragement, at least, that she could take hold of, though now and again stray tones and looks, in their rare meetings, might have whispered hope to her heart.

"You have not seen Mrs. Dawkes lately?" observed Millicent.

"Not since her child died. What a blow that was!"

"A worse one for her than we can even imagine, I fear," said Millicent. "She looks fearfully ill; but we very rarely meet. You have come down, I suppose, to see her?"

"Not so. I came down, Millicent, to see you."

A hot blush in her face, a startled look, visible even in the dim twilight. Mr. Kage touched her arm, and drew her down a side-path they were passing.

"Let us walk here for a few minutes, Millicent."

Seated by her dressing-room fire, with little prevision of the surprises in store for her, was Olive Canterbury. The door opened softly, and Millicent came in.

"Olive, will you go into the drawing-room?" she said. "Some one is there."

"Who is it, Leta?" asked Miss Canterbury, wondering what could have sent the young lady's face into its scarlet glow.

"Thomas Kage. He came down by train. He wants to see you."

Down sat Millicent as she spoke: *she* was not wanted in the drawing-room. Olive Canterbury took notice of the signs—of the faltering tones and the downcast eyes—drew her conclusions, and passed out of the room with a stately step. As to Mrs. Dunn, she had gone out of Leta's mind wholesale.

"Your visit is unexpected, but I am very glad to see you," said Olive, shaking Mr. Kage's hand heartily, for he was a great favourite of hers.

"My visit is to Millicent," he answered, plunging at once into the matter that had brought him down. "I have come to ask her to be my wife. I should have asked it long ago, but that briefs did not come in so quickly as I wished. They have taken a turn for the better of late."

"And what does Millicent say?"

"Millicent ran away and said nothing," he answered with a smile; "nothing very decisive, at any rate. So I called out that I had better see you."

"A good sign," laughed Miss Canterbury. "I fancy you and Leta have understood each other for some time," she added. "I know I used to think so when we were in London."

"Tacitly, I believe we have; and I hope Millicent has understood why it was only tacitly. I was too poor to speak."

"Millicent's fortune would have helped you on, Mr. Kage."

"It is that fortune which has kept me from her," he replied.

"It need not. It is only ten thousand pounds."

Thomas Kage raised his eyes, bright with amusement, to Miss Canterbury's face. "*Only* ten thousand! A very paltry sum, no doubt, to the Miss Canterburys, reared to their hundreds of thousands, but a Golconda to a struggling barrister."

"*Reared* to their hundreds of thousands; yes!" retorted Miss Canterbury, with a swelling heart, "but not enjoying them."

Sitting down, he went briefly over his position with her; showing her what his present income was; saying how greatly the bequest of the two houses from Mrs. Garston had helped him on. He should scarcely think himself justified yet in removing to the larger of the two, according to the wish expressed by his kind old friend, he said; but Millicent should decide the point for herself. Both of them evidently took her consent to the marriage for granted. Miss Canterbury asked him to stay and partake of dinner, without ceremony.

But ere that meal could be announced, even now as they were talking together, up dashed Mrs. Dunn's fly, with part of the luggage, taking the house by storm. The other part had been left at the Rectory, for she meant to divide her time between them, she told Olive. Olive was delighted to see her; it seemed an age since they met.

Not a greater contrast than of yore did the three sisters present, sitting down to dinner together. Olive, lofty in mind, lofty in manner, tall, handsome, always self-possessed; Lydia Dunn, stout, restless, an inveterate talker; Millicent, much younger than either, quiet and graceful. But Millicent would never see twenty-seven again. Time passes swiftly: year follows year, each with a more rapid wing than its precursor. Miss Canterbury took as usual the head of her table, requesting Thomas Kage to face her.

"Now then, Mr. Kage, I am going to cross-question you," impatiently began Mrs. Dunn, the instant the servants had left them alone after dinner. "Who gave the poison to that child, little Tom Canterbury?"

"That is a problem I cannot solve," was his reply.

"You were on the spot at the time."

"I was in London."

"And I abroad," pursued Mrs. Dunn in a tone of much resentment. "It was a dreadful occurrence; and all the information I could gain of it was by letters or hearsay. Do you tell me the particulars. I had a great mind to come over and ascertain them for myself; but it would have answered no end. Begin at the beginning, please. Had he been ill?"

"He had been dangerously ill with inflammation of the chest, but was getting better; in fact, was nearly well," said Mr. Kage, obeying her implicitly, and recalling the facts. "Mrs. Dawkes was about to take him to the Rock for change of air. That same morning, the one they ought to have started, he was found dead in his bed."

"And had died from a dose of opium. But now, who gave it him?"

"The facts were shrouded in mystery," continued Mr. Kage, "and the coroner's jury returned an open verdict. The nurse was perfectly trustworthy, and the child had not been out of her sight the whole of the previous day. She undressed him, gave him his regular medicine, and put him into his bed by the side of her own. She heard nothing of him in the night;

and in the morning, when she came to take him up, he was dead."

"What was that medicine?" suspiciously asked Mrs. Dunn.

"Harmless, proper medicine, as was proved at the inquest. He had been taking a dessert-spoonful of it three times a-day."

"Some one must have got into the bedroom and administered the poison; that's clear," said Mrs. Dunn. "The nurse Judith was trustworthy; I'll give her that due. She was one of the housemaids at the Rock before we left it, or my father had made a simpleton of himself by marrying that flighty child Caroline Kage. When the changes came, and the new baby was born, Judith became its nurse. Yes, she was to be trusted. But somebody must have got into the chamber while she slept."

"No one went in; that seems to have been certain," observed Mr. Kage.

"O, ay, I know it was so asserted," contemptuously returned Mrs. Dunn; "but the boy could not have found a bottle of laudanum in his bed, uncorked ready for use, and swallowed it down. It does not stand to reason, Mr. Kage."

"Judith deposed that she never left the room for more than a couple of minutes after the boy was in bed, and then no one could have got to him. She put up some things that would be wanted for the journey in the morning, and then went to bed herself, the doors being locked; and they were so locked when she rose in the morning. No person could have entered."

"Well, all I know is, that poison cannot be taken

into a child's mouth without its being put there; and you are the first person that ever I heard say it could, Mr. Kage."

He glanced at the angry lady with a spice of merriment; but for the grave subject, he might have laughed outright. "Did I say it could, Mrs. Dunn?"

"Just as good, when you assert that nobody was near him but Judith."

"Judith never left him; that appears to be a fact," interposed Miss Canterbury, speaking for the first time. "The medical men thought the poison had been taken about evening time, did they not, Mr. Kage?"

Thomas Kage nodded.

"Now, Olive, pray let me speak," broke in her impatient sister. "You were in the way of hearing about it at the time, remember. Mr. Kage, I want to know what your opinion is—how *did* he come by the poison? Do you suspect *any* one of having given it to him? Answer me frankly amidst ourselves."

"Frankly speaking, Mrs. Dunn, I cannot answer you. As to suspecting any one—No. The child seems to have been so entirely encompassed about by protection, that I do not see how it was possible for harm, whether in the shape of mankind or womankind, to approach him. The matter to me appears to be one of those mysteries that cannot be accounted for."

"Then you positively know nothing more to tell me!" cried the exasperated Mrs. Dunn.

"I really do not."

"Well, I'm sure I never heard of such a thing. So unsatisfactory! Where's Judith now?"

"Judith took another situation afterwards," said Miss Canterbury. "Somewhere in Essex, I think."

"Mrs. Dawkes has been a fine gainer. The death gave her all the splendid Canterbury fortune."

"Hush, Lydia!" interrupted Olive. "However much we may have felt disposed to cast previous reflections on Mrs. Dawkes, we can but have the sincerest sympathy for her in her great misfortune. I believe she idolised the child."

"She was very fond of him," said Mr. Kage, "and her grief was pitiable to witness. She clung round me, and asked if I could not bring him back to life. Fry sent for me in the afternoon, and I found Caroline almost beside herself. Major Dawkes had gone out, about some of the necessary arrangements, they said, and she was alone. She clung to me, as I tell you, in a sad state; I hardly knew what to do with her."

"She came down to the Rock, a mere skeleton, the day after the funeral," remarked Miss Canterbury. "We were shocked when we called upon her. She briefly and shrinkingly told us the particulars, tallying with what you have now related, and said she should never recover the blow during life. I thought, as she spoke, that she little knew how time heals the worst pangs; but I fear my thoughts were too fast, for she does not recover either strength or spirits. We scarcely ever see her; there seems to be an unwillingness on her part to receive visitors, and she leads a very secluded life. I do not think it can be good for her."

"The Major passes most of his time in London," abruptly remarked Thomas Kage.

"He passes it somewhere," replied Miss Canterbury; "he is rarely at the Rock."

"At any rate, *he* has gained by the bargain," cried the incorrigible Mrs. Dunn. "It is a magnificent fortune for him to have dropped into, all unexpectedly, through the demise of a little stepson."

"It is his wife who has dropped into it, not he," remarked Miss Canterbury.

"As if he did not have the fingering of it!" retorted Mrs. Dunn.

And Thomas Kage drew in his lips, compressing them to silence. Fingering, ay!

"Keziah Dawkes, that sister of his, lives with her, I hear," said Mrs. Dunn. "Austin Rufort told me. A nice wet blanket she must be, judging by her face, to live with an invalid!"

"A cold, gray, hard-looking woman," acquiesced Olive Canterbury. "Caroline comes abroad but rarely; when she does, it is but to walk or drive to her mother's cottage and home again; and Miss Dawkes is always with her like her shadow. Poor Caroline seems as though she could never more find comfort in life; it is a sadness painful to look upon."

"O my goodness! And what satisfaction has the fortune brought her, that she so schemed for?" cried Lydia Dunn. "Only a few short years, and to have it believed that there's no more comfort for her in life! And her mother—the worse plotter of the two—a nice miserable object she is, by all account! Austin Rufort came in from seeing her this afternoon while I was there. We are better off than they are, with all their wealth. As to that Dawkes, Mrs. Garston knew what she was about when she left her fortune away from him. *She* was an insolent old woman to the last, though. Fancy a Bible and Prayer-book the legacy to me, and to Olive a case of diamonds! I'm sick of the world at times. Let us go to the drawing-room, if nobody wants to take anything more."

In her unceremonious fashion, she rose at once and went away. When Mr. Kage followed them, he found Millicent alone near the fire; her sisters were at the far end of the room, examining some presents brought by Mrs. Dunn from Germany.

"Millicent, I have had no direct answer, remember," he said in a low tone. "But I am easy on the score; for I know the signs of rejection well, and you do not wear them."

"Have you been rejected, that you know them well?"

"Once—years ago."

"By Caroline Kage?" she whispered.

"Even so. I thought you must have known it at the time. I loved her, Millicent; how deeply, matters little now, and has not mattered since that time. She broke the spell too rudely."

"When she left you to marry my father—or rather, his fortune; for that was what in truth she married. But she did love you, Thomas: I saw it then; and she continued to love you, or I am mistaken, after papa's death."

He knew she had. But he was strictly honourable; and that love and its acknowledgment would be buried within the archives of his own breast for ever.

"I shall not make you the less fond husband, Millicent, for having indulged a dream in the days gone by."

She felt that to be true. But there's a dash of

coquetry in all women, and will be to the end of time. Millicent affected to doubt.

"If Major Dawkes were to die to-morrow, leaving Caroline free, you might wish then you had not spoken to me."

Mr. Kage looked at her.

"That contingency has arisen once—when your father died."

No answer.

"Millicent, seeing as I see now, loving one of you as I do now, and not the other, were you and Caroline standing before me for my choice, and she had never been else than free, never a wife, it is you I should take. Time has worked its changes within me, as well as in life's events. My darling, you need not doubt me!"

Her hand was sheltered in his; a sweet smile parted her lips; and on her cheek, partly turned from him, shone a bright glow of rose-colour.

It was rather cruel abruptly to interrupt the interview; and perhaps Olive Canterbury herself thought so, but she had no other resource. A servant had come in, bringing a note for Mr. Kage, marked "Immediate." He wondered who could be writing to him there and then; but when he looked at the superscription, he saw it was from Mrs. Dawkes.

"Open your note, Mr. Kage; don't stand on ceremony."

He was opening it as Mrs. Dunn spoke. She watched him, feeling curious. It contained a request, than which none more earnest had ever been penned, that he would go at once to the Rock, would return with the messenger, and *not* speak of it to any one.

"Who has brought this?" he asked of the servant.

"It's Fry, sir, Mrs. Dawkes's maid. She is waiting at the door; she'd not come in."

With a word of apology to Miss Canterbury for his departure, but none of explanation, Mr. Kage withdrew. Outside he found Fry. She said that Mrs. Dawkes wanted to see him for something very particular indeed, if he would be so kind as go back to the Rock with her. Mr. Kage acquiesced, and they proceeded on the way together.

"I hear your mistress is not in a good state of health," he observed.

"She's just in that state, sir, that unless a change takes place more speedier than it's possible, she will not last long," was the maid's answer.

He was deeply shocked, but he made no comment; though he could not but think there was something unreasonable in her thus grieving to death for the loss of a fragile child.

"Is the Major at the Rock just now?" he inquired.

"No, sir. His sister is with us; she came down here the day following the one me and my mistress came, and she has never gone away since. As to the Major, it's not often he troubles the Rock."

"But with his wife in this precarious state?" debated Thomas Kage.

"O, as to that, my poor mistress would as lieve have his room as his company. They are not too good friends, sir."

Fry gave her head a toss in the starlight. It seemed evident that she was not too good a friend of the Major's either. Mr. Kage said nothing.

"My mistress has been wanting to see you so much, sir, that she was talking of sending to London for you," resumed Fry. "When I told her to-night that you were at Chilling, she said it was nothing but a Providence that had brought you down."

"How did you know I was here?"

"Neel brought me word, sir. He went to the station after a parcel of books Miss Dawkes expected, and saw you there. I went round to the inn first, and they said they thought you had gone to Miss Canterbury's."

"Is it the grieving for the child that has brought your mistress into this sad state of health?"

"It can't be anything else, sir. She has never looked up, so to say, since he was put into his grave. Not that she ever speaks of it, even to me. I have ventured once or twice to say that she ought not to let it prey upon her mind so, as the dear little boy is better off; but she answers nothing—only tells me to hold my tongue."

"She wants cheerful society, and change."

"Just what I say, sir," returned Fry. "Always alone, and brooding upon it, it stands to reason that she can't shake it off. I'm sure the way she tosses and turns and moans in her sleep is enough to make her ill, let alone anything else. I sleep in her room now, sir. The day the inquest took place in London, she says to me, "Fry, get a bed put up in my room to-night; I am ill, and may want attendance in the night." Since that she has never let me go out of her room again. If she moves her room—and she has twice since she came to the Rock—my bed has to be moved too."

16*

"Is Miss Dawkes a sufficiently cheerful companion for your mistress?" asked Mr. Kage, a doubtful accent in his voice.

"Well, sir, I believe she does her best to amuse her. But my mistress sits a great deal alone in her own rooms, where she won't always admit Miss Dawkes: she never liked her, and that's the fact."

Walking quickly, they had approached the Rock, and were close to the front entrance. Fry took a sudden detour to the right.

"This way, if you please, sir," she whispered.

"This way!" echoed Mr. Kage; for the way led direct into the wilderness of trees that bordered the south wing of the Rock. "Wherefore?"

"It's all right, sir."

Glancing back at the house, he saw how dull it looked; scarcely any lights to be seen in its windows; just like the dwelling of one who lives a sick life, secluded from the world. Fry plunged into a labyrinth of trees, and Mr. Kage followed her.

"My mistress does not wish your visit to her known, sir; and I am going to take you in by the small iron postern-door in the south wing," said Fry in a confidential tone. "A rare trouble I had to unlock it to-night, for it has never been used—no, nor opened either—since the time of young Mr. Edgar Canterbury. I thought I should have had to call Neel, but my mistress said do it myself, if I could. You've heard of the door, sir, I daresay; it opens on a staircase which leads right up to the rooms in the south wing: and Mr. Edgar used to steal in and out that way, when his father wanted to keep too tight a hand upon him. My mistress has changed her apartments

for these. I didn't want her to. Edgar Canterbury
died in them, and I thought it looked like a bad omen;
but Miss Dawkes said she was to go into them if she
liked, and not be checked in such a trifle. But for
her being in them, I'm sure I don't know how ever
you would have got to her to-night, sir, unbeknown."

"To whom does Mrs. Dawkes not wish my visit
known?" he asked. "To the servants?"

"Chiefly to Miss Dawkes, sir. But there's none
of *them* she'd trust, except me and Neel; they are all
regular gossips. Mind your face, sir."

It all sounded mysterious enough, especially Fry's
voice. The shrubs were dense just here, and the re-
commendation as to his face was connected with the
spreading brambles, the door—a small iron door—
being completely hidden by them. Fry dexterously
fought her way to it, took a key from her pocket, and
turned it in the lock. After a great deal of creaking
and groaning, the door allowed itself to be pushed
open. Mr. Kage saw a flight of narrow stairs, on one
of which stood a lighted hand-lamp.

"You must excuse the dust, sir. It's an inch
thick."

Locking the door behind her, she took the lamp
to light him up. At the top of the stairs another
door had to be opened, and a dark closet passed
through. This brought them to the habitable part of
the south wing. Crossing the richly-carpeted corridor.
Thomas Kage found himself in the presence of Mrs.
Dawkes.

CHAPTER XVIII.

In the South Wing.

SHOCKED though Mr. Kage had been by Fry's account of her mistress's state, far, far more shocked was he to see her. The room was small but handsome, and replete with every comfort. Mrs. Dawkes sat on a sofa near the fire; her features where white and attenuated, her cheeks and lips scarlet with inward fever, and a dark circle surrounded her wild bright eyes. The black-silk dress she wore sat loosely; her beautiful golden hair, bound back by a bit of black ribbon, fell carelessly on her shoulders. She did not rise from the sofa, but held out both her hands to Thomas Kage. He advanced and took them in silence.

"Fry," said Mrs. Dawkes, bending aside to look beyond him, "remain in the room next the baize door. If she comes to the door, call out to her that I am not visible to-night; but don't unlock it to answer her. I am too unwell to go down, say, and can see no one here."

"All right, ma'am," answered Fry, as she went out and closed the door.

Thomas Kage still retained her hands, looking the pity he would not express. He thought her culpably wrong to give way to this intense grief, but supposed it had become morbid. She gazed up into his face with a yearning look.

"Years ago, in this very house," she began, "you said that you would henceforth from that time be unto me as a brother, other relationship between us being barred. You said that if ever I were in need of a true friend, I was to apply to you. I have put aside the old feelings—I have indeed; but I want a friend. Will you be one?"

"You know I will, Caroline. Your best and truest friend: your brother."

He relinquished her hands, and sat down by her.

"I have had a door put up—you might have seen it had you looked to the other end of the corridor—a strong green-baize door that fastens inside. I made the excuse that the apartments in this wing were cold, and I would have them shut in from the draught."

It was not so much the words that struck upon Thomas Kage as being unpleasantly singular; it was the manner, the tone in which they were uttered. She spoke in a hushed whisper, and turned her eyes to different parts of the room, as if in dread of being watched from the walls.

"I think I dreamt of this evening—of your coming here," she continued; "I am sure it has been presented indistinctly to my mind. And I knew that I could not talk to you undisturbed, so I had the door put up for that, as well as to keep her out—and him, when he is down here."

"You—dreamt of this evening?" asked Thomas Kage, not catching distinctly the thread of the sense.

"I seem to have foreseen it. I knew that I should need to see you before I die—for who else is there that I can trust?—and I knew that so long as she could get access to me there was no chance of any private conversation. Besides, I wanted to be alone, all to myself; away from the weariness of her continual

presence, from her observant eyes.   She's a spy upon
me.   She is."

A strange fear came over Thomas Kage as he
listened.   Had she in any degree lost her mind?
Something in the words and the unconnected tone
suggested the thought to him.   But he was wrong.
Highly feverish she was; her mind restless, her manner
nervous; but nothing more.

"I know she is placed over me as a spy.   I can
see it, and so can Fry; but I am now in that state of
nervous weakness that any great scene of agitation
might kill me, so I do not exert my authority to turn
her out.   But I am the Rock's mistress, and I will be
as long as I live; and I sent for the man, and gave
my orders, and had the door put up."

"You speak of Miss Dawkes?"

"Yes.   She watches me like a cat by night and by
day.   What do you think?—she actually proposed to
take Fry's place in my room at night.   It was the first
time *he* was down after we came here.   That did arouse
me.   I told him, that if his sister pushed herself too
much on me—and he knew I had never cared for her
—I should apply for a separation from him, and be
rid of both of them.   I can't think how I ever took
courage to say it; but Mr. Carlton had called that day,
and Miss Canterbury had called, and it seemed to
make me think I was not quite without friends, and
that I need not be so much afraid.   We have moments
of inspiration, you know.   It answered too; for nothing
more was said about her sleeping in my room.   And
then the time went on, and I moved into this wing,
and had the door put up.   She does not know of the
postern staircase."

"Caroline, you are feverish; your imagination is excited," he soothingly said. "Can I get you anything to calm you, my dear?"

"I am no more feverish than usual. And as to excitement—let any one lose a child in the way I did, and see if imagination would ever calm down again."

"But you do very wrong to indulge this excessive grief. I must point out your errors, Caroline: you know I have always spoken for your good, your welfare."

"O yes, I know you have," she interrupted, in a tone of anguished remorse. "If I had but heeded you! You told me such a will ought not to be made; you told me the money would not bring me good. If I had but heeded you! You told me Captain Dawkes was not a fit husband for me. Thomas, I accepted him in a fit of angry passion; of pique against you."

"These events are past; why recall them?"

"Why *not* recall them? I am passing from the world, and I would not that you should think I go blindfold to the grave; though I may have lived blindfold, or partially so. When you quitted the Rock, after that decisive interview had taken place between us, which I am sure you remember as vividly as I, I seemed not to care what became of me. I was bitterly angry with you; and when the man proposed again to me, I believe I accepted him only because you had warned me not to do it, and I hoped it would vex you. God has punished me."

"It cannot be recalled, Caroline; surely you may let it rest," he rejoined. "I ask you why you give way to this unaccountable sorrow. It is a positive sin to

talk of grief sending you into the grave. Your child
is better off. He is at rest; he is in happiness."

"I am not grieving for him. I have learnt to be
glad that he went before me."

"Then what is all this? You are seriously ill in
mind as well as in body; what distress is it that you
are suffering from?"

"I must have inherited a touch of papa's complaint;
he died of consumption, I believe. Before Tom went
I was very ill and weak, as you may remember; and—
and—the shock, I suppose, prevented my rallying. In
short, it is that which has killed me."

"The grief?"

"No, not the grief."

"The shock, then?"

"No, not the shock. It's the wretchedness altogether. Then things are preying upon me; things
which I cannot speak of; and whenever *he* is at the
Rock, I am in a dreadful state of nervousness. And
no one knows how *her* being here angers me and
worries me."

Mrs. Dawkes's words were by no means intelligible
to their hearer. He could not help remarking, either,
the strange avoidance of her husband's and Miss Dawkes's
names.

"I do not comprehend the half of what you say,
Caroline. What things are they that prey upon you?"

Mrs. Dawkes shuddered.

"I tell you I cannot speak of them. Thomas, will
you serve me?"

"Certainly I will. What is it that you wish me
to do?"

Mrs. Dawkes glanced over her shoulder, in apparent

dread of being heard. Which was quite a foolish apprehension; for the south wing, enclosed within its strong walls, was entirely apart from the rest of the house, and Fry, the only present inmate save themselves, sat in her far-off chamber, near the green-baize entrance-door. Caroline bent towards her cousin and spoke; but in so low a tone that he did not catch the words, and had to ask her again.

"I—want—a—will—made," she slowly repeated.

"Have you not made one since the child died?"

"No—no."

"Then it is right and proper that you should make one. And without delay."

"Will you contrive that I shall do it? Will you help me? Will you take my instructions, and get it executed?"

"My dear, what ails you?" he rejoined. "The shortest way, the best way, will be for you to send for Mr. Norris, and give your instructions to him."

"That is the very thing I cannot do," she said. "She will take care that I don't make one."

He knew she alluded still to Miss Dawkes.

"But she must let you make one; she cannot hinder you."

"Thomas, she is here to see that I don't make one. For no other purpose whatever, than that, is she put here to keep guard over me."

"Caroline, how can you have taken these ideas into your head?" he remonstrated, reverting again to the doubt whether her nervous state did not border on insanity. "A woman, possessing the immense property that you do, is bound to make a will."

"If I die without one, it goes to my husband—

money, and land, and the Rock. Everything, nearly, would go to him."

"Of course, if you leave no will."

"Then do you not see now why he does not want me to make one; *why he will not permit me to make one;* why he puts his sister here, to watch over me that I don't make one? It would be too wearisome for *him* to remain on guard—let alone the issue we might come to—and so he leaves *her* on duty."

"I hope you are mistaken," Thomas Kage gravely replied. "Major Dawkes must feel that he has little right to the whole vast fortune of Mr. Canterbury."

"He has no right to it, and he shall not have it!" she vehemently broke forth. "O Thomas, Thomas," she continued, changing her tone to one of wailing, "why did I not listen to you, when you begged me not to suffer the money to be so left—not to inherit it, contingent on the death of my child?"

"Hush, Caroline! Do not, I say, recall the past."

"What possessed Mr. Canterbury to make so dangerous a will? what possessed my mother to incite him to it, and I to second her?" she went on, paying no attention to the interruption. "I wish it had been burnt; I wish the money and the Rock had been sunk at the bottom of the sea!"

"It was an unjust will, bordering, as I think, on iniquity; but why do you call it a dangerous one? How am I to understand the term as applied to Mr. Canterbury's will?"

"Do you *not* understand it?" she asked, with pointed emphasis. "I sit here in my solitude, in my terrible nervousness, and dwell on many things, real and unreal, on the past and on the future; and I have fancied that you foresaw how it might become dangerous. There was a day, in this very house, when you earnestly warned me against suffering such a will to stand; when you seemed to be buried in a vision of the time to come, if I *did* let it stand, and shrank from it as from a black shadow, from a haunting dream. I have not forgotten it, Thomas, or your words."

Neither had he; but he did not choose to say so. The past was past; and for many reasons he thought it well not to bring it back again.

"Caroline, we were speaking of the real, not of the ideal. I am unable to comprehend your position, as you seem to put it. You are mistress of this house, and of its servants. It is your own absolutely; your husband has legally no authority in it. If the presence of Miss Dawkes is not agreeable to you, politely request her to terminate her visit. Try and shake off this nervousness, my dear; for nervousness it must be, and nothing else."

"If I only stirred in the matter, if I only said to her, Go, it would bring *him*. They are acting in concert."

"What if it did? Though he is your husband, he cannot take from you your freedom of action. The whole property is yours, remember; not subject to Major Dawkes's control."

"But there would be dreadful scenes, I say, and they would shatter me. Besides," she added, sinking her voice and glancing round with another of those looks of apprehensive terror, "I might be poisoned."

"O Caroline!"

"Tom was, you know," she continued, staring at

him with her wild eyes. "And I must make the will first."

Was she wandering now? Thomas Kage mentally debated the question, and with intense pain.

"I wish to leave this wretched fortune—wretched it has been to me and mine—to its rightful owners: I wish to repair the injustice that was committed on the Miss Canterburys. Will you advise me whether Olive—"

"I cannot advise you on the disposal of your money," he interrupted, in a voice almost of alarm; "neither will I inherit any of it, neither will I be the executor. Leave it as you think well yourself; I must decline all interference. The money has lapsed to you, Caroline; my trusteeship is over; do not now request me to take it up again."

"But you will advise me how to leave my money?"

"No."

"Not advise me! What can be the motive for your refusal?"

"The motive is of no consequence, Caroline. You have experience to guide you now; you can take advice of yourself."

"But you must have a motive. Tell it me. If you do not, the wondering what it can be will worry me for days and nights; you don't know how weak I have grown. Thomas, I conjure you, tell it me."

He would have preferred not to tell her; at least, during this interview. But she left him no resource. In his straightforward truth he spoke; his voice somewhat low and unwilling.

"I am to marry Millicent Canterbury."

She looked down upon her thin white hands, clasped together, and did not speak. But for the crimson hue that stole over her face and neck, he would have thought she did not hear. Surely she must love him still! In spite of her two marriages, hers must indeed have been an enduring love.

"Well, be it so," she said at length. "Thomas, I am glad to hear it; or I shall be when the brunt of the news has a little passed. Do not mistake me; the old remembrances are upon me to-night, or I should not feel this. You could not have chosen a better girl than Leta. Indeed I am glad of it; I have never been so selfish as to wish you not to marry."

"You see, therefore, why I cannot and will not advise, as to leaving money to the Miss Canterburys," explained Mr. Kage, in a very matter-of-fact tone. "Individually, I would prefer that you did not, for it may be the means of separating me from Millicent; on the other hand, they have claims on their father's estate. I cannot advise or interfere."

"Chivalrous and honourable as usual! You are too much so, Thomas. Had you been less so—"

"What then?" he asked, for she did not continue.

"This conversation never would have had place, and my child would be here by my side, and I should not be dying."

What she said was too true; and he knew it. They had not been able to fight against fate. Little use, then, to picture now what might have been. Caroline had played him false to marry a wealthy man; and all the regret in the world, and the bitter repentance, would not alter it.

"I must get a will made," she resumed, breaking the silence. "Can you show me how it may be done? I am virtually a wretched prisoner, remember."

He thought it over for a moment. Assuming what she said to be a fact, there was difficulty in the prospect.

"Let Mr. Norris come to you in the way I have done to-night, and take your instructions, Caroline."

She appeared to catch eagerly at the suggestion.

"So he might! I had not thought of it. The fact is, it was only when I heard you were in the neighbourhood, and I was worrying myself to contrive how I could get to see you alone, that Fry suggested the opening of the postern-door. Yes, yes; Norris is honest, and I will send for him. I shall leave my husband nothing, Thomas."

"Leave him nothing!" exclaimed Mr. Kage, surprised into the remark. "Nothing? Would that be justice?"

"Justice and mercy too. I leave him my *silence;* and that is more mercy than he deserves. He poisoned my child."

"Hush!" rebuked Mr. Kage.

"He poisoned my child," she persisted, beginning to tremble.

They gazed into each other's eyes. Hers were fixed, wild, bright; his seriously questioning.

"Caroline, this is an awfully grave charge."

"It is a true one," she affirmed. "I have known it all along. I knew it when the coroner's inquest was sitting; I knew it when you all went to put him in the grave. He had a bottle of laudanum in his dressing-room, but I believe none of the inmates of the house, save myself, had noticed that he had it; and lucky for him they had not. That laudanum-bottle had been there for weeks, untouched; but it was missing from its place the evening Tom died. I looked for it, and it was gone; I wanted some to put to my tooth. Was it not strange that that very night, of all others, I should have looked for it, and only that night?"

Mr. Kage made no reply. He was lost in thought.

"I went to bed early that night, at eight o'clock; and after I was in bed, I got up to fetch the laudanum-bottle from his dressing-room. It was not there. I was amazed at its absence, because I knew it always was there, and I had seen it earlier in the day. Soon afterwards *he* came in; and when he saw me he started like a guilty man, and hurried something under his coat as he went through to his dressing-room. It must have been the bottle—it was the bottle! The next morning I saw the bottle in its place again. No one but himself had gone through my room that night; and therefore I knew that it was he who had replaced it. I thought nothing of it at the moment; no, nor even when the alarm of the death came."

"Allowing all this to be true—and I cannot disbelieve you—how could he have administered it to the child? Judith never left him."

"He did not administer it; Judith did that."

"*Judith!*" uttered Thomas Kage.

"Judith; but not intentionally. She believed, poor woman, when she gave him his dessert-spoonful of mixture that evening, that she was giving him his proper medicine. When she brought the child down to me, I did not send her back, but kept her talking; the nursery was therefore vacant. That was his opportunity. The mixture-bottle must have been then taken away, and the laudanum-bottle substituted. O, I assure you, Thomas, I have gone over all this so often since in my mind, that I seem to have seen it all done. Judith gave him a dessert-spoonful of the opium instead of his proper medicine. Major Dawkes must have waited in his room opposite; and when she had shut herself into the night-nursery; he went softly in and changed the bottles again, having taken out the same quantity of the rightful physic. I daresay he swallowed it. Then he came sneaking down with the laudanum-bottle in his hand, little thinking I had been searching for it, or that I was in my room. I saw the next morning that some of the contents had been taken out."

"Were the bottles alike?"

"Exactly alike. Green-glass bottles, with about the same quantity of stuff in each; and the colour of the mixture and of the laudanum tallied. The labels were not alike, but Judith cannot read writing."

"I know she cannot."

" 'Tincture of Opium. Major Dawkes,' was on the one; 'The Mixture. Master Canterbury,' was on the other. Some days after the dreadful truth had revealed itself to me, I had Judith alone, and cautiously questioned her. She was in much distress, and confessed that a matter was preying on her mind. It was this: after she had given the mixture to the child that evening, he shook his head and said it was 'nasty,' which had never been his complaint before. In putting in the cork, her eye fell on the words of the label, and she thought they looked different—not the same she was accustomed to see; but in the impossibility (as she supposed) of its being any other label or bottle, she had concluded it was her fancy. The next morning by daylight, the old familiar writing seemed to be returned to the bottle. Not until after the child was buried, she said, did this incident recur to her memory. It was strange that it should not; but I could not disbelieve her, for Judith was ever truthful."

"Did you do well to conceal these circumstances?" inquired Mr. Kage, in a low tone. "They might have been investigated."

"Had I known them—had they presented themselves to my mind at the moment of my boy's death, I should inevitably have proclaimed them to the world. But Fry was hasty with her opinion that he must have died in a fit; the Major seconded it; and I thought it was so, in my wild grief. When the doctors had held their post-mortem examination, and declared the cause of his death to be opium, the news of which was brought in by Fry, then the truth flashed upon me—in a confusion of ideas at first; but, little by little, each distinct point grew, and stood out with awful clearness."

"He came down to my chambers that night, asking me to advance some of the child's money," murmured Thomas Kage.

"O yes, that was a part of his cunning scheme," was Mrs. Dawkes's bitter answer. "He had laid his plans well, be you sure of that, to divert suspicion from himself. He went to you, that you might testify, if needful, he was away in the evening; he asked to borrow the money—knowing that you were not likely to lend it—that it might be assumed he saw no prospect at that, the eleventh hour, of succeeding to my boy's. He slept out, that it should be seen *he* had not gone near Tom to harm him, and hoping to be away when the alarm occurred."

"And you have not spoken of this!"

"Never, until this night. How could I? No one suspects the part he took, unless it be Judith, and—no

17*

doubt—Miss Dawkes. Fry does not; she would abuse
the doctors by the hour together in my presence, for
saying Tom died from opium, seeing he could not have
got at any; but I stop her always. Can you wonder,"
added Caroline in an altered tone, "that I have lived
since in fear—in nervous dread—and thàt I dare not
provoke an open rupture with the man I once called
husband?"

"Did you ever hint at your suspicions to him?"

"Only once. If ever I thought to do it, my tongue
seemed to dry in my mouth, my heart to sicken. On
the day of the inquest, he came in to condole with me
after it was over—the false hypocrite! and I suddenly
spoke to him. 'That bottle of laudanum you kept in
your dressing-room was away from its place the evening
Tom died; where was it?' He was taken by surprise,
and turned as white as ashes; his lips were ghastly and
tremulous, as they strove to say it was not away from
it, so far as he knew. That look alone would be sufficient to prove his guilt. I said no more; I only gazed
steadily at him, and he turned away. I could not be
the first to accuse him; he had been my husband; had
any one else done so, I should have said what I knew.
We have lived an estranged life since then; to appearance outwardly civil. I came here the next day, with
my dreadful secret; he has been down once or twice,
and we go through the ceremony of hand-shaking
at his arrival and departure; and she is here—my
keeper."

Mr. Kage leaned his head upon his hand.

"Yes I am here with my dreadful secret," she
reiterated; "and he is living in a whirl of gaiety, of
sin. I sometimes wonder whether the past lies, a

burden, upon him also, in the silence of the accusing night."

"A dreadful secret indeed!" Thomas Kage echoed, wiping his brow. "Caroline, why did you tell it me?"

"Not for you to accuse and betray him; not to repeat again. When this conversation shall be over, you can bury it in the solitude of your own breast, and leave him to his conscience and the future. But I could not go to my grave without telling *you* what has sent me there."

Mr. Kage sat thinking—thinking over the chain of events from their commencement. The foolish marriage of Mr. Canterbury with this young girl; the unjust will; the dangerous clause of the great fortune reverting to her should the child die. Yes, dangerous; Mrs. Dawkes had called it by its right name. Dangerous if she married a needy and unscrupulous second husband.

"O, but it was an awful temptation!" he exclaimed aloud; not to her, but in self-communing. "Awful, awful, to such a one as Dawkes. Poor man!"

"You say 'poor man!' You pity him?"

"Not his guilty weakness in yielding to it; not his wicked sin; but I pity him for his exposure to the temptation. Better that Mr. Canterbury had left his money to revert to his daughters after the child; better that he had left it to the county hospital."

"Did you think of this horrible contingency when you urged me, almost with a prayer, not to inherit after my child?"

"Do not recur to what I thought," he sharply cried, as if the question struck an unpleasant chord within him. "I am given to flights of fancy, and don't know what I may have thought."

"I will send for Norris," she resumed; "he must come in as you came to-night. You see now why I dare not venture to let it be known I wish to make a will. Major Dawkes comes into all after my death; he sees that I cannot last long, *she* sees it. Of course they will not let me make a will."

"Yes, I see, Caroline."

"Were I to insist upon it—were they only to suspect that I wished to make one, that I so much as thought of it, they—he—might put me out of the way as he put Tom," she said with glistening eyes.

It was altogether so strange and sad a thing, that Thomas Kage scarcely liked to leave her. But it must be. He took her hands in his when he rose to say farewell, bending over her.

"I shall come in state to the front entrance to-morrow, Caroline, and pay you a formal visit, as though we had not met since you left London."

"Since the day of my boy's funeral! Do so. She will be in the room all the time; there's no chance of any visitor being allowed to see me alone. Good-night, good-night; we shall not meet many more times in this world."

"Caroline," he lingered to whisper, an anxious look arising to his own face, "are you prepared for the next?"

"I think of it as a rest from weary sorrow; I think of it as a place of loving pardon and peace. I wish I was better fitted for it."

"Why do you not send for Mr. Rufort?"

"She would not let him come to be with me alone."

"She must let him; she shall let him."

"Thomas, let me get the will made first, and I shall be more at ease. I am in no immediate danger."

"Good-night, my dear child. Keep up your spirits."

Mrs. Dawkes touched a silver hand-bell, and Fry came flying out of a room at the end of the corridor, one close to the new baize door. Thomas Kage saw the door as he looked that way. Fry conducted him down the dusty stairs, and out at the rusty postern entrance to the mass of entangled shrubs; and he picked his way through them lost in thought, deeply pondering on the revelations his visit had brought forth.

CHAPTER XIX.

On the Watch.

An enemy could not have said that Keziah Dawkes was unkind to her brother's wife. With the exception that she never quitted that unhappy lady for more than two minutes together throughout the day, she was as kind to her as kind could be. Keziah, made of as hard iron as it is possible for a woman to be, could not but have some grains of compassion for the delicate girl (she was little more than a girl yet) wasting away to death under her eyes. It might be that she had qualms of remorse also. Not for the watching: Keziah thought her sister-in-law none the worse for that. Not on her own score at all; but for a certain event that might be lying on her brother's conscience, and of which she strove to drive out intruding suspicions.

They were too dreadful even for Keziah. Caroline's
grief for her poor child was pitiable to witness, and
Keziah felt for her in regard to that.

When Mrs. Dawkes would come downstairs in the
morning, be it early or be it late, there sat Keziah
waiting for her, and beguiling the waiting with some
everlasting knitting. After that, she stuck to Mrs.
Dawkes throughout the day, her very shadow. If
Caroline strolled out in the garden, to sit on the
autumn-wintry bench, wrapped up in furs (a rare occurrence), Keziah and her knitting went too; when
Caroline walked or drove over to see her mother,
Keziah was her companion; if, by rare chance, visitors
called at the Rock, Keziah sat in the drawing-room by
the side of its mistress. Only in her own chamber was
Caroline free. It was this disagreeable espionage that
caused her to remove into the south wing, and have a
barrier-door erected. *Not*, at that time, had the slightest thought of the postern-door, as a possible means
of admittance to her own friends, crossed her mind.
It never might have been thought of, or used as such,
but for the happy suggestion of her maid Fry. Fry
lived in a chronic state of resentment against Miss
Dawkes, and was warmly attached to her mistress.
Any way, then, that she could find to "circumvent"
the former (Fry's own word, in her whispered con-
fidences to the butler) was more welcome to her than
flowers in May.

But Fry had opposed the removal to the south
wing. Edgar Canterbury had died in those rooms;
they had never been inhabited since; and for her
mistress to go into them she looked upon as boding
ill-luck—nothing less than an omen that she would die

in them, in her turn. Keziah came to the rescue, and
said Mrs. Dawkes might remove into them if she liked
—why not? All unconscious was she of the heavy
blow it might be the means of eventually dealing her
brother. And so poor Caroline took up her abode in
the long-unused wing; and very shortly afterwards
caused that intervening door, covered with green baize,
to be erected, shutting out the wing from the rest of
the house and from Keziah. Keziah did not care: if
Mrs. Dawkes chose to pass part of her days in seclusion,
with Fry in attendance upon her, why, let her; it was
only a relief to Keziah. *She* could take care that no
chance visitor was admitted to the south wing unac-
companied by herself. Never did it enter into Keziah's
imagination—no, not in its wildest dreams—that an
outer door existed to that south wing. She had never
heard of it.

The postern-door, encompassed by the wilderness
of trees and shrubs around, was invisible to the eye.
In the midst of this wilderness (as was related earlier
in the story) stood the Lady's Well; and this had so
sure a reputation for being haunted—the lady's ghost,
as was well known, appearing at will, and shrieking
frightfully on windy nights—that no one ever thought
of penetrating to that side of the house. And therefore, in the lapse of time, the postern-door came to be
entirely forgotten by the few who had been cognisant
of its existence. In after-life, Fry was wont to say that
nothing less than a special revelation had made *her*
remember it the evening when Thomas Kage was at
Chilling. But Keziah Dawkes knew nothing of the
postern-door; and when her sister-in-law was shut up
within that wing, she supposed her to be as safe as if

she were in her own presence. What though Caroline did take freaks at times to bar the green door against her? She was welcome to do it for Keziah, who supposed it arose from simple caprice, or a real desire for solitude.

Caroline was correct in the opinion she had expressed to Thomas Kage, that what they feared was, that she might make a will. Of course this could not, in the Major's interests, be allowed; neither did they intend it should be. All the watching was on this score: there existed no other cause for it. Keziah had little fear. Caroline seemed to be overwhelmed with apathy—to have no more thought or care for the future disposal of her property than if it had been a tract of land in the wilds of Africa. She seemed to care for nothing. She had never attempted to write a letter since she came to the Rock; her days were passed in inert sadness—in one long monotony; and Keziah believed this would continue to the end. As well, perhaps, that she did not attempt to write letters: they would not have been permitted to go out of the house without a supervision, so that it might have come to the same in the end. Keziah watched always; she would never relinquish the watching so long as Caroline lingered in life; but she was as sure as sure can be that it was an entirely superfluous precaution. And meanwhile she did not intend that Mrs. Dawkes should see she was watched, and had no suspicion Caroline had already detected it.

"What ever can your mistress do with herself, shut in all alone evening after evening, with not a soul to speak to?" Keziah had said to Fry only a day or two before this visit of Thomas Kage's. "She must be frightfully lonesome."

"For the matter of that, Miss Dawkes, she has been nothing else but lonesome ever since the poor boy died," was Fry's answer. "As to what she does, she mostly lies on the sofa, sometimes with a book, oftener without one. All she wants is to lie in quiet, where folks won't come in to bother her with talking."

A hint for Keziah. Fry's words were honest; and Miss Dawkes was aware she had always been objectionable to her young sister-in-law. Caroline dared not order her out of the house, as she would have done in former days. In her broken spirit, and with the remembrance of the child's death and its attendant circumstances ever upon her, she had grown to be terribly afraid of Keziah and Barnaby. She removed to the south wing from no other motive than to be sometimes free of the former's presence, and stayed there as a refuge. But as the days went on, and she was drawing (as she fully believed) nearer to death, the obligation to make a will pressed itself with greater urgency upon her, until it seemed to grow into a religious duty that she must not fail in if she would find peace with Heaven.

A fine bright morning—the one following the secret visit of Mr. Kage—and Keziah Dawkes sat at her solitary but sumptuous breakfast full of complacency. Caroline took hers in her own chamber. Fry urged her to take it in bed; but there seemed to be ever a restlessness upon her that prevented her lying long once morning had dawned. Sitting in her arm-chair by the fire, partially dressed only, and wrapped in her dressing-gown of lavender silk, Mrs. Dawkes generally took her breakfast from the small low stand drawn close before her.

"I wonder what she'll do to-day?" thought Keziah, as, her meal over, she sat with her head upon her hand. "She said something yesterday about wanting to call on the Miss Canterburys. I'm sure I hope she'll not. "Don't let her get intimate with those women," said Barby to me when he was down here last; and he is quite right. On the other hand, if she *will* call, I suppose she must: it may not do to draw the reins too tight. I wish to goodness the downright cold weather would set in!"

Rising from her chair, Keziah gave a shake to the folds of her gray-merino morning-dress with its black trimmings, and passed out to betake herself to the south wing. Ascending the stairs, she went through the picture-gallery to a small corridor which brought her to the green-baize door. Opening it at will, she was in the south wing. It contained four rooms only, and a dark lumber-closet, panelled with oak, in which receptacle were stowed away sundry articles that had belonged to Edgar Canterbury. The door of the staircase descending to the postern entrance was in this closet; and Keziah had seen it one day that she chose to take a look round on Mrs. Dawkes's first removal; but it looked exactly like one of the panels, and Keziah suspected nothing. Of these four rooms two were Caroline's—her sitting- and bed-rooms; the small one next the baize door Fry sat in; the fourth was not used. Keziah walked along the passage, carpeted lately, and knocked at Mrs. Dawkes's chamber.

"Come in," came the faint spiritless answer.

Caroline sat in the elbow-chair, in the pretty silk gown, her golden hair falling upon it in curly waves, as it was mostly let fall now. Keziah took her hand.

"How are you, my dear, this morning?"

"O, about the same, I think," was the listless reply. "I've not coughed much to-night. It's very fine—is it not?"

"Beautifully fine; but so sharp and cold. I don't think it will do for you to venture into the air to-day, Caroline."

"I am not thinking of venturing into it, that I know of," returned Caroline peevishly. "I shall see when I come down."

"And, my dear, is there anything particular that you could fancy for your luncheon?"

"No."

A few more of these questions and answers, a little chat on Keziah's part—items of news she had read in the journal last night—and then she withdrew; and Caroline was left alone, to have her dressing completed by Fry. About twelve o'clock she went downstairs, dressed for the day in her black silk, her hair gathered up in order. Keziah drew a warm chair to the fire, and hastened to bring one of the rich-painted white-velvet foot-stools. Close upon this the old doctor came in. He had been medical attendant to the Rock as long as the Canterburys had inhabited it—a hale simple-minded gentleman, turned seventy now, with fresh-coloured cheeks and white hair. Mr. Owen's daily visits were the only break in Caroline's monotonous life. As he sat there to-day, telling of various out-door interests, he mentioned the arrival of Mrs. Dunn and of Mr. Kage.

Caroline's cheeks grew scarlet, knowing that she had to appear as if it were *news;* and her attempt at doing so was rather a poor one; but Keziah failed to notice: in her own intense, and not pleasurable surprise, she observed nothing.

"Mr. Kage!" exclaimed Keziah. "What!—Thomas Kage?"

"Yes; I don't know any other Mr. Kage," was the surgeon's answer. "He got here yesterday evening, he tells me, and is staying at the inn."

"But, Mr. Owen, what has he come for?"

"To see the old place again, I suppose, Miss Dawkes. I didn't ask him."

Keziah lapsed into silence, pondering over certain interests with herself. She thought it very undesirable that any communication should take place between Mr. Kage and Caroline, and wondered what ill wind could have blown him to Chilling just now. Who was to know that he, connected as he had been with the child's property, might not get urging his cousin to make a will?

"Of course, he will come to call on me," suddenly spoke Caroline, the first words she had uttered. "Mr. Owen, if you see him, tell him that he must not go away without calling on me."

Rather lame words; as Keziah might have thought, but that she was so preoccupied with her own reflections. For Thomas Kage to come to Chilling and *not* call to see Caroline would have been an anomaly.

When Mr. Owen left, Keziah, as was her frequent custom, went with him to the hall. She was in the habit of evincing much anxiety that Caroline's health should be restored, her life prolonged.

"No, I do not think her any better, Miss Dawkes," was the doctor's answer to the query put; and at the same moment Fry, happening to see them from the back of the hall, came forward to join in the colloquy. "Looks brighter, you fancy? Nonsense! She's flushed, if you will; flushed with nervousness and sleeplessness. I tell you she is nearly as weak as a woman can be, my dear madam, short of absolute helplessness. The poor young thing is eating away her heart with grief for her child; and my emphatic opinion is—and has been, you know, Miss Dawkes, for some time—that the solitude she lives in is not good for her."

"And so I say," put in Fry, who did not at all like the solitude on her own account. "To mope all alone cannot be good for any one. She never does an earthly thing but read a bit—as I've told you, Mr. Owen—and that not for five minutes together. But if she *won't* be roused, why, she won't—and there it is."

"Ah, concluded the doctor, as he took his departure, "it's one of those sad cases, I'm afraid, that all our care and skill, exert them as we will, are unable to touch."

A comforting assurance for the interests of Barnaby Dawkes. Keziah heard it with an unruffled face, and turned indoors.

The next visitor to make his appearance was Thomas Kage. The sun was at its meridian height when he was shown in, and poor Caroline sat where its rays could fall on her wan face. She seemed strangely passive; a little faint colouring might flush into the face, but she did not rise from her chair; only let him take her hand in silence. The emotion of the meeting had spent itself the previous night: Caroline, besides, was afraid lest an incautious word should betray that it had taken place, and so kept still. Keziah Dawkes, sitting quite inconveniently near, was agreeably surprised at the apathetic character of the interview.

Keziah talked. Mr. Kage talked. Caroline scarcely spoke a word. But the conversation turned solely on commonplace nothings; and, so far as Keziah could see, Mr. Kage's visit to Chilling had been made without reference to Mrs. Dawkes. She would have liked to knit a thanksgiving for it into her knitting.

"Caroline," he said, "do you know that you are looking quite painfully thin?"

"Yes; painfully so; you have used the right word, Thomas. I know it more and more every day when they dress me, for my things hang upon me now like bags."

"You should have some change; staying in this solitude at the Rock cannot be good for you. Miss Dawkes, I think you might have perceived this before, and suggested to Major Dawkes that something should be tried."

Miss Dawkes let her knitting fall on her gown, and stared at Caroline with a face of concern, as if she saw the signs of sickness for the first time. As her eye met, quite accidentally, that of Mr. Kage, a vivid recollection of the interview she had once held with him in her sick despair flashed into her mind, bringing a tinge to her leaden cheek. Perhaps she thought of the contrast between Barnaby's hopeless condition then and his flourishing state now; or—perhaps the flush arose because she feared Mr. Kage must be thinking of it.

"Caroline does look thin; unusually so to-day," she quietly replied; "I hope a little time will see an improvement. She is unwilling to stir from home."

"I shall never stir from home until I am carried out of it," interposed Caroline. "What does it matter where I am—here or elsewhere? It won't be for so very long."

"But, Caroline, you should not indulge this kind of thought," said Mr. Kage, in a tone of remonstrance.

"Why not? I do not wish to live. And if I did wish it, it would be all the same, for I know that nothing can prolong my existence. When they took my boy's life, they virtually took mine."

The last sentence was evidently not spoken with any invidious meaning. Mr. Kage made no observation; Keziah was picking-up some stitches that had dropped.

"I should like to go to Tom. When he used to wish to be with the angels, I wondered greatly. I could not understand it. But I wish it now myself—to go away and be with the angels—and with him."

Keziah lifted her eyes and telegraphed a confidential look to Mr. Kage. It meant to say, "Don't notice her; this comes of low spirits." He made no answering sign: he believed it came of the *truth*—and that she was following her little son as quickly as was possible.

"Caroline, do you see Mr. Rufort?"

"No."

"But you ought to do so. Speaking in a worldly point of view only, his visit would do you good; he is

a very agreeable man. And—if there be any graver
necessity—"

"The last time he came, Miss Dawkes sent word
out I was too poorly to be seen," interrupted Caroline.

"And so you were, my dear," cried that affectionate lady in a sweetly soothing tone.

"And the time before that you went out and met
him, and he turned back again; and another time you
told me he had been to the cottages on the common
where the scarlet-fever was, and that it would not do
for him to come in to me then," quietly went on
Caroline.

Mr. Kage turned his luminous eyes on Miss Dawkes.
Questioning eyes just then.

"My dear Caroline, Mr. Rufort can come to you
every day, if you like," said the guardian dragon, who
felt scared out of the best part of her equanimity in
the presence of Mr. Kage. "I'll drop him a note, my
dear, to-day."

A little more conversation, bringing forth no
particular fruit, and then luncheon was announced.
Mr. Kage rose to leave, declining the invitation to stay.
Caroline got up as he took her hands. She was visibly
agitated.

"Shall I see you again, Thomas? Shall I ever see
you again?"

"Ever?—yes, I hope so. Not this time, I fear, for
I leave for London to-morrow morning. You can
write to me news of how you go on, and—"

"I never write," interrupted Caroline. "It is too
much exertion for me now. I have not written a word
to anybody, Thomas, since the blow fell."

"Perhaps Miss Dawkes, then, will drop me a line,

should there be any change," he rejoined, glancing at that lady. "Should you need me in any way, Caroline, I will come."

Miss Dawkes graciously acceded: promising and vowing to write on any and every occasion that Mr. Kage could possibly be wished for. Without, however, having the smallest intention of doing it.

"Why are you going so soon?" resumed Caroline. "I think you might take this one meal with me."

"I agreed to take it at Miss Canterbury's."

"As you please, of course. I am nothing to any one now, and shall soon be less."

Her subdued voice spoke of pain, hot tears stood in her eyes. Thomas Kage held out his arm to lead her to the dining-room, and sat down by her side. His heart smote him for the unkindness he would have committed. Never again, in all probability, would the opportunity be afforded him of taking the meal with her; whereas he would most likely often take it in future times and seasons with the Miss Canterburys.

And she was gratified: there was no doubt of that. A soft pink shone on her cheeks, a light in her eyes; and she talked a little. Keziah, almost ignored, glanced up again and again surreptitiously from her place below, as she revelled in the delicacies provided.

But Caroline ate nothing. The wing of a partridge was on her plate, but she merely toyed with it; and the pink faded again, and the bright eyes grew dim. Every soothing attention that Thomas Kage could give, he did give. Perhaps the remembrance of the first dinner he had ever eaten in this magnificent room, when she was by his side, but not then the Rock's mistress, lay on both of them. Could they have fore-

seen at that happy banquet the fruits that a few years
would bring forth! Time does indeed work strange
changes.

The meal over, Mr. Kage, preparing finally to depart, held out his hand again to Caroline. Instead of
responding to it, she took his arm, and went with him
outside the door. Keziah came flying up with a warm
cloak—the ostensible plea—and stuck herself close to
Caroline's side. It was a warm lovely day for late
autumn: quite a contrast to the cold of the preceding
one, the wind—what slight wind there was—being in
its softest quarter. Mr. Kage turned his steps to the
right, towards the side gate.

"Why are you going this way, Thomas?"

"I shall cross over to your mamma's cottage,
Caroline. I must see her this afternoon, and this is
the nearest way."

At the gate, to which they walked in silence,
Caroline halted, not loosing his arm. Miss Dawkes,
making pretty remarks upon the scenery and the
weather, was patient as any tame lap-dog.

"I think I will go with you, Thomas. I can walk
as far as that."

This did arouse Miss Dawkes. In the first place,
the continued companionship with Thomas Kage was
not desirable; every minute she was on greater thorns
lest he might accidentally hit on so undesirable a topic
of conversation as the ultimate disposal of the vast
property on which he trod. In the second, Keziah had
nothing on her head, and was very subject to face-
ache.

"*Walk* to Mrs. Kage's!" she exclaimed almost with
a scream. "My dear Caroline, you must not attempt

it. The last time you could hardly get home; that's a fortnight ago, and you are weaker since then."

"But I had not my cousin's arm to lean upon, Miss Dawkes," was the cold answer.—"Thomas, I should like to go, if you will not mind the trouble of walking back with me. I feel that it might do me good."

Without a word of dissent he took her through the gate, and bade her lean all her weight upon him. Had there never been any feeling between them but that arising from relationship, he might have passed his arm round her waist to help her on her way. But, the very consciousness of what had been, had made him throughout her married life more carefully respectful to her. And so they walked along—Caroline in her warm woollen cloak and hood, Keziah in nothing.

"There is not the slightest necessity for you to come, Miss Dawkes," said Caroline, stopping to speak. "Mr. Kage will take care of me."

"O, my dear, I *couldn't* be so unkind as suffer you to go alone," returned Keziah. "Don't mind me."

"I am not alone. You have no bonnet on."

"It is quite delightful, dear, to be without a bonnet this sweet day. I'm sure it's like summer," responded Keziah, shivering just a little, and wishing Mrs. Dawkes could be taken with a fit, or any other ailment that might stop the expedition. "Mr. Kage, how is your sister Charlotte?"

"Mrs. Lowther? Quite well, and busy and happy as usual with her many children."

"*Does* Mr. Lowther get on any better?" continued Keziah in a tone of compassion.

"Thank you, he does. Lowther has turned the lane at last, and is in a fair way of accumulating a

fortune.   Mrs. Garston's legacy to his wife has been
the means of effecting it."

"O!" said Keziah.

They came to the barrier in the field where the
stile used to be.   It was a gate now.   How vividly the
spot brought back that unhappy day to Thomas Kage,
when he had found Caroline talking there with George
Canterbury, and the blow she had dealt himself within
a few minutes of it! He had never been the same man
since.   And she, the vain heartless girl, had grown into
this poor, sickly, spiritless shadow, leaning on his
arm, soon, very soon, to die.

Mrs. Kage was a worse spectacle—a miserable
dried-up mummy, who had some little remains of mind
left; but no capability of comfort in life.   She could
not eat and drink as she used; *that* had remained her
chief solace, and that was leaving her.   She sat huddled
up in her chair in the bedroom, close to the fire, and
was the veriest object Mr. Kage had ever looked upon.
At the first moment he started back.   No rouge now,
no teeth, no false hair; when mortals get very near the
grave, these adjuncts are left off.   She was wrapped up
in an old blue-silk cloak lined with ermine, that had
once been young Mrs. Canterbury's; her palsied fingers
kept catching at the fastening cord and tassels.   O,
what a wreck it was! What a wreck both were! What
good had George Canterbury's money, that they so
schemed for, brought to either?   Thomas Kage could
not help a fancy coming over him that it must have
entailed evil.

Blinking upwards, she at length recognised her
visitors.   Caroline and Mr. Kage sat down by her;
Keziah put herself on the other side, nearly into the

fire. The sight of Thomas Kage appeared to reawaken the palsied woman to memories and interests.

"What's the matter with her?" she suddenly asked, touching Caroline, but addressing Mr. Kage.

"I do not know. I am grieved to see her looking so ill."

"She's dying. I know it. Every time she comes to see me there's less life in her.—What do you do to her—you and that false brother of yours?"

The latter query was directed with a raised voice and menacing gesture to Miss Dawkes. That lady, receiving it in silence, stared a little; it took her by surprise.

"I'd like *you* to ask it, Thomas; and to require an answer from them. I can't, and I've got nobody here to do it for me or to speak to. They are killing her between them. He'll get all the money, you know."

Keziah's gray face took a tinge of purple. This turn in the conversation was by no means agreeable. Caroline was the one to break the silence.

'Mamma, do not let my state of health trouble you. I am as happy at the Rock as I should be any-where else; happier perhaps. Major Dawkes has gone his own way this many a day, and I have gone mine. As to Miss Dawkes here, she is as attentive to me as can be."

Mrs. Kage blinked out at the three and shook her head. The matter was too complicated for her weakened mind to deal with or retain long. Again she bent towards Thomas Kage, and lowered her voice to a semi-whisper.

"If the time could come over again, Thomas, I'd not urge her to marry into the Rock. We might have been better off had we stayed as we were. Where's the boy?"

"The boy!" stammered Mr. Kage, all too conscious of the secret that lay upon him.

"What did he die of, that sweet little boy? I have dark dreams about it, I can tell you. I wonder if the Major has?"

Caroline rose, pleading fatigue. Keziah—her face a bright purple now—glanced round to see if the curious hint affected the company, and thought *not*, which was satisfactory. One thing Keziah did not bargain for—the strangely-expressive look that sat in Mr. Kage's eyes, as her glance happened to meet his. Keziah had felt cold outside from lack of a bonnet; she turned far colder now.

They got safely out from the presence of the poor old woman, who seemed to have taken up some undesirable fancies, and whose last words were a loud lamentation over her daughter's ill-starred marriage with Barnaby Dawkes. It was now that Thomas Kage contrived to get a couple of minutes' private conversation with Caroline, in spite of Keziah's dragon-like precaution. That bonnetless lady, not daring to risk uncovered the same cold walk back again, stayed behind to borrow a shawl of Mrs. Kage's maid: and the others went on together.

In a few clear, concise, but rapid words, Thomas Kage inquired whether Caroline would wish to be anywhere else than at the Rock—whether she would choose to be an entirely free agent, and relieved of the espionage of Miss Dawkes; if so, he undertook that it should be at once accomplished. The secret he possessed gave him the power to act for her welfare in any way she pleased; and the Major should not dare to lift voice or finger in opposition. But Caroline shook her head and refused; all she wanted was to be left in peace to the end.

The end! Mr. Kage had made it his business to see the surgeon, Owen, that morning, in regard to Mrs. Dawkes's state, and inquired whether anything could be done for her. Nothing at all, the doctor answered; it was too late. She was dying of a complication that Mr. Owen could not well understand— chest-weakness and grief and a kind of nervous irritability; dying slowly, no doubt, but quite surely. Neither Mr. Kage nor any other anxious friend could arrest the fiat. With this knowledge within him, Thomas Kage could not urge any removal upon her.

The lost confidential word was spoken as Keziah's footsteps were heard. When she came hurrying up, a shawl pinned over her head, Mr. Kage was talking about the white clouds floating gently across the deep-blue sky. Keziah began pathetically to deplore the "wandering state" of poor dear Mrs. Kage. Mrs. Kage's daughter agreed that it was very pitiable. Not for the world would Caroline have aroused any suspicions in Keziah; for who could tell what might come of such? The one earnest desire lay on her mind and heart like a nightmare—to succeed in getting a will made.

"God bless and keep you, my dear Caroline!" were the murmured words of Thomas Kage, as he stood to say farewell when they reached the Rock. "I shall see you again, I hope, some time."

"Yes; in heaven," she answered, bursting into tears. "Thank you for your life-long kindness to me, Thomas; thank you for ever."

And in all the phases of their many meetings and separations, never had Thomas Kage's heart ached worse than it did now, when he wrung her hands, and quitted her for the last time. His career in life, so to say, was beginning: hers was ending.

O that miserable will of George Canterbury's! What good had it done to anybody? what ill not wrought?

CHAPTER XX.

Searching for Fencing-sticks.

KEZIAH DAWKES stood at the entrance-door of the Rock, in the light of the afternoon sun. It might have been thought that she was standing there to admire the view, so beautiful as seen from that elevated spot. Perhaps she was; and speculating upon the fast-approaching period when her beloved brother Barby—beloved still, as few brothers have been, in spite of his many sins, real or suspected, against Keziah and the world in general—should have this fine domain in absolute actual possession. Her mood was one of complacency. Thomas Kage had gone away without any undesirable interference—he was barely out of sight even yet—and, so far as Keziah could understand, he was not likely to trouble them with a visit soon again. As to poor Mrs. Dawkes, Keziah, in her hard way, did feel some pity for her. She was very young to die; but Keziah comforted herself with this consolation—that *she* could not help it. If Mrs. Dawkes was sick with a sickness that would, apparently, only end in death, and not long first either, it was

certainly no fault of hers; she had not helped her to
the sickness or the sorrow—was not responsible for it
in any way whatsoever.

Upon coming in from the walk, and parting with
Thomas Kage just within the hall, Caroline said she
felt weary and would go to her room to rest, desiring
not to be disturbed. Keziah acquiesced, speaking
some kind words, and accompanied her to the foot of
the stairs quite affectionately. It was in returning,
that the rays from the western sun, streaming into the
hall through the open entrance-door, drew Keziah out
by their brightness. The shawl, borrowed from Mrs.
Kage's maid, was wrapped round her still; Keziah felt
quite comfortable, and stayed there thinking, as if she
meant to make it her abode for the rest of the day.

"Quite the best thing she could do," murmured
Keziah, and the words applied to the retreat of her
sister-in-law to rest in the south wing. "She is quiet
there, and Fry's at hand to wait on her, and it saves
me an immense deal of trouble. It *is* a strain to have
to make conversation without ceasing for a person
with whom you have no sympathies in common; or,
rather, who has none with you. As to that horrible
old Mrs. Kage, I could have found it in my heart to
put a pitch-plaster on her mouth. She is more knave
than fool. Talk of her being imbecile, indeed! Just
because Thomas Kage was present, she said—that!
Caroline did not take it up; that was a blessing;
neither did he: but there was a look in his eyes I did
not like to see. Thanks be to all the saints that the
man has gone again! If he were to stay in the neighbourhood, mischief might come of it. Only to think
of her walking there and back because *he* was going

to walk! He has great influence over her. And he is one of those inconveniently straightforward men that might prove troublesome if his suspicions were aroused as to—to anything. I should like to know what brings him down here. Not Caroline's interests, though—as I feared when old Owen first said he was come. I'm sure my heart leaped into my mouth; I felt that I ought to telegraph to Barby. But it's all right. I'll just mention that he has been here when I write to Barby presently; and if Barby chooses—my goodness! why, there he is!"

The last words applied to Barby himself. An open fly had driven in and was approaching the hall-steps; in its inmate—a gentleman who leaned back with rather a pompous air—Keziah surely thought she recognised Barby. Did the sun's rays deceive her?— they were shining right into her eyes, dazzling her sight—and she thought it must be so. The traveller took off his hat, and gave it a gentle wave by way of greeting. It was Barby. Keziah sounded a peal on the visitors' bell to bring out the servants.

Major Dawkes came up the steps, and Keziah received him with a warm embrace—which he did not seem to appreciate sufficiently. She led the way to the sitting-room, and stirred the fire into a blaze.

"All well?" asked the Major, taking off his over-coat, and standing on the hearth-rug to warm his hands.

"Quite well," answered Keziah. "Except that I fear Caroline grows weaker."

"Does she?—dear me! Where is she?" added the Major, looking round the room.

"She has just gone to lie down, Barnaby. What will you take?"

"Nothing at present. Is Kage down here?"

And, with the last question, Keziah's understanding was opened: Major Dawkes must have heard of Mr. Kage's visit, and had come to checkmate it.

Even so. Keziah was an accurate guesser. On the previous afternoon, chance, or luck, or whatever the genius might be that presided over the interests of Barnaby Dawkes, had taken that gentleman's lawyer to Mr. Kage's chambers. So vast a property as the Major had dropped into—or, to be correct, his wife, but it came to the same practically—had its complications. More than once, Mr. Kage, as the previous acting trustee, had to be referred to for details connected with the past management. Some need of this kind took lawyer Jessup to the barrister's chambers, and there he heard that Mr. Kage had just gone down to Chilling. Later in the day, another chance, or accident, caused Major Dawkes to call at his lawyer's —the objects of the two visits being quite unconnected with each other. While there, the lawyer incidentally mentioned the item of news he had heard—that Mr. Kage had gone to Chilling.

"To see your wife, Major, no doubt," innocently quoth old Jessup, who had not the faintest notion of anything that might be involved, or of the sudden turn the suggestion gave the Major.

"Ah, yes, possibly so; they are cousins," drawled the Major, stroking his black moustache, and relieving his feelings by a little mental swearing.

The Major would have liked to drive direct to the Paddington Station and take the first train for Chilling.

That might not be, however; but he made arrangements to leave in the morning. Down he came, as fast as the engine would bring him; his mind rather inconveniently tormenting itself as to the motive that had taken Thomas Kage thither. That it was to see Mrs. Dawkes he assumed to be a matter of course; but— with what object? Conscience makes cowards of the best of us—it made a coward of the Major oftener than his friends might think—and is apt to suggest all kinds of improbabilities. The least he feared was, that Mr. Kage had gone down to inform his wife she ought to make a will. There might be one or two things in life Major Dawkes dreaded more than that, but he dreaded it quite enough.

She might be leaving half the fortune away from him, once she got the idea of a will put into her head, as the Major's common sense told. He did not intend she should. Having come to revel in the sweets of wealth, it would not be pleasant to relinquish any of it. Major Dawkes was living rather a fast life, spending the late Mr. Canterbury's money wholesale. The principal he could not touch; but he made free as air with the large amount returned as interest.

Keziah, feeling at rest as to the reason of his sudden appearance, slipped off the shawl, and took up her knitting.

"Is Kage down here?"

"Yes."

"What has he come for?"

"I was asking the very same question of myself just as you arrived, Barnaby. I don't know."

"Where the deuce is he staying? In the house?"

"Certainly not," quietly answered Keziah, as she

told, in a few words, all she knew of the matter—the hearing of his arrival from Owen the doctor, and Mr. Kage's subsequent visit. Major Dawkes listened with a gloomy brow.

"O, yes, I daresay! It's all very well for you to tell me he is going back to-morrow morning, and will not call here again. I don't believe it."

"You may depend upon one thing, I think, Barnaby: that, whatever business may have brought him here, it is not connected with Caroline."

"You are a fool, Keziah," politely rejoined the Major.

"Not where you are concerned," was Keziah's composed answer. "You had never cause to charge me with being that in the years gone by."

"Do you suppose she wrote for him?"

"Who?—Caroline? I am sure she did not. She has never put pen to paper since we came to the Rock. Had you seen the quiet apathetic manner with which she received him when he came in this morning, you would put aside all idea of her having sent for him—or of her wishing to see him either."

"The man must want something, Keziah. He'd not come all this cursed long railway journey for pleasure. What interests has he in Chilling but Caroline? Don't tell me."

Keziah, knitting always, silently revolved the points in her mind. There was reason in what Barby said. On the other hand, she could not disbelieve her sight, and ears, and senses generally. Thomas Kage had paid but a formal call, as any other stranger might do, and was certainly not coming again.

"That man has been a sort of enemy to me through

life; cropping up at all kinds of unseasonable times," observed the Major, giving the rich and thick hearthrug a passionate kick.

"But you have always managed to hold your own against him in the long-run," quietly returned Keziah.

"Yes, and will still. I'm sure I wish the fellow was buried; there's no man living I——"

Major Dawkes came to a sudden pause. "I dread so much as him," had been the words on the tip of his tongue. But it was not always convenient to speak out his full thoughts, even to Keziah.

"Look here, Keziah. The man must have come down on some matter connected with Caroline; and I don't care what you say to the contrary. He may have got it in his head—and my firm belief is that he has —that she ought to make a will. Considering the faculty he has for mixing himself up with other people's affairs, it's only what he might be expected to do. He has come here to see whether she has done it, and to suggest it to her."

"I tell you no, Barnaby," reiterated Keziah. "He did not hint at such a thing; he never said a word to her that anybody could disapprove of. The conversation was upon the most indifferent topics you can imagine. I was with them all the time."

Major Dawkes twirled the corners of his moustache savagely. Things did not look absolutely clear.

"Does *she* ever express a wish to make one?"

"Never. I do not suppose the thought or wish has occurred to her. I feel quite sure she looks upon you as her legal successor here."

"And of course I am such," interjected the Major.

"One day last week we were on the lawn; Caroline

sat down to rest; things were looking beautiful. A remark slipped from me quite involuntarily, that I hoped you, when you were sole master here, would keep the gardeners to their duty, as they were kept now. 'Yes, indeed; if I thought otherwise, I should be sorry to leave the place,' she answered. Barnaby, rely upon it, she has no thought of leaving anything away from you."

The Major felt a little reassured.

"A will is an inconvenient article, you see, Keziah. Once a man (or woman) sets himself to make one, he may be led away to leave no end of property to individuals indiscriminately."

"Ease your mind," was Keziah's assuring answer. "Caroline has no thought of doing it; and if she had, I am at hand, remember. She is in a state of complete apathy; I don't believe she cares one iota whose the property is, or who will inherit it after her."

The Major let fall his coat-tails, which he had picked up under his arm, and moved off the hearth-rug.

"I'll go up and see her. South wing, isn't it? A curious freak, to take up her abode in that gloomy place."

"She is quiet there, you see; and to be quiet is all she cares for now. As to the wing being gloomy, I think the rooms are very nice and comfortable."

"And look out on a howling wilderness," observed the Major. "If I recollect rightly, that is the chief prospect the windows possess."

"There are some charming hills and other scenery in the distance."

"Every one to his taste: distant hills possess no attractions for me."

Without giving himself the trouble to knock, the Major opened the green-baize door, which was rarely bolted in the day-time, and entered. Fry came flying out of the room close by, and stood in utter astonishment at sight of the visitor.

"Which room is your mistress in?"

"She—she's in her sitting-room, sir," was Fry's answer, when her surprise allowed her to speak. "I'll tell her you are here."

Caroline was lying on the sofa. She felt equally surprised with Fry at sight of the Major, but did not evince it. Rising from the sofa, she coldly shook hands with him, and then sat down on it. The Major had seemed to understand for some time now that he must not attempt any warmer greeting.

"How are you, my dear?" inquired the Major, taking up the position he had taken below—his back to the fire.

"Middling. I am not very strong."

"Dear me! You look pretty well, too."

At that moment perhaps she did. A red flush, born of aversion and other complicated feelings, had risen to her face latterly whenever he appeared in her presence, and was illumining it now.

"I've been wanting to run down for this week past; couldn't get the time until yesterday," cried the truthful Major. "Lots of duties on hand just now in town."

"A pity you left them."

"Came down to see you, and Kez, and how things

were getting on here. Wish you could pick up a bit, my dear."

Mrs. Dawkes, sitting in what seemed to be the completest state of apathy, made no response. He began again:

"Hear you've had a visitor to-day—Kage. Awfully astonished to find he was down here. Passed him in the street in town but a few days ago."

Again no answer.

"What has Kage come to Chilling for?"

"I did not ask him."

"Lively and agreeable this," thought the Major. And no doubt it was.

"I hope Kage came for the purpose of seeing you, Caroline, my dear. It's good to be remembered by one's old acquaintances."

"He did not come to see me. If he had come for that, he would have said so."

"Does he make a long stay?"

"He goes again to-night, or to-morrow; I forget which he said. Keziah would know."

Beyond these short answers, nothing could the Major get. He strove to make himself agreeable; told an amusing anecdote or two; but they sufficed not to arouse Caroline from her cold resentful state. The Major swallowed down about fifteen yawns.

"By the way," said he briskly, "there used to be some fencing-sticks of mine here. Do you happen to know where they were put?"

"I don't know anything about them."

"I had them here when we were first married, Caroline. Briscoe came down to stay, you may remember; and we used to come up to the big room of this wing—the one you make your bed-chamber now, I suppose—and have a fencing-bout."

"I don't know anything about them," repeated she, in the same inert tone.

The Major walked to the door and called Fry, telling her what he was inquiring after.

"There was a lumber-closet somewhere here; we used to throw them into it when done with. Perhaps they are in it yet."

Fry felt discomposed. It was from this self-same lumber-closet that the way led down to the postern entrance. The Major, suddenly remembering the position of the closet, threw open the door.

A way had been cleared inside it for Mr. Kage to come through on the previous night, consigning all the "lumber" on either side. It lay indiscriminately, one thing upon another. As the Major stood contemplating the interior from the door—as well as the semi-light enabled him — he faced exactly the panelled entrance, so bare now. Well indeed was it, for the sake of justice, that the panel gave to the eye no indication of its secret opening.

Fry, her eyes dilating a little, made a furious onslaught on the lumber, and blocked up the cleared passage. The Major, standing just inside, suddenly saw his wife at the entrance-door, her face pale and scared.

"What is it?" she asked. "What is the matter?"

"We are looking for the fencing-sticks. Don't you come, my dear."

"Look here," said Fry, stopping in her work. "If the Major would leave me, and you'd leave me, ma'am, perhaps I might find 'em. I think I've seen 'em here."

"Whereabouts?" cried the Major eagerly.

"I never can do anything when I'm looked at and bothered; my mistress knows I can't," was Fry's answer. "Both of you just leave me to myself, sir, and I'll find the sticks if they are to be found."

But, as she spoke, something caught the Major's quick eye. He drew it up; it proved to be one of the fencing-sticks. This gave an indication to the locality of the other, and it came to light soon. When Caroline went back after the investigation, her chest was heaving with ominous quickness.

"The commotion has disturbed you, I fear," observed the Major. "I'm really very sorry. These fencing-sticks—"

He was interrupted. Neel had come up to say that a visitor was below—Mrs. Dunn.

"Plague take it! who wants to see her?" cried the Major. "Mrs. Dunn! I thought she was abroad."

"The family thought so too, sir," observed Neel, who considered the old family far more than he did the new one. "Mrs. Dunn came to Chilling yesterday, and surprised them."

"She's a horrid woman," cried the Major.—"Will you come down, my dear?"

"No," was Mrs. Dawkes's answer.—"Just say, if you please, Neel, that I am very tired and poorly. I do not feel equal to it."

"I can say that. I suppose I must go," grumbled the Major, stalking off with his fencing-sticks.

Mrs. Dunn, in very fashionable foreign attire—quite a contrast to anything ever assumed by Keziah Dawkes —sat on a sofa in the grand drawing-room, to which Neel had shown her. There was no fire; at which she gave her head a disdainful toss, and remarked to Neel that the ways of the house appeared to be altered.

"And so they are, ma'am," answered Neel confidentially. "Miss Dawkes is manager."

"O! Mrs. Dawkes gives it up to her, then?"

"Mrs. Dawkes has never gave a single blessed order since she came into the house this last time," was Neel's reply. "She don't care who gives 'em, and who don't; she's too ill for it, ma'am."

Major and Miss Dawkes, the latter with her knitting, presented themselves together; and Mrs. Dunn condescended to give each in succession the tip of her forefinger. Neel could not despise these new people half as much as she did. The feeling peeped out in her manner too, in spite of her surface civility.

"Too ill to come down to me, is she!" cried Mrs. Dunn, receiving the apologies for the non-appearance of the Rock's mistress. "I hear she *is* ill, and I am sorry for her."

"Too tired to come, I said," corrected the Major. "On the whole, she is rather poorly."

"If what I am told be true, she is a great deal more than poorly, Major Dawkes," retorted Mrs. Dunn. "Owen, with whom I was talking this morning, fears you'll not have her very long amidst you."

"Dear me!" cried the Major, with a start of dismay. "But Owen always did look on the black side of things, I remember. *I* think her somewhat better than she was when I was here last."

"*You* know, I suppose, how it is—that she is alarmingly ill?" resumed Mrs. Dunn, turning the fire of her tongue on Keziah.

"I do not know that she is alarmingly ill," was Keziah's composed answer, given very slowly, for she was picking up some stitches in the everlasting knitting. "Mrs. Dawkes is certainly weak and languid; but I hope she will soon regain strength."

"It was the state she is represented to me as being in that brought me here this afternoon. I should have liked to see her, poor thing; I knew her when she was a child. It is her boy's death, they say, that has brought on her illness."

But the Major denied this rather vehemently. His wife had been at death's door before the boy died, he observed; her lungs and chest were weak.

Mrs. Dunn left her sofa without ceremony, and took a seat that faced the Major and Miss Dawkes. It was this same magnificent room that had witnessed the contention about the will between Olive Canterbury and her father. Not an executed will at that time, only a purposed one. Caroline had no doubt remembered the scene often enough since, when sitting there.

"What did that boy die of, Major Dawkes?"

The question was a pointed one; especially so as Mrs. Dunn put it. Bending forward, her eyes fixed on the Major, save when they wandered to Keziah, her voice low and full of meaning, — it was thus she asked it.

"It's of no use to recall it now," replied the Major, looking down on the rich carpet—out at the window —to the walls of the room. Anywhere except at her.

"But it is of use. I ask to know. You were in the midst of it; I was abroad, shut out from all news, except hearsay. As I remarked to Mr. Kage at our

dinner-table last night, when I besought him to tell
me."

"And pray what might he have told you, Mrs.
Dunn?" inquired the Major, not with so much polite
indifference as Keziah would have liked to hear.

"He said he could tell me nothing, except what I
knew before—that the doctors said the boy died from
poison."

"Ah, yes," replied the Major, "they did say it.
But doctors are mistaken sometimes, and I think they
were."

"That's rubbish, Major Dawkes," was Mrs. Dunn's
complimentary answer. "You don't really think so.
The doctors could not have dreamt they found opium
within the boy, if none was there. Do you mean to
charge them with telling a falsehood?"

Keziah's knitting was trembling a little. But she
kept her attention on it. As to her lips, they seemed
to be compressed into nothing. Happening to glance
at her, Mrs. Dunn thought she was unusually gray.

"I don't charge them with anything, Mrs. Dunn,"
resumed the Major. "I only think they were mistaken."

"And I say I don't believe you think it. The
opium was in the child, safe enough; it was proved so.
What I want to ask you is—who gave it him?"

Keziah looked off her knitting and took up the
answer. She could bear it no longer. Her lips were
turning strangely white.

"That never was ascertained. It was proved beyond all dispute or doubt that the child had not taken
anything of the kind; had not been in the way of tak-

ing it. It was an absolute impossibility that any such
thing had come near him."

"An absolute fiddlestick," said Mrs. Dunn. "Of
course it is to your sister's interest and yours, Major
Dawkes, to uphold this view and stifle farther inquiry;
but you cannot expect commonsense people to believe it."

"To my—my interest!" retorted the Major, with
a kind of stammer.

"To be sure it is. Haven't you come in for the
child's money?"

"Certainly I have not," said the Major boldly.
"The money reverted to the boy's mother, not to me."

"It reverted to her in name. Not, I expect, in
fact. Who draws the cheques, pray? Major Dawkes,
you cannot play at sophistry with me."

Major Dawkes rose and walked to the window with
an air of easy carelessness, gazing out upon the setting
sun. Keziah looked as if she were going to be sick.

"Had I been in England, I should have caused
the investigation to be reopened," said Mrs. Dunn.
"Mr. Kage, as the boy's trustee, was culpably careless
not to enforce a more searching one. One would
think it would be as satisfactory to you to come to the
bottom of it, as to us," she added, throwing a full
look after him.

"Immensely so," acquiesced the Major. "I begged
the medical men not to leave a stone unturned. The
authority lay in my hands, not in Mr. Kage's; but he
could have done no more than I did."

"Had I been he, I should have tried at it. There's
a secret in the matter somewhere, Major Dawkes, and

it ought to have been got at. It ought to be still. For two pins, I'd reopen the inquiry myself."

"It would do no earthly good, and be a frightful amount of trouble," spoke the Major, somewhat hurriedly.

"It would be a trouble, of course; but I think I should rather like it. He stood to me in the light of half-brother, absurd though it sounds to say it of a little fellow of that age."

"My firm persuasion is, that the boy died from nothing but his illness," said the Major in a candid tone, as he returned to his seat. "I went over the matter fully, point after point, at the time, and since, and I am quite unable, as my sister here knows, to arrive at any other conclusion. It was very much to be regretted that I was away from home."

"Well, it strikes me as being one of the most unaccountably mysterious cases I ever came across: nothing satisfactory about it in any way. But I can't stay to talk farther of it now," concluded Mrs. Dunn, rising to depart. "The rectory people and Thomas Kage are coming in to dine with us, and I like to take my time in dressing."

"Is Mr. Kage's visit at Chilling to you?" asked the Major on the impulse of the moment.

"I suppose it may be considered to my sister Millicent; they are engaged to be married," she replied.

And as Barnaby Dawkes heard the avowal, he felt as if a whole weight of lead had been lifted from his heart.

In an airy, graceful, sprightly manner, as though no care or dread had ever oppressed his soul, he attended Mrs. Dunn to the very extreme gates of the Rock, chatting amicably, and sending his respects to the Miss Canterburys. Keziah had disappeared when he returned, and he did not see her again until dinner. They took the meal together; Caroline remaining in her own room.

"*That's* what has brought Kage down," he observed to Keziah, alluding to the information volunteered by Mrs. Dunn of the engagement to Millicent.

"Yes, Barby dear. I knew it had nothing to do with us."

"Wish him joy of her! I'd not like one of the Canterburys for my wife. And, Keziah—keep that woman, civilly, at arm's distance; the Dunn. Don't let her get near Caroline, if you can help it. Her tongue's made of fire."

"All right," nodded Keziah.

With the morning Mr. Kage started for London. The Major stayed to see the coast clear of him, and then departed himself, his fears dispersed. Disagreeable doubts were over; and Barnaby Dawkes went gleefully back into the sunshine of the London streets, that to him might be said to be paved with gold.

CHAPTER XXI.

The Lawyer's secret Visit.

MAJOR DAWKES departed, and the Rock was its own quiet self again. A strangely monotonous abode now, its attractions, its fine rooms, its natural beauties, going for naught to those two silent women living in it—the one so hard and gray, something like a block of stone; the other passing swiftly and surely on to the tomb that must soon incase her. That each had her inward cares, was indisputable. Keziah was never quite free from a living dread—a dread of some vague danger on Barby's account—that would not quite keep itself down; it tinted the charming landscape, it gave a bitter taste to the dishes she ate of, it poisoned her pleasure sleeping and waking. It seemed to her that this danger would pass with Mrs. Dawkes's life; once she was beyond speaking, the fear would be nearly completely over. Barby would be in full possession of the Rock and its large revenues then, and who might dare to breathe a slander on him? Never a word had passed between her and her brother on that inconvenient subject, the death of the child; but Keziah, a shrewd sensible woman, had discerned odds and ends of things for herself. What Caroline knew or knew not, she did not dare to glance at; *something*, she feared; else why the life of estrangement she had lived ever since from her husband, and which he acquiesced in as a matter of course, without a dissenting word? Strangers could not be more entirely separate than they were; and Mrs. Dawkes took no trouble to hide the fact. There were moments when Keziah awoke out of her sleep in a great horror—a sleep in which she had seen Barnaby in the hands of men who are the administrators of England's criminal laws; and Caroline was invariably the Nemesis that brought him to his punishment. Keziah knew these were but miserable dreams, the result of the waking nightmare that was ever upon her; but nevertheless her limbs would shake in the bed with terror, her hair be wet with a cold perspiration. There could be no true safety for Barby, or peace for her, until Mrs. Dawkes should have been removed from the world; and Keziah, while pitying her, saw every fresh sign of weakness with a feeling that was certainly not sorrow. Barnaby's sins might be very great; but he was dearer to Keziah's heart than all the rest of the world. Had the whole inhabitants of the globe been ranged on one side, and Barnaby on the other, she would have sacrificed them all to him, had there been need of it.

Major Dawkes might well return to town in full reliance on his sister. No undesirable visitors would be admitted to any private interview at the Rock; no opportunity afforded for so much as a documentary line being executed, let alone a will. Keziah was a sure and vigilant keeper. The strain on herself, taking one hidden thing with another, was great just now; but she looked for the time when it should be removed for ever, and she and Barnaby be at liberty to breathe again. One great consolation attended it all: Caroline's state of inert apathy. It was quite apparent that she intended no active ill to her husband; it was equally apparent that never a thought of leaving her money away from him had place within her. It some-

times crossed Keziah's mind to question whether Mrs.
Dawkes remembered the fact, that the disposal of her
property lay in her own power.

What with Caroline's almost certain denial to visitors—between her own distaste for it and Keziah's
manœuvring, that was sure to be the result when callers
came—the Rock had been deserted by such before the
time of Mr. Kage's visit. After his departure, Mr.
Rufort took to come with rather inconvenient persistency. The fact was, Thomas Kage had told him
he ought to see Mrs. Dawkes occasionally, considering
the uncertain state of health she was in—or, rather, its
too certain state; and Mr. Rufort acted on it. He got
at length to see the mistress of the Rock, going in
and out with tolerable regularity. But, like the doctor,
he never got to see her alone. Just as Keziah invariably accompanied Mr. Owen to the rooms in the south
wing, so did she accompany Mr. Rufort. Mr. Rufort
hinted that he should like to be, in his capacity as
Christ's minister, alone with the sick lady. Keziah
practically refused to take the hint. She liked Mr.
Rufort's visits, she said; they did her good. When
Mr. Rufort said, that in praying with his sick parish-
ioners he preferred to be alone with them, Keziah
rejoined that she liked prayers. Mr. Rufort yielded:
for Caroline besought him in a private whisper—with
anxious eyes of entreaty, and a clasp of the hand to
pain—not to insist on the point; at least, at present:
time enough for it when she should be nearer death.
Mr. Rufort felt altogether a little puzzled, but said no
more; and Keziah enjoyed the personal benefit of the
prayers.

Had Keziah Dawkes been told that her sister-in-law was, in one sense, acting a part, she had refused credence to it. With all her knowledge of human nature, its wiles and concealments, its tricks and its turns, she had never believed that Caroline was deceiving her; or that the weak woman lying in the south wing, to all appearance in utter inertness, in complete apathy, could be plotting and planning as anxiously as the best of them. But it was so.

Caroline set about what she had to do with more cautious dread than there was a necessity for. From the moment she had parted with Thomas Kage, the night of his secret visit by the postern-door, her mind and brain had been incessantly on the rack, thinking how she could get Mr. Norris the solicitor to her. The unexpected visit of her husband startled her so effectually, that for some days she let the matter rest. Over and over again she asked herself the question: Had he suspected what she was about to do, and come down in consequence? Fully did Caroline believe that nothing, save the watching over his own interests, would bring him away from London. The terror she had felt when he went to the lumber-closet in search of the fencing-sticks, she felt still: it had seemed a confirmation of her fears. The Major's departure, after only one clear day's stay, somewhat reassured her; but even then, for some days, she did not dare to move in it. The time came, however. And while Keziah was knitting fresh patterns into her woollen work below, congratulating herself, rather than the contrary, that her sister-in-law was lying more of her hours away than usual in inert listlessness, shut up alone in the south wing, with Fry within hearing of the silver bell, Caroline was up and doing. Not that the term "up and doing" could be applied to poor Caroline in any but the slightest degree.

"My dear Mr. Norris,—I have an urgent reason for wishing to see you, and to see you alone. It is essential that your visit to me should be kept entirely private, from my household as well as from people in general. Please *note this*. Will you be at the postern-gate of the south wing to-morrow evening at seven o'clock? Fry will be waiting for you, and bring you up to me. She will take this note to you, and carry back your verbal answer. I rely upon you, as my first husband's legal adviser, and I may add friend: I have no one else to rely upon. Be very cautious.

"Very sincerely yours,
"Caroline Dawkes."

Mrs. Dawkes sat reading this note after it was written. It was the third she had attempted. Neither of the others pleased her, and they were already in the fire.

"I think it will do," she murmured, as she folded and sealed it.

Fry had her instructions. It was necessary for Caroline to place some confidence in her; but she did not tell her what she wanted with Mr. Norris. Fry was trustworthy; and thought the little private programme as good as a play.

Caroline went down to dinner that day; she said she felt better. Keziah thought she looked it: the fact was that the excitement caused by the consciousness of what she was doing imparted some life and colouring to the faded countenance. Rather to Keziah's surprise, Caroline did not go up after dinner, but settled herself in an arm-chair. It was not often she dined below now; but if so, she went away when the meal was over. Of course, Keziah was full of congratulation; she talked to her sister-in-law, and read to her a short story from a magazine. Just as it had concluded, Caroline was taken with a shivering fit, and Miss Dawkes rang for a warm shawl. Mr. Owen did not much like these attacks of shivering—they had come on three or four times lately; he thought, though, they were purely nervous.

"Where's Fry?" demanded Miss Dawkes, when the shawl was brought in by the upper housemaid.

"Fry's gone out, ma'am. She said she wanted to buy herself some aprons."

"She has no right to go out when she knows her mistress may want her at any moment," sharply returned Keziah. "Did she ask your leave, Caroline?"

"I forget," answered poor Caroline. "I heard her say she wanted some new aprons."

"She ought to have gone in the day-time," persisted Keziah, who had no notion of Fry's doing as she pleased without permission. "Suppose you had wanted to go to bed?"

"Don't be angry with her, Keziah. I keep her in so very much; except to church, she never goes out; and she must buy herself necessary things."

Keziah let the matter drop. Fry was gone, as the reader knows quite well, to Mr. Norris. It was only in the evening she could see him; for he was all day long at his office at Aberton. Fry had cleverly made the aprons the ostensible excuse to the household.

The reader may think that all comment might have

been avoided by Fry's going out by way of the postern-
door.   But the truth was, poor Caroline had got into
that nervous state, that she was afraid to be alone in
the south wing after dark.   What with the surroundings
of little Tom's death (so dreadful to her imagination),
and the reputation of the ghost that was wont to hover
around the Lady's Well outside the windows, Caroline
preferred company to solitude.

It was a bright starlight night when Fry went forth.
Mr. Norris's residence was situated a little beyond the
rectory, as the reader may remember; for he once went
to it with Miss Canterbury.   She knoked at the door
and asked for the lawyer.

"Not at home."

"Not at home?" retorted Fry, as if the man, an
old acquaintance of hers, were telling a story.   "Mr.
Norris gets home before this."

"He do mostly.   He's late to-night.   Is it anything
I can say to him?"

"No—I think not," replied Fry, as if in delibera-
tion.   "I just wanted to say a word to him myself.   It
can wait."

But, even as she was speaking, Mr. Norris himself approached the door.   He had come from Aberton by the usual train, but had called on some friend
at Chilling.

"To see me, Fry?   Come in, then.   I suppose
it's about that money you let your brother have?"
added the lawyer, as he led the way to a sitting-
room.

"Yes, sir," was Fry's bold answer, for the benefit
of any ears that might be open.   "If he can't give

me the money back, he might try and pay me interest."

But, when the door was closed, she presented the note in silence, and waited. Mr. Norris read it, glanced at Fry, and read it again.

"Do you know the purport of this?" he asked.

"Well, sir, I b'lieve it is to ask you to come to the Rock to-morrow night; and I am to let you in by the postern-door."

"Just so. Your mistress says she wishes to see me."

He looked at Fry, and she looked at him. Each of them would have liked to speak out pretty freely to the other.

"I fancied that postern entrance was wholly unused, Fry. It's years since I've heard it mentioned; I'm not sure but I had half forgotten there was such an entrance."

"It was me that thought of it," said Fry, proud of being able so far to compliment her own memory. "There's folks in our house no better than watchful cats, and the servants be nothing but tattling gossipers."

"And your mistress is virtually a prisoner, eh, Fry?"

"Well, I don't know but she is, sir. For one thing, she don't seem to care to be anything else. As to the Rock, that was once so gay, it seems no better now than a dungeon. A rare bother I had to get that postern-door open. What message am I to take back, sir?"

"Say to Mrs. Dawkes that I will come. She men-

20*

tions seven: at that hour I will be at the postern-door."

"All right," said Fry. "If you will come into the grounds, sir, by that little private gate on the south side, it will bring you past the Lady's Well to the postern-door; and you'll not be likely to meet anybody, my mistress says. I don't suppose you mind about what used to be talked of—that the way was haunted?"

"Not very much," said Mr. Norris, with a silent laugh. "I hear your mistress is looking very ill, Fry."

"She is just as ill as she looks," was Fry's answer. "It won't be long, sir, as far as I believe, before she goes after the poor child she's always regretting."

Mr. Norris saw Fry out himself, whispering to her a last charge, to be at her post in readiness for him on the following night. Fry dashed on to the general shop in the village—for her wanting the new aprons had been no false excuse—and went home with the checked muslin in triumph. Keziah said a sharp word to her—poor Caroline was in weary waiting for her bed—which Fry flung back again.

And when the next day came, circumstances seemed really to be favouring Caroline. She was so weak, and looked so ill, that Keziah, paying her morning visit, advised her not to move out of her room all day. At dusk Fry was downstairs; and coming in contact with Miss Dawkes, said her mistress was still in bed, and had given her orders to close up the green-baize door for the night, wishing for perfect quiet in the wing. Miss Dawkes nodded her head complacently, and told Fry to be cautious not to make any noise herself.

But the first thing Fry did, after bolting and barring the said door, was to assist her mistress to dress and proceed to the sitting-room. The fire burnt with a bright blaze, the room had its full amount of light. Caroline, sipping her tea, looked the only faded thing in it. She wore her usual black-silk gown—a mile too large for her; it was covered with a shawl; and her beautiful hair hung carelessly. Excitement lent her both heat and colour. In the state of sickness she was, bodily and mentally, this coming interview with the lawyer, and what she must say at it, put her into a veritable fever.

"Fry! Fry!"

Fry came in at the nervous covert call.

"It is seven o'clock, Fry. You ought to be down at the postern-door."

Mrs. Dawkes had sat with her feverish eyes fixed on the mantelpiece clock. The hands were fast approaching the hour.

"It wants six minutes good, ma'am, by the right time; that clock is five minutes too fast. Mr. Owen said so when he was here to-day; and I know it besides."

"Mr. Norris's watch may be fast also. He must not be kept waiting, Fry."

"No fear. Them lawyers are never afore their time, ma'am, unless it is to sue a poor man for money."

"Fry, I tell you to go down. Better for you to wait than for Mr. Norris. He might go away again."

Fry, grumbling a little, took her lamp, and went down. Waiting at that dusty door, with the wind moaning amid the trees outside, and the ghost farther off—it was said to come always on a windy night— was not altogether agreeable. But she had not stood there long when footsteps were heard, the boughs were pushed aside, and Mr. Norris stood there.

"All right," he said. "How is your mistress to-night?"

"She is just as fidgety as she can be, thinking I should not be down here in time, and you might go away again," was Fry's answer. "I'll tell you what it is, sir: if the excitement of folks coming to her this way was to last, she'd just be in her grave before her time. All day long she has kept her bed, through nothing but the fever and worry she was in last night from knowing I had come to you. Can you see, sir? I'll go on with the lamp."

"These stairs don't get wider with age," remarked the lawyer, in a low tone.

"They are the steepest and narrowest stairs it was ever a lady's lot to go up or down," was Fry's answer; "which stands to reason, seeing they are built in the wall. I'd as soon come down a ladder: and sooner— there'd be less danger of pitching over."

"As I did once," said Mr. Norris.

"You!" exclaimed Fry, stopping to turn and look at him in the midst of the said stairs. "Were you ever here before, sir?"

"Yes; in the days of Edgar Canterbury. The place has never been dusted since that time, I should think, Fry. My gloves are covered."

"It has never been as much as opened, let alone dusted," answered Fry. "Here we are, sir."

With a light tread the lawyer stepped through the lumber-closet, and into the presence of Mrs. Dawkes. The shawl had slipped from her shoulders. Very thin and worn and shadowy did she look; and Mr. Norris could but contrast the poor faded thing before him with the beautiful and blooming girl whose entrance into the Canterbury family had caused so much trouble and heart-burning. He had hated the intruder in his heart of hearts, for a love of justice was implanted strongly within him; but in this moment his resentment passed away with a cry of pity, for he almost thought he was looking on the dead.

"Poor thing!" he involuntarily murmured, as he took her hand. "My dear, you are very ill."

"Yes," she answered, "the time is getting short now. That is why I was so anxious to see you."

Mr. Norris sat down by her, and they talked together in a low tone. The consciousness of the necessity of secrecy lay upon them, otherwise both knew it was impossible they could be overheard. Mr. Norris had been cognisant of the past troubles connected with Edgar Canterbury, and he knew this part of the house just as well as its present mistress.

Caroline told him what she wanted—a will made that would in a degree repair the injustice of the last one. Without speaking with the express plainness she had used to Thomas Kage, Mr. Norris gathered a vast deal. He nodded his head, and drew in his lips, and thought it was altogether about the most remarkable case he had ever come across.

"I could not die in peace if I did not make the

will," she said with feverish lips. "I should never rest
in my grave."

"My dear lady," he said, "there's no earthly reason
why you should not make one. It's what you ought
to do. As to that watchful person downstairs, I think
we can manage to keep her in the dark. If you were
in stronger health, I should advise a totally different
course of procedure; but—"

"But I am not strong enough for it," interrupted
Caroline with painful eagerness. "You mean open
opposition, the asserting of my own position and
rights; but if matters came to that, it would kill me."

"Yes, yes."

"Will you write down my instructions? I have
thought of all I wish to do—and say."

Mr. Norris took some paper from his pocket, a
pen, and a tiny ink-bottle. He began unscrewing the
stopper.

"I suppose it will be legal?" she said.

He did not understand. "What legal? the will?
Most certainly. Why should it not be?"

"I thought—because it is made in secret."

"As a vast many wills are made. Trust to me for
its being in due order. And now—"

What Mr. Norris was about to say received a most
startling interruption—startling, at least, to one who
heard it. It was a loud knocking at the green-baize
door, followed by the voice of Keziah Dawkes.

Caroline gave a faint cry. Were Mr. Norris to be
seen with her, all was at an end.

With her trembling hands clasped upon her bosom
—with her poor face whiter than ashes—with steps
that tottered as she stood, and a sick faintness that

seemed as if it must overpower her, Caroline looked forth.

"Don't answer, don't answer!" she breathed to Fry, who had appeared at her own door with a carelessly-defiant countenance.

"Not going to," nodded Fry in a whisper. "Let her think I've gone to bed myself.—That's right, Madam Dawkes; you can knock again."

"Fry! Fry!" cried out Keziah, "it's a letter for your mistress; it has "Immediate" marked upon it."

No response. Keziah went away grumbling. Things were come to a pretty pass, she thought, when servants went to bed at seven o'clock in the evening.

"All right, Madam Dawkes!" said impudent Fry; "you don't get over me. The letter will have to keep, though it came from the Pope o' Rome."

But later, when Mr. Norris, his business for the night accomplished, had been escorted down the postern-stairs and was safely away, Fry went to Miss Dawkes with a face as bold as brass. Asking whether, or not, anybody had knocked: she fancied to have heard it, but was engaged at the time with her mistress.

And the letter proved to be nothing but a note from Mr. Owen, containing some instructions in regard to the medicine Mrs. Dawkes was taking that he had omitted to give in the morning when paying his visit to the Rock.

"Shall I get the will executed, or not?" murmured poor Caroline from her sleepless bed, when the household was hushed in sleep. "It seems a great chance. Perhaps Heaven will help me!"

CHAPTER XXII.

The last and final Will.

IN the comfortable compartment of a first-class carriage, one of a train that was on its way to Chilling, sat Major Dawkes. It was not a cold day by any means, for spring sunshine lay on the earth, wooing the hedges to start into bud, the flowers to blossom; but Major Dawkes liked to travel warmly, and a rich fur wrapper, lined with wool and scarlet silk, lay on his knees. His cheeks wore their usual bloom, his whiskers were of the same old purple richness, and the Major was decidedly getting plump; but he composed his countenance to a grave sadness befitting the occasion, for he was hastening down to his wife's deathbed.

At least, he would have told you he was hastening —as he did incidentally tell the old lady and gentleman seated opposite to him in the carriage—for he was rather given to indulge in little boasts of fiction. But the real fact was, that instead of hastening down, he had so contrived to retard his movements, that the closing scene would in all probability be over before he arrived. Which was what he secretly wished.

Mrs. Dawkes had lingered longer than was expected by herself, by her medical attendants, or by any one about her. Strange somewhat to say, with the cold weather of the winter she had rallied a little. If it could not be said that she grew materially better, at least she did not appear worse; her progress to the grave seemed to have made a halt—to have become for the time stationary. But the life she led was not any the less secluded; with the exception of the doctors and Mr. Rufort, she scarcely saw any one; visitors to her were, she acknowledged, utterly distasteful. The former restlessness of mind and manner had subsided, and given place to a still calmness. Very peacefully did she seem to wait for the coming death. Nay, to welcome it.

In February Mrs. Kage died. Keziah Dawkes, who took upon herself the ordering of matters, let her be buried without any needless ceremony; neither Major Dawkes nor Thomas Kage was invited to attend the funeral. Caroline seemed not to care one way or the other, and did not interfere; her poor mother was "better off," she said to Mr. Rufort, and it seemed to be her whole feeling in regard to it. So Keziah had it all her own way. Later, Mrs. Dawkes began herself to droop again; and when it became apparent that the end was close at hand, Keziah sent up a telegram to her brother. The Major telegraphed back to say he was "on duty," but would get away as immediately as he could. He had always made "duty" a standing plea of excuse. Quietly suffering two days to elapse, the Major then went down.

The first person he saw at Chilling station was Mr. Carlton of the Hall: quite a young man in activity still, in spite of his more than seventy years. He happened to be on the platform when Major Dawkes alighted. The latter (privately wishing him a hundred miles off) went up with outstretched hand and a face as long as a walking-stick, mournfully hoping his dear wife was better.

"She is dead," said Mr. Carlton, privately believ-

ing just as much and as little of the displayed concern
as he chose.

"Dead! My wife dead!"

"She died at five o'clock this morning, Major
Dawkes. So you are somewhat late, you see. Some
of us thought you might have been coming earlier."

"Duty," groaned the Major, bolting into the
only fly waiting. "Dear me!—Richard, see to my
portmanteau."

Keziah, gray in face as ever, but intensely calm,
received him in one of the smallest and snuggest
sitting-rooms. He went through the same farce here
—the plea of "duty." *She* believed just as much as
she chose; but she held his hand in hers, and murmured her heartfelt thanks that he, her ever-beloved
brother, was free at last.

"Got any of the brown sherry up, Keziah?"

"Yes dear."

"I'll take some."

Miss Dawkes went and brought it in herself. The
Major drank two glasses of it at once, Keziah fondly
watching him.

"All's right, I suppose, Keziah?"

"All is quite right. But I don't exactly know what
you mean."

"She expressed no wish at the last about the
property, I suppose?"

"None. It was the same as usual to the last hour
of her life—utter indifference to all worldly things.
She never mentioned her property at all; I feel sure
she did not so much as think of it."

"All's mine, then."

"Everything, Barby dear, *everything*."

The Major tossed off another glass of the famous brown sherry—the same that Mr. Canterbury in his life-time used to boast of. Major Dawkes's head was strong; a few glasses more or less of good old wine made no difference to him.

"You see now the utility of my taking care that Caroline had no opportunity of making a will, Keziah. She might have got bequeathing some of her money to those Canterbury women."

"As if I should have allowed it!" responded Keziah. "Barnaby, it is an *immense* inheritance."

The Major smacked his lips; partly at the sherry, partly at the suggested thought. He liked to be reminded that he was a millionaire.

"You shall have a share in it, Kéz. I shall set you up in comfort for life. This is real property, you see; what I came into when I married was but a limited income."

Keziah smiled. "Limited!"

"Well, it *was;* in comparison. The bulk of the property lay in Kage's hands then, as the child's trustee. I wonder what he'll think now—hang him! Have you seen anything of the fellow lately?"

"No. He has not been down since that one visit. When Mrs. Dunn went up to her house in London for Christmas, she took the Miss Canterburys with her; and they have not long come back again. Lydia Dunn is with them. Kage has written to Caroline two or three times, but she gave me the letters to answer."

"What was in his letters?"

"Nothing much. Inquiries after health, and that. It is all right, Barby; it has all been smooth as glass."

Barby stroked his whiskers complacently. Yes, it

had all been smooth, his heart responded, and he was a vast inheritor.

"I wish to goodness that miserable old woman was alive now, Keziah; our ancient aunt. She'd open her eyes at my wealth. Her own, that she grudged me, was a flea-bite by the side of it."

"I wish she was, Barby. 'Twould give her a fit of the spleen."

There was a short pause. Major Dawkes turned and gave the fire a knock with his boot.

"Did she suffer much at the last?"

"O no," was the reply, for Keziah knew he was speaking of his wife. "She drifted out of life very quietly and calmly."

The conversation was interrupted by the entrance of Mr. Rufort. Hearing of the Major's arrival, he had come up to see him, having been charged with a note from Mrs. Dawkes. The Major took it wonderingly, perhaps with some inward trepidation; but it proved to be a very harmless missive indeed—merely expressing some wishes about her funeral.

She had first of all expressed them to Mr. Rufort in the presence of Keziah, though Keziah only partially gathered their purport, for she had been engaged at the moment in a wordy war with Fry. Mr. Rufort had suggested to Mrs. Dawkes that she should convey them in a note to her husband; and she so far complied as to pencil down the wishes on paper, put it in an envelope, and direct it to the Major, charging Mr. Rufort to deliver it.

It appeared that she desired the same friends and relatives to attend her funeral who had attended her former husband's—Mr. Canterbury. She wished the

Miss Canterburys to be invited to spend the day of the funeral at the Rock—as they had been at the former one—also Mrs. Rufort; and Mrs. Dunn, as she was staying at Chilling. In short, she directed that the arrangements for this funeral, with one notable exception, should be similar to the last that went out of the Rock. Mr. Canterbury had been put into his grave with all the pomp and pageantry of a theatrical show: she was to be taken to it with the smallest ceremony and expense that should be deemed consistent.

Major Dawkes, relieved of any private doubts, was all suavity. Had his late wife wished that the whole parish should be at the Rock that day, he would cordially have invited them.

"Your late wife's wishes appear very simple ones, Major Dawkes; I presume there will be no difficulty put in the way of their being carried out," observed the Rector.

"None in the world," heartily replied the Major.

"She seemed to make a great point of it—the dying have these fancies, you know—and begged me to see them carried out. I told her I could only urge it upon you, Major, and that she had better write to you herself."

"They are precisely my own wishes," spoke the complaisant Major. "Only the half of any wish, expressed by my dear departed wife, I can but look upon as a solemn charge, strictly to be complied with. Perhaps you will 'oblige me by giving in the list of people yourself, Mr. Rufort; I was not at Mr. Canterbury's funeral, and might make a mistake over it."

But, in one sense, he had been at Mr. Canterbury's funeral. For he had watched the pageant along the road, and made his comments. The recollection flashed into his mind now, bringing a flush to his face. His hopeless condition then, and his flourishing state now, were indeed a strange contrast.

"Who conducts the funeral?" he asked, turning to Keziah.

"I have given no orders," she replied. "I waited for you."

"I wonder who conducted Mr. Canterbury's?"

"I can tell you about that," said the Rector. "Young Mrs. Canterbury was inexperienced; and at her request Norris the solicitor undertook all the trouble of it, transmitting her wishes himself to the proper quarters. Of course he charged for his time."

"Then I think Norris had better undertake this one," spoke the Major in a fit of liberality. "You can write to him, Keziah."

In his anxiety that things should go smoothly, that all unpleasant reminiscences of the past should be kept down, as well as reflections on the present, Major Dawkes was eagerly desirous that these wishes of his wife's should be carried out to the letter. A conviction darted across him that it would be anything but agreeable to have the Canterbury family at the Rock on the day of the funeral, and he would very much indeed dislike the presence of Thomas Kage; but there was no help for it. If he refused compliance, how could he tell that something would not be made of it?—tongues were so venomous: and the very idea of any inquiry or unpleasantness turned him sick with an undefined fear. Refuse concession in this little matter, and people might but ask how he had come into all the money, and what right he had to it. No; the very consciousness that it might be suspected he had wished for his wife's death, made him all the more scrupulous, if only from prudential considerations, to carry out her wishes to the extreme letter. Had they been transmitted to him in private, he would simply have put them and the paper they were written on into the nearest fire; but they came publicly, through the Honourable and Reverend Austin Rufort.

"I should have refused, Barnaby, had I been you," remarked Keziah, as she finished the note to Mr. Norris, after they were left alone. "It will be frightfully disagreeable to have the Canterbury family here."

"You are a fool, Keziah."

"For myself I don't mind; but I am sure you will not like it, Barby dear," she resumed, passing over in silence the compliment to herself.

"Don't you see there was no help for it?"

"Yes, there was. You are now sole master here, and need fear no one."

"I don't know about fear," said the Major dreamily. "One likes to stand well in the world's opinion. The invitation must be given to them, and Kage also; but I should think the Canterburys will not accept it. They must feel that they have no business here, and will be quite out of place. How she came to think of so foolish a thing, is beyond me to imagine."

"Some idea of respect to their father and to them must have been floating in her weakened head, poor creature," surmised Keziah. "She was Mr. Canterbury's wife once, and would not have his daughters quite ignored at her funeral. I wish the day was over. Barnaby, if I were you I should let the Rock."

"I shall sell it," said the Major, improving upon
the suggestion. "If I can get my price for it."

He rather wished with Keziah that the funeral-day
was over; and it was fixed for an early one. The presence of those ladies and of Thomas Kage would no
doubt a little put him out of ease. But it could not
last more than its appointed hours, and he determined
to make the best of it, and act the host with courteous
grace. The anticipation did not disturb him; he was
in too gracious a mood for that. His golden dreams
were at last realised, and with the death of his wife all
tormenting dread had passed away. This magnificent
mansion and its magnificent revenues were his; his
only, as Keziah said; it was a costly nugget to have
come into: and that there could be any doubt that he
had come into it, never for the faintest shadow of a
moment crossed Major Dawkes's mind.

Once more a stately funeral issued from the Rock.
In one respect Major Dawkes ignored his dead wife's
commands, and abandoned the simplicity she had expressed a wish for. If the funeral procession was not
quite of the gorgeous nature that had characterised Mr.
Canterbury's, the show was at least sumptuous to look
at. In a coach all to himself, following next the hearse,
sat the bereaved Major, black with all the trappings of
woe. In the next were Thomas Kage and Austin
Rufort; the latter attending as mourner and relative
to-day, not as pastor. And so on, a string of coaches
and carriages imposing to the eye.

George Canterbury's daughters had accepted the
invitation to the Rock, very much to Major and Miss
Dawkes's secret surprise, as well as to that of the neigh-

bourhood. The only one of them who had fought against it was Mrs. Dunn. Millicent was passive as usual. Olive decided that they should go. After this day, all connection with the Rock and with the second family would be at an end, she observed; and it was well for the parting to have a peaceful feeling about it. Besides which, it was the last expressed wish of poor Caroline Dawkes, and therefore to be complied with.

So the four sisters, attired in suitable mourning, arrived at the Rock a short while before the hour fixed on for the funeral. They sat in the grand drawing-room—Olive, Mrs. Rufort, Mrs. Dunn, and Millicent. Keziah, in deep black, also was there, playing the hostess. Civility reigned, of course; but, in spite of effort, the conversation flagged, only a remark being made now and then. Once Mrs. Dunn, in her free way, found fault with some arrangement at the lodge, saying their carriage had waited at least three minutes for the gates to be opened. She could not tell, for her part, why they were closed at all.

"The keeper is getting negligent," observed Keziah; "my brother intends to discharge him. There are several alterations and changes he means to make; but he thought it as well to let them be during Mrs. Dawkes's life."

No answer from anybody. Mrs. Dunn had to bite her rebellious tongue though, which had a mind to tell Keziah that the power to make alterations before lay with the Major's wife, not with him.

A weary while it seemed to wait; and, in truth, even Olive wondered why they should have been summoned to the Rock, and thought it was somewhat of a mistake. But the coaches were coming back at last, with their slow tread, bearing the immediate personal friends of the family. The comparative strangers were taken home direct from the churchyard.

As the coaches stopped at the entrance, Major Dawkes (who had been privately hoping nobody would alight) found that everybody did alight, and that Norris the solicitor was taking upon himself to invite the company to enter. The Major turned rather red, and would have liked to resent the liberty; but, in the face of the gentlemen, could not say he did not want them to come in. While he hesitated, Mr. Norris walked forward, threw open the door of the library—a room scarcely used since Mr. Canterbury's time—and marshalled the people to it: Lord Rufort and his son, Mr. Carlton and Mr. Kage. Major Dawkes brought up the rear, and politely asked them if they would like to sit down. He could not imagine why they need have entered, or what fit of officiousness had taken Norris.

But Norris had disappeared. Only for an instant, when he came in with the ladies—Mr. Canterbury's daughters and Keziah. They all sat down; and then the lawyer addressed Major Dawkes.

"Shall we proceed now, sir, to read the will?"

Major Dawkes looked at him.

"Whose will?"

"Your late wife's, sir."

"Mrs. Dawkes made no will."

"Pardon me, Major; Mrs. Dawkes executed a will, all in due order. She wrote to me a few days before her death, stating it would be found in the large drawer of this bureau, quite at the bottom, beneath the old leases and the other out-of-date papers."

The lawyer touched a piece of furniture as he

spoke; but the widower smiled with incredulity. The attention of the whole room was aroused, and drawn to Mr. Norris.

"There is no will, I tell you," persisted the Major. "My wife never made one."

"Major Dawkes, she *did*."

"When and where?"

"In this house, some months ago," replied the lawyer. "I made it."

Miss Dawkes half rose from her seat. Her gray face had a scornful look on it; the gruffness of her voice was unpleasantly perceptible.

"Mrs. Dawkes made no will in this house; I can take upon myself to assert it; and you never were here, Mr. Norris."

"I beg your pardon, madam. I came here and took Mrs. Dawkes's instructions for a will. When it was prepared, I came again, and brought witnesses with me to attest her signature."

The words were spoken so calmly, in so matter-of-fact a tone, that the Major was startled. He turned a look, full of evil, upon his sister.

"It is false!" she cried, utterly refusing credence. "It is a conspiracy concocted amongst the Canterbury family to deprive you of your rights, Barnaby. I will pledge myself to the fact that Mrs. Dawkes made no will: she could not have done so without my knowledge."

"Your not having been cognisant of this is easily explained, madam," returned Mr. Norris. "Mrs. Dawkes became possessed of an idea that she was not quite a free agent in her own house: certainly was not permitted to be so much alone as she desired to be. She there-

fore retired to the south wing, and caused the baize
door to be erected to shut in her apartments.   This,
so far, is patent to you and to all.   Later, when she
had occasion to see a friend or two in private, she
ordered the small postern-door to be unfastened.   It
leads direct up to those apartments, and by that means
she was enabled to receive her visitors.   They were
confined, however, to one or two.   That is how I got
access to her."

"The postern-door?" gasped Miss Dawkes, after
taking in the sense of the lawyer's words with a
sickening heart.   "What postern-door? I did not know
there was one."

"Possibly not, madam.   You are, comparatively
speaking, a stranger here.   The door is hidden by
trees, and has never been used of late years."

Major Dawkes, amidst a multitude of feelings that
were anything but agreeable, began wondering whether
he had ever known of the postern-door.   At first he
could not decide; but a thought began to dawn over
him that he did once hear of this, and had afterwards
forgotten it.

"I can assure you Mrs. Dawkes made her will,"
persisted Mr. Norris.

"And I can assure you she never did," uselessly
persisted Keziah.

"The shortest way to settle it is to look in the
drawer and see if there is a will," interrupted Mr.
Carlton.   "Norris told me, coming back in the coach,
that I am one of the executors."

"You are," said Mr. Norris; "and Lord Rufort is
the other."

Lord Rufort sat still in his chair, too stately to be

moved by that, or by any other information; and there was a pause.

"We wait, sir," he said to Major Dawkes.

Major Dawkes was at bay.

"My lord, there is no will. I will equally pledge myself to it with my sister. It will be useless to examine the place."

"As you please, Major Dawkes," said Mr. Norris. "The will was made, and signed, in duplicate; and I took charge of the other copy. "To guard against possible accidents," Mrs. Dawkes said. I have it with me."

Major Dawkes, foiled, and doubly at bay, searched for the key and opened the drawer. There was the will. He could have gnashed his teeth, but for those around. He sat down, and bit one of the fingers of his black-kid glove.

"She may have left half the money away from me," he murmured in Keziah's ear, dashing his hair from his damp brow.

Mr. Norris opened the deed and put on his spectacles.

The will began by premising that no person whatever was a party to its contents: that it was the testatrix's own uncounselled act and deed, biassed by a sense of justice alone. There were a few legacies to servants and friends; the largest was one, fifty pounds a-year, to the nurse Judith for her life, and for her disposal at death; and there was a command that the remains of her little boy should be brought from the cemetery at Brompton, to be finally laid by herself and his father.

Mr. Norris then cleared his throat, and the Major turned red with expectation.

"I bequeath this mansion, the Rock, and all that it contains,—plate, furniture, books, pictures, together with the lands and revenues pertaining to it,—to Olive Canterbury, absolutely. I bequeath the whole of the money of which I may die possessed, the remainder of the lands, the houses (save and except the Rock), to the four daughters of my late husband, George Canterbury, to be shared by them in equal portions. I bequeath to Thomas Kage my gold watch and chain, with the locket, key, and seal attached; and I beg him to accept them a token of gratitude for his unvarying kindness to me and his solicitude for my best welfare. And I bequeath to my present husband, Barnaby Dawkes, the sum of five-and-twenty pounds, wherewith to purchase a mourning-ring, which he will wear in remembrance of my dear child, Thomas Canterbury."

Such, shorn of its technicalities, was the substance of the will.

An intense silence prevailed in the room. The surprise of all present was so great, that every tongue was tied. Only with their eyes did people look at each other, and seem to question whether it was a dream.

Major Dawkes sat, a pitiable object to look upon, like unto a man who has received his death-blow. Suddenly the perspiration, great drops of it, began breaking out on his livid face. Was it the fact of his entire disinheritance, or the peculiar allnsion to Thomas Canterbury, that caused his face to wear that deathly hue? He was a ruined man: yesterday he stood on a high pinnacle, vaunting his wealth and position; to-day he was hurled from it, and hurled from it for ever.

He felt reckless. "I dispute the will!" cried he, in his desperation. "Mr. Norris, you will take my instructions preparatory to setting it aside."

Mr. Norris smiled. "You forget that I am solicitor to the Canterbury family.—I presume I may say so much?" he added, turning to Miss Canterbury.

Olive bowed.

"Why, you might just as well tell the sun not to shine, as attempt to set aside a plain will like that, Major," cried Mr. Carlton. "Though I sympathise with your disappointment, Dawkes," he added, "I cannot imagine how you could so mortally have offended your wife, as to be cut off with nothing."

"Very strange indeed!" remarked Lord Rufort. And "Very strange indeed!" murmured everybody else, with the exception of the lawyer and Thomas Kage.

Mr. Rufort stepped forward, and held out a small parcel towards Mr. Kage.

"It is the legacy mentioned in the will," said he; "the watch and chain. Mrs. Dawkes gave it into my charge to convey to you."

And Thomas Kage rose and took it, a vivid flush of bygone recollections dyeing his face.

"I wonder you had not a better memento than that; a good thumping sum of money, for instance," exclaimed the unceremonious Mr. Carlton to Thomas Kage. "You were her nearest relative, save her mother; her only relative living. The chronometer is valuable, but counts for nothing as a legacy."

"In legacies from friends we do not look at value,

Mr. Carlton," was Thomas Kage's reply, given in a low tone.

But Miss Dawkes, only now beginning to recover her scared senses, could not let the matter rest. She must fight it out to the last.

"When my brother gives it as his opinion that this will has been concocted, he only states what is no doubt the fact. Perhaps *you* were her adviser, sir?"—turning sharply on Mr. Rufort.

"Indeed, no," Mr. Rufort quietly replied; "I had nothing to do with the will in any way. Mrs. Dawkes once said to me that her pecuniary affairs were settled, and that is all I ever heard. Had any one asked me, previous to this hour, to whom her fortune was most likely left, I should have answered, to her husband. I never supposed there was a doubt that he would have it."

"Were you one of the visitors we now hear of as sneaking in through the postern-door?" continued the angry lady.

"Certainly not. There was no necessity. I never knew the postern-door had been unfastened. Allow me to remind you, Miss Dawkes, that you invariably made a third at my interviews with Mrs. Dawkes, up to the last," pointedly concluded Mr. Rufort. "Had she wished for any private conversation with me, or I with her, the opportunity was not afforded for it."

True; very true. Keziah drew in her thin lips as she mentally acknowledged it. And O, of what avail had been all the precaution? Of all moments of Keziah's life, this was perhaps the most hopelessly miserable.

A general rise to leave shortly took place: to say

the truth, neither the Canterbury family nor the Dawkeses felt at ease. That this was but a restitution of the justice so long diverted, Olive knew; but it seemed to be harder than it need have been on Major Dawkes. Unless—a suspicion was crossing her mind that she started from with horror; and would willingly have put far away, but that thoughts are not under our own control. Mr. Norris approached the Major.

"You will be prepared to give up possession at your earliest convenience, Major," he said. "Not at your inconvenience, you know: I am sure Miss Canterbury would not wish that."

And perhaps, of all the shocks he had received during the past half-hour, this practical one was the most startling. Give up possession? Ay, give up possession of all: Major Dawkes's day was over.

It seemed impossible to realise it. Watching the carriages away, through the half-raised blind, it seemed simply impossible that it could be reality. A man of almost unlimited wealth when he rose that morning; his, the fair domain, stretched out far and wide; numerous servants who called him master; carriages and horses at his sole command! And now—all had been dashed down at one fell swoop, and he was—what he was.

Turning to Keziah with a stamp and an evil frown, he cursed her. It was something to have an object for blame to stand upon. Cursed her want of vigilance, that he said had wrought the mischief.

"Stay, Barnaby," she interposed. "The fault lies with you—if anywhere; certainly not with me. I could not *divine* there existed a private door to the wing;

there was no inspiration to tell it me. If you knew
of it, you should have warned me."

Ay. But then his memory had played him treacher-
ously.

"It appears to me to be just one of those unhappy
chances of life for which there is no human preven-
tion," resumed Keziah, her tone low from intense inward pain. "I'd *never* have failed you, Barnaby, fair
play being given me; but how could I combat with
shadows that I did not know were there?"

Must he give all up? Was there no possible loop-
hole by which he could right matters again—or at least
fight for it? The Major was deeply engaged in this
mental calculation when Mr. Norris came into the room.
Instead of departing with the others, he had remained
to give sundry private charges to Neel, as to the looking closely after valuables. He trusted neither the
Major nor Miss Dawkes.

"I have resolved upon my course of conduct,"
spoke the Major, overcoming his surprise; for he too
thought Mr. Norris had departed. "Mrs. Dawkes was,
beyond all doubt, insane when she made the will; that
is, so mentally weakened as not to be of lucid capacity. On those grounds, I shall dispute it."

Mr. Norris sent Miss Dawkes from the room, saying that he must speak a word to her brother in private.
He made the Major sit down, and drew a chair for
himself in front of him.

"Look here, Major Dawkes," he whispered in a
cautious tone; "your best and only policy will be to
give up quietly. I say this for your own sake. Lying
down deep in a chest of mine is another paper of your
wife's, not a will. She wrote it lest some such con-

tingency as what you speak of should arise. I have
not read it; it is signed and sealed; and my word is
passed to your dead wife that that paper shall never
see the light of day, and that human eye shall never
rest on its contents, unless you force it. It contains a
full and explicit statement of the causes and reasons
for her disinheriting you. I guess what they are; in
fact, I gathered them from her, perhaps unintentionally
on her part, when she was giving me the directions
for her will. I fancy Mr. Kage could say something,
and the nurse-girl Judith. This is private information
to you. Take my advice: we lawyers have to give
such sometimes, you know; and I shall never speak of
it to living soul. That paper, in your own solemn interests, must not be dislodged from its resting-place.
You, perhaps, know what the consequences would be:
it would not be a question of the loss of property then,
Major, but of something more. If I speak plainly, it
is for your own sake. Make no fight; don't stir up
muddy waters."

The Major's eyes were bent on the ground, and his
face wore again its livid tinge. But Mr. Norris, accustomed to read countenances, saw that all idea of
opposition was perforce abandoned. O, they were
bitter—the pills that unhappy sinner had to swallow!

"And you will give up possession, Major. Miss
Canterbury said at your convenience; I say do it *soon*.
It will be more agreeable for you, I feel sure, to be
away from here. What I looked in to say was, that I
considered it my duty to place Neel in charge, as it
were, of the family valuables and that. This is a very
exceptional case, you see, Major Dawkes; so I hope
you will pardon exceptional measures. And look here:

I have no ill-will to you, Heaven knows. Man gets led into all sorts of queer corners thoughtlessly; and if I can do you a good turn, I will. Miss Canterbury is of a nobly-generous nature, and I think she'd do something for you, if she were asked. There!"

The lawyer disappeared with the last words, waiting for neither comment nor answer. Major Dawkes sat on, still as a statue, plunging into a vista of the future —a future encompassed about with the stings of remorse and bitter disappointment. What had he gained by that dark deed he had accomplished in secrecy and silence? Not the golden Utopia, the luxurious freedom he had pictured to himself; but poverty, and guilt, and shame. His wife gone—her money gone—the Rock gone—position gone—all the good things were wrested from him for ever! And Major Dawkes started up wildly, and pulled at his hair with vengeful hands, as the thought suddenly flashed over him that, but for that woful deed, he would have been revelling in them yet.

It is often thus. Satan lures us on to commit evil that good may come, and then turns on us with a mocking laugh. Of all men living, perhaps, Major Dawkes was in that hour the most miserable.

CHAPTER XXIII.

Conclusion.

THOMAS KAGE had quitted the Rock in the Miss Canterburys' carriage; Mrs. Dunn would go with the Rector and his wife. Scarcely a word was spoken on the way home. The strange event of the day seemed very startling yet.

"Shall I come in?" he asked when he had assisted them to alight. And he spoke it with so much deprecation, that Olive looked at him.

"Shall you!" she repeated; "why should you not?"

"What has passed this morning bars my right to do so—at least, on the previous footing," he continued when they had entered.—"Millicent," he added, turning to her, "this is a cruel blow; for it ought, in justice, to deprive me of you. But it is only what I looked for."

"What now?" cried Olive.

"I possess, by dint of scraping and saving, a thousand pounds laid by in the bank, to purchase chairs and tables. Millicent is now worth, at least, a hundred thousand—how much more, I dare not guess. Can I, in honour, still hold her to her promise to become my wife?"

Millicent Canterbury turned red and white, and hot and sick, and finally burst into tears. Olive, on the contrary, felt inclined to laugh.

"It is the first time I ever heard a rising barrister —looking forward to the Woolsack, no doubt, in his own vain heart—say that a hundred thousand pounds was a thing to reject or quarrel with. Would you have liked it to be a million, sir?"

"Miss Canterbury."

"Ay, Miss Canterbury indeed! Look at Leta. I daresay she has had her visions, as well as you. The Lord Chancellor and his wig rule England, and she rules the Lord Chancellor, may have been one of her ambitious idealities for the far-off future. No slight temptation to a young lady, let me tell you, Mr. Kage. And now you want to upset it all!"

"It is the money which upsets it."

"Poor child!" cried Olive, advancing and stroking Millicent's hair; "you have cause for tears. He says he will not give you a home now; and I am sure I will not give you one. I won't harbour a rejected and forlorn damsel at the Rock."

"You are making a joke of it," he said; and that she should do so rather jarred upon his very serious mood.

"Of all fastidious men you are the most absurd, sir. I don't suppose it is the first time the accusation has been brought against you."

"What would you have me do, Miss Canterbury?"

"Do!" she echoed, in a changed tone. "Ask Millicent. Money separate you! What next? I never was ashamed of you until now, Thomas Kage."

She left the room; and the next minute Millicent was sobbing on his breast. Separate, indeed!

With a commotion of rustling skirts, and a fierce bang, in came Mrs. Dunn, who had chosen to alight at Thornhedge Villa instead of going on to the Rectory. Millicent was then seated, her face bent over a book (held upside down); Thomas Kage was looking demurely from the window.

"Olive! Where's Olive? I want Olive.—Why, Leta, you look as though you had been crying!"

"I!" stammered poor Leta.

"I'm sure it's nothing to cry about," reprimanded Mrs. Dunn, who had not parted with her propensity to set the world to rights. "Poor Caroline Dawkes had been as good as dead so long, that one can't feel it much at last. Don't be stupid, child.—O, here you are, Olive!"

Olive would have liked them to have a few minutes' conversation to themselves, that they might get reconciled to the new state of things; and she thought Mrs. Dunn was a great marplot. But there was no help for it. Miss Canterbury sat down by Mr. Kage, and began talking.

"Mrs. Dawkes's will, in a different way, is as strange a one as my father's," she observed to him. "Can you account for it?"

"I do not wish to account for it," was the evasive reply of Thomas Kage.

"There's one part I can't account for, and that is why she should have cut off her husband absolutely," put in Mrs. Dunn, tilting her black bonnet off the back of her head. "Who can?"

There was no reply. She had not addressed the question to any one in particular, so an answer was saved. Miss Canterbury was occupied with her jet chain; Thomas Kage had turned to the window again.

"One thing strikes me as being remarkably curious," pursued Lydia Dunn. "That Mrs. Garston at the last altered her will, so that the pittance she left the Major should be paid to him weekly. It was just as though she foresaw what has come to pass, and would secure him from absolute starvation."

"Yes, that was curious," warmly assented Thomas Kage, a strange light in his luminous eyes.

"It strikes me that you know more than you will tell us, Mr. Kage," she rejoined suddenly.

"That I know more? What of?"

"Why, of the *reason* for Mrs. Dawkes's cutting him off. He was her husband: nobody can deny that. I see you won't admit anything, Mr. Kage. You law-people are closer than wax. But I have my own thoughts about it now and again. Odd ones, too."

"I cannot help feeling sorry for Major Dawkes," observed Olive. "His present position must be a pitiable one. As to its cause—I mean his wife's motive —I do not think we are called upon to speculate upon it, Lydia."

"He'll quit the army—that's a matter of course," went on Lydia. "He and Keziah will club their means together, and go over the water and live. You'll see. He has his four pounds a-week; she has about the same. They won't quite starve."

"No, I must take care of that," murmured Miss Canterbury. "I think, with Mr. Carlton, that it is very strange Caroline left nothing to you," she added to Thomas Kage. "I have a suspicion that you prevented it yourself."

"I told her I would not accept it if she did."

"But why?"

"The money, in point of right, was not Caroline's

to leave; and what claim had I on Mr. Canterbury's property?"

"A small slice of it would not have been missed."

"Perhaps not," he said; "but I had no claim to a slice, small or large. No; I would not have accepted a shilling."

"Well, you *are* fastidious," cried Olive, looking at him; "chivalrously honourable."

"I think I am only just, Miss Canterbury."

"But O, what a strange thing it is, that our own money should have come back to us!" she exclaimed with enthusiasm. "I cannot yet realise it: when I wake up to-morrow morning, I shall not believe it's true. It did not bring altogether luck or happiness to those to whom it was left when papa disinherited his own people."

"Indeed it did not," warmly replied Thomas Kage: and he knew it, far better than she did. "Be assured of one thing, Miss Canterbury: that an unjust will never prospers the inheritors. All my experience in life has proved it to me."

And do you be assured of it also, my readers, for it is a stern truth. Look out for yourselves in life, and mark these cases. Years may go by, all apparently flourishing, justice may seem to have flagging wings; but when the final result shall come—as it surely will —you will see what it brings. Over and over again has the bitter truth been spoken—"It brought no blessing with it."

Summer sunshine lay around the Rock; summer brightness glistened on it. The old family were within

its walls again, and wrongs had been righted.   There
had been no trouble: Major Dawkes had given up
early possession, betaking himself off one morning
quietly with Keziah at his heels.   He was no longer
Major now, except by courtesy.   As Mrs. Dunn pre-
dicted, he had made haste to sell out of the army,
never again to reënter it; and had taken up his residence across the Channel with his sister, on a very fair
and sufficient income.   Were men generally rewarded
here in accordance with their deserts, Major Dawkes
might perhaps have confessed to himself that, after all,
he was more lucky than he deserved to be.

Not quite all the family back at the Rock who had
been turned out of it; for Miss Canterbury alone was
left of them.   Mrs. Rufort was at the Rectory; Millicent was already on the verge of entering a new
home.

For this was the wedding-day—as might be seen
by the gay carriages passing to and fro, and the gala
dresses within them.   In vain Millicent had pleaded
for a quiet wedding; in vain Thomas Kage had
threatened to run away with Leta beforehand if they
were to be subjected to display: Miss Canterbury willed
it otherwise.   They had had enough of quiet weddings,
she said, and decided for a grand one.   A gracious
mistress, she, reigning in her own birthplace, the Rock;
but rather an autocrat still in the matter of taking her
own way.   And grand it was, especially considering
that two lords were at it.

Lord Rufort begged to be allowed to give the bride
away.   Percival, Earl of Hartledon, invited himself,
and came down with Mr. Kage—the two close and
confidential friends of many years.   Richard Dunn and

his wife Sarah came to it; Lydia Dunn was of course there, busier and finer than anybody. Lord Rufort's stiffness had somewhat relaxed of late; for the fortune his daughter-in-law had come into afforded him the most intense gratification.

But the ceremony was over, and the breakfast was eaten, and the bridal-carriage was at length off amidst its cloud of old shoes. The out-door groups were cheering, the church-bells were ringing.

"Thank goodness, it's at an end," laughed Thomas Kage, as he leaned back in the carriage, leaving the noise and excitement behind. "Leta, I vow I'll never get married again."

"I think one time quite enough," she answered, with a shy laugh, and a blush.

"Farewell to Chilling," he murmured, three parts to himself; "farewell to all the old reminiscences, sad ones most of them, that the place has wrought into its history. Henceforth we begin a new life, Leta. I trust a happy one."

"I am sure of it," she breathed.

"Ay, yes; with Heaven's blessing."

A very short bridal tour was to be theirs, for Thomas Kage had chosen to get married in the busy season when the law-courts were sitting, instead of waiting sensibly for the autumn. And then the house that had been Mrs. Garston's would receive them, henceforth to be their home.

The sunshine lay, white and calm, on the road; the birds sang, the swallows dipping as they flew; the yellow corn was ripening; the summer flowers threw up their sweet perfume; the trees waved gently against the blue sky; the mountains basked in their hues of light and shade: on all things there seemed to rest a holy gladness, speaking to the heart of peace.

And the horses, spanking along, carried the chariot away in the distance.

THE END.